2059

Naif Makmi

NaifBooks

Copyrighted by Naif M. Alruwaili © 2022
Library of Congress Control Number: 2022908830

Cover design by Eugene Chugunov at 99designs by Vista.
Book Layout by Marcelo Cimadamore.

Printed in the United States of America
A 2 Z Press LLC
PO Box 582
Deleon Springs, FL 32130
bestlittleonlinebookstore.com
sizemore3630@aol.com
440-241-3126
ISBN: 978-1-946908-69-3

NaifBooks

www.naifbooks.com

To my brother Osamah Makmi,
the great video gamer.

CHAPTER ONE

"Ya know? It's been more than a bit boring lately," Olivia declared loudly from where she sat bent over a microscope. Andrew rolled his eyes and continued taking his notes, trying to decide for perhaps the millionth time if Olivia was talking to him or herself.

"Andrew? I'm not used to you having so much focus that you don't even hear me," she said in her thick, deep, almost masculine voice. He turned to see her staring at him. Even through her glasses, her brown eyes were deeply unnerving and there was a certain frustration to her countenance that he didn't know she could muster.

Not that she couldn't be frustrated, of course, it was merely that her face never showed it. Even now, she was a picture of quick and meticulous efficiency. Her raven-black hair was cut to her shoulders and still tied up and pulled away from the sides of her face. There was barely any makeup on her face that was neither beautiful nor ugly. Like every other part of her, it was merely attractive. The only thing standing out was her eyes. She was neither lean nor fat and Andrew knew that in her head was a mind that could think clear circles around him. She had graduated top of her class and was now doing her graduate studies in astrobiology, researching alien viruses.

"Perhaps you have been rubbing off on me," Andrew replied and pulled his lean, tall body up from the chair he was sitting on. Unlike Olivia, who seemed to be cut precisely to the size that would keep her at peak efficiency, Andrew was far too tall and too thin but he had a boyish pretty face that made him seem several years younger than his age.

He hadn't exactly vied for a position as an assistant for Olivia, but since he started, deep respect for her had grown within him.

"Nah, that can't be the case," Olivia said and looked upwards then sighed; a gesture that Andrew had seen her perform frequently.

"What is it?" Andrew asked.

Olivia shrugged and asked, "You know how it was ten years ago when they first came?"

Andrew raised his eyebrows in mild confusion. Olivia shook her head and placed a palm on her forehead as if checking her temperature. He knew that she was wondering if his mind had evolved fully and he was actually surprised. Olivia was never this expressive.

"The aliens? The immensely tall beings with skin like it was pulled directly out of Michelangelo's mind? Ring a bell?" Olivia asked.

Andrew nodded and simply said, "Yes."

"Good. What I'm saying is that there was so much excitement, so much buzz; from the government wondering if they would go back on their peace treaty and attack to watching them settle in their cities and sharing mysteries of science and technology with us. Ah, the press and the engineers had a field day. The military too. Keep in mind they'd never readily admit it. It was… exciting and I was actually scared that all the fun would pass before I was old enough to join it. Turns out, it actually did. Who'd have thought?" she said and walked to a high chair and sat on it, her eyes darker from the thoughts that swirled in her mind.

Andrew wasn't exactly sure what to say. He always felt this way whenever he was talking with Olivia. She was not much older than he was but it seemed like there was an infinite gap between how their minds worked. He hadn't put much thought into the arrival of the aliens beyond the personal interest and fascination he felt for them. It wasn't like with Olivia who seemed to eat, breathe, and think solely about the things from another world.

"Boring can be safe, you know?" Andrew said.

She looked at him like she not only realized that he was still there, but also like he had grown a tail.

Andrew continued, "I mean, what if others come and they're not as friendly as Elk and his friends. It's not like we're superbly prepared for that kind of threat, you see? I mean, what if Elk and his people decided that they didn't want to share their tech with us and decided to fight us instead? It'd take all the effort of an afterthought to thoroughly and permanently squash us."

Olivia gave him that look that told him that she agreed but didn't want to agree. Her ability to communicate with an assorted variety of glares and stares both impressed and scared him. She nodded and exhaled through puffed cheeks, looking up.

"Yeah. Boring is probably safer. Besides, only someone like me would want an invasion from outer space anyway," she said and shrugged; then went back to her corner.

Andrew could guess the real source of her agitation, but he kept his mouth shut and went back to his notes. Agitated or not, she would skin him alive if they weren't ready for her perusal by the impossible deadline she'd given.

Olivia stepped out of the lab and waited, tapping her feet on the ground then stopping once she realized she was doing it. Andrew had left a couple of hours earlier and the sky was already dark now. She remembered that she had promised herself she would cut back on the hours she worked. *'Too bad'* she thought and shrugged, her mood seemingly growing darker with the sky.

A taxi cab pulled over and Olivia got in. It wasn't manually driven anymore, of course. She just told it where she wanted to go and it went there, another ingenious contribution made by the aliens that now lived among, but not actually among them. She wondered why they preferred the borders of the cities given to them. Did they enjoy living their lives like caged exotic animals? Though it wasn't exactly a cage if it was self-imposed.

Feeling pressure mounting on her shoulders, Olivia sighed and cracked her neck; ignoring the snacks being offered to her by the robotic plate. She had no appetite even though she knew she was famished.

Olivia stopped in front of the general hospital and walked in. She never really liked hospitals. She always had a claustrophobic feeling in them no matter how spacious they were inside and it was made worse by the fact that this hospital seemed to have changed significantly since her last visit just a couple of days ago.

Olivia had not foreseen how bad her claustrophobia had gotten and a mild headache started at the sides of her head. The place seemed crowded and parts of some especially wide corridors were turned into makeshift wards. For it to be this bad here meant that it was worse in other areas. She stepped lightly, careful to take measured breaths, fighting against the feeling of being trapped. She hoped that the place hadn't changed too much so she wouldn't have to ask for help from the nurses who would probably be overworked and unpleasant.

One of the nurses saw Olivia and smiled widely. She walked to her.

"Hello, Olivia. How are you feeling today?" she asked.

Olivia felt slightly annoyed. She wasn't a patient. She wasn't sick and there was no need for that question.

"How is he?" Olivia asked.

The nurse's smile faded a little. Whether it was from the news of her brother's condition or from the slight rudeness, Olivia couldn't tell.

"There's been no development. He's still in the induced coma to slow down the spread of the virus and we are working…"

"It's fine, thank you…" Olivia started then stopped and rubbed her forehead then inhaled deeply. "I'm sorry. It's just that today's his birthday and… he shouldn't have to spend it in an isolated center, you know?"

The nurse nodded and replied, "I completely understand. It's fine." Olivia was grateful she didn't say more or make any further attempts to console her. Then, she was shown to the semi-lit room that held her brother.

Olivia had to see him from behind a glass enclosure and watched the heart monitor to make sure he was still alive. He looked so frail; his handsome face was calm and serene. He looked dead and just the thought of that caused Olivia to panic a little but she remembered her deep breaths and calmed herself down.

Eric turned eighteen today and he didn't even know it. She remembered how he held on to her after their parents left, clutching her as tightly as his arms could. She hadn't seen her parents since their mysterious departure. Eric was the only family she had and he was being ravaged by this virus that was unidentified and had no cure. A weaker, less contagious strain had been around for a while, hence the patients everywhere. But, this was the first of a potentially lethal strain and she wondered what rotten luck she had that it would affect her brother.

When Olivia finally couldn't bear watching him in that state any longer, she left the hospital, deciding to walk a little and feel the fresh air. There were holographic sign boards along with bright lights lighting up the night. There was the noise of people and machines and the smell of life, change, and dust. It was cool outside and she looked up, seeing only the brightest stars from the light pollution.

Olivia wondered if the people from before, the Egyptians, the Romans, and every other civilization, felt the same wonder as she did. If they wondered if they were alone. Perhaps they did. No, they actually did and they wrote about it. It was comforting to know that they weren't alone, but it was also scary.

Olivia shook her head, wondering why she was thinking about this while her brother was dying. Perhaps it was her mind's way of escaping but she wouldn't allow herself such luxury while her brother wasn't getting any better. She decided to find a way to heal him while working on her project. She needed a way to cure him. Eric was everything she had.

Then Olivia stopped, feeling weary all of a sudden. She closed her eyes briefly, collecting herself, then she looked up at the stars and exhaled through puffed cheeks. She would have to put aside her musings and aspirations. Olivia had to save her family.

***

Olivia felt like her brain was pulled out of her head and a truck had driven over it. Her hair was a mess and there were dark circles under her eyes. She seemed to think in slow motion and, after she had all but snarled at Andrew, he'd kept his concerns to himself. Though she felt worse than she had in years, Olivia also felt a glow of elation in her heart. She found out that the lethal strain of the virus was passed through water and not necessarily by drinking it.

"Olivia?" Andrew called tentatively from behind her. She turned to stare at him, feeling like she could fall off to sleep at any second. She maintained a clear head and a straight face through her weariness but she could see that Andrew was not so easily fooled. "I know that you might chew my head off for saying this but I think…. Don't you think that you should rest a little? I mean…"

"Know what, Andrew? Your head really is starting to look quite obnoxious. There are thousands of people currently being infected by this disease and some of them by the lethal strain that has taken hold of my brother. He's not dead but he might as well be. His condition has only gotten worse and you're asking me to lie down comfortably and snore my time away while my brother dies slowly. Is that right?" she snapped and his face grew ashen.

Olivia felt a bit remorseful for being sharp with him and she softened her face and voice slightly. This lack of sleep was really getting to her. "I just…. I'm sorry," she said quietly.

Andrew's face was brightened by a smile. Olivia wondered if he knew how much he looked like a kid at that moment.

"You got your audience," he said.

She stared at him curiously.

"What audience?"

Andrew shrugged. "Well, you know how the disease is spreading very fast and no one has found out anything worthwhile, not even its mode of propagation? And how you also complained that the aliens have been keeping awfully quiet about the whole matter. And, I believe you threw a pen at me when you were frustrated over the fact that they seem reluctant to help us with some antidote for...."

"Get to the freaking point, Andrew," Olivia shouted, becoming impatient.

Andrew nodded and cleared his throat. "What I'm trying to say is that I personally reached out to the aliens and requested an audience on your behalf, and you know how they rarely grant it unless it's worth their time. Well, I sent them our work here and they reached out saying that they would be, and get this, delighted to meet you. Do you…"

Andrew didn't finish before Olivia shot up from her seat, eyes wide. He grinned tentatively, not sure if she would break his nose or hug him. She did something entirely unexpected.

"Thank you, Andrew. I am grateful," she said with all the sincerity her normally piercing eyes could muster; which was far too much for Andrew to handle. He looked down. She had never thanked him in their whole year of working together.

"They would like to meet tomorrow, though," Andrew said.

Olivia raised her eyebrows, but her face had gone into that perfect stillness that had grown very familiar over their time working together. She nodded silently and he smiled, then turned to leave.

"Good work, Andrew," Olivia said. He laughed a little. "Things had gotten so boring on the alien front I was considering switching my career entirely."

"How do you study people you can't even see?" Andrew asked.

And the shadow of a smile passed across Olivia's face.

"Now you're getting it. Besides, they may have some insight into this virus and could maybe get us that much closer to cracking it," Olivia added.

Andrew nodded and walked away; back to his corner.

Olivia's mind wandered to her brother currently struggling for his life and she shuddered a little. "I just need more time. A little more time," she muttered to no one in particular.

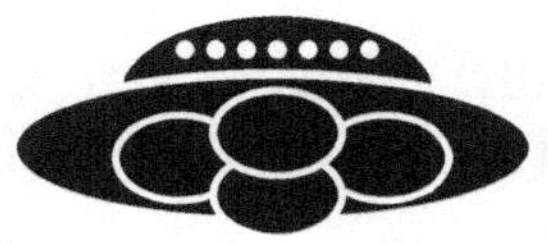

CHAPTER TWO

Eko-Neh seemed like something directly out of a sci-fi movie. When Olivia stood within this city that seldom saw direct sunlight, she felt like she had been pulled from the Earth and thrust into another place entirely. Her guide had given her the appropriate suit to compensate for the higher pressure and denser air that had a little too much carbon for her body's taste.

The entire city was roofed with some type of glass structure that yellowed the sunlight that came through. The roof seemed so high in order to accommodate the very interesting architecture that was present.

There were buildings that spiraled upwards and some that seemed hollow, almost like they'd collapse, but they stood perfectly still. There were also smaller, sturdier, dome-shaped buildings and she noticed there were barely any cars, just hovercrafts. Most of the sounds seemed muffled and dulled.

Olivia's guide was an almost eight-foot-tall alien, and to her, it seemed almost as if she was being guided by a strange sculpture. Once they had crossed into the city bounds, a hovercraft landed in front of them and the alien beside her made a buzzing sound. It seemed the entire hovercraft buzzed a reply. Then the hatch opened and he slowly walked in with her.

"Hello. I'm sorry. I never did get your name," Olivia said to the guide who sat still, staring at a wall like he had the intention of burning through it with his eyes. Perhaps he could. Olivia knew next to nothing about his kind.

"It was never asked," the alien responded with a startlingly musical voice; like notes were being played within its vocal mechanisms.

"So, umm. Would you like to tell me then?" Olivia asked.

It turned to look at her with its small, yellow eyes. "I am Zek, in your language… no, in your pronunciation," he clarified and made a gesture with his head that was halfway between a nod and a rolling of the head.

Zek spoke mechanically, like there were many things that were left out because they wouldn't fit into the English language. Olivia suspected that the case wasn't any different with other languages.

"Why is everywhere yellow?" Olivia asked suddenly.

Zek, ever expressionless, looked at her and then back at the wall. "Easier for the eyes. Easier on the body as well," he said and tilted his head to the side though Olivia suspected that this perhaps meant something utterly different from what it usually meant among humans.

The fact that it was a familiar gesture didn't mean Olivia understood it. She decided to leave the questions on hold as her guide, or perhaps the entire tribe of aliens, didn't find talking a very appealing exercise.

They landed in front of one of the spiraling structures that felt strangely alive to Olivia. They seemed to be pulsing with some sort of energy. The door opened as they approached and they walked in.

Olivia felt like a toddler among these towering giants around her. Her guide didn't say much and she wondered what the others would be like if someone that was selected to be her guide was so averse to speech.

Olivia was led to a hall that was bare except for a roundish chair and a ridiculously wide table upon which holographic images of different places on Earth and outside were displayed. The lights were a lighter yellow than the tints outside and there was a low hum.

Olivia remembered that energy that seemed to be in all the buildings. The guide went to the wall and pushed some buttons then turned to her.

"Make yourself comfortable. Drinks will be brought to you and you can take off your helmet now. The air here has been adjusted to suit you," Zek said matter-of-factly. He tilted his head slightly then walked away.

Olivia was about to ask where the person she was supposed to meet was but she had a feeling that there would be no reply.

"I like your hair," a deep, musical voice said from somewhere to her left.

Olivia turned sharply. A dark figure detached itself from the darkness behind it and she saw that it was one of them; his eyes regarding her with such flatness that she was a bit startled. The eyes revealed nothing at all and, after a while, he smiled in a way that was more a display of silvery teeth than a smile.

"Why did you do that?" Olivia asked. He just nodded.

Olivia was about to ask why he nodded then remembered again that their gestures were different. He made a low noise that sounded like boiling water.

"It is a behavioral trait among your kind that you do to show friendliness. I have been practicing in front of a mirror for a while now and I thought that it was pretty good. Seems like I was wrong," he said.

Olivia frowned. "Very wrong," she blurted.

He nodded again, deeper than before, and Olivia suspected that it might be a gesture of embarrassment.

"Your associate reached out to me and I must say that your work was fascinating. It actually mirrors some of ours and I wanted to congratulate you personally," he began and walked to the round chair and sat, setting his limbs in unnatural angles. Then he stared at her through those flat eyes.

"Just that?" Olivia asked.

He tilted his head to the side. Olivia suspected that was confirmation. She realized that a chair was not set out for her and she began to get annoyed and scared that this was not meant to be a long visit.

"I have decided to reward you with an audience, Olivia. You are an interesting human and a very brilliant one. I will answer five questions that you may have," he said.

Olivia paused, realizing what a gold mine this was. Most of the information about aliens was shrouded in mystery. Though they had even placed monitoring devices in and around the aliens' domain, they found nothing. She suspected that they knew that they were being monitored but put up with it in order to assuage any fears the humans might have had.

"Why did you leave!?" Olivia shouted.

He nodded as if this was a question he expected. Olivia had decided that he was a he because his mannerisms and voice were masculine although his clothes were neutral and she didn't understand the biological subtleties that differentiated any genders the aliens might have; if they had any genders at all.

"My planet was a beautiful place and, unlike yours that is very vast and large with different cultures and peoples and everything, mine was small, about one third the size of yours and three-fifths of our population were the ones like me and another… I wonder what your kind would term it… species? No… tribe perhaps? Yes, that seems fine. We had two tribes. One of them was like me and the other… was different. A misunderstanding started and a war ensued in all of the greatest civilizations. We destroyed ourselves and we had to find another place, a place to rebuild. That is when we found your planet. It is common among your kind to say '*and the rest is history*,'" he said.

He never gestured while he spoke. His entire body remained perfectly still and it seemed like only his lips were capable of movement.

Olivia wondered what it must have been like to be in an alien war and, although a part of her acknowledged the possible devastating destruction that could cause, she decided that it would be something she'd love to see. She cleared the thoughts from her head, realizing that this alien before her had never for once looked away from her. His eyes were much too unnerving.

"What's your name?" Olivia finally asked.

He made a sound like a muffled whistle in his throat. Olivia didn't know why, but she felt like she had offended him in some way. She was about to apologize when he answered with something between the rumble of thunder and the sound of pianos playing. A puzzled expression passed over her face and he laced his fingers together.

"Or, in your speech, Elk," he said softly.

Olivia suddenly felt uncomfortable, but she had another question she wanted to ask. "Do you know anything about the virus, anything you would like to share that we don't already know? I can't believe that a civilization as advanced as yours wouldn't be able to crack something as simple as a virus," she rambled a little.

Elk remained still, watching Olivia for such a long time. She was beginning to doubt that he had heard her question.

"We know a few things," Elk replied and made a low whistling sound in his throat.

Olivia resolved that she would find out what those sounds meant. She already hypothesized that it might be their own version of facial expressions. She almost asked him *what* things, but she suspected that he would count it as a question so she remained silent and hoped he would continue.

"We do know a few things," Elk continued, to her relief. "The things we have found out are quite strange and… interesting. And when it is time to share it, we will. Your kind has a certain affinity for disorganization and mindless squabbles, and anything that will be given to them has to be… properly packaged and complete."

There was no condescension or mockery in his voice, but, for some reason, Olivia felt herself growing annoyed.

"I am sorry if this offends you, but it is true and your reaction towards this truth has further proved its accuracy," Elk said curtly.

His calm logic cut through Olivia's anger. She nodded and inhaled deeply, calming herself.

"So, you'd watch people die and waste away and you won't give us anything to work with because we're temperamental children that find it impossible to leash our own excitement and anger? I wonder if you'd react in this manner if it were your own people that were being affected and losing their lives. You know that in some circles, they whisper that your kind might be responsible for this ailment," Olivia said, glad that she had maintained a calm and collected presence.

Elk made the muffled whistle sound again and slowly stood, unfolding himself from his chair. Even from that distance, he seemed to look over Olivia. "Miss Olivia, I am a warrior among my people and my first loyalty is to them. I have seen them suffer before and I have seen them die, but I have withheld sources of relief because a part of protecting something is also knowing when to protect it from itself. Sometimes in a bid to ease pain or to solve a problem, we worsen it," he snapped.

"And what makes you think that you can make that decision for them? That somehow you know what's best for other people?" Olivia demanded.

A sound like the muffled hissing of a snake came from him and Olivia knew then that he was angry. Maybe only mildly, but he definitely was.

"My people gave me that right when they chose me to defend, protect, and do whatever is best for them. Your kind would say they trusted me and they still trust me to do the right thing. If I do anything other than that which I perceive to be right, I would be doing them a disservice and that is something I absolutely shall not do," he said softly and confidently.

Elk waited a few moments before he spoke again. "Five questions, according to my count. I respect and admire you, Olivia, and I look forward to meeting you again soon. I have no doubt that you will be in a better light and able to see things from my view."

The door swung open almost immediately and the one Olivia had known to be her guide walked in.

"Piece of advice," Elk said flatly, "keep your mind very open. Do not merely think outside the box. You have to think outside the room that the box is in. Do you understand?"

Olivia nodded, letting her guide lead her toward the door.

***

"I'm so glad we brought the sub bots," Andrew said, leaning against the truck, fiddling with one of the robots that looked like mini-submarines.

Olivia thought that Andrew lent a certain aesthetic to the art of learning. It was almost instinctive for him. As his blue eyes scrutinized the machine, she wondered if that was what the Terrans – the new term that they had begun to use for the aliens – had become; a crutch to lean on for humanity.

"You would have to drive if we hadn't brought them, you know?" Olivia said and turned to stare at Andrew, whose eyes searched hers for any sign of a joke, then turned shocked when he saw that she wasn't joking.

"I know that I'm a pretty decent diver, but seriously? Nothing can go that deep. You wouldn't make me," Andrew replied as Olivia shrugged.

"Wouldn't I?" Olivia asked and he gave a mock gasp.

Olivia turned to look at the body of water they had chosen. This virus was something that she couldn't wrap her mind around and it seemed to adapt and change at very convenient times. As Olivia would get closer to an antidote, it would turn into something entirely different at about the same time. Almost like it had a mind of its own. It was terrifying and frustrating to say the least, and Olivia exhaled through puffed cheeks as she imagined Eric still struggling for his life.

When the university found out about Olivia's interest in the virus, they cut her funding, but an "anonymous" supporter continued from where they stopped. Her space was still hers and, if anything, she could afford more efficient equipment now. Olivia wondered why Elk would fund her, but then she rationalized it by admitting that she had no hope of understanding how the alien mind worked. At least not yet.

"Do you think that human beings don't enjoy free will?" Olivia asked.

Andrew raised an eyebrow at her as he walked to the water and lowered the bot and then monitored its movement from the screen of the device he held in his hands. "Where's that coming from?" he asked.

Olivia turned to look at him, causing him to flinch. She had no idea why he did that whenever she gave him a serious look but she secretly enjoyed it.

"Think about it. Ever since the beginning of humanity's existence, we've always looked for something greater than ourselves that we accord respect and defer to. We take people from among us and raise them to be our leaders and almost become their slaves in both action and thought. We give them the right to make decisions concerning our lives and we begin to think them superior to ourselves. Perhaps that was how religion came to be, you know? The people choose a king and, from among the kings, rises an emperor and he needs someone above himself that he can serve and enslave himself to, so he creates the concept of an all-powerful and all-knowing being. It's almost as if we do not want to be free," she said.

Andrew raised an eyebrow. "Wow. That's a lot," he remarked.

Olivia shook her head slowly. Andrew must have sensed her disappointment because he waved one hand frantically. "I'm so sorry, but I've never thought about it in that manner before. I don't know and I have to think about it while making sure that these bots pick up the samples and don't crash while at it."

Olivia nodded. "I understand," she said.

"Wow," Andrew said under his breath.

Olivia's eyes flew wide open as she knew what that sound meant; that he had seen something interesting. She stood beside him, silently annoyed that he was so tall that he had to lower his arms just for her to see what was on the screen.

Olivia's eyes widened as well and she looked up at him. The entire floor of the lake was covered in blood-red moss and it seemed to glow from time to time.

"Do you know what it is?" he asked.

Olivia shook her head, her mind working already on what it could be. "I don't know. Not yet anyway, but that can easily be changed," she said, feeling excitement spread from her chest into the rest of her body. She could feel her head throbbing with small explosions of color following each throb.

"What is this?" Olivia asked herself mostly. Her annoyance flaring as she reviewed the results again and again. Each strand of the moss was like a sack loaded with microbes that were unlike anything she had ever seen or known.

Olivia had run it through all the available databases but she found nothing similar to what she was seeing. Olivia wondered if she was the first to have noticed this and if she wasn't, why had no one mentioned it before. It seemed too strange. Even the microbes seemed to have a mind of their own, almost like they were actively trying to evade detection. Nothing natural would be able to do this, or at least, nothing natural to her.

"Andrew!" Olivia called sharply.

The young man sat up from where he had dozed off, his eyes red and puffy from lack of sleep, his hair in disarray. Olivia almost pitied him then but she was angry and confused and there was work to be done.

"Contact Elk," Olivia barked.

Andrew nodded, then stopped. "Contact who?" he asked.

Olivia snapped her fingers, thinking about how she would start explaining. "Just contact the aliens somehow. Do the same thing you did before, only tell them that it is Olivia and I want to speak to Elk."

Andrew went to work immediately on his holophone, although she didn't miss the worried and strange look he had shot at her.

Olivia wondered what she was going to do while she waited for their reply. She was already half sure that these things were extraterrestrial and decided that she'd contact her former friend and colleague, Sam, but she hesitated. Sam wasn't exactly someone she wanted to entrust something important to. She decided to wait for Elk.

"Anything?" she asked Andrew.

He shook his head slowly, more out of confusion than anything. "Ummm. I think we'll have to…"

"Miss Olivia," the low, deep musical voice said from behind her. She turned to see a full miniature holographic image of Elk observing her from the holophone. "You asked for me?"

Olivia turned to him, fighting for control of the anger she felt at seeing him although she was unsure why exactly she was angry. "What are those microbes?" she asked earnestly.

He remained silent, watching her.

"We have been working on those," Elk informed her as she drew closer to him.

"Is that like a Terran reply to deny the importance, or is that just you?" she asked.

He remained silent then, after a while, spoke. "These are very strange, very delicate matters and we have made our own assumptions and deductions, but we are still unsure. But we are working on it. I assure you though that those did not follow us from our planet, they seemed to have gotten here some other way. And I will not divulge any more information until I am sure."

"What if you're the ones that planted this? What if that's your way of slowly wiping out humanity? What if these microbes are like a Pandora's box of diseases and..."

"You must think us to be of unlimited patience and resources to mount such a slow and wasteful attack when we could just have used faster methods to subdue your entire population. Do not misunderstand this as arrogance, no, it is a mere statement of the truth and I assure you that you have nothing to fear from us. We are not the only ones in space, you see. You must understand that many things have happened on the galactic scale and your planet has been away from it all, but I believe that attention has been drawn to you since our landing here, and for that, I am truly sorry. Information will be revealed soon but until..."

"Elk. My brother is sick. He was the first person to be infected and I don't know what miracle is keeping him alive but I'm thankful for it. Time is running out and I need anything you can give me. Anything, please," she begged.

Olivia heard the sound like the murmuring of many people from Elk. She didn't know what it meant and didn't care at the moment.

"I know," Elk said simply, and, at that moment, if he were actually there, she would have slapped him. "A certain tribe among your people have a saying that *hot broth is eaten slowly,* and this broth is indeed hot. I urge you to show restraint and patience. We will talk again." Then, he vanished from before her.

Olivia stood there, feeling empty and tired and all she wanted to do was to cry, but she'd not cried in years and she wasn't going to begin now. She blinked a few times and inhaled deeply, collecting herself.

CHAPTER THREE

Elk sat in the back of his hovercraft with his second sitting perfectly still beside him, communicating logs into his consciousness. He felt a certain irritation within him and the low sharp whistle was in his buzzer. A whistle is the alien's way of expression because they don't have facial muscles.

Elk wondered if they could understand the efficiency of expressing emotion through sound. He was astounded when he found out that the Earthlings expressed most of their emotion on their faces and had such a limited vocabulary that couldn't begin to scratch the surface of efficient and meaningful communication, making misunderstanding very easy.

Elk was very sure that he hadn't assuaged Olivia's worries and, for a brief moment, he wished that she was one of his kind so he could communicate all the subtleties of thought and feelings that had prompted his decision to her.

Olivia was a bright spark and was one of the few he had deemed fit for direct coalition with his kind. Most of humanity was irrational and supremely selfish. He didn't blame them for it but he wouldn't entrust more than they could handle into their hands either. He thought about Olivia again, then quickly wiped her from his mind. In the grand scale of things, she was still another insignificant Earthling. And no single part is to be out above the whole.

This bore some similarities to home, Elk pondered. He had seen the slow infiltration, the confusion, the fear; and his people were far more united and organized than the Earthlings. He turned to his second who was still attached to his line of thought and slowly removed him. There was no reaction from him as usual, but Elk could sense his disapproval. It didn't matter what he thought at this moment though. He wanted some privacy of thought and he felt a little amusement at the idea. The humans were indeed rubbing off on him.

Their arrival was communicated by his second, who bore the name Tekka when forced into the boundaries of human speech. Tekka, as all Terrans were, was neither male nor female in the manner of the humans. They wore just whatever suited the needs of their race and their convenience and preference. He preferred the male form as most of their race did, as many of that gender was wiped off during the wars that preceded the destruction of their planet. And he could still decide to undergo the brief process of transforming into another gender if he wished, as their race had four genders.

Elk stepped out of his hovercraft and felt the harshness and brightness of the unfiltered sun fiercely for a moment before his body adjusted accordingly, though it still made him uncomfortable. This was part of the reason most of his kind never left their cities. Their young and tenderers had features that could not easily adapt to the low carbon in the atmosphere and the harshness of the sun. For Elk and most of the others, it was an inconvenience that could be endured. The stark white building wasn't helping his mood either and he whistled low and quick. Tekka made subtle attempts to soothe his mood and he allowed it, although grudgingly.

They walked through the doors, down the immense white corridor, and through clusters of people that still stared wide-eyed at them despite their presence on this planet for slightly over a decade.

A team of men came to meet them and exchanged pleasantries with Elk, who had split his mind in two as only a warrior could do. He let a part go through the torture of the mundanities of human ritual and let the other analyze the place. He appreciated the courtesy of the lights turning yellow and dimming as soon as he entered and he appreciated the cooler condition of the entire place though he knew that it must be an inconvenience for every human present within.

"They have all arrived and await your presence," the man said to him.

Elk let his attention focus on the man who was short, even for his kind, with rodent-like features and a huge seeing aid on his face. Elk wondered why he hadn't gotten robotic contact lenses or undergone laser surgery but he put that out of his mind for now. Humans were strange.

Elk was led to the door fashioned out of the finest, heaviest wood and he wondered, again, why they valued physical displays of wealth and beauty. He never did understand it though he had studied them intensively over the years.

Elk walked into a room that held precisely 88 delegates from each of the Commonwealths that had emerged from the unification and dissolution of many of the countries of the world. He could feel their expectation, annoyance, and their awe as well and, from a rare few, respect.

Elk didn't feel himself to be in the mood to pass through all the pleasantries and rituals so he got directly to the point.

"There have been some developments recently and careful research into these developments has led me to believe that it would not be a far-fetched assumption that this planet is currently under attack," Elk began.

He listened as gasps and murmurs rippled through everyone gathered. He deciphered each sentence and stored them for perusal at a later time.

"What makes you think this?" a heavy-set man with a bald shaved head and about four chins asked.

Elk regarded him silently for a while before he spoke. "This bears similarities to something I have witnessed before. I would advise that every one of the Commonwealths be on high military alert," he said. Another murmur arose, louder than the last.

After a while, relative silence returned and a man black as wet coal with thick glasses wearing an agbada rose. "How sure are you of these assumptions. It would be foolishness to cause panic and worry on mere assumptions. Is there anything concrete that we can lay our hands upon? Something that would be able to validate the amount of unrest that this would cause?" he asked.

Elk waited a while as he found that it made them think that he was weighing and considering their words. "This assumption is a safe one to be made and it is worth the unrest that would follow because it is better to be prepared and have nothing happen than not to be prepared when something does," he patiently responded.

The man shook his head. "Do you even know what you're asking? And in the midst of a pandemic?" he asked.

Elk nodded, a gesture he had learned from them. "I understand exactly what I am asking," he said. A few arguments erupted on different fronts but were later quieted.

"Under attack from whom exactly?" a thin, Asian woman asked

And, without hesitation, he answered, "I am not sure of that."

"You do understand how ridiculous this is, right? You are asking us to prepare for a war that you're not sure is here, against a foe you're not sure exists…. Is that correct?" another woman asked.

"Yes."

"Why then should we take your advice? Why should we terrify our people and cause instability and doubt? And why should we do all of this on the word of an extraterrestrial such as yourself?" another man asked.

Elk felt a bit of anger, but he quickly let it dissipate as he found and held the questioner's gaze. "This extraterrestrial has seen the destruction of not only one, but several planets. He has witnessed and fought in battles on galactic scales and he has been attuned by technologies far beyond what you can imagine to the symptoms and signs of war and violence. It is the word of an extraterrestrial that has contributed, with the entire might and zeal of his people, to the development of this planet that we now call home. If that is not enough for you, then I do not know what is. I advise you to be practical," Elk said.

There was quiet for a while, then the spokesman and moderator spoke to him. "We'll need to convene and make a decision on this matter. Our decision will be forwarded to you," he said.

Elk nodded respectfully and uttered his thanks before he left them and walked back to his hovercraft. There was something about the engineering of the machine that soothed him. Perhaps it was the way it resembled his house back home or just because after the inconveniences of temperature and atmosphere and the bickering of humans, anything from home would be an improvement.

Elk caught his condescension and regretted it immediately. If anything, these humans had taken them in without major protest and that spoke of something very positive about them. He reminded himself not to let his race's superiority in some areas make him conceited.

"You know that they will refuse," Tekka said in human speech.

Elk made a noise like the rumbling of thunder to show mild amusement. Tekka made the same sound, then moved directly to their own mode of communication. Elk shared the murmurs with him and they analyzed it along with everything he had seen and they knew with a startling amount of certainty that the humans wouldn't listen.

"What do we do?" Tekka asked

Elk closed his eyes, feeling the need to rest for a long while. "We prepare," he said softly and was glad that Tekka didn't push the conversation further and slowly left his consciousness to give himself a few moments of rest.

***

There was no rest in Olivia's laboratory. At times, Andrew felt that he would go crazy. He felt that she was already insane. Nothing was left to chance, nothing was left for later, nothing was done that wasn't checked at least thrice and it felt like running a marathon, but he endured it because he understood that this was personal for her.

Andrew knew that if he was under the same circumstance as Olivia, he probably would be no different. He brought her food often and was glad that she ate, although she only did so after several reminders. There were dark circles around her eyes and she kept taking some kind of medication that he knew nothing of. He didn't know of any friend or family that she had that he could report her condition to and request for immediate intervention, so he resolved to be available as much as he could. He hunkered down and bore it.

Andrew almost staggered into the laboratory one day, thinking of how to juggle his own assignments when he heard Olivia call him.

"Andrew?" Olivia's voice was low and quiet, almost as if she feared that raising it too loud would disturb something.

"Olivia?" Andrew called.

He could feel tense energy in the air. He walked around the corner and saw her staring at something inside a tube that was also inside a glass case, or what seemed like a glass case. It was never safe to assume anymore.

"Andrew?" Olivia called again.

Andrew could see that she was wide-eyed with a fierce look of excitement and pleasure in her eyes and something of pride as well. "What is it?" he asked and dropped his back.

Olivia shook her head like he was distracting her so he remained silent and watched instead. "I have found a way to predict, with a fairly decent degree of accuracy, how the virus will transmit. I have really found it!" Her voice turned into a high squeal.

Olivia was clearly excited, but Andrew was more worried about her health than anything and he was glad the breakthrough was made. Maybe now he could convince her to sleep for longer than an hour.

"Wow! That's great! I mean, how *did* you do it?" he asked.

Olivia stood slowly, then turned towards him and rattled off for a solid ten minutes on genetic sequencing and cross-referencing and so many things that it made his head hurt. But, he maintained a stoic, thoughtful expression though he probably missed seventy percent of what was being said.

"We should post it on S.net," he said.

Olivia raised an eyebrow at him then shook her head vehemently.

"You've been working in isolation since, Olivia. Besides, the whole world would still know that you were the one that found it. It would be prudent to let organizations more equipped, staffed, and funded than us to take it from here. You should rest."

Olivia placed her hand on the table and gritted her teeth so loudly Andrew felt shivers go down his spine.

"They would just shut it down and try to invalidate it. They would just argue more than anything. I feel like they argue more than they actually do anything else and I will not leave my brother's fate into the hands of those jokers. That's why I never got an S.net account," Olivia stammered.

Andrew shoved down the impulse to tell Olivia that she already had the one that he'd created for her. A small part of him told him that she wouldn't take that very well. She turned away from him and barely took three steps before she collapsed to the floor.

CHAPTER FOUR

Olivia felt the mother of headaches pounding away at her head when she woke and she groaned as the lights were much too bright for her eyes. She stretched a hand towards it as if she would close the shutters with her mind.

It seemed that was what happened because the shutters suddenly closed and Olivia frowned in puzzlement when saw it was Andrew, not her mind, that closed it.

"Where am I?" she asked and stretched her hand, though, for what she didn't know.

Andrew pressed a cup into her palm and without thinking, Olivia gulped down the contents. Her mind seemed to explode into wakefulness, but not the kind that enabled her to actually stand up and get back to work. It was just enough that she could actually hear what he was saying.

"You've been asleep for eighteen hours. You really passed out back there. I brought you something to eat." There was a mild tension to his words; like he was annoyed but trying to hide it.

Olivia was almost affronted then she realized that he had every right to be annoyed. She'd worked him to the bone and herself half to death. The least she could do was eat a meal and try to get her mind off work for a while. It was some kind of soup that warmed her from the inside out while being superbly filling. She wondered why she had never tasted anything like it before. She tried to remember the last time she ate and after a while, she shrugged, giving up.

"I have to talk to you about something," Andrew said. His voice was grave and detached and, for no reason that she could understand, Olivia felt herself grow scared and worried. "Never do this again, Olivia. I mean, one second you were telling me how S.net is trash and the next you're out cold on the floor. Yes, I understand that Eric is your first priority now and you are doing everything you can to save him, but it gives you absolutely no right to burn yourself out and work yourself to death. It gives you no right to starve your body of sleep and food and expect me to go along with it. No one would go along with it. You should care more about yourself Olivia because if what happened here repeats itself, I'm sorry but you're going to have to find yourself a new associate."

Olivia knew that he meant it. A dismissive reply almost left her lips, but she kept it there, realizing that she didn't actually want Andrew to leave. His presence around the lab was a comfortable thing although she didn't think about it often. He was perhaps the only friend she had at the moment. Not that she was planning to get anymore in the foreseeable future.

"I understand," Olivia said quietly, and she saw relief pass quickly across his face. Andrew had obviously been expecting something else and she was glad that his fear wasn't realized.

Andrew sat back on his chair and gestured towards the soup. "I eat there every Tuesday and Friday. Their soup is out of this world. Just perfect," he said, pinching his thumb and forefinger together.

Olivia nodded as she quickly made the soup disappear and drank the bluish stuff inside the cup that Andrew had kept beside the plate. It both satisfied her thirst and gave her something of warmth through her bones, though she had become sleepy again and was sure she'd fall back asleep. She worried a little that she was sleeping while the world crumbled around her, but she rationalized that she would rather be alert when it crumbled than to keep on passing out embarrassingly.

"Oh. After a lot of thinking and studying your notes, I think I got the gist of your breakthrough and I posted it on S.net," Andrew said.

Olivia's eyes flew wide open, and she looked at his straight face, almost as if he had prepared for the worst already and she felt a small headache come back to her. "What?!" she screamed.

He nodded. "It was the best thing to do rather than see you slave away at it alone. It would be much faster and efficient if you got help. Except if you are chasing glory or fame; which I know you aren't."

Olivia clasped her head with both hands then took some deep, calming breaths. "How long ago did you upload it?" she asked.

He shrugged. "Eleven, maybe twelve hours ago?"

Olivia shook her head repeatedly then sighed. "Any reviews yet?" she asked.

He shrugged again. "Honestly? I haven't checked. I just kind of uploaded it and went back to the arduous task of keeping you alive."

He smiled a little, but she felt none of his humor.

"I didn't even know that I had an S.net account," she said.

"Yeaaah about that..."

Olivia waved his words away and snapped her fingers repeatedly. "Get a holophone. I need to see those reviews," she demanded.

Andrew nodded, taking out what looked like a small stick from his pocket. He then clicked it on and a holographic screen emerged which he operated with a neural transmitter previously implanted.

Olivia scoffed at this in her mind. She didn't see what it was about those flashy gadgets anyway and she realized with more than a little bit of embarrassment that she was beginning to think like an old lady despite not even properly reaching her mid-twenties yet.

Andrew's eyes widened and he mouthed something then looked at Olivia who grew immediately worried and snapped her fingers for the phone. He looked back at the screen that was blurred from behind so no one could actually read it from afar. Then he slowly handed it over, looking resigned and more than a bit older.

Olivia looked at the reviews and her eyes nearly bulged out. Almost all of them were negative. It seemed that the entire scientific community on S.net had abandoned whatever it was that they were doing for the sole purpose of taking her down.

Some even called Olivia a clout chaser and called her research farfetched and amateurish. She inhaled deeply, feeling tears well up in her eyes then she pushed them down, clearing her throat instead. She felt like the world had indeed crumbled but on a smaller scale than she had first imagined.

She looked up at Andrew, whose head was hung low in shame and embarrassment. She thought of scolding him but she realized that he was as clueless as she. There was no harm in his intention, so she shrugged.

"At least I tried, right?" she finally said. Her voice broke a little, but she mastered it quickly.

Andrew's eyes widened then turned almost angry. "You did more than that and I believe there's a lot to your discovery. You're right. I should never have posted on S.net. What was I even thinking? Of course, those big shot corporations wouldn't take kindly to the fact that an individual working alone would best their entire think tanks with limitless funding. We should just block them out and continue working,"

Olivia nodded a little. "Yeah, yeah I think we should probably do that…" She paused and inhaled deeply. "After I have slept and eaten more of that soup."

Olivia smiled a little to ease the tension though she could feel her heart break from within.

Andrew smiled in return and stood. "I'll go get it then. You rest." he said sweetly and left.

Olivia wondered what the Terrans would do. Would they withdraw their funding because of the embarrassment she must have brought upon herself? She couldn't decide as they were utterly unpredictable. Besides, any error in her methods was partly due to their secrecy. If Elk had just told her something that she could actually use….

Olivia rubbed her forehead as sparks of light and a headache swarmed it. She flopped back down against the bed and fatigue, stress, worry, and pain overtook her then she began to weep. The tears came and, all of the sudden, it seemed that they would never stop.

Olivia cried for her parents, for her brother, for her incompetence and helplessness, and she cried for this feeling of worthlessness that suddenly filled every inch of her heart. For the first time since she was a child, she cried herself back to sleep.

***

It had been so long since Olivia was in a bar. She didn't feel at all comfortable in the short moment they'd been there. She kept looking around, uneasy about the people and the odors; mostly the people, as she was unused to being among a lot of them unless it was in a classroom or a lecture hall.

"You know, it's very antisocial to stare or frown at people so openly," Andrew said.

Olivia frowned at him as well, causing him to chuckle.

"How do people enjoy this? Just sitting around ingesting alcohol?" she asked and shuddered a little.

Andrew leaned back in his chair. "Your skill at oversimplification can be very impressive. For some people, it's their way of relaxation, you know. Just kick back and have a few beers with friends and let the problems of your life slide down your shoulders like dirt under a shower."

He closed his eyes. Olivia grimaced.

"Your skill at metaphors is not impressive at all," she remarked and peered into the glass in front of her then shook her head. "There's no way I'm putting that in my system," she said.

Andrew shrugged. "I just brought you out to see people. I thought it must be boring, you know? Stuck in a laboratory with only me and microbes all day for company. I know human beings are hardly as interesting as the microbes can be, but they do have their own flavor of interesting, don't you think?"

She raised an eyebrow then shook her head. "In fact, I do think a lot and I think this is nonsense. Let's get out of here. Take a walk perhaps?"

Andrew pulled in his long legs, then nodded. Outside was cold but not the unpleasant kind. It was more like the kind that cleared the head and brought calming thoughts into focus. It was the kind that Olivia preferred.

"Do you have family, Andrew?" Olivia asked out of nowhere then realized, to her own embarrassment, that it would have been more appropriate to ask sooner.

Andrew didn't seem to mind as he answered her mildly. "My mother and my sister. They live a bit far from the school, so I had to get a lodge. Dorms don't actually do it for me, you know?"

Dorms didn't do it for Olivia either, but she suspected that it was for a different reason than Andrew's.

"Do you see them often?" she asked.

He shrugged and stuck out his lower lip briefly, making him look like a child. "Yeah, a decent amount. Not had enough time lately to visit, but we make a lot of calls so… I don't think I'm missing much per say."

She nodded. They walked in silence for a while before she spoke again.

"Why did you choose astrobiology?" she asked.

He raised an eyebrow at her.

She shrugged, suddenly feeling the need to explain. "I mean, it's not exactly an old science. In fact, it didn't exist until three years after the arrival of the Terrans and those weird plant-like things that they brought with them. Even though they've refused to be studied, which I guess is okay because I would object to being examined in a table within a lab as well but…, you get the point. So why did you choose it?" she asked again.

He shrugged again, seeming to lean backward, almost as if he was leaning on something and she frowned. She didn't enjoy his terrible posture at all.

"You know? It was new and I like biology and stuff. I was good at it actually and thought of being a doctor or a marine biologist 'cuz, you know? water? diving? Anyway, I wasn't really excited by the prospects but the idea of studying stuff from outer space was very exciting and fascinating to me so… here I am. Though sometimes I do regret it because there's not much to study." He gave a self-conscious laugh as he answered her.

"I regret it too. Sometimes I wish I'd just decided to be a virologist," she said

He nodded and asked, "Because of your brother?"

She nodded and replied, "Don't get me wrong. I love astrobiology or at least the idea of it but… it's not really practical many times and most of what we do is indistinguishable from microbiology anyway. I'm thinking maybe I could take up a degree in that after all this."

Olivia laughed a little like it was a joke, though she knew that somewhere within her, she probably meant it.

Olivia's holophone buzzed and she tapped it into the audio receiver in her back tooth that she had installed more out of convenience than anything. She wouldn't let anything into her brain though. And she wasn't to be moved from that decision.

"Hello, Miss Olivia?" a soft voice came from the other side and she recognized it immediately as one of the nurses on Daniel's case; the one that was always nice to her.

"Hi…" Olivia stopped and almost slapped her forehead, remembering that she had not even asked for the nurse's name.

"It's Beatrice from the isocenter. I'm calling to inform you that your brother and some of the other patients broke out of their wards. I'm so sorry, but it would be good if you could come over here immediately so we can better explain. Would you like us to send a taxicab to pick you up? Could you inform us of your location?"

Olivia stood rooted into the concrete for a while before she finally croaked out a few words and sent her location. She wondered what it meant that her brother *broke out. Had his health been magically re-*

stored? Was this some Terran cure? Why did Eric break out if he had recovered though? What exactly was happening?

She finally croaked out a few words and sent her location. She wondered what it meant that her brother broke out. He wasn't even conscious the last time that she'd seen him. Did the Terrans find a cure that she didn't know about? Even if they did, why did he break out? Eric escaped to join Ork's army as a recruited zombie. The virus did its intended objective now.

Olivia jumped as she felt a hand on her shoulder and looked up into Andrew's concerned face. She almost snapped at him but the pure worry and concern in his eyes made her shut up. "I need to get to the isocenter. Something's wrong… with Eric."

"I'm coming with you then."

She shook her head. "You really don't have to. You have other stuff to do. I can handle this."

Olivia could even hear the shakiness in her own voice.

He gave her a flat stare then calmly shook his head. "I'm coming," he said simply.

Olivia nodded, grateful that he insisted.

The isocenter was in disarray when they got there. There were shattered windows and signs of struggles all over the place. There were smashed monitors and lights and some of the staff were wounded.

"What happened here? Where's Eric?" Olivia asked as Beatrice ran up to her.

Beatrice's eyes were wide like she had just seen something absolutely awful and she placed a hand on Olivia's shoulder. Olivia thought of shrugging it off, but let it rest as she tried to keep herself from panicking.

"Come with me somewhere quieter. I'll explain everything," Beatrice said.

Olivia followed her down the hallway into an office where a man, obviously a doctor from his lab coat and weary appearance, stood with his eyes fixed on the wall like there was an invisible procedure there that he was trying to make sense of. He seemed to snap out of his trance with a visible jolt when Beatrice tapped him on the shoulder. She whispered something to him and his gaze fell on Olivia. There was a mixture of embarrassment, worry, and annoyance in his eyes as he gestured for her to sit.

"Who's this?" he asked, pointing at Andrew.

"A friend," Olivia said and realized that she meant it.

The doctor nodded and adjusted his spectacles.

Olivia didn't sit. "What happened to my brother, doctor?" she asked, fighting to maintain her cool and ignore the absurdity in the idea that her comatosed brother somehow broke out of the isocenter.

"My name is Doctor Farukh. I was in charge of your brother's care and development. He was normal until two days ago when we began to see his skin turning gray. At first, we thought it was a mild effect of the virus, but it spread rapidly. We tried contacting you, but we couldn't. It wasn't until much later that he woke up. His eyes were entirely white and he had unnatural strength. We did our best to restrain him, but it didn't amount to much. Six of the earliest victims also showed the same signs and before we could do much about it, they overpowered our security and escaped. We have been keeping a close eye on the others. We've requested assistance but, for now, we have barricaded their doors and sealed them shut until we know what…."

"You're trying to say that my brother woke up all of a sudden and escaped? Is that what you're telling me?" Olivia demanded.

Dr. Farukh nodded slowly, clearly embarrassed. He also looked very weary and sad, but Olivia was beyond the point of caring. "We don't know much about the virus at all. There was no way we could have…"

"Actually, you do," a voice said from outside the door and it slowly opened to let a seven-foot-tall alien in. He stretched to his full height after passing in a stoop through the door.

Olivia saw that it was Elk. There was no change to his person or demeanor, but she had the feeling that he was infuriated.

"Her research provided the procedure by which this strain of the virus could be predicted and appropriate measures could have been taken. But I will not bother you with that as it is not your fault," Elk continued.

He turned to Olivia, who was surprised to see him away from his city.

Andrew was looking up at the alien in barely disguised awe and Beatrice looked like all the blood had been pulled from her entire body.

"I apologize for not contacting you sooner but there were matters to tend to. Your brother is being tracked down as we speak, and in a short while, he will be taken into our own custody where he will receive the best care available." Elk spoke calmly.

Olivia was relieved and at the same time, frustrated, angry, and very tired.

"I told the Commonwealths and all those conceited fools at the S.net that you were not far off the mark and with a little modification, your research would have been the break we needed, but they would not listen and could not get over their own pride and ego to admit it. I expect that a few of them have taken your research under closer study, will modify it and add a little something and declare it theirs, but that is not something we have to worry about now. The same thing that happened to your brother has been replicated in isocenters all over the world," Elk spoke.

"What? Why? How is this even happening?" Olivia asked.

Elk gestured towards the door. "Let us discuss this on our way out of here. Soon, the Commonwealths will declare a lockdown on all isocenters and this city, in fact, as it was ground zero. It would be a fair assumption that they are already pointing fingers at each other and squabbling as usual. I expect that my kind would be the object of their suspicion soon and that is a possibility I have to prepare for. Come, there is little time to waste." As he said this, he walked out the door briskly.

It was an arduous task to keep up with Elk's inhumanly long gait and they stepped into a hovercraft that was waiting outside. The inside was *way* larger than the outside suggested and looked like a small house.

"I have adjusted the atmosphere to suit you," a Terran who stood close to Elk immediately walked in and said to them.

"This is Tekka, my second. More of an assistant in your terms," Elk said and proceeded to a table upon which things like threads moved quickly past his vision.

It was only after careful thought that Olivia realized that this was their own equivalent of reading. She didn't even notice when the hovercraft took to the air. "Where are we going?" she asked.

"I'm taking you to a laboratory outside the city. Trust me, you do not want to be caught within the city by the time the Commonwealths start with it. They have also demanded an explanation from my people and are, in fact, waiting for me back at my city. This will be tricky." Elk said this quietly and made a hum and a sharp whistle escaped him.

Tekka made a sound like the purring of many cats and Olivia thought that the atmosphere seemed to ease a little.

"Why me? Why did you come take me?" she asked.

Elk turned to look at her. The neutrality of his face unnerved her sometimes, but it was something she imagined she would soon get used to.

"Actually, I came for both of you."

Olivia looked behind to see a surprised Andrew staring at Elk.

"When we came here, we began monitoring some of the young, brightest, and most curious people with the right combination of character traits. Yours was nearly ruined when your parents left you, but you proved to be stronger than we expected and became a very special and interesting specimen among your kind. There are a few dozen others and I have relocated them to safe spots as well. I cannot work with the current people at the helm of affairs… not entirely anyways, but in time, I believe I can work with you and others like you." After Elk said this, he then made a low buzzing sound. He gestured to a protrusion around his neck. It was about the diameter of a coin and an inch thick. "This is my buzzer and it conveys what is the equivalent of expression to your kind. The buzzing sound, in very rigid terms, is the equivalent of a smile," he said and buzzed again.

Olivia nodded and felt a bit of elation. The fact that he had shared this with her seemed to validate her hard work somehow.

Elk stepped out of his hovercraft. They had just dropped Olivia and Andrew off, and he felt his shoulders tighten with the strain of having to leash his anger and hold his patience this long as it was necessary to deal with humans. His temper wasn't like theirs and it felt like he was almost always angry, even at the slightest irritation.

Elk was not tendered for this. In his home planet he was meant for only one thing: war and leadership in war. The war had wiped out all of the diplomats which forced him to have to learn and refine his ways to suit the ways of diplomacy. It wasn't an easy thing and it still disturbed him even now, but it was a sacrifice for his people. It was necessary and his personal discomfort didn't matter.

Even from this distance, he could sense their anger, their suspicion, and their resentment. He could also sense envy in some, and it irked him. He walked down the narrow hall into his office and saw several of them lounging in chairs.

Elk had not missed the armed soldiers and the military hovercrafts camped outside his city. Normally, that would have been enough for him to launch an attack, but they were not his enemies. They were frightened and confused, and their natural inclinations worsened those feelings.

"Gentlemen," Elk said.

One of them, a tall broad man with grayish hair and a thick beard, wearing a full military uniform that signified him as General of the Unified Military of the Commonwealths, came to stand before him. Elk looked down at the man and found a measure of respect for him. This was a warrior such as himself and that was something he could respect.

"Good afternoon, Elk. I do apologize for this intrusion into your home and I assure you it would never have happened if it had not been due to the, ah, recent events around the world," he said.

Elk nodded. "You want to check our laboratories, search our offices, and mount an inquisition on my tribe, yes?" he asked.

The man looked away for a brief moment before he met Elk's flat eyes and nodded. Elk felt Tekka's calmness hit him like a wave before he could react impulsively and he calmed himself, forcing his mind to approach the situation logically.

"You are welcome to look and search and anything you find confusing. You can ask any of the guides that will be given to you, but I expect a lot of it will be strange, considering the disparity between our races," Elk said.

The General nodded and said, "Thank you and please accept my apologies."

"You're just doing your job. Might I also add that this is a gross waste of time because if it is what I think it is, then we should devote our time to other things. This could be..." Elk began.

"An attack from extraterrestrials? In that case, I should think our time and resources are being spent quite well," one of the men interrupted.

Elk let the insult roll off him before he spoke again. "I do not know you. Who are you?" he asked.

The man straightened himself and approached Elk and said, "My name is Mashood. I am an advisor to the North African Commonwealth on military and defense affairs."

Elk nodded. "I see. I assure you, Moshood, that by the time this is over, you will wish you had listened to me. That is if you remain capable of making wishes. Do not think I threaten you for that is not my intent. I am just stating the truth."

As Elk said this, the man's face twisted into a frown. "I suppose you would also like to interrogate me?" Elk asked.

The man nodded, not being able to keep away the satisfaction in his eyes. Elk tilted his head to the side very slowly.

"That would not be possible, I'm afraid. There are pressing matters to tend to. In fact, while we have been wasting time here, more of the infected have broken out of their hospitals and isocenters and are currently walking the streets, wreaking havoc. This is a grievous waste of time," Elk said and turned to leave.

"You will remain here, Elk. By order of the Union of the Commonwealths," Moshood bellowed.

A sound like metals clanging together came from Elk's buzzer as he stopped. "No, I do not think I will remain. Careful not to disrupt too much in your inspection," he said and continued to walk, leaving his office.

CHAPTER FIVE

Olivia watched the world literally break apart before her very eyes. It was like watching a horror movie. She kept on searching the faces of the infected shown on the news and was fractionally glad that Eric's face was not among them yet she knew that somewhere he looked just like them and probably led some of them, considering…

Olivia tried to push the thoughts away from the forefront of her mind and focus on work instead. She had three assistants now and a bigger, well-equipped space, but she had lost a lot of her focus, most of it being replaced with worry.

They noticed that almost all the infected seemed to be traveling in one direction. Their movements were anything but haphazard. It was almost as if they knew exactly where they were going and it was a place that Olivia knew because she'd been there before; the lake with the microbes.

Olivia wondered what exactly was there as the population of infected grew and they pressed against each other until they were basically a swarming mass. She couldn't remove her mind from the fact that somewhere among them was Eric, growling and sapped of his own ability to think. She stifled a shudder. Andrew kept an eye on her like an overprotective parent and would occasionally offer her coffee or something like that out of the blue.

Elk walked in wearing a dark robe that was buttoned at the sides of the chest. He walked straight to where Olivia stood and remained silent, watching her for such a long time. It seemed like he was deciding something.

Finally, he spoke, "I told you before that we were under attack. I did not know who it was exactly that was attacking us, but I am sure of who it is now. And, I must say, Olivia, though it is not my intention to cause panic at all. This enemy is one of the worst that could have taken an interest in Earth,"

Olivia's eyes widened as she watched him wordlessly zoom in on the lake with cameras that were previously installed around the site. Most of the ones installed by the Commonwealths had been found and taken apart by the infected, but Elk's scientists were a tad better at camouflage and their cameras had gone unnoticed.

They watched as bubbles seemed to ripple across the lake and increase steadily in frequency until it seemed like the entire lake was boiling. Then, black forms began to appear from it. They looked like hovercrafts but were so black they seemed to absorb even the light around them and seemed like holes of blackness more than anything else.

"Elk?" Olivia croaked when the worst of her speechlessness and terror had passed. "What are those?"

She heard the sound of metal clanging from Elk's buzzer and needed no explanation to understand that it wasn't even remotely friendly.

"They are pods. Stealth pods to be precise. I know of only one kind that has such rare technology so handy that he can afford fifty vehicles equipped with it," Elk said.

Olivia turned back to the camera and was startled to see that even more of the pods had popped out on the water. They glided towards the shore and the infected gave way for them. They seemed to remain there, almost as if they were paused in time. Then, they began to open, making sounds like cracking eggs followed by long hisses and a letting out of what looked like red steam from within.

Then, creatures emerged that were twice a man's height, had tawny, leathery bodies, rounded eyes as if sealed into their oblong heads and noses that were nasally interlocked with their mouths, imbued to stream whatever it was that they breathed. They also had small, enclosed hands, but with an aperture in each and mind-reading abilities.

The latter Olivia found out from Elk shortly before he left. It was more a warning than anything and she felt her chest begin to hurt and her head spin. Yes, she had wanted something from outer space, but not this. Certainly not this.

***

Ork stood in what used to be a stadium, taking in all the strangeness of this new world. Had it not been for his peoples' superior skills at adaptation and their months of preparation, this would have been a bit too much. The sky had little yellow in it and the sun was far too bright for their sensitive eyes, but the worst of it was the screaming thoughts of everyone on this planet. They never guarded their thoughts and images and words and songs kept floating into his consciousness in such torrents that he had to block most of it out. Even then, it felt like too much to handle.

Ork watched as the infected worked hard at building something resembling an abode. He entertained the thought of actually attacking the alien base, but decided that it would be much too soon and he had brought only forty of his best, but that would have to do. He had taken out planets with far less.

"You have infiltrated Earth's atmosphere and have made adjustments to her infrastructure without permission. The Union of Commonwealths demands an audience with your leader," a voice boomed from somewhere outside the stadium.

Mastering their languages and modes of communication was a trivial thing as it was too simple and basic, too limited. Ork analyzed the voice that spoke and perceived fear. In every species, in every civilization, there was always that common denominator; the perception of a superior force and the instinctive wariness of that force. He cherished that and took strength from it and began to walk outside.

They were so small. Small in both mind and body. And, as it would appear, Ork thought they were extremely fragile as well, with skeletons that could be crushed with all the force of an afterthought. How they were still able to survive up to this moment was a mystery to him. He watched as they made their demands to know him and his intentions.

It was a truly amusing thing and Ork buzzed accordingly. He could see their military hovercrafts, planes, and tanks and could smell some of the technology of his home planet on them.

It didn't matter though. They would fall just as the others had fallen before them and he would make a spectacle of it. Ork could hear their thoughts growing more frantic and he could perceive their fear rising. When it had gotten to a sufficiently high degree, it could cause irrationality, which was what he hoped for.

It was Ork's creed never to be the first to use force on a planet, but they were always the first to use force on him. And, it was interesting because whenever they took that route, they were unable to sustain it.

Ork was pleased when they finally felt threatened and he still watched them, basking under the illusion that they had him outnumbered. They would pay for that foolish idea soon. He would make sure of it.

Almost immediately, a missile was fired from one of the hover-crafts. Ork watched as the weak thing hit the barrier that his men had set up around the stadium and dissolved harmlessly into ash. He wondered how something as big as a hovercraft could possibly wield such little power.

Ork mentally switched in the lasers in the gauntlet of his armor and stretched out his arm. An overpoweringly bright yellow beam shot out of the gauntlet and melted the tank and flesh alike. He raised it up and brought down the hovercrafts from the sky, exulting in the destruction he was causing.

When Ork had finished, he turned around and went back to his business silently. Here was a civilization ripe for the taking and, in a little while, they would learn to fear and worship him, leaving their will at his feet.

The only possible hindrance was the race of aliens, a cousin species to his own people who now lived among the humans. He thought about Elk and was excited. It would be good to match wits and will with him again he thought and went back to the supervision of the construction.

***

"What is the meaning of this?!" the man yelled and slammed the table.

Elk slowly turned towards him. What point did that display of aggression serve? They were always wasting their energy on the wrong things. He was thinking about Ork, who was almost surely behind this. Elk felt like this was the universe offering him a chance to redeem himself.

Elk thought of all the lives that were lost, all of the destruction Ork had brought, and he thought about his own inability to stop him. They would meet again and there would be an end to this. Elk brought back all of his faculties to the argument. They were considering whether to mount a direct offensive or to try and negotiate for a truce.

Many of them had witnessed first-hand Ork's might and it had frightened and intimidated them. Elk wished that their fears were unfounded, but they actually were. Most of the technologies and the materials of his people had been lost during the war, and, when they had made their great retreat across the stars, more was also lost. So they had arrived here with only a miserly fraction of their normal strength.

Already, the best minds among Elk's people were hard at work to try to retrieve what was lost, but much couldn't be retrieved and much would take far longer than the time Ork would give them before he launched his full-scale attack.

Still, they couldn't sit around and wait while he gathered strength. They must attack the very moment his foot is not yet steady on this planet.

"I think it would be prudent for us to attack first. We have the advantage at this point, no matter how slim it might look. We do have the advantage and it is quickly slipping from us. We must attack, and soon. With the Terrans' help, we can push this alien filth back into the deepest, darkest gutters of the galaxy where they crawled out from!" a woman boomed.

Elk knew her well and respected her greatly. Field Marshal Willows was as efficient and as calculating as humans came. And she was a warrior to the roots of her soul.

"I support her," Elk said.

Willows turned to him, her gray eyes looking over him once before she nodded.

"I have fought Ork before, and I assure you that the only reason he has not attacked yet is because he is trying to build a base, to get a grip on affairs and when he does, whatever he does will be swift and ruthless and will bring such destruction that you could never imagine. Even if you're successful in getting anything akin to a treaty, it would just be buying him more time. If we are to do anything, we must do it now," Elk said. Willows nodded her agreement.

"You say you have battled this Ork before, yes? Do you perhaps have any ideas as to why he has chosen to attack us? Perhaps it could be because of his issue with you and your people. Perhaps you can take your battle back into the farthest reaches of the galaxy and leave our planet the heck out of it," another man questioned.

It was in moments like these that Elk wondered exactly how humans chose their generals. "Ork doesn't care if I am here or not. He might, but it would be very low on his list. Ork is a single-minded, aggressive, and extremely intelligent commander who somehow has decided that free will is a gift that must be granted only to those who absolutely have proven worthy of it and has decided to make himself a master of wills and of every intelligent life in the universe. He has been going from planet to planet. Some have been destroyed when they showed little potential or have proven too strong for easy manipulation. Some, he has decided to rule. It does not matter if I leave or stay. Earth has caught his attention and that is the end of the matter."

The man grumbled a little then fell silent.

"I guess it comes down to a vote then," Willows said and sighed. "All in favor of attacking?" she asked and raised her hand, along with around fifty-six generals there. She smiled a crooked, wicked smile then shrugged. "I guess that settles it then," she added and turned to Elk. "You are the only one among us who has fought on this scale before. I shall defer to you in the matter of talking. Now tell us, what's your plan?"

***

Olivia paced the entire length of the laboratory a few times, then finally plopped down into a chair to think. In a way, it was mildly exciting to know that there were other races, other beings strewed across the galaxy, and, though she wondered why they had waited this long to make themselves known, she was also terrified to death for her brother's life.

Olivia wondered if the infection was even reversible. She wondered a lot of things and, though she knew that this was probably crippling her analytical thinking, she didn't care. She saw the tall shadow blocking out the light from the hallway before Elk stepped in.

Olivia had some difficulty recognizing Elk and her mouth dropped at the changes that had taken place in his physique. His face was leaner, meaner, and his eyes had a reddish tint to them. His muscles were fuller and he seemed to have added a full foot with spikes jutting out of his shoulders and forearms.

"Pardon my appearance. This is how my body changes when a battle is close. It is a more efficient form for the rigors of the field," Elk said.

Olivia's eyes widened even more as she stared at him and understood the full meaning of his words. "You… you are going to fight him? What if he gets angry? What if he decided to kill everyone that has been infected?" she asked.

Elk made a sound that she couldn't describe, then stepped closer to her. "He has no interest in them, Olivia. He does not understand things in that manner and he would not see their lives as worth much unless we make him think that by our actions. We must pretend that their lives do not matter in order to protect them. You see?"

Olivia thought she might have been imagining it, but his voice was softer. She didn't think it was possible that his voice could be soft and the manner with which he spoke of Ork. "Do you know him?" she asked.

Elk tilted his head to the side. She had understood this to be his own equivalent of a nod. "My planet had two species... if you ignore the plant and animal matter, of course. In your planet, only humanity evolved to the pinnacle of intelligence but imagine if the chimpanzees got to that level as well," he said.

Olivia felt her interest peak at what he was saying. She adjusted in order to face him.

"There was us, who lived in the... cleaner, friendlier part of the planet and we had no need to be overly strong or aggressive. But his kind evolved in the parts that were... the badlands, I guess, but that would be a gross understatement. They evolved to be extremely aggressive, with a very limited emotional span, and very manipulative and exploitative, but somehow we had an agreement and lived together. They had their own social systems and we had ours, until... Ork happened. I do not know how and I do not know why but he began to have this understanding that free will was bad and it was more to the detriment of all intelligent life than its absence so he made it his mission to eradicate it. He was also after something else. Something that would make his self-imposed mission easier. He first dominated his people and brainwashed them, then he began to search for the object..."

"What object?" Olivia asked

Elk remained silent for a long while. Then, Olivia understood that he wasn't going to reply to that question. She feared for a while that he wouldn't continue to speak, but he finally did.

"By the time Ork was done with his people, he was no longer content. He came for my people and the war ensued. Billions died because of one creature's ambition and, in the end, our planet was destroyed. Ork has continued since and has shown no signs of stopping. I had hoped that his sights would be turned away from Earth long enough for us to be ready but... well, we have to be ready now," Elk said then went quiet.

Olivia couldn't imagine how much Elk'd lost; his home, family, and most of his people. Up to the point where he had to squat on a foreign planet. Her respect for this Terran deepened in that moment.

Finally, Elk stood and left without another word. Olivia wondered why he bothered to tell her this and she was grateful he did. At the same time she was worried for her brother and didn't trust that Ork would leave him unharmed.

CHAPTER SIX

Ork was far from happy with how slow the construction was going. He had already driven many of the infected to their limits. Some had died, but it didn't matter to him. Their lives were worth nothing in the grand scheme of things.

Ord had already built communication devices to enable him to send messages faster than light-speed into deep space and now he wanted a full base of operations. He needed things to proceed quickly for there were more worlds to conquer and he couldn't afford to waste time on this one.

Ork sensed aggression and human thoughts and knew that planes were headed in their direction; high-speed planes with deadly payloads. Ork wondered if he should send some of the pods to confront them, but decided that would be like killing a rodent with a laser gun. He decided that he would send out a dozen of his men to obliterate them in the sky.

Ork was irritated by their weakness and the fact that they didn't realize and accept his superiority. It was an inconvenience that he would have to deal with.

Ork communicated telepathically with a dozen of his finest soldiers with orders to bring down the planes. He had read their thoughts for any other plan or tactic and found none. He cursed their simplicity in not making a plan within a plan within a plan. Ork soon put them out of his mind. They were dead anyway.

Ork heard the explosions and turned immediately to see holes in his barrier. He watched as the planes that shot them were brought down by the armor lasers of his own shoulders. Other sets of missiles were fired and they further weakened his barrier and his anger surged when he realized the only people who could possibly have been behind this advanced attack.

It was also probable that the pilots didn't even know the type of missiles they were equipped with, so Ork couldn't read their minds and find out. He knew it was something that Elk could do and he felt the old hatred for that creature rise within him again. Ork wished desperately that he had taken Elk's life when the opportunity had first presented itself.

Ork felt something like an earthquake and before he could realize what was happening, the walls of the stadium began to crumble, taken apart from below. He saw them fall apart and knew that the Terrans had joined the fray.

Without their support, most of the barrier collapsed, letting in high-speed hovercrafts that met the full firepower of Ork's weapons including a vacuum laser that crushed whatever it touched into nothing. Ork had no time for his pods to take to the air while his men fought back with their own long-range lasers and guns with their armor made of an alloy that was taken from one of the conquered planets, a hundred times stronger than diamond and as light as a sweater. His men could withstand the fire power of the Terrans. Ork cursed in his language and it sounded harsh and foul, terrible to hear.

Elk stood within his hovercraft overseeing the battle and he realized that it wasn't one that he could win. At least not at the moment. The fire power and technological advancement of the enemy far outranked theirs. And, while they had only succeeded in wounding one of Ork's soldiers, he had taken casualties of about a dozen of his soldiers which, considering the already weak population of the Terrans, was a painful loss.

Elk waited, watching Ork at the center of the field knowing that if he met with Ork now, he would lose and it wouldn't even be the appropriate time, but Elk was already sufficiently weakened that he would probably allow for a truce to give them time to build back stronger.

Only Elk and the Terrans would build faster. Ork's communication devices had been taken out and he was basically lost out here. It was time to call off the battle, for it had served its purpose. Elk contacted Field Marshal Willows and it seemed she had seen the same thing he had because, though it came grudgingly, she agreed to call off the attack.

Elk knew that he would meet Ork again and he would finally redeem himself and take vengeance for his home and his people.

***

Ork couldn't believe it. It seemed that the humans didn't even know the plan of attack of the Terrans, as nothing was in their minds that could give it away.

In one fatal swoop, the Terrans had set him back months. Ork had lost one soldier and didn't know how long it would be until reinforcements came. His anger knew no bounds and he swore then that when the planet became his, he would burn one third of it down and make the rest suffer unimaginable horrors for this humiliation. He would find Elk and publicly execute him and wipe off the race of weaklings that he had once shared a planet with.

Ork fumed with rage as he watched the destruction of his base. It didn't matter that the Terrans retreated. Their work was already done and it wounded Ork's pride. He cultivated restraint, managing to get a modicum of calmness, for he couldn't properly analyze and plan. He knew that they would want a treaty for the moment and he was ready for it. Ork would accept and later he would unleash hell on them for having such guts. He took a little bit of comfort from that.

"I have to go for him," Olivia said suddenly.

Andrew winced like he was slapped, then slowly turned to look at her. It was only when he saw no hint of jest in her face that he began to mildly panic. "Are you mad?" he asked slowly.

Olivia nodded; then nodded again. "Maybe I am mad, you know? But he's my brother. He's everything that I have. Some of the infected died during the attack and some even died before from the labor. If he's alive, I have to find him and get him out of there," she said.

Andrew scratched his hair with his hands and exhaled through puffed cheeks. "What are you saying? That place is heavily guarded and those things can read minds, Olivia. They can read minds! I bet they already know you're coming now that you're thinking about it. Olivia, I know that you don't listen to me often, but please listen to me when I tell you that this is a horrible, awful idea. On a scale of one to ten of horrible ideas, this is a one hundred. Elk will figure this out. Just… just don't do whatever it is that your mind tells you at this moment," he pleaded.

Olivia watched him, seeing the desperation in his eyes. In truth, she hadn't thought much about how to get him out, but she knew that she couldn't sit around while her brother's life remained at risk. She didn't know what she would do if he died. She already didn't know what to do, but she schooled her expression and wiped the panic from her face and nodded. "Yeah, yeah, you're right. It's crazy I know," she said and felt mild pity when she saw the relief that became very visible on Andrew's face.

"Yes, I'm right. Perhaps you need some time off work for a while. Just kick back and relax. This will be over soon and we'll all be fine," he said

Olivia saw something pass quickly across his face, then she realized and was shocked. "Oh my God, Andrew. Your family! Have you heard from them recently?" she asked.

He shook his head, suddenly looking very tired and worn down. "I'm pretty sure that they're fine, you know? I mean, it's not like they're in the center of things."

Olivia nodded, wanting to encourage him but not finding the words to do so.

"It feels weird, though. You know? Leaving them there while I'm in relative safety and comfort here. I really don't know what's happening and it's terrifying. Aliens and battles and freaking zombies. Ork has no army now, so he uses a mysterious virus to transform humans into zombies so that he can recruit them as mercenaries but with no payment whatsoever. But, it would do no good to complicate it further by rushing headlong into the madness. If you go to rescue him, think about who would have to rescue you," Andrew said and sighed heavily.

Olivia bit her lower lip then adjusted her glasses a little.

"You should get some rest," Andrew said.

She agreed. "You should as well," she reminded him.

He nodded and rubbed his hair. "Yeah probably," he said and smiled a little.

Olivia stood and walked away, leaving him there. Her mind worked on how it was possible for Andrew to be so calm while his family was in danger. She wasn't like him. She wouldn't 'get some rest' while her brother was being handled like a puppet on a string by those god-forsaken aliens.

Andrew yawned and stretched, feeling his muscles respond appropriately. He was always grateful for the miracle of sleep and he took great care to participate in that miracle whenever he had the opportunity. He rubbed his eyes and hair and thought about how close they were to finding a cure. It excited him that soon they would get through this and it was mostly because of Olivia's ingenious ideas.

Andrew and Olivia had stripped the virus down to its basic structure and had reverse engineered it with help from the aliens. It was thrilling how much this race had advanced and how working with them made everything easier.

Andrew took a quick shower and went down to the kitchen to eat while thinking about his wife and daughter, wondering if they even had enough to eat. He would ask Elk to try and find anything he could about them. It would make him feel a bit better perhaps to know that they're okay.

Andrew yawned and tapped one of the meals available and it was quickly prepared by the culinary robots in almost the blink of an eye. Then, another robot that was about half a man's height and moved on wheels served him.

Andrew wondered why Olivia was still asleep. She should've been awake at least a couple of hours earlier than him, if she had gotten any sleep at all. He decided to go check on her. She had almost become like family to him recently and he found himself worrying about her welfare like he would a sister and even though this was a nice development, it also scared him because he had never seen someone so good at self-neglect as Olivia.

Andrew got to Olivia's door and pressed the doorbell. After a while, he pressed it again and suspicion began to build in his mind. He tapped into the building's system and asked if Olivia was in her room, a question which got a negative reply.

Andrew felt cold sweat run down his back as he repeatedly asked again if anyone had left the building and he got an affirmative reply. He gasped and felt terror rise in his body.

All the Terrans had left prior to the battle, but he knew he had to contact them now or it was a sure thing that Olivia would get herself killed, if she hadn't already.

Andrew contacted Elk's personal line which was given to him and the others whom Elk had selected. A voice came from the other side which he knew to be Tekka's.

"Andrew," he said by way of greeting.

"Olivia has vanished. I think she went to find her brother. I think she went to collect him or something. She'll die, Tekka. I need your help, I need…"

"Calm yourself. She will be found and brought back. Until then I advise that you maintain a calm and rational head because if you go chasing after her, then I would be truly irritated," Tekka said dryly.

Andrew nodded, though he knew that Tekka couldn't see him as it was merely an audio transmission. "I understand. Umm, yeah, of course I understand. Just... find her, okay?" he said.

The line went off from Tekka's end. Andrew had the feeling that the Terran was annoyed and he understood. He too was annoyed, but more worried and terrified than annoyed. Andrew promised himself that he would give Olivia a piece of his mind if she came back in one piece. It wasn't long before he was pacing the entire length of the living area.

***

Ork stared at the committee that had gathered to make the treaty with him. They looked so small. They seemed like toddlers of his kind and just being in their presence offended him. They smelled wrong and looked wrong, and it was an act of supreme will and restraint that he didn't obliterate all of them sitting there. Not that he was entirely sure he could though because Elk stood at the back, staring at him, his thoughts impenetrable.

As much as Ork hated the Terran, there was a grudging respect for his strength and silent courage. Ork would break all of those soon enough. The humans' minds, though, were naked and bare. He already knew what they would ask him.

"You wish to know why I have come, yes?" Ork asked.

A murmur rippled through them. Ork had chosen a voice that would reverberate through their consciousness and cause an awakening of fear and doubt which would affect their decisions.

"My name is Ork. General Ork in your terms. And, I have come, just as the Terrans before me, to find refuge in your planet as mine was destroyed."

Ork knew that they knew that he was lying but they wouldn't and couldn't call him out now.

"Since that was your intent, why have you decided to use violence instead of communicating your intentions to us directly from the beginning? A lot of destruction and loss would have been avoided if that was done," a woman said from among the delegates.

Ork paused a little, quelling the fires of rage that were common to his kind and usually came unbidden and unprovoked, though there was a little provocation now.

"I was not the first to use force if you would remember. I had just been introduced into a strange world of which I knew nothing about and it was a very disorienting reality that I needed time to adjust to. You must understand my confusion when my base is surrounded by hostiles and my hesitation in replying to them. I was acting only in self-defense when I attacked after they had shot at my base," Ork replied.

Ork loathed the fact that he was explaining himself to these inferior creatures, but took solace from the fact that they would be paying for his humiliation soon enough.

"My home was ruined and, unlike the Terrans before me, I come with only a small number of my people and my stay here is not to be permanent. I only ask for some time to heal and grow before we find a more suitable home among the stars. I apologize for any misunderstanding that happened before, and grieve for your losses as well. All of this could have been easily avoided and I regret the part I played," he said and felt the words burn like flames in his mouth.

"Since it is sanctuary that you wish, and you have apologized for your misdeeds, we have the intention of granting it; provided that our conditions are met of course," the spokesman said.

Ork inclined his head a little; a show of respect he had learned among all the nonsensical subtleties of these people, and it was useful at this point. "As it should be. Please, let me hear them," he said, adjusting his tone to one of respect and deference.

"First, you must agree that no attack will be launched on any property or human or anything within or affiliated with humanity, including the Terrans. You must also agree to keep us up-to-speed on your development as you build and grow and inform us of any help you should need in order to hasten your recovery. You must also stop the progress of the virus that has been, hopefully inadvertently, planted by your arrival amongst our people. As long as you meet these terms, humanity will offer you the sanctuary you request in good faith," he said.

Ork rumbled within himself but was careful to maintain an outward show of understanding and contemplation. "No attack will be launched by me or any of mine upon anything that is, belongs to, or is affiliated with Earth in any manner. I shall also keep you in the loop on all our projects and developments. Though I must warn you, that there would be more than a little complexity in it as the disparity between us in both technology and measures of literacy and culture is far too wide, but we will try our best. As for the virus, we have no known cure at the moment, but we will work hard on that as well; sharing whatever information we gather with your scientists. It has afflicted my kind for a long while and we have bred to become immune to it over time. I am sure that finding a cure would not be a task that would prove too difficult," he said and inclined his head respectfully, hating the motion with every fiber of his being.

"For the damages on my own people, I ask that you release half of the infected currently in your possession," Elk said.

Ork looked up at him and fought to keep the ugly hiss that signaled extreme rage from sounding. He decided that this was not something he was going to do. If Elk wanted it, that was enough reason for him to withhold it. For all he knew, those infected could be part of a strategy that Elk had thought up. Even if it weren't for that, his hatred for Elk would be sufficient for him to deny anything that Elk asked.

"I am afraid that I cannot do that," Ork said.

Elk stepped away from the wall he was leaning on. "What do you mean you 'cannot'? Those people are ill. They should be resting in hospital wards rather than acting as slaves for whatever you are building. They have families and friends. I hear that some of them have already been worked to death. It is because of this that I ask you to release a number of them: the young, the old, and the weak."

All the men there nodded their agreement. Ork knew that this was a request he couldn't easily refuse. If he refused it, then he would have to fight again and he needed to conserve their energy until the rest of his army arrived. Ork needed those infected, but in the long run they didn't mean much to him. It wasn't like the entire fate of this war rested on them. The only effect, visible at least, that it would have would be the reduction in the speed at which his plans moved. And that was probably what Elk was after.

"I currently have six thousand three hundred and twenty-four infected with me. Of those, I will release two thousand," Ork said.

"Four," Elk replied quickly.

"Three, and that is final. I have to hold some as leverage to make sure you do not go back on our agreement."

"And what leverage do we have to make sure you keep yours?" the spokesman asked.

Ork slowly stretched his arms in a wide gesture. "I am on your planet, at the mercy of your armies. What other leverage could you possibly need?"

"Three of your soldiers," Elk said.

Ork almost let out a hiss. He knew that if he did, he wouldn't be able to control himself any longer. He would make sure that none of those filthy human scum currently here with him would make it out alive. "I cannot give you three of my soldiers," he said. Under normal circumstances, he wouldn't mind giving up any of his soldiers. He wasn't like the emotional commanders that were blinded by their supposed loyalty to their men, but he couldn't afford to be as weak as the loss of three men would make him be.

"Two," Elk said.

Ork cursed him in his mind as he slammed his hand on the platform before him. "This cannot be bargained. I will give you none of my soldiers and that is that!" he shouted.

Elk's flat stare remained for a while before he finally nodded and stepped back to lean against the wall like he had not spoken.

Ork noticed that he was still in his battle form which meant that their guards hadn't been lowered one bit. He cursed fate for making him meet the one person who had any chance of foiling his plans. Trying to control his rage was a huge strain on him, but Ork maintained control; imagining the moment he would not have to; the time he would make Elk pay for his insolence and disrespect.

CHAPTER SEVEN

Olivia could smell sweat and blood and some other unnatural smells that made her belly turn. She tried not to venture into the cluster of the infected. She was loitering around the edges instead, praying that she'd be able to spot her brother.

Olivia held a tranquilizer that had enough punch to knock out three men and she hoped that the same thing that had given her brother unnatural strength also gave him unnatural endurance; enough to just pass out after she had given him the injection. Provided that she would find him first.

Olivia didn't know how the infected detected those who were one of them, so she painted herself to look like them. She whipped up a compound that mimicked their stench, hoping they didn't use anything else except their sight and noses to perceive one of their kind. She also kept from talking or making any noise, remaining as perfectly quiet as them with even the absence of the periodic snort that was usual among the infected.

Slowly, she began to grow desperate. Olivia saw a soldier, but he didn't seem to pay too much mind to the infected and she kept her thoughts and fear as quiet as possible. She didn't expect that the infected feared the soldiers, and showing fear would be a beacon to summon all of them.

Olivia began to move deeper into the infected territory and the smell grew so bad under the sun that she couldn't breathe or even think properly. Olivia still forced herself onwards, hoping desperately to see that soft chin and dimpled cheeks, that mess of black hair; but she saw nothing.

After a long while, Olivia was sweaty and on the verge of losing her cool. She saw him, staring vacantly into space. His brown eyes were gone, replaced by an utter block of white. His skin was broken, dry and gray, and his hair had grown to his lower neck. She felt her heart break a hundred times as she saw him, and she slowly started to approach him when she heard a hum that seemed to come from the ground.

Something seemed to press against her mind and she instinctively pushed it out. It was then that she saw the yellowish sheen covering the sky above her and she knew that the barrier was up again. Her heart sank into her chest. It seemed that things were determined to get worse because the infected started moving with more speed and energy, going for various parts of the new stadium that Ork had chosen.

Olivia wondered what it was with Ork and stadiums, but her mind didn't really have time for such trivial thoughts as she looked around. But she didn't find her brother.

Then, Olivia made the mistake of panicking. Before she knew what was happening, a nine-foot-tall shadow covered hers and she looked up to see what was unmistakably one of Ork's soldiers staring down at her.

Olivia knew that it was futile to run, but she did anyway. He merely reached out and caught her leg, pulling her up until she was upside down and swinging from his deathly strong grip. Olivia began to feel heat from his grip and it grew hotter until she felt her feet start to burn.

Olivia let out a scream, then heard a sound like the breaking of rocks and the whirling of a great wind. She was immediately dropped. She whimpered and sobbed in pain, feeling the burn still on her legs.

"Who are you?" Olivia heard a deep, reverberating voice say from somewhere behind her. She turned to see an equally tall alien who she recognized immediately because of his distinctive armor that was designed separately from the rest. Terror filled her chest and made her want to weep as she realized that she was in the presence of Ork, the one that destroyed worlds. The one that had destroyed Elk's world.

"I suppose there is no need to bother asking when I can simply see it," he said.

Olivia felt her mind being pried open. She tried to block him out, but she was helpless against the force of his will. It didn't take long before she felt his mind in hers, turning her thoughts, dreams, desires, and fears over like a potter inspecting a piece of clay. After he was done, he left her. But she felt loose and open like a small shoe that had been worn by a giant.

"Greetings, Olivia. It is really sad and I cannot imagine how hard it must be for creatures like you that are always governed by tender thoughts to the point of irrationality. Look at you, knowing that the chances of you succeeding were almost nonexistent, yet you came. That must be very difficult to live with," Ork said, almost thoughtfully.

Olivia tried to speak but her saliva had dried in her mouth and she couldn't think clearly through the pain on her leg.

"You are important to Elk and I am not sure why, but I would like to find out; which is why I will keep you alive," Ork said and picked her up with all the effort it would take to pick up a rag doll.

Then, he carried her to the platform at the highest point of the stadium that looked more like a throne room with a chair carved out of an unidentifiable metal.

Ork watched her silently while she nursed her wounds, then he looked away. He began to speak to his men in their own tongue, which was fiery and sounded often like tornadoes, grinding clicks, and the clash of metal that evoked feelings of anger, disgust, fear, and a little excitement.

"It is a sad thing, isn't it? How every living thing in this universe wastes a gift given freely. How they have wasted it until it has turned into a curse," Ork said.

Olivia had a feeling that she wasn't to reply, neither did she want to. He waited for a while as if he was contemplating his own words then he spoke again.

"Because they have the ability to choose, they became selfish beings, inefficient and useless in every conceivable way. Chaos becomes the norm and order becomes the aberration. Do you see? I myself am a victim of the curse named free will and I have come to liberate. But they treat me as a villain. They fight me, who brings them nothing but salvation. It is truly sad." Ork sounded truly saddened as he said these words.

Olivia watched him closely. He seemed strange for a while then hardened back up again, returning to himself.

"Do you know the reason for Elk's interest in you? Well, I suppose you would not know. Your mind is far too limited to grasp the undertones of a mind as complex as Elk's. Imagine how little time it took to strip your mind to its essentials and absorb all of it. I am truly disappointed in your kind but, no matter, that will be rectified. You shall no longer have to think with your feeble minds. Rather, you will ascend to a higher purpose and have the great privilege of using minds whose capabilities far exceed yours. Yes… that is perfection." When he finished rambling, he leaned back in his chair.

Olivia looked outwards to the place where people toiled at some monstrous work that she didn't understand, and she thought that somewhere out there was her brother. The pain in her heart mingled with that in her leg and she began to sob.

***

"What are you saying, Andrew?" Elk asked.

The young man had repeated everything that had happened because Elk asked him to. Not because he hadn't heard, but in a misguided attempt to assuage his belief. Elk wondered how much the humans had already rubbed off on him in order for him to behave in such a manner, but he knew that he had to hear the words again.

Elk listened carefully and felt his anger rise. Olivia's mind would surely be invaded by Ork, who would see her value to him and create a very difficult situation for Elk to maneuver out of. In truth, Elk wasn't sure why Ork was drawn to a rare few among the human race.

True, humans had some mental and behavioral characteristics that made them unique, but there was something else and Elk suspected it had something to do with the artifact that had been placed under his care by the Supreme Monarch of his people before their planet was ruined. It was the thing that Ork searched for, but didn't know that it was within his possession.

Elk knew of its abilities and how it was used, but any attempt by him to draw even a little of its power had proved futile. It was said that its will would mingle with the will of its guardian and perhaps that was the cause of this unexplained fondness that he had for these ones, Olivia most of all.

Elk felt for her what was expected to feel for one's offspring and he had resisted this at first, but he had yielded and started to cave to this strangeness. Hearing that Olivia had put herself in harm's way almost drove him to foolish impulsiveness, but Elk managed to restrain himself and nodded at Andrew before leaving.

Andrew said something else, but Elk blocked the young man out, preferring solitude and the clarity of thought that it gave. Elk walked into his hovercraft that would carry him back to his city and, while sitting there, he thought about how he would retrieve Olivia. Elk explored the idea of leaving her there, but it was too hurtful for him to linger on.

He thought of asking for her personally and calling Ork out for a breach of contract, but that would have catastrophic consequences.

Elk came to the conclusion that he would have to leave Olivia, for the moment at least, on her own. Elk swore again that he would kill Ork or he would die in the attempt. He sat in the yellow light and his soul was heavy.

Elk was still sitting there when he heard Tekka's approach. Elk buzzed to show that he wanted to be alone and Tekka communicated the importance of the information he possessed directly into Elk's consciousness. Elk accepted the information, then sat upright in shock, buzzing his surprise. He stood up sharply.

"This is what he's planning? How did you know?" Elk asked.

Tekka communicated directly into his mind that Olivia had carried a micro-camera disguised as a button on her shirt and, with it, they'd seen the device that Ork was building and understood its purpose. Elk was shocked, but at the same time he was relieved because he had found great discomfort from maintaining a treaty with Ork and he now had an excuse to attack.

"Contact Marshal Willows," Elk ordered and walked out.

"What did you say?" Willows boomed, slamming her hand on the table, her face contorted with rage.

"They're building a weapon, yes. It's basically an EMP, but way more advanced than what you might think. Not only will he cripple any electrically powered piece of technology around the globe, but it will also affect the electrical brain signals and will send out a beacon powerful enough for the rest of his people to detect and respond immediately. We would be easily outnumbered and utterly defeated," Elk informed her.

Willows eyed him, some of her rage pouring out on him. Elk was always mildly amazed at the levels to which her anger surged. It was almost like a physical reaction and it burned anyone it touched or anyone around her.

"In what way exactly will it affect brain signals?" she snapped.

Elk paused for a moment before he spoke. "Currently, Ork can see into minds and read them within a particular range, but he cannot exactly control them. After this weapon is deployed, every human mind will be rendered defenseless against his manipulation. His range would also increase and he might be able to control whole countries at a time."

Elk could see the fear pass through Willows' face before being quick-ly replaced by rage. "That overgrown frog," she hissed. Elk felt amused for it was quite an apt description.

"It can safely be concluded that Ork has gone back on the agreements of the treaty and, as such, full offensive actions should be taken against him," the spokesman said.

There was no need for a vote because no one even spoke against it; although Elk wasn't sure that they'd win. He wasn't sure at all.

***

Olivia felt the cold painfully as it seeped through her bones, chilling her blood, fogging her brain and making her wounds hurt even more. Ork didn't seem to care. It was obvious that the basic things that were needed for the survival of his hostages were of no concern to him. He saw them as less than animals, far less than the machine of which he so prized.

Her teeth chattered and her body shook uncontrollably. It seemed ironic that they could burn her with a touch, but she'd die from the cold. Olivia thought about her brother and wondered if he felt the cold as well or if the virus had somehow given him some insulation against that. She hoped desperately that it was the latter.

Ork walked up to her, his heavy footsteps growing louder before he squatted beside her. He watched her for a long moment and she felt how horrible it was to have those black pits focus solely on you and knew that they knew every thought, every whim, every fear that you've ever had; for they had dug up even the memories that were long buried.

"Ah, I had forgotten how fragile your kind can be," Ork said.

Olivia suddenly began to feel warm. She could feel the warmth spread into the atmosphere around her and she knew the warmth was emanat-ing from his suit. The scientist in her wondered how much energy that thing possessed and she decided that it was possibly enough to suffice a small country for a year. He stood up and straightened out.

Olivia marveled at how fast the thing Ork was creating was forming. It was now rising into the air and she knew that no matter what it was, it was probably not for the benefit of Earth, or any planet really.

"I conquered a planet… shortly after mine betrayed me. They were strong, fierce, and the notion that anyone could defeat them was… something they couldn't stomach. Their planet still remains the most hostile one I have visited and I counted it a great victory when I finally bent their will to my pleasure. Many of them serve in my army now. They were worthy foes. Your planet however? There is nothing respectable here, nothing strong, nothing intriguing. It's for only one thing; to be wiped off the surface of the galaxy and blotted out of existence. But I suppose I'm merciful for that isn't the plan I have for them. They will be slaves to superior races as it should be. The strong must always take precedence above the weak." Ork chuckled a little as he said this.

It was forced, a sound practiced more to terrify than to convey amusement and Olivia wondered what kind of obsession Ork must have with dominion and fear that he would learn the nuances of gestures and warp them in such a way that suited his twisted thoughts.

One of Ork's soldiers came to him in apparent haste and the exchange was anything but calm. Ork turned to Olivia and watched her for a while as if he was trying to remember something. Then he finally spoke. "Your people are launching an attack. Fools. They feel that they have an edge because Elk is with them. That is foolish. They don't see the gift being offered to them. They see nothing. If it is war they want then… they will have it."

Ork went back to communicating with his men. Olivia shivered at the amount of havoc these things could bring, and with such few numbers. How much more could they cause when they numbered in the thousands? In the millions?

In the distance, Olivia could see lights in the sky and she knew those to be planes and hovercrafts coming in the hundreds. She felt a bit of elation, but she saw Ork standing and staring at them with such calmness that it worried her. And that worry slowly turned to suspicion and fear. No creature should be calm in the face of such might.

Elk viewed the large stadium from his hovercraft which had been weaponized and modified for military purposes. He felt something was wrong and hoped that they weren't too late to arrive. He hoped that Ork wasn't done with the abomination that he was building because…

A light exploded from the stadium. It was so bright and so powerful that it felt almost tangible. The wave of energy surged past them and Elk was thankful that his view had adjusted, allowing his eyes to be able to handle the intensity of the light. He realized what had happened and felt a flicker of fear before he quickly regained himself.

They had taken precautions to prepare against this but it was still disheartening to see planes drop like birds from the sky. Elk narrowed his eyes and let loose his warrior instincts as he wordlessly ordered the unleashing of their missiles and he exulted in the bombardment of their shields.

When the shields were weakened, Elk uttered the war cry from deep within him. The cry that spoke of death, ruin, destruction, madness, and strength. And it echoed from the other hovercrafts. They saw that this time Ork's pods had taken to the air.

Elk quickly blocked their formations and passed orders across his ranks for his own warriors to adjust accordingly. They had seven pods to contend with, but he knew that it would be close because of the firepower that those things possessed. His own hovercraft maneuvered through the battle and he opened the hatch and leaped out from it when it was still far from the ground.

The impact from Elk's feet hitting the ground flowed upwards and dissipated around his shoulders. It felt good to become who he was, who he was made to be and he braced himself as one of Ork's soldiers launched himself at him.

Elk slipped away and to the side, blasting the soldier in the chest with his palm blaster then rammed into him with all the force his armor and body could gather before he proceeded to focus a concentrated laser beam on his head, pinning his arms to the ground with his powerful legs. When that one was dead, Elk looked up and saw Ork staring at him with flat, black eyes. He almost reflexively let his gaze wander to where Olivia was, but stopped. It was too much of a risk to show open care for her.

"Ah, Elk. How long has it been? Our feud has gone on for far too long, don't you think? I think it's time that we settle it," Ork said and stepped forward.

Elk wondered why Ork was obsessed with giving speeches, both little and great, over every single thing. Perhaps, because of his high opinion of himself, he felt that every thought was profound and should be voiced. Elk shot forward, pushing off his feet, and leaping directly into the air to meet Ork.

It had been a while since Elk actually fought outside of training and it began to show. After a while in his duel with Ork, his armor had multiple cracks and his energy was depleting fast. His armor, powerful as it was, was made of inferior technology to Ork's who took punishment without even a scratch.

Elk analyzed the armor in his mind, looking for weaknesses while fighting Ork. It wasn't long before they had almost destroyed the entire stadium with the force of their battle. Elk took a blast to his side and he knew that it was an injury that he wouldn't be able to shrug off. And, judging from the disadvantage that he presently had, this was a battle he would soon lose. And so, Elk did something that he never thought he would do again, something he swore not to do; he invaded Olivia's mind.

Olivia felt another push on her mind, but it was more subtle, gentler, and less dominating. She recognized Elk once he entered her mind because he didn't go around prodding in places he didn't belong. Elk shared himself with her and Olivia realized that he was in terrible pain and had the awareness that he would lose this battle.

Elk dropped something in Olivia's mind and left and when he did. Her mind instinctively searched for what was left and found a strange piece of information that required urgent attention. Olivia forced herself up and started to walk but knew that she couldn't get anywhere close to where Elk wanted her to be on time. It was then that she felt a presence behind her and she turned to see an alien she knew well.

Tekka looked bigger in his armor, but she knew he didn't have Elk's war form and she realized what the Terrans were sacrificing; to the point they even took some of them that weren't meant for war and put them on the field anyway.

Before Olivia could say anything, Tekka picked her up and began to run. And he ran. Each step he took felt like a long leap and he seemed to have an instinctive knowledge of where debris would fall and smoothly avoided it until they were well outside the heat of the battle. Tekka took her even farther and kept running for what seemed like a lifetime, but she was sure that it was not more than thirty minutes.

Olivia looked around and saw that they had come to a place that had nothing in sight; just a few rocks, some shrubs, and sand. She wondered what she was supposed to find here and, as she was still wondering, Tekka gave a loud shriek and clasped his head, crashing to the ground.

Her eyes widened as she looked around, wondering who attacked him, but then Olivia slowly understood. And, when the realization hit her, she became numb. Time seemed to slow as she slowly defrosted and tears gathered around her eyes as she fell to her knees. There was only one thing that could affect Tekka that way without anyone attacking him and, judging from his connection with Elk, there could be only one explanation – Elk was dead.

Tekka pressed his palm on to the ground, obviously in severe pain, then stood and staggered towards what looked like a common rock, then reached for it. Olivia's eyes widened at what she saw. Tekka reached until his shoulder was nearly swallowed by the depths of the rock. Then, he pulled out a softly-glowing substance that looked like a stone but pulsed with so much energy that she felt all life on Earth begin to resonate with it. Tekka suddenly looked around quickly, obviously in fear.

"He senses it, and he's coming. Elk thought that you can use this, so please use it," Tekka said and pushed the stone against her belly.

Olivia grasped it instinctively then… she felt it. It was almost as if she was spread out, taken up and separated into the tiniest particles of her being; each filled with unimaginable power. She was compressed and filled with intimate knowledge in every tiny particle and she expanded into universal awareness.

Olivia saw through multiple dimensions and time became an object to her that she could manipulate. Space became nothing to her. As she watched Ork approach where she was, he seemed like such a small thing that she wondered why she was ever afraid of this little creature. Olivia thought of killing Ork but that wouldn't end what he had started and it wouldn't truly end him either. So, she inhaled and everything in the universe inhaled with her. Then she acted.

She felt nothing. She saw nothing. For a moment, perhaps, she was nothing. Then, Olivia slowly began to form shape and life. When she opened her eyes, she was in the laboratory back at the school. She stood up from the chair and saw Andrew reading something she couldn't make out, nodding to some music that was no doubt playing through his neural streams.

"Wha… what happened?" she asked.

Andrew turned to look at her then stood up, smiling. "You're awake! You know, I was worried when you said you needed to get some shut eye. I thought the world was ending."

Olivia narrowed her eyes at him. The world was ending. What the heck was he talking about? Before she could ask any questions, the door to her lab opened and a gigantic figure stopped to walk through. Her eyes widened as she saw it was Elk. Had he not died that night? What was happening?

"Olivia. Pardon my intrusion, but I thought to drop by and check up on you. Maybe get a few words in perhaps?" He gestured towards the door.

She nodded and followed him. Outside the sun was bright and everything seemed normal. There were no hovercrafts, no deaths, nothing.

"What… what happened?" she asked.

Elk paused his signature pause before he spoke. "You reversed time, but not all of it," he said simply.

"What do you mean, 'I reversed time?'"

Elk slowly turned to give her a flat look with his yellow eyes. "You reversed time. You also dumped Ork and his soldiers in outer space while at it. He still retains all the damage. There wouldn't have been much choice but… it's impressive."

"What do you mean? What did I do? What was that thing that Tekka gave me?" She scrambled to make sense of it all.

Elk turned to look at her. "That thing was a treasure. It is one of the treasures of the universe with some of the powers that formed the universe and can grant the wielder with the ability to do… certain things. There are four of them in existence and Ork has been searching for them. If he gets them…" He stopped and tilted his head to the side.

"Why didn't you use it to restore your people?" she interrupted softly.

He looked at her and she thought she imagined it, but she saw real pain in his eyes. "Because none of my people can use it. It seems that only humans, a specific type of human, can wield it," he said and looked away.

"I could use it, you know? To restore your people? If you want."

Elk shook his head slowly. An oddly human gesture. "Too many threads have been interwoven into that pattern now. Besides, you cannot use it again for a long while. It has to regain its depleted energy. It's no small thing to tug on the threads of time."

Olivia began thinking about all the things she didn't know existed, all the things that even Elk didn't know existed. And she felt like her head was on the verge of spinning. "How many people know?" she asked.

"All of my people. Their minds are more in tune with the cosmos. None of your kind. Not even the Commonwealths. And I think it's best that we let it remain that way. For now, at least."

"You enjoy keeping secrets far too much, Elk," she said.

He made a mild buzzing sound and then said, "It's safer that way."

They remained in silence for a while until Elk turned to look at her. "It will be hard keeping two timelines in your mind. Just knowing that I died…. It's too much. But I admit that it can be relieving. All the… responsibilities were gone."

Somehow, she understood him. It would indeed be blissful to leave everything and let all the responsibility pass to other people. She couldn't fathom the weight of his burdens, but she understood in her own way. They stood in silence while she tried to make sense of how strange her life had gotten and found it amusing that only a couple months ago she was looking for excitement from outer space. For now, she would savor and enjoy all the peace and quiet she could get.

"Elk?"

"Yes?"

"How old are you?"

"It's hard to tell."

"In Earth years," she added.

He was silent for a moment, but it was a thoughtful silence; like he was truly computing his age in Earth years. Then he nodded, which meant something different from Olivia's reflexive understanding of what a nod meant before he spoke. "Two thousand years, give or take a few decades. That was very hard to compute, you know? Now that I think about it, it's very long in your time." He was oblivious to Olivia's wide-eyed stare.

"I would, with your permission of course, like to make some utterly noninvasive observations of your people. I'm an astrobiologist after all," she said,

Elk looked sideways at her then asked flatly, "You want to observe us like they do animals in the wild or in the zoo?"

Olivia gasped in shock and waved her hands frantically. "No, no… I didn't mean…" She stopped when she heard the buzzing sound Elk was making.

"Of course, you have my permission but, for your own sake, keep them strictly noninvasive."

She nodded. He waited a while then slowly nodded as well.

"Olivia?"

She heard a voice say behind her and turned to see her brother just as he was before the virus infected him. His hair was cut short and his brilliant brown eyes were staring at her with laughter in them, although he cast mistrustful, strange looks at Elk.

Olivia felt her heart leap as she ran and embraced him in a hug. He smelled like flowers and oranges and she realized how much she had missed his scent. She held him there in her arms and he held her before he whispered in her ear. "It's my birthday tomorrow."

She smiled and hugged him.

CHAPTER EIGHT

The job of an astrobiologist is almost evenly split – like night and day. Split between research conducted inside labs or observatories, and work that's conducted in the field at often, remote locations.

Olivia had now been retained by the university and was a scientist at the lab, whereas Andrew was now a graduate student who often spoke of his frustration in matters of his physical appearance, specifically about his lack of facial hair and how his face remained infantile no matter what he tried.

Andrew still tried to introduce himself to Olivia as much as possible, even as the semester had only just begun. As was detailed in the job description, Olivia was hardly present at the university these days. It'd been so throughout the weekends also. He thought, like any sane person, that she was working way too much. She said that curiosity couldn't be compared with work per say, it was only a meaningful adventure or like skydiving with a purpose, as she put it. And, as it was a hierarchical sin to indulge in these arguments with someone who'd learned more than you, Andrew didn't push it. He simply let her be. He followed her somewhat at his own pace; being stuck at school was lame anyway.

Olivia represented something else. There was the intriguing jeopardy with which she touted curiosity and the quest for knowledge. She pursued and hinted at whatever it was she wanted in order to complete an experiment or theory. She brought nothing less than the spirit of an investigator to science; always needing to touch and feel the truth.

With this nature, Olivia was sure to get to the bottom of anything. Many depths of study abounded that were yet unreached and the prospect of this excited Andrew very much. He couldn't wait to be out there on a field trip, even though it was mostly an excuse for him to see the world. Olivia knew he simply wanted to see the world and she didn't mind. Coming from a small and restrictive family, he could only let his imagination fulfill its desires.

Naturally, the places they visited weren't the most fanciful. That wasn't necessarily disappointing for him though, as these things were to be expected. They toured caves, deserts, natural parks, forests, and even Antarctica. However, he hated most of these missions, whereas Olivia was exasperated at what she was unable to find. Some days they'd almost spend the night at these places, as a matter of fact.

"Oh, Olivia," Andrew would ask, "are we looking for some organismic treasure? Come on!"

They'd always leave unfulfilled, taunted by near-misses, close calls and lookalikes and the abundance of clues that may or may not have been pointing to the real thing. She sucked it in every time and went her way. The Earth's been here for archeologists-know-how-many-years, what could she possibly be missing? She consoled herself with these words while she went her way each time.

The university's satellites had pointed her in this direction. She didn't know what was going wrong now and she couldn't tell how large a margin of error she was dealing with at all. But, at least these slowdowns made her decelerate as her body needed. Such times enabled her to be reflective of things, to strategize, and to remember why she felt the need to continue.

Or, perhaps it was the lack of resources. She should have been working for a bigger, better, and wealthier lab. A private or a secret one owned by the government. And then, she wouldn't have as many issues. But, then they would hardly be interested in the things that held her own interest. For the resources, she would have to utterly lose control of the direction of things, wouldn't she? She believed she was at the right place.

"Funding is so hard to secure for the things that actually matter. But I guess they think I'm kidding," she said offhandedly. "You're always thought to be kidding when it's not in their best interest," she said to herself.

"Or you're just paranoid," Andrew answered her. "I don't know why you refused help from Elk anyway. It's not like he has anything better to do with all the money he makes in revenue from the tech that his people develop. I don't think he actually values money. I used his help now and then, you know. Generous man… alien… thing."

Olivia smiled a little, then shook her head slowly. "I can't take help from Elk, not anymore. I don't want to feel like… like he owns me, you know? I mean there's only so much you can take from a person before you find it impossible to turn down any request they make of you."

Andrew raised an eyebrow, then slowly shook his own head while making a clicking sound with his tongue. "Why do you have to over-complicate everything?"

She shrugged. "Maybe I don't. Maybe you're the one with the over-simplification and everything is actually terribly complex."

He pointed at her then clapped and said, "Aha! There you go again!"

She smiled a little then looked upwards at the ceiling.

Andrew sighed and rubbed his forehead. "What? You're about to wonder why there has been no excitement from outer space?"

Olivia almost replied, but she remembered that Andrew didn't know. Then, a sudden headache passed across her head, making her wince. It was hard for the human mind to keep two timelines within itself for an extended period. Elk said that the headaches would increase for a while then subside.

"Do you think that we're being too complacent?" she asked.

Andrew pouted a little then narrowed his eyes. "What do you mean?"

She shrugged and then said, "I mean what if excitement actually comes from outer space and it's not the pleasant kind like the Terrans? What if it's the kind of excitement that would require the deaths of many, destruction, and loss? What if instead of friends, we're visited by enemies?" She shuddered a little as she thought of Ork's eyes.

"Perhaps, but you must admit that technological advancement has been growing quite exponentially since the arrival of the Terrans,"

She eyed him then raised a single eyebrow. "In a battle, who do you think would win? The Terrans or humans?"

Andrew frowned. "That's a very disturbing thought, Olivia."

She nodded like that was exactly what she expected.

"You see? It is disturbing because you know that we would lose… badly. Imagine something powerful enough to destroy their planet and nearly wipe out their race, which we have decided is a very powerful race. Imagine if that force turns on us. What would we be able to do in the face of that? Anything we attempted would be like cavemen carrying sticks to a nuclear bomb. We'd have absolutely no chance," she said.

Andrew nodded. "Well, it's the truth, what you say. But wouldn't you agree that it would be a less than exciting endeavor to try to pass across that idea to the Commonwealths?"

She wondered if he fully grasped the seriousness of what she was saying. Then again, how could he? He hadn't seen the death and the loss that had happened in the other timeline. She hoped that there would be enough time for them to grow strong enough to resist Ork should he try to return.

"Elk could," she said.

Andrew sucked his teeth. "I thought we weren't asking for Elk's help."

"This isn't for me. It's for all of us." she replied.

***

Elk sat in his office, studying the strings that spread out before him on his holodeck. It was sometimes exhausting to study the reports from the different members of his people, but it was satisfying to see that his people were growing; and they were growing fast. Already some young ones had been tendered.

Some of his people had already been looking to him to tender young, but he wasn't ready for it yet. He forced his mind to focus again and realized that he was finding it more difficult to focus these days. It was hard to maintain his mind on this timeline but it had reduced from the first few days in which he was in confusion and distraction, It was the same with the rest of his people.

Elk wondered how Olivia would be taking it. Her strength marveled him again. She was the only one of her kind that knew what happened and she was bearing it with admirable courage. Elk tried smiling again but it was a difficult thing to do, and he knew that he was more showing his teeth than anything.

Elk returned his mind to the strings and, just when he was beginning to settle back into focus, he was interrupted by Tekka, who was somewhere outside his door. Tekka communicated that Olivia had come to visit. Elk buzzed with happiness. Since she had turned down his sponsorship, he had been more than a bit worried and slightly annoyed. But, Elk supposed that he understood her need for independence. Olivia was not a child, but among his people, she would still be considered as barely more than an infant.

Olivia had dark circles around her eyes when she walked in, she looked pale, and more than a bit tired.

"Hello, Olivia," he said and realized that his voice was maybe a bit too flat. He had considered learning to infuse more emotion into it, but it was a very difficult task and he abandoned it altogether.

"Hi. How have you been?" she asked.

Elk stood. He walked up to her, then held her small head in his hands. He saw her tense as if she would resist, then she subsided and he peered into her eyes, seeing her weariness and lack of sleep. "You have been overworking again. You make me a bit regretful about giving you the samples taken from our plants and those charts…. Such horrible sources of addiction for a mind like yours."

She rolled her eyes. Elk left her face and stepped back. "Lovely seeing you too, Elk," she said.

"How's your brother?" he asked.

She shrugged. "Preparing for his exams. He needs to get admitted into college this year."

Elk tilted his head to the side. She had understood this to be his own equivalent of a nod.

"Elk, I want to talk to you about something," she started.

Elk waved a hand and a small opening appeared from the ground and a chair rose out. Elk saw surprise in Olivia's expression because he never offered chairs to anyone that came to his office. At first, it had been because he didn't understand that it was part of their culture but, as time proceeded, he had realized that they left quicker when no chairs were offered.

She sat down, looking a bit nervous. Olivia was never nervous, not really, and he wondered what would make her nervous. Perhaps she wanted to ask for her funding back, but he didn't want to assume. Only the very young and the very stupid did that hastily, so he decided to wait.

"Aren't you bothered?" she asked.

He remained silent, as was his habit, waiting for her to explain the reason behind her question. "I mean, are you not bothered by the apparent laxness of the Commonwealths, of everyone? It takes a long time for the treasure to recharge and we can't count on it to save us next time. And even if we could, Ork knows we have it, so he'll be very prepared. As it is, we would lose to any extraterrestrial threat devastatingly. We need better space programs. We need accelerated advancements in technology. We need to come together on this in order to stand a chance against anything that comes; and something will definitely come. We have seen it. And next time, it will be much worse than what we saw before," she said, noticing that she appeared to be rambling.

Elk tilted his head to the side, agreeing with what she said. Then, he waited to be sure that she was done speaking before he began to speak. "I have been trying to put the words in the right places, but they don't see the urgency, the need. I have told them of threats from outside but they have never seen it, experienced it. They don't really know that it's more than a hypothetical situation."

He paused a little, then began talking again. "Convincing them to be less complacent would be difficult, but it's something that I'm working on, and trust me, my people aren't complacent at all."

Olivia nodded slowly, seeing his point and understanding his meaning, but the worry in her refused to be quelled.

"You know, you should ease up on the work for a while," Elk suggested. Olivia frowned at him. "You should relax. True, the world needs to work harder at securing itself, but that doesn't mean that in their present complacence, that you'll do it alone. It's wrong to push yourself in that manner. Go on a vacation perhaps."

She narrowed her eyes. "Vacation? Do your people go on vacations?"

Elk buzzed. "Something close, but not quite."

"By that you mean…?"

"Hibernation," he said.

She raised an eyebrow. "I didn't know that you hibernated."

He tilted his head a little. "I do hibernate. I have hibernated about a few dozen times and that's because I don't need it much with my heightened endurance and tolerance for stress, but many of my people do frequently."

Olivia nodded. "But that's not similar to a vacation."

Elk leaned backwards into his chair. "You go on vacations so that you can ease the stress and tension from your normal life and, if done right, you're supposed to feel better and refreshed when you return, yes?"

She nodded.

"Well, hibernation does that for us. You go in and come out feeling new." He slowly stood up. "There is one man that I should talk to. Yes.

He probably would listen and, if we start with one of the Common-wealths, it would be easier to spread from there."

Olivia stood and sighed a little, then sighed and glanced at Elk's table again. "When will you send someone to teach me this?" she asked playfully, but there was slight seriousness in her voice. She had secretly hoped that there was a way that Elk would be able to enlighten her in the strange mysteries of his people's writing system.

He looked at the well-tuned holographic strings that shifted and moved across his table, then looked back at Olivia who still had the half smile on her face.

"You are a very smart, intelligent woman, Olivia, but some things cannot be taught. No matter how hard we try to teach it. Your alphabet is formed from the rudiments of basic sounds that your kind makes, sounds ingrained in the process of your evolution. Our language is made up of other things… sounds and states of consciousness and awareness that cannot possibly be taught because you simply don't have the capacity to understand it."

Olivia had suspected that was the case and she was a little bit saddened by the fact that she would be unable to learn it, but she nodded again. "Thank you, Elk." Olivia started to leave before she stopped and turned back. "What does it feel like? Trying to make my kind see and understand things from your perspective, to make us see past our limited experiences and understand the things you try to communicate?"

He looked at her for such a long time that she was about to excuse herself. Then he answered quietly. "Frustrating," he said quietly.

She understood immediately. She was human and, even to her, humanity could be frustratingly short-sighted. She stood there for a few more seconds in silence before she excused herself.

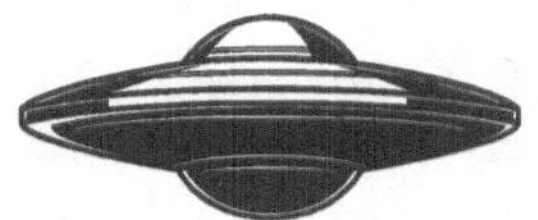

CHAPTER NINE

Andrew sipped from his cup and frowned, but bore it silently. He had been made to take a few sips every morning by his wife, who had been informed by some herbalist with whom Andrew wanted to have a few words, that drinking that specific mixture of herbs would increase strength, reduce stress, and double vitality. An elixir of youth.

He had passed it through his very own team of doctors who said it was a harmless potion of herbs that actually could be beneficial to his health, but obviously not as much as his wife had been made to believe. He could have spent the next hour wondering when the bitter aftertaste would vanish from his mouth, but there were other matters on his mind that seemed to dull the horrible taste.

Andrew Jimoh was a tall, slim man with brown eyes and a strong, square chin. He was also an engineering genius that had risen by virtue of his intellect and powerful family connections to become the Chief Engineer of the Commonwealth of West Africa. He was soon appointed advisor to the Committee of Science and Technology, a position he'd held for five years. He stared at himself in the mirror, then adjusted his tie a little; satisfied at how he still looked trim and healthy at nearly fifty years old. And, he thought that maybe he would point out to his wife that there was no herb involved in that beyond decent diet and exercise. A bit of good genes helped a lot as well.

Andrew's assistant walked in and he frowned, thinking that now he would have to meet the most distasteful set of creatures on the planet – the aliens. He shook his head a little as he thought of sitting even for a few minutes with those weird creatures who knew far too much and held far too much power for the safety of Earth. And, to think that it was their leader that he would be meeting. As if there couldn't be enough unpleasant things in one man's day.

He walked out, flanked closely by his assistant, Peter, who was the only one he permitted to be part of his daily activities. He didn't fancy the idea of walking around with an army of advisors and all that nonsense that offered nothing but distractions.

Peter was a very efficient and intuitive young man who had served under Andrew since he was selected as his adviser and Andrew hadn't faulted the man's service in any way since Peter had entered his service. They walked into Andrew's office, where Elk was already seated. The chair that was set out for him wasn't chosen with consideration for his size though because it looked more like a children's plastic seat given to an adult man, but Elk sat in it with so much grace and composure that it seemed like a throne. Andrew disliked him a little bit more for that, but he greeted him with a polite smile and a handshake; hating how his normally large hand was lost in Elk's gigantic hand.

"Thank you for meeting me, Your Excellency," Elk said.

Andrew smiled a bit wider, though he didn't really have a choice. He had already turned him down too many times and had reached the limit of politeness. But the creature's tone gave no hint of mockery or flattery or anything. It was just flat and toneless.

"It's always a pleasure. Please, sit down. Tea?" Andrew asked as he walked to his own chair and sat as the tea that was being steeped was poured into little mugs and placed before them.

Elk stared at his for a while then looked back at Andrew. "Your culinary tastes differ very much from mine, but I appreciate the gesture."

Andrew gave him a look of embarrassment. "Oh, I should have gotten something more appropriate. Forgive this error."

Elk started to tilt his head, stopped, then nodded. "I sent a message to you highlighting the purpose of my visit," he said

Andrew nodded and said, "Ah, yes, I did get it, and I must say those are very interesting things you have brought my attention to, but they're also not urgent and nor important. The Commonwealth has other pressing matters and, while I see the need for this, it will have to be taken under advisement and delegated to a later date."

Elk nodded slowly. "Excellency, might I ask you a question?"

Andrew raised an eyebrow then nodded.

"Have you ever heard of the name Ork or Vol?"

Andrew bore a confused expression then slowly shook his head. "No. I don't believe I have."

Elk paused for a while before he continued to speak. "Ork is a member of a race that is cousin to mine and he was responsible for the destruction of my planet. He is what you would call a madman, a creature that has committed the type of genocide that would make what Hitler did the equivalent of a child using a curse word. He moves from planet to planet doing the same thing. He does not relent. He does not stop. He does not see life as something to be valued and he believes freewill is something that should be exterminated. Vol is what you would call a psychopath and, though I have never met him, I have seen his work and I'll tell you that his technological ingenuity has built weapons that could level entire solar systems. No one has been able to work with or capture him because he's too dangerous to work with due to his utter insanity. And he's too smart to be captured." Elk paused and continued, "These two are the most dangerous that I know of, but I assure you that there are also pirates, criminals, and warlords from different planets, solar systems, and different galaxies that roam the universe. But they avoid smaller, poorer planets such as yours because it simply is not worth their while. But with the recent overall development of Earth, there is need to defend it now." Elk said this carefully omitting the fact that there was also one of the most coveted treasures in the universe currently on their planet.

Andrew had not perceived a change in tone from Elk, yet somehow, he understood that the creature was serious. He admitted that there was little he knew of anything beyond Earth and the idea of a creature that could obliterate solar systems worried him very much, yet this was not an easy task to embark on. "I understand that this is very much possible, but the idea of preparing for a war that may never come is unsettling. There would be panic, the financial impact would be substantial, and there's the matter of getting the committee to approve it in the first place. The disadvantages outweigh the advantages," he said.

"I beg to differ, Your Excellency. It could be masqueraded as a space program and even if there is no war, with the support my people would give you for this project, your space program would far outrank that of other Commonwealths. If the war does happen, then you would be applauded as the ones who started Earth's preparation. Either way, you lose very little and gain very much. And, for a long while, your part of the world has lagged in technological advancement. Imagine that reversed. Not only now, but permanently."

Andrew's interest heightened at the prospects outlined by Elk. It was good that there was no emotion in the alien's voice because there was no impression that was given that he was trying to manipulate or cajole. He seemed sincere. "What about you?"

"Yes?"

"What do you get out of all this if I agree?" Andrew asked.

Elk paused for a while as if he was considering his answer, but that might not have been entirely the case as the alien was in the habit of short pauses before he spoke, almost as if every word was carefully chosen. "I have seen the threat. I have fought quite a number of them and so have my people. The knowledge that my people are safe and that another planet will not be lost on my watch is enough payment."

Andrew stared intently at him, trying to find any insincerity, but he got as much information out of his eyes as one could hope to get from a conversation with a rock. He knew that he was going to agree, he just needed to present a front of hesitation. "Well, Elk, I'd like a couple of days to consider this. It's not a light project and I want to be sure that I have carefully considered all the variables."

Elk stared at him for a while then nodded. It was almost as if he had to remember to do it. He stood with as much grace as when he sat and Andrew was a bit jealous that a creature not even from Earth could have so much regality, but still have a hard edge that could crush him as easily as an insect. He still didn't like Elk in the slightest, but he did like what he was selling, so he put out his hand and Elk shook it a little.

"Thank you for your time," Elk said and left.

Andrew sat back on his chair and realized that the aftertaste of his wife's tea remained. He cursed under his breath.

***

"The food here is good," Andrew said quietly. Olivia frowned. He looked up and shrugged. "The food is good. You're letting the thoughts in your mind ruin the taste of the food," he added.

She gave him her best scowl. He chuckled. She remembered when that scowl would have shut him up and made him cower. There were a lot of benefits of having him as a friend rather than a subordinate, but she still missed being able to shut him up with just a glance.

"Any news from Elk?" he asked.

She shrugged and said, "He's been very busy and not been replying to my messages, but I think that he has begun seeing some of the leaders of the Commonwealths. Fingers crossed." Andrew nodded, leaning back in his chair. "Why did you stay?" she asked suddenly.

He raised an eyebrow. "Stay where?"

"I mean, why did you stay with me, working in the lab, even after you graduated? You could have moved into Elk's think tank."

Andrew stared at his hands, then looked back at her and shrugged. "I really don't know. I just like it here, all of the work we do together. Besides, it's not like I'm strapped for cash or anything. Elk still pays generously for the freelance work I do for him and stuff. So, yeah..." he shrugged again then ran his hand through his hair. "Besides, I don't want to hear one day on the news that a renowned scientist works herself to death or just come up on you one day and find you scribbling stuff on the wall and muttering the name of some obscure microbe."

Olivia smiled a little, grateful for his presence. She was beginning to consider Andrew family and she would have been terribly sad if he had left. "But if you ever get any of those wonderful offers…"

"If it's not extremely boring and limiting and bans me from working closely with aliens or mandates me to use my contacts there to spy on their tech? Then yeah, why not?"

Olivia didn't know why, but that made her mildly sad. They ate in silence for a while until a figure entered the door and she looked to see that it was an alien; one of the ones she didn't know. This one had clearly chosen to be female from the way she walked and the clothes she wore. She walked to them, stared at the chair for a long moment, then pulled it backward and sat gently on it, clearly uncomfortable. Olivia was a bit annoyed at the way the people there gawked at the alien and some even made rude gestures and others scowled openly.

"Hi," Andrew said. The alien turned slowly to look at him then smiled brightly, a smile that was way better than Elk's and almost as good as some humans with severe social awkwardness. But, it was an effort and Olivia admired it, considering in the back of her mind that she would try to imitate some of their sounds.

"My name is Akya. I am a friend of Elk and a tenderer currently learning the diplomatic ways. He sent me here to speak with you as a test of sorts," she said. Her tone wasn't as robotic as Elk's. There were some subtleties of tone and infusions of emotions at appropriate places. It seemed stiff, but for entirely different reasons.

"Oh, that's wonderful. So basically, Elk is training you to handle diplomacy, am I right?" Andrew asked, and she nodded and smiled again.

Olivia wished she wouldn't smile so much, but practice made perfection so maybe it could be excused.

"You're smart. Well, Elk said that the both of you are very smart. What exactly are you eating?" Akya asked.

Andrew looked down at his plate and smiled a little. "Fish sauce and rice."

She nodded, peering at his plate with what came very close to curiosity.

Olivia could see that she was methodically testing out each part of her training. "Why exactly did Elk ask you to meet us here, Akya?"

Akya looked at her, then smiled in a way that Olivia suspected was meant to be embarrassment but just came off as slightly manic. "Look at me going on and on. He actually asked me to inform you that there was progress from the Commonwealth of West Africa. They have decided to accept his proposal and are currently working hard along with our people to launch probes and satellites in space equipped with military equipment of course, but that's not information that should be shared lest panic start. And I don't think that would be beneficial to anyone," she said.

Olivia felt more than a little bit of elation, but wondered why Elk hadn't told her before. But then again, she couldn't fault him as he was very busy. She glanced at Akya again, who was staring strangely at her, then she remembered that Akya's memory of the events of before weren't lost and she knew exactly who she was. She couldn't decide if that was a good or bad thing.

"He could have sent a message," Olivia said.

Akya nodded. Thankfully, she didn't smile this time. "It was part of my training. This is actually my first time engaging with people, you know. It's too loud out here and the sun is too bright and it's too… everything. Yes, there are lotions we apply to lessen the effects but it's still very uncomfortable. And, breathing can be hard except that there is this thin film within my nostrils that infuses more carbon into the air I breathe. But it will soon run out and breathing would be very exhausting."

Akya inadvertently let out a sound that Olivia recognized to mean embarrassment. Before she could say anything, Andrew reached out to hold her hand. She seemed startled but she calmly turned to look at him.

"You will get used to it. I know everything about us can be too much, but you will get used to it and maybe even love it… hopefully. You're doing great already. I love your smile," Andrew said. Olivia almost winced but she maintained an expressionless face.

"Thank you, Andrew. I worked and still work hard on that smile," she said and added one more smile to her practice. "You don't talk much, Olivia," Akya added.

Olivia shrugged a little then drank from her glass and was very glad that it was water as she had neither looked nor listened when Andrew had ordered for her. "I don't think we're moving fast enough."

Andrew shot her a meaningful glance, but Akya nodded solemnly and said, "I honestly don't think we are either. Your people can be quite slow in decision making. They seem to value their own interests above the interest of the entire planet. It's shocking because I didn't know that such a thing was possible until I came here. There was so much selfishness that I was among the people that advocated for us to leave and find a better place, but Elk believed in you, and he still does. To a great extent, his belief has made us also believe." She paused a little and continued, "I just wish you didn't make it so hard."

Olivia thought that she should be annoyed, but she understood perfectly. Then, she nodded and, after a while, Andrew excused himself to use the bathroom.

"How has it been?" Akya asked almost immediately as Andrew was out of earshot.

"How has what been?"

Akya shrugged. "Your mind. It must not be easy keeping two timelines in your consciousness. At times there is time displacement, confusion, and outright pain when the headaches come. You could have our physicians check you. They…"

"No. No, that won't be necessary. There's so much left to do. I can't afford to waste any time now."

Akya nodded like she understood. "I was informed about your study into extremophiles."

Olivia's eyes widened as she stared at Akya, remembering that the only other person she had ever informed about that was…. Well, she had actually never really let anyone, even Andrew, know exactly what she was researching. "How do you…"

"Elk has this ability to read minds, as all warriors of our kind can, but he does it very selectively and he only did it to you to make sure your mind was stable after what happened. But those things aren't exact and he picked up some information along the way."

Olivia was visibly angry now and she clenched her fists under the table until they hurt. She exhaled slowly, letting some of her anger out. The fact that Elk knew that she was studying the same kind of virus that affected humanity before and had pretended like he didn't know, coupled with the fact that he kept his kind's reading capabilities a secret, was shocking. But, then again, it wasn't like he owed her any information, yet she couldn't stop herself from remaining angry.

Andrew returned then, took one look at her face, then politely turned to Akya. "We should be back at the lab now. We've taken far too much time than was planned. I really do hope to meet you again, Akya. It has been delightful talking to you."

She smiled, then took his hands in hers, making them seem so tiny. She stood, nodded once to Olivia, who nodded back, and she walked away.

"What happened?" Andrew whispered to her as they left the restaurant.

"Nothing," she said and gritted her teeth.

Olivia couldn't deny that she'd changed since that event, and she had changed drastically. She looked at Eric's face when he spoke, when he laughed, when he was sad and worried, and when he slept. How perfect his visage was compared to that grotesque zombie-like state he was in once before. She had to protect this version of Eric by any means possible. She studied his features, how calmly they brought his face to life, and for a moment there, she wept softly.

While at the university, her eyes endearingly explored the tiny bright lights from the spectrum of dust laying on the telescope at the observatory and she came to deeply appreciate all over again the incubator of research that the lab was – this enclosure designed to isolate, simulate, and study the reality of things.

As she walked on the streets, she beheld the technology on the streets; how efficiently they functioned to alleviate much of mankind's stress. Such a jewel should never have to be taken away. Imagine what the world would look like without these jewels, how unbearable life would come to be for many – for technology had become the fabric of society, weaving connections into everything and everyone.

All of this and more were the things that stood to be lost if a devastation was to occur in the magnitude that she imagined. This was about the world, and not just Eric. There must surely be a portal that is to act as a channel and even if it somehow weren't Eric next time around, it'd be someone else out there.

This sense of a loss of control made her shudder. But what control she had in the meantime hovered over Eric, thereby making Olivia an unnecessarily overbearing sister. She was too careful about everything that concerned Eric. Eric had begun to grow weary of her paranoia or what was starting to appear like an ill-will, an over-cautiousness that was foreboding something unmentioned. He kept asking her what it was that made her so unduly taken with concern and he always found nothing but a blank stare or some trite mumbling about how it was her duty as the older sibling.

Eric got on with his life, thinking nothing too unusual was bound to happen; taking few to zero risks where he could in his daily life, as advised by his dearest sister, Olivia. The best she could do was to convince her mind of the best outcome of things and wait.

Olivia had resolved not to contact Elk but there were many things that she wanted to know, many things that she wanted to ask him and, while she was mad at him, she missed his quiet assurance. She wanted someone with whom she could actually talk to about her worries and he was the only one of the aliens that she had bothered to make a connection with.

There was Tekka, but something about the Terran creeped Olivia out. Maybe the idea that he had no life of his own, preferring to attach himself, like some symbiotic creature, to Elk, or maybe how he never seemed to have or show an actual interest in anything beyond Elk. Maybe that was a normal way for a second to behave, but Olivia saw no reason to have to accept it.

Her holophone signaled a message and she checked it to see that it was from Elk. She felt annoyance and slight fear pass through her as she wondered at what range his mind reading stopped or if it was just purely coincidental that he asked to meet her at the same time she mirrored the same intention. She decided that she would ask him and she messaged back that she would meet him. She was still angry, but it wasn't as much as it was before.

They sat in an orchard, silently looking out into the trees. Elk saw what was on her mind, but he waited for the moment she'd choose to present it to him. "You're so courteous, are you not? Waiting to hear me say out loud what you've already telepathically read."

"Yes, I am courteous. It is necessary that way when you don't exactly have a home." His voice was flat as always and, while that had previously calmed her, she wanted there to be emotion. Regret, perhaps for lying to her.

"Why did you not tell me?" she asked

He waited for a long while, then slowly spoke as if each word meant more than it normally did or as if he was trying to make it be that way. "You wouldn't think freely, behave freely. I have only read your mind twice and the first was that time you came to my office. The second was after what happened with Ork, and I am truly sorry for both, but I wanted you to be you when you were in my presence. I apologize again," he said quietly, and like that, she knew that she had forgiven him.

"Courteousness is necessary when you have no home," she said.

He tilted his head to the side. "Or the hope of keeping the one you're a guest in."

She needed the conversation to ebb to a bleak edge already. All she wanted to talk about was the end of the world, the disintegration of the planet, and the obliteration of the universe.

"You are so bleak-minded. One could mistake you for the protégé of some dark lord."

"I was hoping someone would finally take notice after all these years," she said in a rather crackling tone.

"Months," he corrected calmly.

Olivia nodded absurdly, noting the displacement of time in her head. There was a long silence between them waiting to be emancipated by a voice.

She rubbed her hands nervously. Elk, while sitting, was her height when she stood. It suddenly coursed through her sensibilities what the reality of a sinister extraterrestrial presence might feel like. She considered if the safety she felt around Elk was deceitful and how everything could just flip over. What if somehow their clan of aliens were to be the real threats this time around? What if they always had been the main threat and she just didn't perceive things correctly?

She'd been having these thoughts unguardedly, not setting up the spikes of resistance around her mind to make it unreadable and fortified.

"Those thoughts have crossed the minds of every human who has got the time to think them up," Elk said indifferently.

Olivia didn't know what to ask him and so another long silence prevailed. She shrugged and asked, "Could the collective hunch of a race be so wrong? You tell me."

"It won't be the first time humanity chose a position that wasn't obvious to them and wasn't in their favor. And so, yes, that hunch is wrong."

An appreciative smile tore across her face and involuntarily strode up to her ears. Then, at the recollection of a thought, she grew fidgety. "Do you think they'll be back?" She referred to the bad aliens and their chances of invading Earth.

He shifted uneasily on the wooden bench, searching for an answer. "I should think so." Olivia sighed despondently. "I know this doesn't reassure you," Elk said.

"No, it doesn't."

"The main question would be, 'How do we stop them well ahead of time?'"

She looked at him curiously. "Have you been able to answer that question yet?"

"Unimpressively, no. But, I've been up to something else. I've tried to advise the government on the likely routes and scenarios of an alien invasion."

"And?"

"Some of them have listened and we have been making progress, but you'd be surprised at the amount of stuff they still find preposterous and bizarre." She let out a sad sigh. "They've not quite prepared for anything unnatural, Olivia. And I can't force them to."

"I really wish you weren't courteous with them," Olivia blurted out. "The future doesn't really bode well, Elk, for any of us; for this planet."

"We could have arrived at Earth undetected. But we didn't. Anyone out there can. You have got such inferior and primitive technologies that cannot detect any kind of invasion. And that's a problem."

"You don't say," she answered sourly. That long silence reigned once again, stiffening the atmosphere. And yet she took in the wet air coming from the lush vegetative environment of the orchard. It felt perfect, this peace and harmony within nature. It also felt dreamy, like a transgression on reality itself. She shook off the experience and came back to the conversation. "Why aren't they heeding your advice?"

"Ugh, space politics, I guess."

"Oh, there's that."

"Apparently so."

"So, tell me something…"

"Please, don't ask how many stars there are in the solar system. Or why extraterrestrial life wasn't dully noticed on our planet by your astronomers before our arrival."

Olivia was half-startled. "No," she laughed. "I wanted to ask about your efforts with the government." It was her first true laugh in a while. Elk went quiet then slowly started speaking. Olivia began to guess that he was still not used to words, so they had to be perfectly planned out in his mind before they were given voice.

"Andrew Jimoh has proven himself to be a very dependable associate as long as it's within his Commonwealth's and his own interest. We've launched a few probes and weaponized satellites. Communication has been made even quicker and more fluid. We are embarking on researching force fields big enough to cover cities and advancing hovercraft technology, equipping them against EMPs and other threats. We're also making them fully automated. I believe the progress of the Commonwealth of West Africa is raising some eyebrows and there soon will be a mass movement for technological advancement, a renaissance of sorts." He turned to look at her. She felt a bit of relief within her that there was even a little bit of progress at least.

"It's not fast enough," she said and exhaled through puffed cheeks.

Elk placed a hand on her shoulder. "Calm yourself, Olivia. It's something. At least it's better than when you were doing it alone, researching into extremophiles…. Why extremophiles anyway? You are neither a virologist or an epidemiologist…"

"What I am is a person that cares for her planet and has seen a timeline in which it's ruined, so I have to take certain precautionary measures," she snapped.

Elk sat so still, she thought that he'd turned into stone. Then he made a sound which was unfamiliar to her. "Forgive me for insulting your sense of duty to your planet. Seems I have been spending too much time among the less patriotic of your kind. I perfectly understand what you mean and it's what I would do. In fact, it is what I am doing." He buzzed a little.

"Good that you are training professional diplomats," she said.

Elk tilted his head. "They are very rough now, but we're working on polishing them. I'm very hopeful. Akya is currently our best and most zealous," he said.

Olivia nodded, suddenly feeling remorseful and guilty. "When you see her next, please send my apologies. I'm afraid I was a bit cross with her," she said.

Elk tilted his head to the side and said, "I will," and added, "Things will soon change. They will soon become accelerated and that might be more than even you can handle. At that point it might even… well, it might not be exactly like what we expected or desired. What I do know though is that there is something coming, and it will be big and fast." He tilted his head from side to side.

"That sounds really prophetic," Olivia said.

Elk buzzed. "Sometimes advanced game theory can seem like prophecy and we must not also underestimate our instincts. They were granted to us by evolution for a reason."

Olivia nodded. They remained in silence for another long while before she spoke again. "So, can I ask you about the questions you said I shouldn't…"

"No," he interrupted. She began to laugh. They both sat there until the sun yellowed on its descent. "Looks very much like home on times like this," he said, finally breaking the silence.

She nodded. "Your home must have been beautiful then."

He made a sound she interpreted to be loss and mourning, but it was low which meant that it was mild. "It was very beautiful."

CHAPTER TEN

Within a more-or-less timely period with their newly formed resolve, Olivia was awash with the prevalent news on the various news streams and networks.

The smart band on her wrist was beeping and buzzing with information. She used its AR feature, which popped its feed onto open space, immediately keying her into real-time broadcasts from the news stream.

It was all in alignment with the trend of the time. One might go even further to call it 'zeitgeist.' The incessant reportage pervading human awareness was in sync with what'd been known in the rather fictitious world of science. It was as though fiction and reality were merging. What had once seemed unreal was creeping into what was to be most likely seen in everyday life. It was all on the matter of extraterrestrial possibilities.

Somehow, perhaps with the incident of alien arrival culminating in significant extraterrestrial research on Earth, the times had been rewritten. The lore of science-fiction, alien invasion stories, the reality of multi-planetary species, intergalactic battles, and so forth now abounded more than ever before. The news was covering these facts like it wasn't surreal at all. And what really protruded the news stream was the level of political involvement coming to these things. Things were going to get intense, they warned, with politicians being capable of escalating whatsoever it is that they stepped into.

The problems were simmering from the divide amongst cabinet members, senates, and houses of parliaments, and surely would trickle down to their respective supporters. But why were things breaking onto the scene this way, and why now?

It was because of a draft that had been released by powerful governments. The intent therein was to advance and accelerate the space power programs. The advancements meant surpassing the margins of competitive Commonwealths; the acceleration meant getting there too fast and only in the short-term. These stunned other Commonwealths, or at least they acted like the predisposition was much too radical and provoking. Collaboratively, they initiated a response that would be on course to destabilize international affairs. That was what the news was merely mirroring.

Olivia tried to contact Elk several times but she couldn't. Andrew had also not shown up, but he dropped a message that he'd be out of town for a few days and she could send his work over holophone. She paced the lab and had the idea that she should bury herself in work to help ease the stress of waiting, but she soon found herself pacing again.

She wondered how only a few days of being detached from the internet could have such devastating consequences. Then again, what could she have done? She was the one advocating for speed, but not like this. This was madness. She read the feeds again, then realized that one name kept popping up – hers.

Olivia's essays on the need for preparation in the eventuality of an extraterrestrial invasion had been dug up and publicized. There was one where she had quoted something that Eric had read to her from some book – 'It is far better to be warriors in the garden than to be gardeners in the war.'

It had become one of the most famous and, for the first time, Olivia's own work was being taken seriously on S.net. But instead of elation, the only thing she felt was fear. She wanted to run or vanish.

She needed to contact Elk. She realized that the only reason she wasn't drowned in calls was that she put it on 'do not disturb' mode, and she knew now that there would be a few thousand messages to reply to and far more calls that would follow. She needed to talk to Elk, but it seemed that he too had no time to spare.

***

"What madness is this, Elk?" Andrew fumed, sitting in the vast chair that made him appear to be a toddler. A cup of tea steamed in front of him and his anger seemed to bounce off Elk.

"Sugar? Cream?" Elk asked.

Andrew narrowed his eyes then released his clenched fists, straining for calm and, when he had found it, he shook his head and replied, "Black."

Elk nodded. After a while, during which Elk sipped something unidentifiable from a bowl, he spoke. "I don't understand where the madness is, Your Excellency. You should be glad that they're warming up to the idea of protecting themselves from things that are actually out there, posing threats to their very existence."

"Don't play dumb with me, Elk. You know exactly what I mean. You know that they never embarked upon this space program to protect anything. They did it because my Commonwealth had begun to advance rapidly and they didn't like that. They wanted power, the power that comes with knowledge and you have readily given it to them,"

Elk watched him for a long while in true puzzlement. Then, he subtly penetrated the man's mind and saw the roots of his displeasure; then made a sound of sadness because mere words wouldn't be able to remove this level of selfishness and jealousy.

"What would be the gain in having only one Commonwealth benefit from this knowledge? You all are one species and the only difference is the geographical location or skin color, but does that really matter? You let small things blind you. You are more bothered with scientific superiority, while a great threat approaches. There is a saying among your people that goes 'You're chasing mice while the house is on fire,'" Elk said.

Andrew clenched his teeth, watching the yellow eyes that stared steadily at him. "You know that this will soon become something else. This will spiral even out of your control."

Elk nodded. "I agree but with your help, it won't. I…"

"I will not listen to you, Elk. I have done that, and look where that got us. You still went and told the others the same thing you told me, publicized the true manner of our research, and got their interest," Andrew said and stood up. "Good day, Elk. Lovely tea." Though he hadn't touched it, he turned quickly and left.

A few moments after the door closed behind Andrew, Elk leaned back in his chair and made a weary sound. He had never known a person like this. He couldn't understand it. What was the superiority of one person or people compared to the survival of an entire race? They made the error of looking at the trees and ignoring the forest. Elk knew that he needed to rest or he would burn out. He knew that he was far from sleep unless he manually induced it, but manually induced sleep was always less satisfying. He thought about Olivia and how he should send her a message but he decided to wait a while. He was in no mood to speak to anyone right now.

***

Weeks had passed without any word from Elk except quick messages from Tekka and random visits from Akya. Andrew's return had helped salvage a little of Olivia's sanity, though she still felt like the world was spiraling uncontrollably around her. Every day birthed some new gadget or droid. Some new robot that was better than the last and it took only a month for them to move from version one of something to version six.

Olivia was startled at the hastening that things appeared to have taken. Not so long ago, she was kicking to be heard and, now, she couldn't hear anything else but this. The world had finally opened its eyes and the entire transition seemed rather dreamy to her. Everything was so out there now.

Olivia's voice would be lost, she knew, in the plethora of uprisings and ensuing rage. And, like a lost cause, she wouldn't be able to really sway things the way she'd wanted, despite all the visibility of the cause that'd been flaring up right in her face.

She just couldn't harness the energy, and it was because things were spiraling. Spiraling as politicians wanted them to be. Everything was moving from latency to the hottest degree of temperature that antagonism could reach.

So far, the divide was largely seen in opinionated people, ready to fearlessly vaunt their ideas and rationalities. She never understood why people did this; she supposed that they mistook such things for helpful efforts, or as their most capable efforts to shape the course of things. Either way, these only unnecessarily fanned the flames, oblivious to the fact that danger was readying to encircle them all.

Support groups, hate groups, and conspiracy groups who'd finally been bold enough to come out of the shadows, clashed almost every day wherever they met. They were a prickling lot to contain and so their activities endured. They didn't even listen to their so-called founders anymore who had repeatedly called for peace.

Instead, their reins had been let loose and getting a handle on things was almost impossible. Mostly because of the divide in government. One cabinet would bring forth some law and order and another considered that the chaos was instigated by a faction of people who wanted the law restructured.

This had no sooner led to an era of aggravated surveillance, which was in essence espionage. Drones hovered over homes and borders and droids filled the sidewalks. Citizens grew more concerned that they were slowly descending into fascism and, as such, backlash was delivered to the government.

They rebelled by destroying whatever drones and droids they could find, never minding if the drones and droids were programmed to use lethal force. Whilst in other Commonwealths where these drones sneaked into, they were terminated on sight and political unrest came as a result.

All of this only increased the hostility among the Commonwealths and people. Where a Commonwealth Government was on the side of space power, a significant population of the cabinet and outspoken citizens wouldn't be. Whereas in places where the government was against, on the fence or flippant when it came to space power, the reverse with a great number of their cabinet and vocal citizens would be on their side.

What had earlier turned into hopefulness for Olivia soon convulsed into confusion. And, as with any normal person, she found herself caught in between the two political positions. Before now, she had been clear and unusually objective on where she stood, until things had gotten so muddled by politics. What once seemed like a straightforward path to shared action now depended on the truly exhaustible tools of diplomacy to see the light of day. Of course, she didn't want the proliferation of national arms, particularly at a time when the world had finally chosen to warm up to disarmament. She also didn't want, if truth be told, it to be against fellow Commonwealths, but at otherworldly threats.

Again, it was weird, this thinking. She'd not thought like this before. She'd never had an opinion on weaponry at all. Then she realized what was happening. She was incubating the thoughts of a soldier, one who only knew force to be the most effective stopping mechanism to anything. She was thinking the way Elk was, just from being in his presence so much. Olivia heard a buzz from her wristband and she answered. Elk's flat voice drifted to her ears.

"Where are you?" he asked.

"Good afternoon to you too. I think that you know exactly where I am," she said and saw a taxi pull over beside her.

"There is an issue. Get in. It's for your own safety. Please don't argue," he said.

Olivia determined it would be the wrong decision to argue. She walked in and the taxi moved. "What's happened?" she asked when she was inside the vehicle.

"Forty percent of Western European Commonwealths' satellites have been neutralized. Their communication systems are suffering badly and other systems are down also," Elk said quietly.

Her eyes widened as she froze in shock. Was it happening now? Was this what she had been worried about? "Do you know who did it?" She waited through Elk's signature pause before he spoke again.

"We'll talk when you arrive," he said and clicked off the call.

Olivia sat, feeling like so much was happening so fast that her head spun. She wondered why any of the other Commonwealths would attack the others' satellites. Could it be out of jealousy or a display of superiority? She inhaled deeply and tried to calm herself. Elk would explain. Elk would know what to do.

When she got to the laboratory, which also served as a home for the people Elk chose, she found that it was strangely empty. She then realized that some of them had moved out when they had been helped to achieve greatness in their fields, and some had even moved to Commonwealths to help with the space programs and the advancement of human knowledge.

Olivia was directed to a door by a young lady that seemed familiar, but Olivia couldn't remember her. She walked through to see Elk sitting in a chair, facing a white, empty wall. She didn't know how, but she could feel his anger and disappointment. It covered and wrapped the room like a heavy blanket and it also affected her a little, making her a bit sad and angry as well.

"Elk?" she called, but he remained silent, staring at the wall like the most fascinating piece of art was hung on it.

"Foolish. Utterly foolish and selfish. What kind of race does this? What kind of animal bites its own tail? What kind of creature attacks itself? Its people? Its pack!" he exclaimed and it seemed like with each word, his anger rose until it was more like a tangible thing, making Olivia shrink back. He hadn't even looked at her yet and, somehow, she didn't want him to. As suddenly as it rose, his anger receded and he went quiet. She waited a while before she gathered the nerve to speak directly to him.

"What happened, Elk?"

He paused for a very long while during which she decided to take a seat across the desk that was before him, although his back was to it at the moment.

"Two factions arose over the months: the conspiracy theories and accusers, and the supporters…. All foolish in my opinion. The accusing politicians pointed out that their counterparts only used the alien invasion narrative to proliferate a whole new level of weaponry with such disregard for the accords that'd been signed in recent times towards disarmament. This was what they saw to be the flagrant disregard of the outer space treaty that ratified that no nation would go nuclear in space. They claimed to fight for the Earth, the opposition accused. Meanwhile, their hidden goal was to grow so monstrously that the rest of the Commonwealth would never pick any battle with them. Formulaic deterrence strategies, they noted. They argued that the world was meant to move on to this new, utopian age of harmony and not the stark opposite that was being pushed. Only if the world, just this once, concentrated their might on peace instead, then global harmony would be attainable."

Olivia heard a low whistle from him which signaled mild anger. She thought briefly about calling Tekka in, but she was sure that there was a reason he wasn't there already. Olivia wanted peace as well but she knew that sometimes one had to beg, demand, and then take that peace forcefully at the gateways of resistance and even war. Just sometimes, not all of the time. But, who was to determine how sparingly this should be done? She couldn't tell.

"More and more cabinets around the world, holding the better sway of governance, opted to defund all such units affiliated with space power operations. Previously, their position was to reduce and stretch the funding towards this cause over a period of years. But, now, all they wanted was to suddenly bring those programs to an end. They said they were returning the spontaneity of the head of the cabinet, the President, with this radicalism, however, it didn't entirely bring all related activities to a halt. Those ones which could run on minimal funding still, were underway as well as private firms contracted for these purposes. The defunding was largely ineffectual in stopping the progress of things but it caused a significant pickle anyway," Elk said and turned his chair on its swivel to face her. Although his face was expressionless, she could feel that anger radiated from him and, although she was sure that he wouldn't do anything rash, she still felt fear from such a reaction from him.

"Andrew started it. He started the act of sabotaging other satellites and now he has supporters. They want to turn this into a satellite battle. It's sometimes amusing how they act like children. Do they not see how this would affect them?" Elk asked, then stopped and waited for something she couldn't tell, then spoke. "Please come back to work here. I'll do my best to quell the madness outside, but I need your help here so we can prepare on our own."

Olivia was about to open her mouth to turn him down, but then she realized how she would be sounding; it was the same selfishness Elk had fumed. She would be putting her own needs above the needs of the entire planet. She nodded her assent and he nodded back. He stood and started to leave, then paused at the door.

"Your brother has also been taken care of. He's safe and will be extracted should things turn ugly," Elk said.

Olivia felt her heart drop to her stomach at the idea of things turning ugly. "Let's hope it doesn't come to that," she said and Elk nodded, then walked out, leaving her to sit alone watching the white walls.

"Warbroke" was one of the more prominent messages on the illuminated placards held up throughout the day by the protesters. It referred to the relative level of peace that had spanned the times up until now. Till what was being noted as the space arms race. They hereby touted the end of the infernal madness and mayhem that war was.

Some figureheads of the budding resistance had been detained by the government and, predictably, this caused more unrest among the citizens. This move allowed the government to be cast in a far darker light than before. They now saw the government, the leader of the government especially, as a fiend that didn't belong where he was. One who deserved to be pushed out somehow.

As was with the playbook of these things, pockets of destruction carried out by some elements were wrecked on properties. Many, many streets were aflame and inevitably riotous. It would seem that the rhetoric exchanges by politicians were translated into heated activity by the ones who so steadfastly supported them. There had been no shortage of people to occupy the streets and public places for a cause as detrimental as this one.

It had been a very long time since just a fraction of this population saw each other's eyeballs, patted one another's shoulders, or nudged sweaty chests with the bodies of others in the open. It was because people had come to prefer the comfort of a full-blown virtual life instead of a physical one. They attended concerts and events as virtually as possible. Sometimes, it was even said that these cities were something of a ghost town, and with reason.

The streets had been neatly designed to be practically vacant. The major means of transportation were pods which traveled through surface and subsurface tunnels. The tunnels entangled around the city to various bus stops at certain prominent locations or places where commonly offered services were offered in bulk to the public.

It wasn't so much the disruption of daily activities that held the most indictment for the authorities as much as it was the portentous swathing of people across cities.

The streets bore a nostalgic effect for this lot. Only a handful of their generation had witnessed or been in a real-life protest before. And so, now, they learned how to protest effectively through studying the swiftly receding practice on several digital fronts from their homes.

The Commonwealth where the aliens resided was the hotbed of these issues, given that it was their government who'd made this move so provocative to the rest of the world. One difference in the alien cities where this conflict had largely originated was that it was the government who was being antagonized and left in a berserk manner. And, then came the culmination of the oppositional stance of foreign Commonwealths. So, then it was government versus government, as was with any standard rivalry.

CHAPTER ELEVEN

There were tens of thousands of satellites flying over and warping around the Earth. This constellation of giant spider-like machinery endlessly sent frequencies down the Earth from their geostationary stations. They were more like artificial stars fluttering in space. They belonged to Commonwealths, corporations, business men and women, research facilities, agencies, repositories, metropolises, and individuals. They had long served noble purposes at the frontier of information and communication technology. They had become practically indispensable in their supportive role to modern living.

However, their purposes weren't all civic and entrepreneurial as it was prominently purported. Satellites were strategically placed where they'd been allowed overtime. Spy satellites weren't even the case here. It was something much more powerful; weaponized satellites. This was the deeply disconcerting advancement in space science that made every less empowered Commonwealth shudder at the reality of their own frailness.

This was the Commonwealth where the aliens had sought to upstart a constellation of guardian satellites. For some, it remained to be more worrisome than it was consoling. A closer look at the situation entailed that what was going on was more of an instance of distrust among Commonwealths than anything remotely pacifist. But, the vulnerability in being targeted from outside of the Earth was, to say the least, enormous.

And, this particular Commonwealth was exercising a type of international veto power the rest of the world wasn't aware existed. Their development of advanced and aptly placed weaponry through their space power operations was an effect of their own prerogative. Under the noses of the rest of the world, they placed weapons in orbit. The blatant disregard. It was a call to war for some.

But, others followed. Space power operations were largely a clan-destine effort, but rival Commonwealths privy to being highly suspi-cious of this had equally floated their own arsenals into orbit. This way they hoped to outmatch each other in the eventuality that was to dawn on the respective political leadership. That day had come. That moment was here and nothing was in sight to prevent it.

Some Commonwealths were belligerent towards other Common-wealths, readying to go head-on with them in battle. The civilian class was essentially already at war, the political class was simmering over and about to burst, whilst the military was ever prepared for a 'go.' And this was just in the more bureaucratic Commonwealths where the hi-erarchy of things needed to formally travel down; unlike some other Commonwealths which were already at battle.

It was only between these slim moments that governments reflected and contemplated things; the all-round costs of what they were about to embark upon. In the conflagration of anger and grievances, most of them deemed the costs to be negligible; but the costs of what exact-ly? Surely no one was estimating the cost of rebuilding their various civilizations in the instance of an all-out destructive warfare. But, of course, they were naturally prepared for that. This wasn't the scale of things under review right now. No ground-level provocations had tak-en place because there were no inherent threats to national securities. It was only a hemispherical one, for now.

A confrontation was to be had. So, they reckoned that as far as they could, they'd have to take these punitive strikes to something remote, but endearing, something replaceable but back-seating, something out in space. To the satellites of course. They would take them out in their numbers and perhaps things could return to normal. By normal, they had envisioned the times before; when Commonwealths were yet to acquire an outer space advantage over the others. A time when their various arsenals sort of evened themselves out here on the ground.

Before things had really set off, they should have known how they accelerated to this point; and why screeching to a halt was going to be entirely out of the question. There was going to be no turning back at all. Never again. Just forward thrusting. That was how grave things were to get.

Military heads started the next stage of things and rallied their troops – air force and weapon control system departments alike. They gave pep talks about the purpose of attacks to offset and deter the enemy. They ascertained that their targets were skyward and using radar information, ensured that they locked into their targets accurately. They did this and waited for some time. Waiting for what appeared to be the so-called perfect moment to strike.

***

Nobody had written down what exactly should follow in the event of the defiance of the outer space treaty. Everything was jumbled up in 'consequences' and 'repercussions.' And, since phrases by themselves couldn't do the heavy lifting, people's anger did instead. The anger clouded their hearts more than it ever should have.

There seemed to be an eeriness ringing throughout the world. It was the pervasiveness of suspense, a dangle and flirtatious holdback between indifference and war. A question of who was to go first. And then, the wreckage and inferno would only rapidly follow. Nobody wanted to start a battle or be on the left-hand side of it. Or so they all thought.

Military hastening abroad and hushed statements of political approval accelerated things. "In an attack, we defend." This consensus was declared in order to justify themselves. Now they had all they needed. What was left was nothing other than a countdown. Whilst the political leaders basked in an aura of supremacy at what was to occur, the military jolted with enthusiasm at what these fireworks held in store. There was almost a lust for the inferno.

That not-so-long-ago strange and uncertain spookiness that overlaid the world was about to be upturned once and for all. The platform for RAINBOW was taken outside of a military complex. It was eagerly rolled out by a couple of cocky soldiers and its head was pointed skyward.

RAINBOW was a surface-to-air missile with incredible speed and maneuvering abilities. A countdown rung and RAINBOW was a go.

RAINBOW undocked from its berth with a fiery tail of flame, thrusting into the skies along a vertical trajectory and climbing up against the Earth's gravity, piercing through the troposphere. RAINBOW was a long-range weapon for long shots and it would do the job just fine.

RAINBOW had now traveled out of the Earth's atmosphere and had the satellite constellation in sight. It began to prepare to disintegrate as it got closer to the kill-stage. In a matter of minutes, it made a blistering strike at the first satellite, detonating and shredding it to bits.

Whether that was taken to be some sort of warning strike was yet to be seen. Certainly, it didn't go unnoticed. But, it could've been negligible because it took out a non-military satellite.

And then, there came another. Then another. More strategically targeted strikes were taking out military satellites. This action was worth a retaliation and a counter strike for sure.

Unleashing a nuclear warhead was usually a limited approach, in the sense that a Commonwealth's arsenal was limited and prone to highly discretionary usage. However, in these instances, such considerations were ignored.

Intercontinental ballistic missiles and submarine missiles were released, navigating into space. They rose upwards asymmetrically, honing in on the geostationary targets and other satellites alike.

As was typical of missile defense, missiles were unleashed to seek out the other accelerating ones and take them out before they got to their intended targets. These were particularly sent to protect the satellites from the assault. This was possible by the more advanced Earth-engulfing radar systems of the Commonwealths where the conundrums had originated. They lost some and won some.

The interceptors locked in on other rival military-grade satellites in orbit and a satellite-to-satellite extermination was underway. The missiles progressed aggressively and powerfully through the weightlessness of dark space, locking in on the target satellites that were unprotected. At times, they encircled the Earth seeking and pursuing these other satellites. Their range was just as limitless as it was on Earth and the satellites being taken out couldn't exactly maneuver themselves out of the incoming destruction.

Projectiles kept ricocheting around the Earth's gravitational force, cruising the looming void that was space. It was like fireworks amongst the stars or some sort of comet trail or the rebirth of a solar object.

The debris of these artificial satellites was left littered and hovering in Earth's lower orbit. Some of it had been downed from an upward altitude and was now forcefully falling towards the Earth. Ones that were knocked out of space soon constituted what was a debris shower on the Earth.

If anything, this only spurred them to send even more missiles to disrupt the orbit of even more objects placed above by every other

Commonwealth. In the aftermath, there was hardly any satellite left in space. Mutual destruction made sure of that.

And. in the end, the Earth from the view outside appeared like it was adorned with a crown of fumes. Almost like a volcano had erupted over it.

From the Earth, what could be seen was imagery in the skies of the explosive extinguishment of the manmade stars of technology.

Andrew watched as the night sky was illuminated by the death of the satellites. There wasn't a twinge of regret in him. He did feel sadness at the wastefulness that was occurring, but it was necessary. He wouldn't sit and watch another Commonwealth or other Commonwealth's rise to superiority, then become kings over the rest of them.

He knew that it was also a bit ironic that what had started out as an effort of technological advancement had rapidly handicapped the entire system of the world's technology. Their pods were almost decommissioned and there was little to no transportation or communication anymore. He gritted his teeth and took comfort from the tech he had stashed away in bunkers. Everything would burn and his Commonwealth would rise from the ashes into glory. He smiled grimly and turned to walk back to his desk only to see Elk standing in front of him. He gasped in surprise and took a few startled steps back.

"I suppose there is some aesthetic to it," Elk said and nodded towards the direction of the falling machines.

Andrew wondered how the Terran appeared in his office, but he quickly masked his fear. "You shouldn't be here."

"Neither should this planet. They should be on their way to security and true growth, yet your madness has stopped you from embracing it. It has made you reduce your world into a worse state than it was before; a worse state than it has ever been."

Andrew took a few steps closer to him, his face contorted in rage. "Go ahead and tell me what I should do to protect my planet and how I have ruined it. Of course I would take advice from a creature that let his planet go to waste and now has to squat on another one."

The flatness of the alien's face couldn't tell him if his words had done any real damage, but the utter silence and stillness that came over Elk made Andrew cower a little. His instincts knew what the silence was. It was the stillness before the lion pounced or before a snake struck and, in this case, he was the prey.

"I see," Elk said finally and turned to leave.

"Never enter my office without my permission again," Andrew said, but Elk didn't stop or turn around, he just continued walking.

Andrew made a mental note to fire the chief of his guards. How could they have let something that was eight feet tall slip past them? He turned back to look at the satellites that were hurtling to Earth and those which caused bright spark as they went out of existence. And, perhaps he felt a little, minuscule twinge of guilt.

***

Olivia was watching television, but her eyes weren't really watching the screen. Her eyes were seeing the horrors that were happening around Earth; crashed systems and entire industries. She looked over to where Eric was and she whistled to get his attention.

"Heard from Andrew lately?" she asked.

She had seen that they had grown close and, at times, Eric knew where Andrew was even when she didn't. He shrugged and then sat back in his chair.

"He traveled to go collect his mom and sister. His sister has been having panic attacks due to everything that has been happening. It's messed up though," he said.

Olivia suddenly felt very sad that she hadn't known this and hadn't even bothered to ask about his family. She had always wanted to work on this flaw of hers, but it was actually very difficult for her to get out of her shell and be interested in people; but at least not Andrew. He was such a wonderful person, and it was mandatory that she be interested in his welfare.

"Did you recommend he take her to see a therapist?" she asked

Eric shrugged then shook his head slowly. "I don't know any."

"You don't have to know any to recommend."

He raised an eyebrow. "I guess it slipped my mind then." He looked out the window briefly then sighed.

"I know, right?" Olivia replied. "It has even gotten so much worse since the Commonwealths don't trade with each other anymore and now they have to use middlemen. Some of the goods are even un-branded these days. Don't they see what this warfare is causing?" she asked, and Eric turned to look at her. His face was carefully blank but there was a storm in his eyes. Olivia became worried. "What is it, Eric?"

He shrugged, looking away. "It's their war, let them fight it. I'll be in my room when they're done." Eric started towards the living area. She was surprised at his nonchalance but she suspected it was a mask, a way for him to make sense of and cope with what was happening.

Olivia also needed a way to cope with what was happening and work wasn't doing it anymore, neither was sitting down on the couch and worrying her head off. She was sure she might have aged a couple of decades in the time she'd been indoors. She checked the new wristband that the Terrans issued her and contacted Andrew.

Then, after she had spoken with him, Olivia contacted Elk who surprisingly responded immediately and asked her to come meet him. He sent a pod that would take her as everything about automated transportation had fallen. Even automated prisons were broken and prisoners were unleashed. There was no travel as planes and commercial hovercrafts were grounded. Olivia felt it all pile up on her shoulders and she pulled her legs in and began to cry.

Olivia had stopped by the time she met Elk in the place he had chosen but her eyes were still puffy. It was clear that he noticed but he didn't mention it and she was grateful, thinking a bit how he wasn't human but had a more detailed intuition in handling emotional situations - more than most humans she knew, not that she knew a lot.

"This was not the war we saw," she immediately said to Elk upon entering the room where he was.

He looked at her weirdly. "We saw?" he asked. "I see you're remembering the events of the past as a dream or something merely reminiscent of passing thoughts." He came closer to her, "The treasures tend to have that effect on humans, yes..." he muttered to himself. "How interesting."

Olivia bore a confused, but unconcerned look on her face. "Why is this war going on?" She gestured with her hands toward the world right outside the window. "I've wasted my time... so much time... anticipating a much more rational attack! And from otherworldly beings!"

"Shouldn't you be pleased at this disappointment?"

"How... How could I? I have been utterly wrong." She was confused, searching the ground in despair.

Elk saw her thoughts were disheveled and compounded by powerlessness. At first, he didn't understand just why she felt such a burden of responsibility to her race. It wasn't like she bore real power to significantly turn things around.

"What you did once was purely a happenstance. It didn't bestow upon you saviorhood to mankind." He figured that she'd overworked herself because she once had been able to alter the course of events for her race, using the fate treasure. He saw that the responsibility of that possibility burdened her now as it had always done. "It was never your fault. Do not carry this fault as your own."

She ignored what she perceived to be his soft speaking and platitudes.

"Olivia, think productively. Isn't that what scientists do? I'm quite sure it is."

She paced around impatiently like she was up to something. "But they'll destroy themselves entirely if we don't do something. If we dont intervene."

"That's not the kind of war they're fighting. They're just shooting each other in the foot, that's all. And someday, they'll learn to walk again, I guess."

This didn't satisfy her. She was obsessed with either getting a grip on things or grabbing at anything that might help. She desperately needed a role in the big picture, to at least play punch bag with.

"I think if only the Commonwealths of the world had paused to deliberate," Olivia said.

Elk shrugged. "If only they sat down as acquaintances to hear themselves out."

"Yeah, but missiles bring this adrenaline. And they were all lured in at the idea of power."

Frustrated with the warming indoor space, Olivia came to the enclosed courtyard of the building. It had a transparent roof and a lush garden adorned with meteorites just like the Stonehenge. "Things are really crazy right now. I don't even know where to start. How could we be doing this? And why do I feel like it could only get worse?"

"Because it could."

It was only after a moment that the understanding dawned on her and she quivered. "The pods! They're not coming now, are they?"

"Who says they won't come?" Elk said ominously.

"Oh my God!" She gasped and shook her head. In her thinking, she recounted years of anxiety and months of toiling at various sites around the world, doing all that she could to evade this moment. She found it unbelievable that those moments which she'd long dreaded were coming to life with each unrealized day and hour.

Olivia longed for nothing more than some way to pause time – and then what? She knew she wanted to turn away from the reality that those pods would best them somehow. And, they needed time to change that.

But, because the discounting of time in its form as a delay was a luxury craved for by the desperate, Olivia wouldn't be able to resist a flint of an opportunity to take that chance. So, she went for it, as Elk expected she would. "The treasures. We need to use them."

"What? No."

"We're in a war, and potentially going to have another really soon. We need the treasures!" she cried.

"You wish to use the treasures to alter the fate of many without their consent?" Elk asked her.

"So would our world leaders. A handful of people are powerfully deciding to do all of this." Olivia pointed out the window to the skies, referring to the bombardment of satellites in space and ongoing hostilities on the ground as well. "It's the same strategy. But with different tools," she hoped. Agitated, she told him, "Someone's got to do this."

"You don't just use the treasures whenever you please. Remember that they aren't Earthly artifacts and, so Olivia, you don't understand them. Alright?"

"But they're needed!" her voice croaked.

"Probably. But let me briefly tell you a story. One that may or may not assuage you. Either way, it will offer you ample opportunity to appropriately use your rationality. Over five hundred years ago there was a race of aliens known as the Virzut, who were master engineers and technicians. They had mastered their solar system and subdued their sun, turning it into one of their many batteries that provided the power for much of their technology. They grew so fast and so strong that there was no other race that could hold a candle to them. Well, among their best and brightest was a young Virzutian named Vol. He was among the most intelligent that their kind had ever produced from generations of careful breeding that weeded out any undesirable traits until only perfection was left; but mental perfection is a very fragile thing and, when pushed, it could easily fall into psychopathy. Well, Vol stumbled upon one of the treasures, a different one from the one currently in our possession. He began to study it, to be obsessed by it, figuring out ways to elongate its working time and to grant some other objects, weapons, or people with fragments of its ability. He slowly bent his people, the most intelligent people in the observable universe, to his will and they were an unstoppable force; and he kept studying the treasure. Sometimes using it can alter the events of a battle or an experiment that wasn't going the way he wanted. He began to use it on worlds, on planets, and on civilizations until the treasure rebelled and, in one fatal swoop, erased all his people from the face of the universe and ejected him into the deep recesses of space. His mind became totally unhinged and, even now, he still destroys worlds, uninhabited planets, and he continues making weapons that no one has ever gotten close enough to test their power because he's a madman. That's what the treasures can do."

Olivia was quiet. She didn't know what would happen if they used it again. She had no understanding of these artifacts, and she didn't want to wager the lives on Earth on the probability that everything might turn out fine like it did last time when she wasn't even sure that her mind wouldn't unravel after another reality shift.

"What do we do?" she asked quietly.

Elk looked up then back at her. "We start again."

She smiled a little and looked up at him then nodded. "Yeah. When everything is done, we'll try again." She shrugged a little. "Not like there's anything left anyway. They have literally destroyed decades of careful work and research in just a few months. It would take at least a decade with the help of your people to get back to where we were."

"Then we'll take that decade," Elk said and his flat voice felt reassuring now.

She looked back up again and saw what appeared to be a thousand lights far away in the sky, similar to the stars at night, but shining so brightly that they were seen in the brighter light of the evening.

"What is that?" Olivia asked, pointing.

Elk looked up then she heard the sound of fear and disbelief emanate from his buzzer. "It would seem we don't have a decade. We hardly have a day," he said and his fists clenched as they watched the arrival of a thousand battleships.

CHAPTER TWELVE

Ork heard the hiss as the entrance to his ship opened and, for some reason, he felt fear but he quelled it. He fought against the lies that reputation could tell as he knew those lies intimately and had used them a lot to his advantage. He had known for a long time who Vol was. He had lived through the fear when the Virzutians were at their peak, headed by Vol, who wielded the most powerful and dangerous weapons in the entire universe.

Ork had often imagined himself wielding such power and being in such a position, but the only difference would be that he would not squander it like Vol foolishly did. He did have to admit that the Virzutian wasn't at all foolish; for he had evaded capture, even by Ork's own armadas, and he had destroyed countless ships and armies that have been sent out to find him in order to cajole, coax, or threaten him to divulge the information in his mind, a mind that had been deranged far beyond salvage. Ork knew what he was going up against.

Ork stepped out of his ship into the harshest atmosphere he had witnessed in a long while. He felt the sheer violence of the place as magma erupted from the ground up in the air and lightning sparked; little pebbles of diamonds rained down. Had it not been for this suit that was specifically designed to withstand the harshest conditions conceivable, he would have been torn to shreds just standing there.

Ork stood nine feet tall and was wearing the most impressive armor that the world had ever seen. He was the ruler of a hundred worlds and was waiting for a rebel, a criminal. He was getting angry. Then, he reminded himself that this criminal had been a more powerful ruler than he was and, so, he needed to work with him. And that was something that no other creature had ever achieved.

The Virzutian language was a tongue twister and had many roots in the deepest logic and symmetry. It was formulaic and mathematical and was a bit emotion-based in a way that made learning it an impossibility for Ork. He was displeased at the thought that he was the lesser one between them and was at a disadvantage because Vol somehow knew his tongue and that of thousands of other worlds.

A portal appeared before him; a square through which a form stepped through. Vol was shorter than he had expected and wore a suit that covered the hideous form that all Virzutians had. This suit made it seem like he had two hands and legs and his face was covered in a technician's mask, but Ork had seen naked Virzutians long ago and they were not a sight for the faint hearted. Vol stood there watching him, then raised a finger and whirled it about. Ork didn't understand this, neither did he care to. Trying to understand how someone like Vol thought was just a waste of time.

"This planet will crumble and implode in eight minutes. Say your peace," Vol said.

Vol's tone sent a chill through Ork's spine. This creature was one that had achieved a level of tonal manipulation that allowed anyone to feel his madness and love for destruction. There were no eyes to be seen, but Ork knew that within that mask, three pairs of eyes stared at him and he banished the thought from his mind. He could not afford to show discomfort and fear before something like Vol.

"I'm Ork, the ruler of a hundred worlds and I'm a great admirer of the work you have done. I have great respect for the empire you built and for the work of your great people. And so, I've come to seek your assistance. I seek an alliance with you in order to conquer a planet far off, a planet known as Earth," he said. Vol stood.

A great shriek sounded and a blue light shot up from a distance not far from them. Ork felt a force greater than anything he had ever encountered try to pull him in and he engaged his suit's propellers to get himself back into his ship which immediately launched away from the planet.

He could see the planet cave in on the bright blue light, whirling around it, cracking apart, then it finally imploded. Ork had barely escaped what could well have been his death and the fear he felt gave him great cause for anger. He heard a buzz and saw a flash of light behind him then turned to see Vol step out of a portal. He controlled his shock at the fact that Vol could create portals and just step through them.

"You said eight minutes," Ork said with as much calmness as he could muster. All his soldiers within the ship burst in, weapons ready, but Ork stopped them with a casual wave of his hand. Somehow, he knew that he would be dead if Vol wished it, and that knowledge both terrified and angered him. He would have to find a way to kill this thing before it decided to kill him.

"You said eight minutes," Ork repeated and he heard the slow, rippling sound that was the Virzutian equivalent of laughter.

"I miscalculated," Vol said simply. What kind of creature was this that the destruction of an entire planet was nothing more than a joke to him? "Oh, and I should tell you, the three escort ships that came with you have been sent into portals that were directly above the pulsars. I do not think that they can survive that," Vol added.

Ork fought to control the anger that rose inside him. "Why did you do that?"

"I do not like being hunted."

"I wasn't hunting you. I was just trying to meet with you," Ork said.

"Same thing. You hunt someone down to meet with them. Whether you meet with them alive or dead makes no difference," Vol said. "I've heard of you, Ork, and I've seen your attempts to try and catch me. You're not really a being of much interest, so it never bothered me. But I should think that one planet would be an easy thing for you, or was my underestimation an overestimation in itself?" he asked.

Ork nearly clenched his fists in rage, but he schooled his temper, reminding himself of who was standing before him. "They have something that protects them," he said and saw that Vol was no longer paying attention to him. He had started fiddling with something on his wrist and Ork knew he was rigging up the ship to explode so he spoke a bit louder. "They have protection, Vol. Something that you would be very much interested in, I imagine."

Vol stopped his fiddling, then stared at Ork. "There are very few things that I'm interested in. Be very careful when making that kind of assumption," he said.

Ork stepped closer to him until they were so close he could smell the foulness of the gasses that Vol breathed. "The treasure is there," he said quietly.

Vol went perfectly still. Then, after a while, gas hissed out from a tube attached to his suit. Ork imagined that this primitive design was more to offend than to have any real practicality. "I could just travel there, blast the planet to atoms, and take the treasure," he said quietly as if he was expecting Ork to give him the reason he shouldn't.

"Well, research was carried out and it was easy to gather facts because it was in the possession of the other people with whom we shared my former planet. This treasure can be used by one species and it's the beings that reside on that planet."

"Humans, they're called. I know a fair bit about them," Vol said.

Ork quenched a mild surprise. There was little Vol was expected not to know. "Well, only they can use it, and it grows even more selective. It can be used by only one person," he said.

"What will the death of this person do to the treasure?" Vol asked.

"I don't know. But, is the prospect of gaining a treasure not worth the stress of taking care in handling these creatures?" Ork asked.

Vol went quiet for a while before the gas hissed out again. "I see," he said simply and walked off.

"Where are you going?" Ork asked.

Vol turned swiftly to stare at him, or at least Ork imagined he was staring at him, as none of his features could be seen from behind the mask.

"I saw what looked very much like suitable quarters for me. Inform me when this Earth is in sight," Vol said and walked through a portal that formed in front of him.

Ork bristled at being ordered around, but he needed the Virzutian. After that, he would dispatch of him quickly. He had a plan;, he thought; back to the three Blitzer ships gone to waste in a pulsar. He walked back to his quarters, anger surging restlessly within him.

***

A boy on the steeple of a cathedral was wrangling with the mechanism of a church bell. It was obvious he was weary of the process as he pulled his weight against that of the gigantic bell which clanked disproportionately. The bell rang out loud and far. It was a historic moment for him, one he enjoyed well after the toil. There'd been many who lined up for this opportunity to pull the bells; before now they had nothing to do with the once automated ringing of the bells and, so now, they wanted the medieval feel that came with the iconic church bells. Afterwards, the kids who'd gathered to watch him ring the bells cheered happily, their mirth floating alongside the sounds of the bells.

Andrew's ears followed the sound of the cheering kids as he walked along to the university on this Ash Wednesday morning. For a moment, he admitted to himself that he envied the supposed liberal naivety of those kids; their obliviousness to the truth and the reality pervading them. What it must be like to be a kid again. To not be so drenched in this sad world was nothing but adorable. He walked on, considering the forward course of time, noting to himself that such an era of his life was passed for good. Now all he wanted was merely to live, or was it to survive? Just long enough, no longer well enough, as he once thought.

Churchgoers in bleak clothing walked past him. The morning bore the beam of solemnity. He slowed his pace, not wanting to be seen as defiant, but somewhat adaptive to the tempo of the day. Solemn people moved rather slowly, he figured.

He moved along commuting because it wasn't only cheaper and fairer but probably more efficient and less time-consuming. There just weren't enough solar and mechanical cabs for now and so he sprinted away, making do with his feet.

He passed by a learning facility. 'Of course,' he thought, people certainly were up to figuring out how best to exit this situation. 'Learning,' he said to himself. They held his highest respect. He absolutely approved of it.

Andrew could overhear an instructor speaking to some folks. "The human mind is like a muscle," he said elegantly. "It can be flexed to be unlimited and unending in its might, drive, and possibilities."

He strained his listening some more. It was probably a psychology class. The instructor was most likely answering a question and Andrew couldn't hear it, so he decided to move along. He didn't really like psychology. He reasoned it to be the mind-numbing, so-called re-realization of the human mind.

Lacking the requisite stimulation that made science ambitious. But now he felt a tinge inside of him yearning for that lecture hall. Was that curiosity nudging at him? He'd have really wanted to know what truly was on people's minds at this time: how to read them, empathize with them, reassure them – generally be less abstract than a dry third person narrative or a textbook. He knew people were hurting and only wished he could help somehow.

Then, he passed by a hospitality house. The Grand Hotel, it was called. The name used to be brightly portrayed across the top of the hotel. The property was a broad skyscraper, sprawling freely across a significant square footage. And now, it seemed like something in the works; something yet unopened to the public. But it was as open and functional as it could be.

Andrew was sure management was doing all that they could to make it stay that way. Of course, business had dwindled, primarily from the traveling clients, and it was no easy feat keeping things afloat. He imagined the exasperated guests, the discomfited guests, the forever unsettled guests. All that calamity tolerated at the hotel under the guise of hospitality.

He directed his gaze towards where he could hear a voice humming exhortation from a luxurious steel window someplace midway up the building. What was going on was something that would've been termed a productivity or reevaluation meeting of sorts. And yet it was bound to be futile.

He imagined what it must be like for those staff being goaded to do probably well above what they could do. He could picture the stress – despite the already daunting living conditions. Why would someone want to work there anyway? He couldn't figure it out.

"Better room service," he heard a man say pointedly. The man was probably the manager. Ah, so they were attempting what they could to up the comfort levels of their clients. Comfort was all they could sell at this point anyway. He smiled at his ability to come to this conclusion by himself; he now regarded the hotel as perhaps doing something to quell existing stress after all.

Andrew then passed by an interesting location. He was unusually attentive to anything that was hearable this day. He could hear people begging and bargaining. This was both amusing and so unusual it made him chuckle. But it was understandable. It was the culmination of what had naturally happened. And it was a necessity to most.

It was a makeshift thrift shop with the predominant conversations seeking a discount. He could hear all sorts of back-and-forth. He could equally hear the luxury buyers trying to get ahead of those there to acquire necessities. He could aptly hear how they were being curtailed by the more desperate necessity seekers. He could hear the ceaseless shuffling of feet and the chorus of whining at unfavorable deals. He could hear the rattle of the shop owner and his assistants trying to keep the peace and mediate fairness.

By this time, the chuckle had left his face. "This is serious business," he muttered.

Andrew went on, now comparably closer to the university than when he was by the Cathedral. He was passing by an exercise club whose participants consisted of mostly middle-aged, formerly employed individuals in upstart tech firms, who had now been getting quite sedentary themselves. He could hear the exuberant, noisy, and high-spirited energy with which the trainer had them on.

He wondered if it was effective. For sure, it'll not be something he'd get into doing himself. But he could relate. Andrew could assimilate their desire to engage in seemingly worthwhile activities, pastimes, and the like – all such things that took their minds off the obvious, which was the fact that their present reality sucked. These were those who'd really had their identities and lives tied up in their jobs and now this was the only way they could assure themselves that the world was not closing in on them just yet. That was what unemployment did to them.

The government announced that the unemployment situation was temporary, that they were working on resettling those who'd lost their jobs to the technological onslaught that the world had experienced. But, so far they could only do so much as make a promise. It was difficult to offset the ballooning rates of unemployment. The former executives would be reinstated in low-ranking, low-paying jobs. The prospects weren't bright.

Andrew realized how lucky he and Olivia were to be under Elk's sponsorship. He frowned when he thought of Olivia. She said that she had seen it. And when he asked what exactly she had seen, she said that it was the end. He wondered what end. She had said that she briefly saw the attack as it happened and he wondered what exactly she had seen that had put her so on edge.

Olivia turned a part of the laboratory into an observatory and she viewed the stars every day. Andrew said nothing when he walked into the laboratory. They had taken on a few staff and it made his work easier, but it was strange having more people there. It was only he and Olivia for the most part, and he was happy with that. Not that there was anything against having help around the place. It just felt strange.

Olivia sat in the observatory, peering into the telescope and seeing nothing out of the ordinary. She wondered if it was because she had seen another timeline and lived in it that she was able to catch a glimpse of what was to happen. She knew that they were coming. Elk had all but confirmed it and she studied, worried, and researched obsessively.

But what exactly would she do with anything she found? Did she merely desire to heighten her raging and helpless state? At best, she reasoned that she'd take RPGs, point them skyward, and shoot at whatever alien ships or pods that came. It'd feel like something for sure, even if those ships would be impregnable.

Olivia thought about all she knew regarding the situation and how it felt briefly empowering to know them. For one, she at least knew that they were invading from the skies as anyone had traditionally anticipated for years in science-fiction. She also knew that they'd be more vengeful than ever and likely in better shape than the last time. With any luck, she'd been on Ork's hit list and that made her consider ways she could serve as a useful pawn in the fight that was essentially not hers.

As of yet, she found nothing through those lenses. It was frustrating. This helpless feeling was something she didn't recognize. There was no time, nor need to run to Elk. Elk knew what was to come and he rallied the other aliens in that regard. They were preparing themselves for whatever direction the war might take. As always, they prepared themselves to make a stand, to defend, and push back with all that they've got. They left assorted weaponry in their arsenal, equipping themselves with them as they saw fit. They made haste like ones ready to be outnumbered.

This was the last home of theirs. They couldn't bear yet another journey outside of the galaxy, especially if they had to rely on the primitive human spaceships. They knew that if the invaders succeeded with controlling Earth, their conquest wouldn't just end there. This stand was the only way to stop the planet invaders in their tracks before they rendered this galaxy desolate.

They stood fast, expecting the worst; the worst that vengeance would whip up and they tried their best to be ready.

In increasingly colorful language, she continued cursing the Commonwealths. It got so fierce that Andrew had to talk over her and force her to rest, after which, she seemed to return a little to herself again, although she seemed much thinner and frailer with bags around her eyes. Her eyes seemed less piercing and more dull, almost lifeless, except when fear or worry crossed them.

"Andrew?" she called as she looked up from a specimen she was examining, and rubbed her glasses, frowning a bit at them.

He turned to answer but stopped short. She seemed very small, very vulnerable and it threw him off guard. "What is it?" he asked softly.

Olivia looked out the window, then sighed heavily. She bit her upper lip for a while, then nodded, and nodded again to herself. "I wish the aliens never came. I wish we had never come out of the iron-age because then no one would be interested in us. We would live ignorantly, but safely. It reminds me of what the Bible says, you know? '*He who has much wisdom has much grief, and he who has much knowledge has much sorrow,*'" she quoted from memory.

Andrew started to become truly worried. The truth was, in fact, that he was scared too, terrified even; but of what he wasn't sure. It was Elk's and Olivia's paranoia that had started his fear in the first place. He wondered if staying here was healthy for him. They hadn't seen other aliens apart from the Terrans and he wondered why they would have any need to be afraid but, then again, Elk had seen those beings and he seemed convinced that it was only a matter of time before they were attacked.

"I worry too. I worry that I might be asleep one day and wake up to an invasion. I worry about my family. Everything has taken a turn for the worst lately and, the truth is, that everyone is worried. But I don't think that worry should disrupt and ruin your life. I don't think that you should let it. I think that you should get out from behind that telescope and take a walk, eat some food, and make friends that aren't me or from another galaxy," he said softly.

She peered shortsightedly at him, then slowly nodded.

Andrew shook his head. "You nod, but I know that you'll end up doing nothing about it. Come with me to a party sometime," he said.

She narrowed her eyes at him, anger flashing across her features. "People still have those things? The world is almost ending and people are partying?"

"No. You think the world is ending, Olivia. Elk has infected you with that idea and you have spread that infection. Look at what it has done to you. You can barely focus anymore. You try to spread yourself too thin and you are utterly spent. It's the only thing you talk, think, and read about. Being around you is becoming hard, and it's as if you don't care," he said.

Her eyes went cold, and she nodded slowly, then looked away. "I don't care," she said after a while.

Andrew sighed, rubbing his forehead with his fingers. He hated the fact that he had snapped, but he didn't truly regret it. She was supposed to hear it, and he only regretted not saying it sooner. "I'll leave you to your work, then," he said, then stood up and left, feeling angry and very tired; and it was only morning.

***

Elk was exhausted. It had been a long time since he was truly this exhausted. He wanted nothing more than to slip into hibernation, but who knew what kind of madness the Earth would descend into by the time he came out. He could hear Tekka come in and they both remained in silence for a while.

"You're disturbed," Tekka commented. Elk didn't reply. "You're doing all you can. Our people couldn't ask for a better leader than you."

"It's not enough. It's never been enough. I have just led our people from one disaster to another, and it seems that the time has finally come that I cannot lead them out." Elk closed his eyes, sadness welling up from him so violently that the sound from him was long and loud.

"Elk, I've known you for such a long time that I can barely remember a time that you weren't there. Since the time I have known you, you have always been dependable and strong. You fought with everything you had against Ork, and you led our people across the vast expanse of space and found us a home here. There's no other Terran that could have been able to do as much as you have and I say that with all certainty," Tekka said.

Elk understood that he was trying to encourage him, but he didn't have the strength anymore. It felt like all his strength had been sucked out of him. "These people, this race…. They are unlike anything I've encountered. You put a simple thing among them and they make it spiral into their own undoing. They have created odds that are impossible to surmount."

Tekka made a sound of mild reproach and annoyance. "Apart from the battles that ended our home, you have been undefeated and when there was little and, against impossible odds, you have risen from them and made them work. You will make this one work too and, if they're too great that you can't…, then I don't know any other being who can. You are the best hope we have, so I'll not have you sitting alone and discouraging yourself."

Elk said nothing for a while, but he did feel a little better.

"We could use the treasures," Tekka said.

Elk buzzed his disapproval. "Too risky. There is so much we don't know about it. We were lucky that it didn't do any damage the last time. We should study it until we know more; to find out if there is a way to harness a little of its ability and stop everything. Something tells me that toying with timelines is very risky business and we should be very careful. The pressures of having lived in two timelines is almost driving me crazy and I think that it has succeeded in having that effect on Olivia. How is the research going on erasing those parts from her mind?"

Tekka paused then spoke slowly and softly, "I still don't think that she would give her consent."

Elk nodded, accepting that it would indeed be difficult to get Olivia to remove the knowledge of what she had seen. She'd believe that it was that knowledge that made her more careful, kept her in the light. She wouldn't deliberately relinquish that knowledge.

"Still, it would be good to have it ready. And I also permit the study of the treasure, but only to select people we can trust. People that saw everything from the beginning," Elk said.

Tekka seemed offended. "They are our own people. We can trust all of them..." he said.

Elk shook his head slightly, then realized that he was already adopting human gestures which only supported his point. "They're on a foreign planet that is currently under attack and they're agitated. They could make mistakes in their judgment. Anything could happen in the face of the threat that looms before us. We have to take every eventuality into account."

Tekka stood stiffly for a while, then accepted and turned to leave. Elk watched him for a while, trying to clear his mind. He had lived through a lot. He would see his people through this. He would see the entire planet through this, or die in the process.

CHAPTER THIRTEEN

Ork stood staring at the blue dot on the holofield that served as a display. He found it difficult to believe that he was successfully resisted by something so puny. His anger rose at the idea but he restrained himself, being careful to keep his anger on a leash. He sometimes thought that the constant anger that afflicted his kind was a true nuisance and was more a weakness than a source of inspiration.

Ork thought about the treasure on Earth and the things he would be able to do if it were in his possession. He thought about the way he'd shape the universe if time and reality were his to control. He guarded his thoughts carefully, for he never knew when the Virzutian would appear.

Vol had been restless and he wondered if it was because they were drawing closer to the treasure, and it was affecting him somehow. It wouldn't be strange. The Virzutian had spent the longest time a living being had ever spent with one of those treasures. Perhaps it had bound itself to him in a way and he felt a similar pull by this one. It didn't matter though. The treasure would be Ork's. And once Vol had outlived his usefulness, he would be quickly eliminated.

The air shifted and shimmered around him as he tore through space. Ork was more than a little annoyed and envious at the manner with which the creature broke the basic laws of the universe. Vol stepped closer to him and he smelled the foul stench of the gas from the creature.

"You remind me much of myself," Vol said suddenly.

Ork felt his anger soar, but he fought against his instinctive retort. "I am nothing like you, trust me," he said.

Vol went quiet for such a long while that Ork had to resist the urge to look back and see what abomination he might be up to, but that would make him seem weak so he stood looking at the display, pretending that whatever Vol might be doing behind him was of no importance.

"You remind me of myself," he said again. And the gasses made a bubbling sound then hissed and the foul smell renewed itself. "Not entirely happy memories."

"I doubt any memory of yours is a happy one, if you truly even understand that concept. I don't judge, understand, but it seems that's the truth. Virzutians are incapable of any true emotion beyond the practicality that accompanies logic, and you truly don't know me," Ork snapped.

Vol stepped closer to him, standing a full foot shorter, yet seeming to tower over him. Ork felt a sudden wave hit his mind, but he pushed back against it and braced himself, locking his mind and thoughts away from the force that was Vol. He thought of warning Vol against such attacks, but that would make him seem weak and would achieve nothing. It wasn't like he expected the Virzutian to stop his attacks because he asked him to do so.

"I'm impressed that you resisted my attempt, but I can't say that I'm terribly surprised. I can't get into a mind as well fortified as yours, Ork, but that doesn't mean that I don't know you. It doesn't mean that I don't know a child so gravely misunderstood by his people. A child loved only by his parents and, even they, found no ease in it. A child who lost everything because of the cruelty of existence and he evolved, like all life is expected to do, into a creature of pure will and purpose. Of course, I can't expect to infiltrate a mind protected by such will, but that doesn't mean that I don't understand it. I understand how it works and how it has been motivated by the loneliness and fear of the child within. As time passes you will understand what I mean and you'll see what you do is foolish and you'll grow tired of it," he said softly then buzzed in amusement. "Perhaps you'll lose your mind then and blast your armies into subatomic particles," Vol added.

Ork stood stunned, but masked it with perfect stillness. There was so much truth in what Vol said that he was worried that the Virzutian had gotten a glimpse into his mind, but he knew that wasn't the case. He slowly turned to look at Vol. "You do not know me," he said quietly.

Vol dipped his head a little, managing to make a show of deference look like one of mockery. Then, he stepped into a passage that appeared behind him and vanished. Ork turned back to the planet before him that now appeared the size of a big stone and he felt troubled. It wasn't wise to let Vol get into his head and he reminded himself that more restraint was necessary. It was only a matter of time. Still, flames, weapons, and the body of a dead creature similar to Ork disturbed his mind.

"Tuik," he muttered softly, and found that he was afraid to even think the words and muttering them had taken a lot out of him. This was what his people had been called before he took the name away. This was what the creature who loved him had been called as well. He pushed the thoughts down into the dark depths where they belonged and focused on the task at hand. He wasn't going to let Vol get the better of him.

***

Olivia typed away furiously on the keypad, her fingers a blur as they moved over the final words. She knew that she could have gotten a neural link and made this work much easier or she could just speak the words, but she preferred to type because it sort of cleared her head; transferred her emotions from the cogs in her mind to the movement of her fingers.

Olivia watched as the last period appeared on her work and leaned back in her chair as it was sent over to the large holoscreen and watched the title with pride. A study on the basic Terran microbes. She smiled a little but couldn't help but feel a little guilty. It felt like she had only gotten this research done because Elk granted her exclusive freedom to study his kind. She still had other things she had to work on and she knew that this break had to be short-lived or else the thoughts would return, and the progress she'd made would disappear as her fears and worries about the attack from Ork would resurface; and she'd sink beneath the weight.

She looked around the lab in search of who to share her success with, but there was no one there but other researchers and assistants that aided her. She realized that Andrew was not only her colleague, he was also her only friend and he had not come to work for several days. She wondered if it was because of their last misunderstanding and, after a few moments, she figured that it probably was.

Andrew was too emotional and held some things close that shouldn't be. Olivia wondered who she'd call to have an evening out with. She was surprised that she even needed an evening out and resolved that she'd act on it before the urge faded away. She ended up contacting Akya, who seemed enthusiastic to take her up on the offer. She wondered how it would seem to walk into a restaurant with an alien lady, but she decided that she really didn't care anyway.

Akya seemed very different from the last time Olivia had seen her. She seemed quieter, more withdrawn, and her human gestures were way better than they used to be. Her smile was almost flawless, showing just the right amount of teeth and appearing at appropriate moments. She incorporated very human gestures with unnerving effortlessness. She shrugged, rubbed the back of her neck and chose appropriate times to look people directly in the eyes then look away. When Olivia commented on it, she shrugged and gave a small self-conscious laugh.

"It's like any language. You just have to learn the basics and build on that until you become fluent. Elk says that I'm quickly achieving fluency and he might have something truly challenging for me soon. All I do is work nowadays and I feel like I'm overdue for hibernation, but only a brainless fool would hibernate at such a delicate time." Akya paused as if she just realized something, and her eyes widened. Then, she reached out to gently touch Olivia's forearm. "I forgot that such talks unsettle you. I'm truly sorry."

Olivia shrugged a little. She could feel her worries starting to rise, but she resisted it and bit her lower lip instead. "You might even be more human than I am, Akya," she said quietly.

Akya narrowed her eyes, startling Olivia a little at the fluidity of that reaction. "How so?" she asked.

Olivia shrugged and stabbed at her food with her fork, then rolled it around on the plate. "I don't know. I guess that I've never felt able to really connect with anyone except Andrew. I never really had friends and I just…. human interaction was always too much, you know? The hugging, and checking up, and the parties, and everything left me with nothing but weariness and headaches. I still understand very little about my kind and… I don't think I want friends. I really do sometimes, but it feels like too much. It's too much to handle for me," she said and sighed heavily. Olivia rubbed her hair and pushed some of it off her face, remembering that she still had to cut it.

Akya sat silently and stared at her. She opened her mouth to say something when a sun appeared in the evening sky. They both turned to see what was happening and Olivia's mouth fell open when she realized what was happening. This was it: the object of her nightmares, fears, and worries. It was happening. She wondered where they would land. She thought about the people that would die and her heart constricted as she thought about Eric and Andrew.

"We have to get out of here," Akya said quickly and, before Olivia even knew what was happening, Akya had picked her up like a rag doll and tossed her over one shoulder. Olivia's thoughts ran wild as tears streamed down her face. She thought about their weakness. They could not handle this. They had barely handled a company of forty aliens. This was an army with a full fleet.

Olivia vaguely noticed being thrown into a hovercraft and she heard a little of something Akya was saying, but at that moment the ground began to shake. It was as if the very core of the Earth was thrashing in unrest and she felt the hovercraft go up just before some buildings started collapsing, including the restaurant they had just been inside.

Olivia was in a state of shock and sat in silence for a while until she felt a tap on her shoulder. She looked to see Akya looking down at her with pure worry over her face. She wondered if it was part of training to instinctively let human expressions show on their faces.

"You okay?" Akya asked.

Olivia managed a nod. Her eyes caught the destruction beneath them and widened but, with a gesture, Akya shut it off. She had clearly left the hovercraft on autopilot and she seemed tense. She sat beside Olivia and wrapped her in a very long arm.

"I'm going to need you to calm down, okay? We'll go to the city and Elk will know what to do. Just be okay. I'm sure that preparations have been made for your brother's safety. Such things never slip Tekka's mind, even if they might slip Elk's. Please calm down, okay?" Akya said very softly then stayed there with Olivia for a while. Akya slowly stood and walked to the controls.

"I don't think you should see what is currently happening. It's for your own good," Akya said quietly, and Olivia's stubbornness and curiosity almost got the better of her, prompting her to stand, but she remained where she was, and looked away, terror coursing through her body. Akya seemed so sure that Elk would know what to do. But Olivia wasn't so convinced.

***

Elk clenched his fists as he watched the glowing metal in the distance. It appeared to cover the whole state and above it hovered hundreds of smaller ships the size of airplanes. There was no stable communication system except the one that Elk's engineers had built, and there was no satellite to coordinate an aerial battle. They had nothing. He could see that some delegates had already been sent out and were instantly vaporized. The cities around the landing site had been destroyed, and the invaders didn't seem even vaguely interested in diplomacy or integrity.

Elk turned to look at Tekka, who sent a flurry of data into his consciousness and asked him if it was time to battle. Elk breathed in deeply and looked at the ships again. He knew that there were no fewer than a hundred thousand warriors that had come to battle this time and about twelve thousand ships from what he could see.

"We'll take the second option. Initiate it immediately. The Terrans won't fight today," Elk said quietly. Tekka moved off quickly to communicate the order and set things in motion.

Elk gritted his teeth in anger. He knew that he'd made the right decision, but he really wanted to find Ork and tear him to pieces; but now was not the time. He worried that the time would never show itself as he went to find his hovercraft.

The barrack was in a state of disarray, but work seemed to be going on anyway. Elk could see that some of the communication systems he'd set up were working and he knew that Field Marshal Willows was behind it. A soldier ran up to him.

"She asked that I take you to her as soon as you arrive, sir," the soldier said.

Elk started to tilt his head, then nodded instead. The sun was exceptionally harsh today and it annoyed him. Elk was usually controlled and rational, but he found his temper slipping away from him quicker than usual. He warred against it within his mind. He needed all his faculties working at full capacity if they were going to get through this.

"What in all heck is happening?" Willows bellowed at him as soon as she walked in.

He bristled under her tone and stood silently, staring down at her. It seemed that she realized her mistake because she visibly relaxed and, when she spoke again, her voice was calmer, but still sharp.

"This is what I've been saying would happen. This is what I've been trying to prepare us all for. But that is in the past now. What's the plan?" he asked.

Willows frowned deeply at him. "The Commonwealths have handed over all authority to the military and I've been tasked with spear-heading our offense. Your communication devices have really come in handy and they've been useful in putting war crafts in the air, but we need so much more. What else can you give us?"

Elk looked at the hint of desperation in her gray eyes and found that he didn't want to tell her what was next, but it was for the safety of his people, his race. "Me," he said.

Willow scowled, trying to figure out what he was saying. But, when she realized that he was speaking literally, her eyes widened with a mixture of disbelief and anger. "What do you mean by that? We need communication systems, weapons, hovercrafts. We need everything you have," she shrieked.

Elk stepped closer to her. "I've done my best to prepare you, but your people have refused my advice and help at every turn. My people are a dying race and I have taken measures to prevent that. It even pains me that some were left out in order to help with some of your hovercrafts and planes. I won't give any more of my people, but I will fight alongside you until I can fight no more," he said quietly, enforcing all the sincerity that he could muster into his words. He hoped that his people had successfully gone underground. They needed to be safe until a path was clear.

"It would seem that that will have to do," Willows said softly, but there was so much strain and disappointment in her voice that Elk understood that this conversation was being cut short because of the chronic lack of time.

Elk watched as their planes soared into the sky in crisp formation. He didn't join them. He didn't need to. He already knew how this would end, but that was what it meant to be a soldier; to fight even when you knew that you would lose. He powered up his armor and it spread over his body as he transformed into his war form. He walked into his hovercraft and mentally powered it up. This was his first time in a long while to try it by himself, and it gave him a certain freedom and pleasure that amused and surprised him. He hadn't realized that he missed the thrill and rush of battle.

Within Elk loomed the knowledge that this battle was one they had no chance of winning, for even though the crafts were reinforced and their weapons were updated, their communication systems were very limited and that would limit their coordination and scale. The distraction force had approached and opened fire on the blindingly-bright metal that covered the largest enemy ship.

It seemed like they were throwing pebbles at diamonds as their firepower did little damage and had very little effect on the ship. In turn, they received fire from the hovercrafts around the ship. It was like a rain of fire and lasers that vaporized the ships on contact, except the ones designed by the Terrans.

Elk felt the rush of battle as he maneuvered into the field and brought down three ships with two quick blasts. His hovercraft was equipped with the best firepower the Terrans had created and it proved lethal on the field. He brought down a few more ships and he began to feel the pressure as many other ships disengaged and came for him. He engaged his ship's superior maneuvering abilities, and it wove and spun between ships. Elk released lasers, cutting through ships like butter, burning through them and leaving their debris to hurtle to Earth.

Elk could see that they were taking heavy casualties and their coordination wasn't superb. They were quickly losing this battle, but he knew that this was nothing more than delay tactics. He fought still, cutting through and shooting down ships. He respected the human pilots that fought bravely and with as much coordination as they could manage with the sparse resources available.

The bright ship opened itself with a hiss and a rumble. Elk couldn't wait to find out why as the hatches opened. He flew towards them and attempted to open fire, but was blocked by dozens of ships who defended the opening. He found himself almost overwhelmed and had to pull back.

From within, poured out the black pods he knew and feared. These were marvels of engineering from their first home and they were almost indestructible. Elk could feel their buzz, their subtle pull on his mind. He could see their dark shapes, absorbing all the light around until they were just blobs of darkness hurtling through the air.

Elk felt his morale drop. There would be no victory now. At least there would be no victory at this time. He knew that if he remained, he'd be captured or killed. Neither of which was wise or would bode well for his own people. He needed to survive this battle if the planet had any hope of survival. He closed his eyes and let the shame of leaving the field wash over him.

Then he contacted Willows' pod. "Elk to Spearhead. Pulling out," he said quietly, turned off his communication, and pulled away, fighting against the shame that came upon him. He had to secure the treasure. He had to secure Olivia because of the bond between her and the treasure. It called to her and, though she didn't know it, she was reacting to that call. Maybe there was something there he could use… anything at all would help.

"I never thought I'd see the day," Ork said from within his ship. He had seen Elk's hovercraft pull away and he felt fierce pleasure and pride that he had succeeded in making the famous general flee in battle. Though for him to stay would have been foolishness of the highest magnitude. He had hoped that he would stay and maybe he would have captured Elk and taken the pleasure of torturing him and breaking through his mental and emotional defenses and toying with him. He didn't think that there'd be anything else that would make him as pleased as that. "So he retreats," he added quietly. Ork smelled the foul stench of gasses beside him and turned to see Vol standing silently beside him.

"More than when to attack, a good general must also know when to retreat," Vol said quietly.

Ork was mildly surprised that Vol seemed to know who Elk was. The Virzutian frightened and baffled him at times.

"This was easy. I don't see why you needed me. Except, of course, for matters regarding the treasure. I haven't felt it since we arrived, but I know that it is here," Vol said.

Ork turned to face him. "Since you don't feel it, what makes you sure?" he asked.

Vol waited as if he didn't hear the question, then raised his hand; or at least the part of the suit that served as his hand. Vol's disrespect annoyed Ork, but he maintained an air of quiet restraint.

"A lot of my technology has been destroyed. Basically, anything that violates the normal order of things like the warping of space and time gives me the ability of teleportation, among other things. It has always been a strange phenomenon with the treasures. It is as if they fight anything that unbalances the laws of the universe, yet their existence in itself is a disruption to the balance," Vol said.

Ork felt slight elation at this, but he stashed that away as he was unsure how to use it and he wasn't entirely sure that Vol was being honest. It was unusual that he would reveal his weakness so casually. He watched him, then nodded.

"I see," Ork said and tried to return his attention to the destruction that was taking place just outside the ship, to revel in it. But other thoughts kept tugging at the back of his mind. Why had it been only Elk among the Terrans that had come out to fight? He wondered what it meant. He wondered where the other Terrans were, and he wondered why the resistance of the humans was so weak and uncoordinated. He pushed those thoughts aside to be thought through later.

"What does this mean? Where have the Terrans gone? And what the heck is that demon thing that has come upon us?" the leader of the Commonwealth of Northern Asia thundered.

Andrew sat in his chair, feeling guilt, anger, and hatred boil up within him. He cursed Elk and the Terrans in his mind. If they had just kept the technology and the methods with him, then their satellites wouldn't have failed. They'd have been able to see this attack coming and they would have done something to prevent it.

Andrew hated the other leaders of the Commonwealths that now sat around him. They bristled and foamed, making plans that were just grand displays of foolishness and would amount to nothing. These beings that had invaded their planet were extraterrestrials, aliens, lacking even the vaguest interest in politics or the subtleties of human interaction or culture. They couldn't expect to relate with them in any manner and reasoning with them seemed entirely out of the question. He sighed heavily and watched as the bickering continued.

"Perhaps we should ask them what they want," a thin, tall woman with overly-large glasses said.

"Hostility has already been displayed. I think that we're past asking each other questions and having summits. They don't seem to care about such things and we must focus on resuming battle plans in force. We don't have time, and the time that we're wasting now has bought with it the blood of our soldiers. We can't afford to waste any more time," a broad-shouldered man replied.

"Then, what do you suggest we do? The Terrans have vanished. There's no way for us to fight this foe without their help and they clearly have decided that they won't give it," the woman hissed back.

"We judge them harshly and unfairly. May I bring it back to our memories that these Terrans have been trying to prepare us for this sort of thing, but we just ended up dooming ourselves with small-minded bickering," the man beside Andrew said.

Andrew gritted his teeth but said nothing. There was already too much talk. He slowly began to walk out.

"Perhaps the delegate has more pressing matters than the end of the world to attend to," a thin man with a long mustache and olive skin said.

Andrew turned slowly to look at him. He stared him down for a while, then he felt the words begin to tear out of him. "Do you think it would matter? Do you think that anything we say or do here matters? These creatures are from outer space. And, I urge you to take a moment to think about that. They have cultures different from ours and their minds and even their physical forms differ so vastly from ours that we cannot hope to understand them. We have tried the way of battle and it has failed woefully."

"And might I ask whose fault exactly, that is?" the broad-shouldered man bellowed in his thick voice, hatred dripping from every word.

"It does not matter whose fault it is, but if I must take the blame for it then I shall. And, I'll atone for it by offering myself up as a delegate, should the council decide to listen to me and take the road of peace," Andrew said.

The entire hall erupted into shouts, murmurs, and discussion. Andrew could see that some of them were looking at him with disgust and disbelief, but some seemed to be warming up to his idea; while some maintained perfectly neutral expressions. He knew that he was taking a gamble, but it was a calculated one, and he'd rather be at the helms of power than be trampled underfoot. He wondered where Elk and his band of abominations were. Andrew swore to himself that after all this was over and he survived, he'd find and burn them. He swore it within himself.

CHAPTER FOURTEEN

Olivia watched as Akya stood studying the shifting threads, her angular features illuminated by the soft glow of the threads. Olivia stared down at her hands that had not stopped shaking since the attack and her mind still felt unclear around the edges. She had been offered water and food, but found it impossible for her body to retain anything or even consider the possibility of ingesting anything.

Olivia sat there in terror and struggled to calm her mind. She was in a bunker of sorts, or that would be the only way it would be able to make sense to her. It was much bigger than a bunker and was like an underground city. She wondered how long the Terrans had spent making this place that still felt like the outside without the smells or claustrophobic feeling typical to places like this. The walls didn't seem like walls. They showed images of the outside and the roof showed soft yellow sunlight pouring through cloudy skies and there were unidentifiable flying organisms in the air. Olivia suspected that this was what their home planet must have looked like.

"It was created as more of a hibernation space than anything, but was quickly repurposed after the vision that you and Elk saw before. There's enough food here to feed my kind for a decade and there are weapons and hovercrafts, and the entire thing is a maze with collapsible sections. We're fairly safe here," Akya said.

Olivia nodded a little and thought about what had become of Andrew and his family. She thought about Eric and fear rippled through her. Akya seemed to have read her expression because she shook her head and said, "He couldn't be brought here, but he's somewhere safe. Tekka arranged it. I told you that he would."

"Why couldn't he be brought here?" Olivia asked.

Akya shrugged. "Elk's orders. I don't know what reason he gave it for, but it must have been very important."

"What do you mean? Nowhere up there is safe. Eric needs…"

"I trust Elk's judgment far more than I trust my own, Olivia, and he has never let me down before. If he says that Eric must be kept anywhere other than here, then his reasons are solid and I trust them. Please calm down. I'd advise you to keep how you challenge Elk's orders to a minimum while here. Some of my people can read minds and their senses of perception are far more than you understand. If they sense any insubordination, then…. They can be very loyal," she said softly.

Olivia felt anger burn within her suddenly, giving her strength. She stood up from the floor where she sat and marched to where Akya had arranged her threads of information. "Any news of Elk's whereabouts?" she asked.

Akya shook her head, then pursed her lips. Olivia was still finding it difficult to adjust to Akya's mastery of body language and expressions. "It was last reported to us that he went out to fight against the enemy, but nothing has been reported since then," Akya said.

Olivia felt her heart sink a little. "You don't… You don't think…"

"No, I don't. And you shouldn't either. He's fine and well, and is probably doing something that will set all of this right soon."

Olivia nodded. "Do you know anything about him?" she asked tentatively.

Akya looked at her. There were signs of strain and fatigue on her face and Olivia reminded herself that this Terran was going through a lot as well and was trying her best to maintain her composure and shouldn't be pressed more than was absolutely necessary. "About who?" Akya asked quietly.

Olivia suddenly felt like she shouldn't ask, but she was never one to leave her curiosity unsated. "Ork. Did you know him before now?"

Akya raised her eyes to meet Olivia's then held them in a steady, level gaze that seemed to be a warning and scrutiny at the same time. Olivia was almost annoyed, but then she remembered that there must have been a lot that Akya had lost on her home planet due to Ork's war. She calmed herself and looked away, which seemed to appease Akya because she sighed a little then shrugged.

"Everyone knows him. I know him from afar, though. Well, not really from afar. He was in a meeting in my family home and he rubbed my head when my father introduced me as his offspring. He seemed different. Yes, he was almost always angry in the manner of all Tuik, but he seemed nice enough. This was shortly before the revolution started and his own tribe fell under his authority. And, he wanted our tribe as well. My father… my father was one of the Terrans that spoke for Ork's ideals and goals. Amongst some of my people, I'm still looked upon with suspicion because they feel my father's sounds and essence move within me. They fear I might betray them soon enough, but that would never happen. That vile from the darkest corner of the universe deserves only the cruelest, darkest kind of treatment and I sincerely hope that he gets it."

Akya had forgotten all about human expressions in her anger and made sounds of intense rage and it reverberated through the room, inspiring similar feelings in Olivia. Olivia wondered what Ork had done specifically to her, because this seemed far too personal. But, then again, almost every Terran had lost loved ones at Ork's hand, so it was personal for everyone.

"What are you reading, Akya?"

Akya heard the flat voice behind her and turned to see Elk looking over her in full war form. There was something terribly aggressive about him in this form that frightened her. His eyes were on the threads arranged before Akya, who stood up immediately and made a strange sound like the falling of rain on rooftops that prompted feelings of intense respect from within Olivia as she understood that it was a respectful sound.

"I was reading up on European history," she said.

Olivia almost screamed her surprise. She had thought that Akya had been analyzing information about what was happening above, but she had just decided to relax and do some history reading. "What?" she asked in disbelief.

Elk spared her a quick glance before he walked to the threads and looked over them. "We must not break our routine. It's important that we maintain our way now more than ever. Olivia, your brother has been retrieved and placed under safety. We still haven't found Andrew, but his wife and daughter have been taken care of," he said, his armor easing off him automatically. Underneath he wore black overalls made from some light, but tough fabric that Olivia couldn't identify.

"Why was my brother not brought here?" she asked.

Elk adjusted the collar of his overalls then cracked his neck a few times. His face was blank, but she could sense an unrest within him. "They couldn't be brought here. The fewer the number of humans that know about this place, the safer my people will be," he said.

Olivia almost started to argue, but she restrained herself and nodded silently. "What's the situation up there?" she asked.

Elk remained silent for a while before he spoke. "They will try to reach some form of agreement with Ork and he'll make a pretense of being reasonable in order to figure out the best way to exploit them, but something isn't right. He's waiting, and it's a rare thing for Ork to wait. It means that he wants something. He has some motive that makes him wait and it can't be in our favor."

Olivia wondered what Ork could possibly want that would make him wait. "No," she said.

Elk nodded very slowly.

"The treasure," Akya said quietly.

Elk nodded. "Indeed. It's why this planet is still in one piece. And to keep it that way, we have to keep the treasure away from him," he said.

"But he could just blast everything to bits and take it. The treasure is basically indestructible, so he could just blow everything up and take it," Akya said. Elk nodded his agreement.

"Maybe he doesn't exactly want to waste…" Olivia began.

But Elk shook his head. "Ork doesn't care about waste. He doesn't care how many lives or resources are lost and he doesn't exactly have any love for this planet," he said.

The memories of a different timeline flooded Olivia's consciousness. She rubbed her forehead and tried to massage the headaches away, but she remembered that a battle had been fought before and there was no way Ork would be merciful once he'd gotten what he came for.

"We should use it," she said suddenly.

Elk went perfectly still. Akya's features were also schooled into stillness as she watched Olivia. Olivia suddenly had a feeling that she had said something wrong.

"We cannot use it," Elk said simply, and she wondered what he meant.

"But, I can use it. I used it last time. We can just use it, and…"

"No, Olivia. There's instability in this treasure that makes it a very risky thing to be used right now. Prior to the time you used it, it had been unused for a long time. So, it had time not only to recharge, but to achieve stability. It did what it sensed your intentions wanted it to do. But, if you used it now, things might go very differently from what you would expect."

"How do you know this?" Olivia asked.

"I authorized tentative research on the treasure," he replied.

Her eyes widened about the same time her jaw dropped. "What do you… You didn't tell me?" she asked. She sensed a certain annoyance about Elk which was accompanied by the low whistling sound he was making.

"I am hardly accountable to you, Miss Olivia," he said abruptly.

She nodded, then looked away, suddenly embarrassed and feeling guilty. "Uhm…. Sorry," she muttered.

Elk walked to the door and pulled it open just as Tekka came into view. Olivia wondered how he knew that Tekka was coming, but then she remembered that they could communicate telepathically. It was indeed very convenient.

"Greetings, Miss Olivia. Akya. Should I tell them?" Tekka asked.

The question was meant for Elk who showed some hesitation, and Olivia hoped his inclination toward secrecy wouldn't make him refuse. After a while, he nodded and there seemed to be communication between both of them.

"The treasure has exhibited some qualities that have been extremely intriguing. It remained dormant when brought into contact with our people and with your people as well, but we took certain… samples from you, Miss Olivia – my apologies for that – but it reacted rather vehemently to your cells. We believe that a bond has formed between it and you, and…" Tekka started to say.

"You took samples from me without my permission?" she asked.

Tekka tilted his head. He hadn't grown very accustomed to the nuances of human expression. "I have apologized for taking that liberty, but that's hardly something to get annoyed over, considering the cosmic importance of the matter which we now face," he said and, although Olivia was angry, she saw sense in what Tekka was saying and calmed herself.

"It reacts to me?" she asked.

Tekka tilted his head in agreement. "A theory stands that it might only work when you're the one handling it, but we can't be exactly sure as more experiments are in order," he said.

Olivia felt a slow headache start in her head. "Why?"

"Perhaps it bonds with the person that uses it, or there might be other reasons that we don't know about, but either way, we know that this is happening so even if Ork gets the treasure, without you, it would just be another glowing orb. We need to separate you from it," Elk said.

"What?!" Olivia yelled then reduced her voice when she got a stern glance from Akya. "You want to separate me from it? We should use it. We should…."

"You don't know what you're saying, Olivia. Some of the universe's most advanced civilizations who got one of the treasures in their possession, with all the scientific knowledge that would make even ours seem like animals in comparison, were doomed when they decided to treat the treasures with anything less than the utmost carefulness. I don't want to make such a mistake. There's far too much on the line. This is like handing the codes to a nuclear weapon to a nine-year-old. Do you understand?" Elk asked.

Olivia went perfectly silent for a while, forcing herself to accept Elk's logic. She conceded that some things were just too powerful to be used without the knowledge and perfect understanding of them. But what if Ork decided to just smash the planet to bits? She looked at Elk and decided that she was going to trust him. He had never failed her before and he knew their adversary more than anyone, so she would listen to him.

"Our priority would be to keep you safe. If you die, then maybe the treasure would be able to be used by someone else and that would be… bad. As long as it is bonded to you, then it would be useless to him," Elk said.

Olivia didn't feel right that she was being treated like an egg through this. What did they expect her to do? To just sit around and wait for everything to pass?

"But how do we retaliate? What do we do in the meantime?" she asked.

"When your cells were brought closer to the treasure, it released certain types of… energy. These pockets of energy make certain types of things possible and we've been harnessing them, but we have been careful not to let things get out of hand," Tekka said.

Olivia felt some relief, but Elk was perfectly silent, like he was thinking through something. He nodded and walked out of the room. She wondered what he was thinking, but she felt that it would be wrong to ask now.

Tekka followed and she was left again with Akya, who didn't seem to be in the mood for discussion. She sat on one of the oversized chairs and let the consistent weariness wash over her. For so long she had had this nightmare. And now she was living it.

CHAPTER FIFTEEN

Andrew walked within the ruins, his body badly shaken from the explosion that had thrown him into a wall. He felt pains in every part of his body as his ears whistled, his head throbbed, and he bled from cuts on his cheek and arms. He looked around to see charred bodies, burning buildings, and the foul stench of some gas, death, and mangled metal.

He had been asleep in his hotel room when he was awakened by a sound so loud it seemed to make the entire Earth vibrate. And, in the distance a light had shone so bright. And, from that light came a wave of sorts that he was sure had weakened by the time it had gotten to where he was. He had tried to run out of his room, but the wave slammed against him like a train from behind and pushed him into the wall.

He had woken in rubble and ruin, and it had taken him a few hours before he was able to think properly, let alone walk. He wondered what happened, where he was. He suspected that he might not even be alive. In the distance, he could see something that looked like a vast mirror. Just looking at it threatened to ruin his eyesight. He felt his feet give out and he fell to the ground, his head mercifully hitting sand as he lay there, shirtless, his trousers torn, and his head spinning so fast that he felt like he would soon slip back into unconsciousness.

When he woke, the stars were in the sky. He felt a bit of cold amusement at that. He remembered thinking when he was younger that nighttime was the default setting of the universe. And, the only reason there was any daytime was because the Earth happened to be exposed to the light and heat of a relatively close star. There was a low buzzing in his ears. He tried to stand but found that he couldn't. He could hear nothing, and that was the strange part. Since he was a child, the night was never quiet. It was either the sound of pods or taxicabs from the street or crickets and birds whenever they were in the woods.

There was nothing of that sort now, except for the wind, which seemed more like a soundtrack of doom in a horror movie than anything else. Andrew coughed and the sound echoed. Then he heard it. It was like footsteps, but it moved far too fast to be footsteps. No person could move that fast, and no footstep should sound that heavy. He felt something grip his shoulder and, in the blink of an eye, he found himself lifted clean off the ground, and he was facing what he immediately decided was the foulest looking creature he had ever seen. Its eyes were dark as the blackest night, reflecting nothing. And, it had two slits for a nose. What served for its mouth seemed to be a crooked line drawn across its face. Its skin was scaled like that of a crocodile. It looked at him and he felt fear course through his bones as he sensed the weight of something far different from anything he had ever experienced. He could feel a presence slowly creep into his mind, an invasion in his thoughts and, even though he instinctively pushed against it, it was like invisible fingers were slowly prying his thoughts open and tearing his defenses apart until he was naked and open before this force that quickly overtook his mind. He didn't exactly experience pain, but he felt loose and helpless. He felt the sort of grief that came from expansion.

Andrew was thrown down to the ground again. He knew then that his death had come, or maybe he had died already, and this was hell. He'd never been religious, but what else could this be? His mind vaguely reminded him of Olivia's rants about attacks from outer space, but this couldn't be it, could it? That couldn't have happened.

It didn't matter now as he closed his eyes and awaited his death. Thoughts of his wife and daughter flashed through his mind but he was not exactly sad, remorseful, or regretful. There was just emptiness and something that wasn't quite peace, but came close to it. He waited for death, but it didn't come. Instead, he felt himself lifted again and he could see the ground move past him, and he knew he was moving. His mind couldn't handle it. It shut off.

***

Ork watched the little human that had been brought to speak with him. He was tall by the standards of his people and he wore those ridiculous clothes that granted them neither protection nor comfort. Just looking at this human was revolting, but Vol had counseled that as he sat through the talk. Their search for the treasure and Olivia had proven futile so far and there was no one better suited to root out these creatures than one of them.

Andrew watched silently as the man walked up to the table placed before him, but refrained from sitting. It was clearly out of respect to Ork, but Ork didn't take kindly to them yet, so the mere act of respect infuriated him. Suddenly, one of the men beside their leader began to gasp and thrash for air. His skin began to dissolve, his youth quickly vanishing from him. By the time he fell to the ground, he was mostly just a skeleton in a suit. Vol was standing over the body.

"My apologies. I don't enjoy pranks," he said in the human language, and their leader let out a wave of fear that both pleased and annoyed Ork. It was good that they knew that their lives meant nothing here and each breath was a gift, an act of supreme magnanimity on his part for letting them breathe it, but he didn't appreciate the fact that it was Vol who had taught them that lesson.

"Greetings…" Andrew started in a low voice, but a beam shot out from Ork's staff and vaporized the man next to him. The fear was now visible on his face as he turned to look at the space where the man had stood.

"You will not speak unless granted permission to speak," Ork said evenly.

Andrew nodded, beads of sweat slipped down his brow and Ork felt a little admiration at how the man conducted himself, even under such circumstances.

"You may sit," Ork said.

Andrew sat, careful to remain silent.

"You have come, no doubt, with your pleas and bargains and everything of that sort, but I have something to ask before we get into all of that," Ork said and leaned forward slightly, dropping his voice so Andrew had to strain to hear. "Do you know of a woman named, Olivia, and a Terran named, Elk?" he asked.

Andrew nodded quickly.

"You may speak," Ork said.

Andrew inhaled deeply, gathering himself. He tried to speak, but his mouth suddenly went slack and his eyes began to look frantically around the room, a vein appeared on his forehead. After a while, he slumped and gasped, holding his head as if he was trying to keep it from exploding.

Ork sifted quickly through the thoughts he had taken from Andrew. Then, when he had thoroughly reviewed them, he leaned back into his chair. "I believe that you are in a unique position to get me what I want. Get yourself together and listen. This planet has disrespected me before and, as such, I don't intend to leave them unscathed, but I will consider reducing the magnitude of their suffering if you bring me the girl, Olivia, and Elk. They have something that I need and, when I get it, instead of being wiped out completely from the universe, you will serve as slaves to my empire. It will be difficult, but you will have your lives," he said very slowly. Vol stood off to the side, watching them, more like a sculpture than a living thing.

"I…" Andrew began, but Vol interrupted him.

"Tread carefully, human," he said and Andrew subsided.

Ork went into his thoughts to see what he wanted to say but, whatever it was, Vol had gotten there first and wiped it out. "Also, tell your people that if any sign of aggression is noticed, or if any sinister plans are discovered, the repercussions will be outsized, swift, and merciless," he said.

Andrew nodded.

"Leave," Ork said, and they all scampered away.

"This will not do," Vol said softly. "If Elk is as competent a general as you say he is, he will not be caught by creatures so unsophisticated."

"We would have found them already if you proved to be of any use," Ork snapped.

Vol went silent as if he was contemplating something, but there was a force slowly rising from him that seemed to swell until it pressed against the walls of the room. "Do you insult me?" he asked almost casually.

Ork heard the threat there and, although it enraged him, he knew that this wasn't the time to show pride. He had to swallow it. "I'm just expressing my disappointment," he finally said and felt the force calm down a little.

"The treasure impedes my abilities and technologies as I have informed you, but this doesn't mean that I have stopped seeking a way to bypass this hindrance. Tell me now, what do you know about this… Elk? I only knew him when his career blossomed during the war on your planet. What exactly do you know about him?"

Ork contemplated not replying but, after a brief and careful analysis, he established that he had nothing to lose from sharing this information and it could help Vol actually find Elk. Who knew how Virzutians operated? Least of all, this Virzutian. "Elk was formed from the highest Terran blood, or Uyak, which they were called before their name changed when they came here. He should have been in line for the supreme ruler of the Uyak race, but his bloodline was not pure. It turns out, that the one that contributed the male seed was partly of my race, and that tainted Elk, forcing him out from the line of succession. He became a soldier instead and his ranks grew rapidly until he became one of the most superior generals on the planet. And that is all I know about his background."

Vol stood silently, then muttered something in the harsh, but strangely rhythmic language of the Virzutians; then slowly walked away. Ork took comfort from the fact that he could no longer teleport and, as such, his powers of creeping up on him were limited. It also helped his mood that the Virzutian would have to endure the monotony of having to walk everywhere.

The doors slowly hissed open again and Ork turned to see a soldier of his walking in with a bundle over his shoulder. Upon closer inspection, Ork could see that it was a human. He wondered what was special about this one that this soldier had risked drawing his wrath.

"Great Lord, Ork," the soldier said in the language of his people that was the most pleasant thing to Ork's senses. He didn't much regret their annihilation, but he did miss the language and any of his soldiers that were from his old planet or that had managed to learn the language gained some favor.

"Speak," he said to the soldier who had refrained from looking at his face, looking down instead.

"I beg your pardon for this intrusion, but I was among the forty that came with you during our first campaign here and I came in contact with the human, Olivia. This here is a man that has a lot of her held in his mind. She was a strong presence in his mind when I went through it, but the details are yet unclear to me."

This was one of the things that had made Ork strange among his people. He had developed the abilities of mind intrusion and, reading to the point that even forgotten thoughts were clear to him. He could sort through them in moments. He didn't have to guess or wait long moments for what he had seen to be clear.

Ork reached tentatively as this human was already injured and weak. If he moved aggressively and quickly, the mind might break and the human may die. By the time he had explored the mind of the man, he felt a bit of excitement. There was something here, but he was not entirely sure how he was going to exploit it. This man was of great value to Olivia and Elk, but he knew that holding him hostage was a futile thing because Elk was too practical to value the safety of this human over that of the treasure.

"Do you know what to do with them yet?" Ork heard Vol ask from behind him. He turned sharply to see the Virzutian standing behind him. He wondered if Vol had lied about the loss of his abilities and technologies but, if he had them, he would have found the treasure by now. Ork wondered if this was some scheme that Vol was concocting.

"You can be very focused at times; too focused that it distracts you; a weakness in a soldier. I simply walked around to stand beside you. Don't be so surprised," Vol said quietly.

Ork settled down a little, but his mind was still disturbed. "Do you have any suggestions?" he asked.

Vol walked past him, down the stairs, and around the table to the figure now on the ground. "We Virzutians used to have certain contraptions that slipped into the minds of our victims and made them spies for us against their own will, without their knowledge even. If this man is indeed close to Olivia, then the chip that I'll implant in his brain will lead us directly to her and Elk. It's a clean thing and would be very difficult to detect, except if the other person is a Virzutian."

Ork nodded, but decided that precautions would be taken.

"My scientists and engineers will look over this implant and oversee the process of implantation," Vol replied.

Vol turned to stare at him and again Andrew imagined those eyes looking him over, conceiving countless manners for him to die. He brushed it off his mind. He wouldn't let some Virzutian play mind games with him. He maintained his resolve as he stared back.

After a while, Vol relented and gave a hiss of gasses. "Agreed," he said quietly and walked away.

Ork noticed that his feet made no sound, not even faint ones. He wondered if that was the secret of Vol being able to sneak around so perfectly. It didn't matter. He would be more alert and place more guards around himself. It didn't matter if that showed weakness. It was better than being gutted by a Virzutian.

Andrew sat in his chair, the entire number of Commonwealth representatives looking at him with rapt attention. He still felt hollow, loose from the ravaging of his mind. It was difficult to form words, and even thinking straight took effort. Whatever he had expected, it had not been what he experienced in Ork's presence. There would be no explanation that would suffice. Nothing he could tell these people could make them understand what he had been through. There was no reasoning with these demons. There was just obedience and a desperate hope for mercy or leniency. He hated everything that happened to them.

"What?! They read minds?" one of the representatives asked.

Andrew stared blankly at him. He wondered why some people chose to be stupid, wasting time with rhetorical questions inspired by disbelief.

"Well… we should obey, I think. What are the lives of an alien and one person compared to the lives of the entire population of Earth?" a woman stated as a question.

"He would have every living thing enslaved," the broad-shouldered man said in a deep, thoughtful tone. His face was blank, but there was a storm in his eyes. "Slavery is the same as death. For so long we have fought against the idea of it. We have worked on the liberation of all life, and now we would throw all that work into the bin, and passively walk into a life of chains?" the man continued.

"Slaves at least can have hopes of freedom. A dead man can never hope to rise from the dead. He would obliterate us and no one would ever know that Earth existed."

"That would be better than to live as nothing less than the enemy's toy," the man thundered.

Through the arguments that ensued, Andrew sat cold and quiet, thinking of the powers he'd faced in that room. Ork didn't even consider humanity anything of value and it was even a testament to his restraint that any of them still drew enough breath to argue.

"I believe a vote would be in order," the moderator said.

The broad-shouldered man stood from his seat, his eyes wide and his entire presence like a man going into battle. Andrew decided that he must have been a soldier before. "I can't believe that we would vote on our own freedom. This… this is unbelievable and I will not cast my vote in a matter so obvious," this man said and walked out of the room.

Andrew watched him leave and thought that he was the most stupid man he had ever encountered. What man would choose death over slavery? Slavery was temporary. True, some of his ancestors had chosen death but…. he sighed and watched as a vote was taken. In the end, it was decided that they would obey Ork.

'It was the inevitable choice anyway.' Andrew mused.

***

Olivia read through the book she was given several times, trying to pretend that the world above wasn't in a mess. Ork had begun shooting missiles at cities that seemed prosperous. He had razed seven major cities of the world to the ground, wiping them out so completely that nothing but sand and smoke remained. He had also taken out almost all the nuclear silos in the world, but he had shown that it wasn't in his intention to wipe out whatever was left of humanity by containing the blasts so the surrounding cities weren't affected.

Olivia stood and began to face what seemed to have become her body's favorite thing to do these days as it even did it unconsciously.

"There is now a worn spot in that carpet, you know?" Akya said from behind her and pointed to the slightly faded line that ran from wall to wall. "How does pacing help your kind deal with stress? It doesn't actually do anything…"

"Hush, Akya. I'm thinking," Olivia said. Akya went quiet in the manner that hinted that she had taken offense. Olivia collapsed into the nearest chair with a heavy sigh and added, "I'm sorry. All of this… It's just too much to take. My planet is on the verge of being removed from existence. I don't know how much longer I can sit by and do nothing."

"You're not actually doing nothing. By helping us keep you safe, you're keeping Ork from the one thing that would make him unstoppable. He would transcend from just another maniac with too much power to… well, an even bigger maniac with more power," Akya said. Olivia felt a slight flash of amusement cross her. "I know how you feel," Akya added, her voice low. "I felt the same way the day we lost the battle of Trakei. Our aircrafts rained from the sky and more lives were lost that day than at any period in the history of my kind. I sat in my family's bunker while the battle, which had begun many leagues away, raged just above me. It wasn't long before it was officially declared that we had lost; that the monarch had been beheaded. My parents and siblings died that day. If it hadn't been for Elk…" she stopped and waited a while, then spoke again. Her voice was flat, but there was a sound like the ripping of cloth coming from her. "I understand perfectly how you feel. I wanted to go out. I wanted to fight alongside my parents and my warrior siblings, but of what use would that have been? I would have died, and it would all have been useless."

Olivia sat silently, not knowing what she should do. She asked herself what Andrew would do, and she knew that he would have gone to Akya and made attempts at consoling her, but she wasn't Andrew. The only thing that could come out of her was… "I'm not useless. I can do something apart from sitting here and waiting for all of my people to die. In fact, I've done something before. I'm the reason why we weren't annihilated in the beginning."

"You're not the reason," Akya said quietly. Olivia glared up at her. "It would be selfish, arrogant, and foolish to think you were the reason that Earth survived that day. Elk has protected the treasure since it was given to him. He decided the right moment for it to be wielded and gave the order. Tekka carried you to where it was kept while Elk fought to hold Ork off. All of your efforts saved the planet, not just yours, and it would be respectful for you to keep that in your mind." Akya's voice was quiet as ever.

Olivia started to open her mouth, but nothing came to her mind and she felt immense shame instead. She looked down, bit her lip, and looked away.

After she could no longer bear the weight of Akya's presence and the claustrophobic feeling in the room, big as it was, Olivia walked through the obscenely wide passages and looked at the carvings that were meant to decorate and beautify. She could smell something strange, but not unpleasant and she heard the hum of communication and machinery. She felt small as their gigantic forms passed by her. They soared over her with barely a glance, going about their work with unwavering focus. She was still walking when she felt a heavy hand on her shoulder. She looked up to see Akya looking down at her.

"I'm sorry," Akya said quietly, and that was enough. It was all Olivia needed at that moment. She swallowed heavily before she replied.

"I'm sorry too," Olivia said. Akya nodded. "What do these carvings mean?" Olivia asked.

Akya looked around as if she was just seeing them for the first time. "They are depictions of emotion," she said.

Olivia frowned slightly. "How can emotions be depicted physically? I thought they weren't physical?"

Akya nodded and replied, "To your kind they are, but the threads convey more than a physical meaning. They also convey an emotional quality and that's a component of what you see in the threads. That component is isolated and carved into stone and metal. Some of these are sadness, but more complex than the expressions that mere words can convey. Have you not ever thought that when we say that we're sad or happy or lonely… it isn't just those things? Sometimes many emotions can be tangled up into one and there are gray emotions in between that we haven't explored. To convey those requires something far more complex than words and the words of your kind are not quite… expressive enough. No offense."

Olivia smiled a little. She found it comforting to listen to Akya speak and it gave her mind something else to think of.

"There's something you must see," Akya said.

Olivia walked with her, noticing she reduced the length of her strides to accommodate Olivia's far shorter legs. "What is it?"

Akya shrugged and answered, "A surprise of sorts." She laughed a little.

They walked through a wide door into a room lit with soft blue light, which was a welcome change from the soft yellow that was everywhere, though it was obvious that Akya didn't enjoy it. Special concessions had been made to accommodate Olivia. She wore special clothing to accommodate the pressure and there were special tubes that led up to her nose that made the air breathable. It made her nose ache after prolonged use, after which she had to go to her quarters in order to breathe without aid.

Olivia saw a man with his head on the table and an unknown alien standing over him while another looked over him, checking him carefully. Olivia knew that frame, she knew those long fingers and that hair and, when he slowly raised his head from the table, she gasped at how his eyes had sunken and his face had grown thin, but it was him and he was alive.

Olivia jogged across the room then stopped just a few paces from where he sat, recovering herself before realizing that she didn't know what to do. She reached out slowly and touched his shoulder as his eyes stared blankly at her, almost as if he didn't recognize her.

"Andrew?" she called out softly and he slowly raised his hand to hold hers that was on his shoulder. He slowly stood and, before she knew what was happening, pulled her into an embrace. She had forgotten how comforting his presence was, but she decided that his embrace was even more comforting although his ribs jutted out and he seemed far skinnier than the last time she had met him, even though it had barely been two weeks. "You're okay," Olivia said, and he pulled her in a little tighter.

"I'm alive," he said then pulled away, leaving her feeling a bit disappointed and naked. "You look as good as you've ever been. Same goes for you, Akya. You're glowing actually."

Akya supported him with a smile. Olivia watched him closely and realized that his eyes seemed haunted. He had wrinkles around his eyes that weren't there before and he looked so tired that it was as if he would drop right there and pass out.

"Have you eaten? What did you eat? You should rest," Olivia said.

He nodded. "I was given some nutrition packs that enabled me to be able to stand and be capable of any coherent thought. And I think that a few moments of rest should be in order, but I'm curious and..."

"That curiosity can wait, my friend," Tekka said from somewhere close to the door.

Olivia wondered how he and Elk kept on sneaking in and out, almost as if it was intentional and since when did Tekka refer to anyone as a friend?

"Ah, Tekka. You're always a positive ray of sunshine. I suppose now that you have interfered, I must sleep, but only for a brief moment. There are mad things happening above us. I cannot afford to sleep for long," Andrew said. The final words came out with weight and graveness.

"I understand," Tekka said simply.

Andrew smiled at him and turned to face Olivia. His eyes glazed over briefly and he would have collapsed had the Terran behind him not been fast enough to support him and slowly lower him back to the chair.

"You can talk to him later. He's much too frail and we will now take him to his bed," it said softly.

Olivia couldn't decide if it was male or female, but it didn't matter. Andrew was here. He was alive and he would regain his strength soon. She wondered what horrors he must have faced.

***

Elk stood before the glowing orb, feeling small before it as he always did. It was little more than the size of a basketball, but there was so much power to it that made him feel like little more than a speck of dust. He thought of the formidable missiles they were able to create just from residues of its power and he wondered what force created something like this.

He was tempted to use it, but in its current state, he had no clue as to what the outcome would be. He could end up obliterating Earth. He could make matters worse than they already were and, the worst part was, that it wouldn't be him doing it, it would be Olivia.

Elk could understand her passion and desire to save her people, but he didn't think that there was any wisdom in turning to the treasure now. There was no wisdom at all in it. He had decided that he would battle Ork in chunks; weakening him in the meantime, diverting his attention and learning all that he could while buying time.

Flashes of emotion and memory surged through him, memories of a similar time when he had fought against the same enemy. Elk could hear the explosions, feel the fear and rage, taste the pain and the madness of battle, and he could see the smoke and destruction that was left. He was trying to avoid something similar from happening here. He was trying to contain the explosion that would surely happen. He spent a few more moments watching the orb before he turned away and left.

Elk's armor formed over his body and the cool, calculating manner of a general fell upon him as he approached his hovercraft. There were two pilots there waiting for him and, although their skills were not yet tested because they were exceedingly young, he could trust their training and passion. The engines were powered up and he turned on the technology that amplified telepathic communication to all units.

He heard Ork was beginning to build something a few hundred miles north of where he had landed, so Elk decided that he was going to cause the construction to cease and inflict as much damage as possible in one quick, lethal burst.

They cloaked themselves sufficiently with the latest cloaking technology developed by Elk's engineers. And, before there could be any reaction, they were already within firing range. Elk aligned his hovercrafts in a V-formation and the firing began. They had been tested before, but the firepower of the new missiles still surprised Elk.

First, there was an outward explosion which immediately imploded, then exploded outwards with such force that nothing close to it survived. They flew and fired with deadly precision and, in a matter of moments, they retreated.

Elk knew that they would be long gone before Ork's soldiers could organize themselves enough to give chase. The reckless part of him wished that they had done more but he silenced it, preferring the safety that caution provided.

He could perceive frantic signals from one of the crafts at the extreme left flank and when he accessed it, Elk saw what should have been impossible. About ten pods were closing in on them and were almost within firing range.

He signaled his pilots to initiate evasive tactics, which they proceeded to do immediately. The pods had excellent pilots and flew with almost flawless precision, but the coordination that had been drilled into Elk's pilots were superior to theirs.

In a few minutes, six of the pods were down, taking with them one of Elk's crafts. Those were good numbers, but they weren't good enough for Elk. He permitted the pilots to be a bit more reckless, but still maintain flight precision and, after a few more precious minutes, they cleared the remaining pods and proceeded to fly to safety.

Elk sat in his hovercraft, both exhilarated and worried. He had not known pods to have such speed and firepower before. He wondered how they were able to put enough crafts in the air in such a short amount of time and he wondered from what new planet Ork had gathered his engineers. He decided that it would be good to have eyes within Ork's organization, but that would be very difficult to do. Very difficult indeed.

Once Elk had gotten close to the bunker, he received signals from below. He accessed them and spread out the long-range scanners to see a fleet of airships heading directly for the bunker. His mind grew angry but stopped abruptly as he forced himself into cold calculation, refusing to allow the madness of emotions to hinder his good judgment; a lesson he was taught in the academy where he was trained.

Reflex and emotion were weaknesses for a general. Elk immediately sent word down to Tekka and ordered their movement even deeper, shutting off the bunker above. He called on the crafts still below for backup. He flew towards the direction of the fleet to try to buy time for his people to escape.

"What are your orders, General?" one of his pilots asked.

Elk waited for a while as they flew towards the enemy. "You remember those reckless flying drills they had us do back in the academy?" he asked. The men buzzed in amusement. They had been juniors, but it was routine to put off any recklessness in flying patterns. "Well, we're going to bring them back, just for a bit. They put the strongest ships in the center to be unbreakable, but if we hit them from the flanks then we can chip away at them, generally making a nuisance. That is what we shall do now."

***

Olivia felt fear course through her as she bounced on Akya's shoulders. She had tried to protest, but Akya, who was well over seven feet tall, simply picked her up and threw Olivia over her shoulders. Even in the panic, there was an efficiency to the way the Terrans organized themselves in the evacuation.

Tools and materials for engineering went down on very swift, but careful robotic machines. The young and very old also bore down on those, while the rest used their legs through passageways that seemed like a maze of madness to Olivia. That was until she realized that Tekka must have been communicating the routes telepathically to them.

Olivia thought about Andrew, but she knew that he was safe now and probably sleeping it all off below. She watched the Terrans move calmly but quickly and she couldn't help but admire and pity them at the same time. They deserved rest. They deserved to grow and thrive, not to be hunted down and having to move from one planet to the other, never knowing simple peace and safety. In that moment, Olivia hated Ork with every fiber of her being, with every muscle within her, which was not much.

The section beneath the bunker was darker, but still efficiently built. It was smaller too, but it would suffice. There was the smell of Earth, chemicals, and some foul odor that came off Terrans when they had neither cured nor shed their skin in a long time. Olivia was comforted by these smells, comforted that she was around them and they made her feel safe. She worried about Eric because if she wasn't safe, even among these people, how could he be safe up there where the madness was in full swing.

"Akya?" she called softly.

Akya replied with an "Mm?" Her tone was cool and calm, but there was some tension there. There was raw emotion, and the only reason she hadn't answered with actual words was probably because it was keeping her from having a breakdown.

"Will this place be able to resist steady bombardment?"

Akya nodded. "It was built for that very purpose, but I don't believe that it will come to that. Elk has it all under control," she said slowly and carefully, like she was avoiding landmines with her speech.

Personally, Olivia didn't feel that Elk was doing enough. He could just let her use the treasure and end all of this for good. She wondered if she really even needed his permission to use the treasure, but part of her feared the fact that he was right. She might bring down calamity on her planet, on the universe. Olivia couldn't decide if it was a risk worth taking. She didn't know when the treasure would be stable and they were losing far more than she could bear. She gasped and her eyes widened.

"Wasn't it above? Where is it?" Olivia asked in a harsh whisper.

Akya remained silent for a while, then spoke with the same obvious restraint, so that Olivia wouldn't ask her any more questions. "It is safe."

Olivia fell silent, her mind working. Something had to be done. She wondered if Akya's faith in Elk wasn't misplaced.

***

Elk gave quick orders, even as his hovercraft was hit. It started to self-repair, weakening its shield in the process. Elk wondered how they knew where his people hid and, for a very brief and frightening moment, he wondered if they had fallen victim to sabotage.

His pilots flew well and they had inflicted substantial damage on the enemy, but Elk knew that wouldn't be enough. They were beginning to take on heavy fire and he knew that the time to retreat was close. But they had to buy enough time for the evacuation first. Elk saw one more of his crafts go down and he lost the telepathic link to its pilots.

Elk turned off his emotions; analyzing and giving rational, logical commands, but there was a nagging worry within him that, if left unchecked, could ruin his attack. He banked to the left and fired under an armored warship, blasting it open with the superior missiles from the treasure's energy. He fired a few more, causing it to explode and parts started to hurtle towards Earth.

****

Olivia sat in the cold room while Terrans kept flooding in. Akya wasn't there, neither was Tekka. She wondered how the battle above was going and she knew that Elk might well lose his life trying to buy them enough time. She wondered what would happen without Elk's guidance and she quickly erased the thought from her mind.

Olivia stood and slowly started making her way to where the infirmary was. She wanted to see Andrew. Talking to him might help her quell the turmoil in her mind. She felt a tremor run through the entire bunker and Olivia knew instinctively that it was from the crash of an exceptionally heavy aircraft. She bit her lip and continued walking, careful to keep her thoughts under guard. She was pretty sure that any Terran that caught a glimpse of what she was thinking wouldn't be exceptionally happy with her.

Elk could feel the jolt as his ship was hit and he knew that it had taken serious damage. They had lost one of their boosters, a considerable amount of their speed, shields, and maneuverability, which led to subsequent hits until one smashed through their engines. His pilots lost control of the ship as they hurdled to the Earth.

Elk kept calm as he leaped from one space to another, landing on his feet. The armor absorbed most of the shock, but he still lost his balance and crashed through the debris and sand. He ended up smashing into a wall, of which he felt nothing. He looked up and saw that most of his ships had been cleared and routed. The few that still fought showed skill and courage, but it was hopeless. They were losing. They had lost.

Elk felt a sharp pain and a force that threw him high into the air. He crashed against the ground and tried to move, but he saw that he was restrained by a pod and another leashed his other arm and legs. It would be futile to try to fight against pods but he fought, firing lasers and engaging his thrusters trying to pull away, but it was no use. They carried him away and he thought about his people and hoped desperately that they were safe.

***

"Hey," Olivia said.

Andrew gave her a crooked smile. He seemed better, but he still looked tired and worn out. "Hey," he replied softly. He was sitting up on the bed and his boyish face seemed less boyish. He seemed older, which made him even more attractive except for the hollowness of his eyes. "What is this world turning into, Olivia?" His smile faded a little. She sat silently beside him, unsure of what to say. "I saw charred bodies and burned buildings. I was almost dead myself. I was… I don't know how I survived but… what has this world turned into? Just thirty years ago, there was still debate as to whether aliens existed or not. Now… now they have overrun our planet." He smiled sadly. "At least it's some consolation that humanity won't be the planet's doom, you know?" He chuckled a little.

"Are you okay?" Olivia asked, unsure if it was the right thing to ask, but it was what she had seen many people ask under similar circumstances.

"I'll survive," he said softly and rubbed his forehead. "I'm not okay, Olivia. I just wish that I would wake up and this would all be a dream. Then I'd write one heck of a science-fiction novel out of it, but I sleep and wake up and the nightmares are no longer in my sleep. The nightmares are out here, in reality," he said very softly.

Olivia listened to the soft hum that seemed to emanate from the walls of the room and she listened to the muffled noises outside. She could feel her own fear as well as Andrew's. "We have always survived. Through wars and disease and everything that could be thrown at us. We have always kept it together and we will continue to do that. We'll get past this," she said.

Andrew looked at her, frowned, and narrowed his eyes. "Who are you and what have you done with Olivia?" She felt a small laughter bubble up from within her. "It would be one interesting book now, wouldn't it?" he asked.

She shrugged. "Probably."

"Always the skeptic," he said and laughed.

They sat there in comfortable silence for a while before the door burst open and Akya waked in. She was more agitated than Olivia had ever seen her. "We have to go! Now!" she shouted.

Olivia looked at her with shock and asked, "Go? Go where? Why?"

Akya gripped her arm with such force that she winced. "Elk's defense has fallen. We fear Elk is dead and, somehow, they have found out about this place and have come for us. Tekka has asked me to take you to safety. You must come, now. The bombardment might begin at any moment."

Olivia turned to look at Andrew, whose face was both filled with horror and anger. "What about Andrew?" she asked.

Akya shook her head. "He can barely walk. He'll be kept safe, but you must understand we can't let the enemy get his hands on you. You are too important." The urgency in her tone was terribly unnerving.

"I won't leave without Andrew," Olivia said.

Akya made a sound that was harsh and swift. Olivia was briefly frightened by her frustration and half expected her to lift her up and run, but she felt a hand on her wrist. She turned to see Andrew staring at her with pleading eyes.

"You must go. I don't know why you're important, but they've almost never been wrong before. I'll be fine. You must go now, Olivia," he said.

Olivia stared at him for a while, tears gathering in her eyes, but a tremor ran through the building and bits of debris started to cover the floor. She barely had time to process what was happening before she felt herself hoisted up over Akya's shoulder and they were off.

Akya ran faster than anything Olivia had ever experienced, making her way through the maze of corridors that cut through the bunker until they entered a passage that was dark with a few dim yellow light bulbs. They rushed through and Akya threw herself against the door with Olivia still on her shoulder. Olivia had never seen her in this state before, and it was slightly terrifying.

Akya slammed herself against the door again and it buckled. The third time came with a sound like ancient creatures snarling and the door gave way to a small staircase. A dim light shone from above and got brighter the higher they ascended until they came out to the open. The ground seemed to be shaking and smoke filled the air.

Akya broke into a run and kept running while Olivia wondered about the Terrans and what would become of them. She thought about Andrew and her brother and she buried her face in Akya's shoulder and wept.

CHAPTER SIXTEEN

Ork ran a webbed finger over Elk's face. His yellow eyes stared impassively at Ork. There was no buzz, no emotion, no thoughts or weaknesses in his mind. Elk was as disciplined and controlled as a machine and that infuriated Ork. Even his defeat had not weakened his mind or resolve.

"You failed the first test into the military academy. I found that interesting. I thought that you were a model of perfection, but I find that you failed the first time… It was surprising. You have failed many times since then, no? Failed at defending your monarch, your planet, your people. Some might say that you have made it a habit," Ork said. Elk remained perfectly silent and tranquil.

"Why have you even bothered all these years? I see no need for all the time and energy that you have devoted to being a nuisance to me. You have greatly annoyed and disrespected me, and for that you will suffer. For defying my authority and using the treasure against me, your people will suffer. Unless, of course, you're willing to tell me where the treasure is and where the girl is being hidden. Then, and, I give you my word, I will hurt none of your people, and I'll give you this planet to own and all will be forgiven," Ork continued.

Elk's yellow eyes turned to focus on him and Ork felt a glow of pleasure because it seemed that he had broken through Elk's stoic reserve and captured his interest.

"Yes. These people that you have devoted everything to will be spared, and you can go on protecting them without any further challenge or stress. You will have a home, a place to rebuild and grow if you deliver the treasure and the girl to me."

Elk said nothing for several moments then spoke very slowly, "You talk far too much for a soldier. You should have been a diplomat."

Ork lashed out with his right arm, hitting him across the cheek with such force that his head snapped to the side. He hit him a few more times, but there wasn't even a faint crack in Elk's tranquil presence. Ork felt an inner frustration at the standards to which Terran soldiers were trained but there was also excitement in the potential of breaking him.

"You will tell me either way, Elk. Don't worry," he said.

Elk remained silent as if he hadn't heard what Ork had said.

"I'll let you take it from here, Vol," Ork said and stepped away.

Ork felt a small, minute flicker that was quickly and efficiently concealed as soon as Vol entered the room. The lights slowly changed in brightness from a soft yellow until it was purely white and emanated so much heat and ultraviolet light that Elk felt his entire body scream to get away from under it. His muscles constricted on their own and his vision dimmed until he could barely see. He maintained calm, coaxing his mind into imagining the softest yellow light and the cool air and serenity of hibernation. His muscles slowly stopped straining and relaxed into a hypnotic peacefulness.

"Ah, this one is a challenge, I see. How exciting. I have heard a lot about Terran soldiers. You are trained to detach your mind from your body, they say; to the point that you can endure the highest level of physical torture while keeping your mind intact, divulging nothing. I admire that, I really do, as it creates a challenging task for me to exploit your mind," Vol said slowly, but his voice was filled with excitement.

Elk felt a hand drop something small, almost the size of a grain of sand into his skin. He fought the fear that started to rise, because he knew exactly what it was. They were very rare and it took a lot to build one, but today, the lunatic called Vol had elected to use one on him.

Elk felt its effects slowly at first. He felt a warm sensation all over his body. He felt the warmth intensify to heat, then to pain; mind-shattering, tormenting pain. The purpose of the chip was to trick the body into thinking it was dying by causing all of the pain receptors to flood the mind with signals, making every single part of Elk's body flood with pain. Elk tried to detach his mind and maintain control, but it was getting more difficult with each passing moment. He focused on raw endurance and held his own against the almost overwhelming pain, maintaining control of his mind and not letting it slip open for Vol's or Ork's perusal.

"Ha! Interesting. I think I would enjoy your company very much," Vol said.

***

Andrew watched as the different pods were sent out in search of Olivia. He also made sure that a huge bounty was placed on her head. The aliens had somehow missed her, but he would find her and bring her to them and solidify his usefulness. Andrew would make them trust him so that when this all blew up into a whirlpool of chaos, he, his family, and Commonwealth would be safe.

Andrew picked up the cup and stared at the black, bitter liquid inside. Then, on impulse, he threw it out the window and placed the empty cup back on the table. His mood was already foul, and he didn't need anything else to make it worse.

"Sir?" a voice called from the doorway.

Andrew turned to see his assistant. "Yes, Peter. What is it?" he asked.

The man hesitated a little, which was odd, then spoke rapid-fire; like he wanted the message to get out of him as soon as possible. "There have been protests and riots since the aliens' arrival and they have been quelled repeatedly. But, some of these rioters have organized themselves into a sort of militia. And, they are aided by some of the military and now they have added to their force a growing number of escaped Terrans. They attacked a military base today and took planes, supplies, and recruited some of the youth in the area as well."

"Fools," Andrew hissed under his breath. He loosened his tie and placed both palms on the table.

"Has the counsel heard of this?"

Peter replied instantly. "I think they have, sir. But, they are yet to reach a conclusion about what to do. It's happening across the Commonwealths, but ours currently has the highest number of militia men," he said.

Fury arose within Andrew as he tightened his fists on the table. "They want to ruin everything. I must meet with the council at once," he said.

Peter nodded quickly and left, no doubt to arrange a meeting. Andrew stood up and walked to the window, his brow furrowed and his nostrils flared as he thought about what this could mean. The alliance he was trying to build, and the favor he was trying to gain from Ork would be ruined. His Commonwealth was to be buried deep within the sands and forgotten.

"Stupid, stupid!" Andrew hissed and ran his hand over his face. He wouldn't tolerate this madness. He wouldn't let these militia men ruin the future he was trying so desperately to protect.

***

Olivia watched the man carry what looked to be an aircraft part. He was built like a small house, well over six feet tall with a chest broader than any she had ever seen; and muscles that threatened to tear the shirt he was wearing. His face was plain and he had dark brown eyes that seemed tired and exhausted.

"This place is where we can be safe for now," Akya said quietly.

Olivia looked around and felt a little reassurance. Yes, it was built from concrete with reinforced walls. The outside and the entrance were masked as a decrepit building but, still, she didn't think something like this would stop Ork and his people.

"Elk has been helping some of these militia men with bits of Terran technology should a time come when we would need them. That time is now. Don't worry, we'll be safe," Akya said.

Olivia didn't know how, but she suddenly realized that Akya was also exhausted. "What will we do now?" she asked.

Akya looked around slowly then sniffed. The lights were a bit harsh and Olivia knew that it was affecting her.

"Special rooms have been made for you," the man said, noticing the same thing.

Akya nodded gratefully. "We rest and wait for Tekka's orders," she said.

Olivia frowned. "How do we know if Tekka is even still… you know? Umm…" she said.

Akya watched her the same way a psychiatrist would observe a patient. "He's fine," she said simply then turned to the man.

"Please show me to my room, thank you very much." Olivia stood there until a girl, a little shorter than her, walked up to her. She wore long dreadlocks. Her black skin glowed under the light and her muscles were firm and toned. She wasn't a stranger to physical exertion and Olivia suddenly felt entirely out of shape next to her.

"Follow me," she said and Olivia followed. Her mind was too weary and confused to argue.

***

Tekka didn't know how to feel without Elk's presence. He had known him since they were at the academy together. Tekka had been training to assist monarchs and he actually did assist some of them, but aided Elk whenever he needed it. Elk's presence had always been there but now it felt like he had been blinded and pushed into a desert alone and stranded.

Everyone looked to him, or at least the ones he'd managed to rescue. Tekka watched them as they moved through the underground trailer and he felt, for the first time, the entire weight of what Elk must have felt. He felt the responsibility and pain for those left behind and the responsibility for the ones that remained. Each of them had lives, families, and ambitions. They all looked to him, and he had no one to take orders from. He had aided leaders before. So, he thought, how hard could it be? Yet he knew that it was terribly difficult.

Tekka wished desperately that Elk was here, but he wasn't, and their survival demanded that he remove his emotion and only reason logically. He walked over to where Andrew sat and placed a hand on the man's fragile shoulder.

"How are you feeling?" he asked.

Andrew grinned and said, "Like I could run a thousand miles while carrying this entire trailer on my back."

Tekka patted his shoulder. "What do you think your people are doing now?"

Andrew shrugged and replied, "I don't know. Probably arguing or coming up with some new law to pass that'll make everything seem bearable. Really though, what could they do? They all but ruined themselves even before those aliens arrived. They just… let's just say that I'm not very proud of humanity right now."

Tekka nodded. "I found it very strange when I came here. There was no defined place for things and it caused a gross lack of order. It meant that there was no true trust, no true loyalties. It was… intriguing and frightening. And, it has proven to be a grave disadvantage to your kind. Their lack of defined purpose ruins them. It is the way of such things," he said quietly.

Andrew nodded. "So… back on your planet, everyone had a place and a defined task?" he asked.

Tekka tilted his head in affirmation and said, "There were really no males or females or tenderers in between. You just chose the shape that the system needed the most. I could change to female if that's what was needed and I could change to a tenderer."

"What's a tenderer?" Andrew asked.

Tekka focused his yellow eyes on him then slowly tilted his head. "They have the responsibility of grooming the offspring when they are formed; guiding and nourishing them. It was their own purpose and it was an all-consuming task, unlike being male or female, which allowed us to function in other ways. A female could still have a war form and be a soldier. A male could still be a diplomat, but a tenderer was nothing else. Everything was clear and straightforward."

"Oh wow! So you can change into a female at will?" Andrew asked.

Tekka tilted his head a few times and then replied, "It would require a few complicated processes but, yes, that's the idea."

Andrew gave a mischievous smile. "Very convenient," he said.

Tekka gave him a flat stare and, after a while, realization dawned on his face and he made a soft hissing sound. "The fact that you thought of it that way is proof of your humanity." Andrew laughed. "Are you ready?" Tekka asked.

Andrew nodded, flashing his white teeth.

"Has anyone ever told you that you smile a little too much?" Tekka asked.

Andrew shrugged and asked, "Who doesn't love a smile?" He smiled again.

***

Andrew couldn't believe what he was hearing. He sat very still, struggling to keep a leash on his temper. He looked at the men and women who sat before him and sneered inwardly. They knew nothing of the sacrifices he was making; nothing of the things he had done for them. They just sat in their air-conditioned offices and gave orders. But, they knew nothing of the dirty work that was required to keep the cogs of affairs running smoothly.

"Andrew Jimoh. This decision is final and effective immediately. You have been deposed from your position as Minister of Engineering following your failure to establish a base of cyber and space security for the Commonwealth and for, in fact, helping destroy it," one of the councilmen said.

Andrew looked at him and nodded slowly. "I see," he said and stood, buttoning his suit. "I'll leave my office immediately and go wherever I may be reassigned." He then walked away, anger washing over him.

He would show them just how important he was, how he kept their boundaries safe, safer than even the military could. They had also spoken of meeting with the leaders of the militia men and making a sort of arrangement to reach an understanding and compromise. Andrew gritted his teeth at the idea as he walked out of the building, not bothering to go back to his office. He wasn't moving out, not yet. The office was still his and it would remain that way for a long time.

****

Elk felt like he had been cast into a world made entirely of pain and suffering. Every last bit of him was in pain. Everything he felt, saw, and touched was forged from pain. And, even the brief moments of relief were painful in themselves because he now waited in torture for the expectation of pain. He measured his breathing, kept his thoughts controlled, and tried to imagine himself in a void of nothingness; a void that held neither peace nor altercation, just nothing. The pain was beginning to slowly be blocked out when it changed form again and became more intense. He released a terrible hiss with something similar to a moan and Vol smiled a little with glee.

"That is the first sound I have gotten out of you. Wonderful, no? I must say that you have a very admirable endurance, the best I've seen. Quite impressive for you to hold out this long, but now you've cracked and you'll continue cracking until I break down the bars with which the gates of your mind are sealed. You could also make this stop by just telling us where the girl and the treasure are."

"Vol," Elk said slowly. He felt Vol's excitement soar, for this was the first time he had spoken since the beginning of his torment. "I heard of you," he said quietly.

Vol dipped his head in mock respect. "I'm very flattered, Elk, that your illustrious self was made aware of my existence and exploits. I'm sure, then, that you know what I'm capable of? And, as such, it would be the wisest course and in your best interest for you to tell me what I need to know. Wouldn't you agree?"

Elk waited for a long while then spoke again. "You have been called the destroyer of worlds. And, back when I was but an infant, you held the largest empire that the universe had ever known. You were like a physical force. I admired you a little back then. How does it feel to have fallen so low? To watch that which gave you power destroy and drive you to madness? To cast you out to the edges of the observable universe and wipe out all of your kind, leaving you as the last Virzutian? One could wander the length and breadth of space in entirety and not find a single being like you. They're all gone." His words came out in guarded, weary bursts, and he avoided using telepathy because that would be like giving Vol a free pass into his mind. "You're just a lonely, miserable, insane creature that simply wanders the universe seeking something to make your existence more meaningful. And, I'll tell you now that the treasure won't. Instead, it will finish the job that the other has started. It will ruin and end you."

Vol remained perfectly still for a moment, then uttered something in the ugly Virzutian language, followed closely by a casual backhand that tore into Elk's face. Elk was shocked by the force the blow carried, but he had already primed his mind to absorb pain, so it didn't hurt him as much as it otherwise would have.

"Insolent... foolish... desperately foolish. You would risk antagonizing me? You would risk awakening my anger? I would have every last one of your people killed before your eyes. I could devote myself to erasing your race. I could blast this planet to smithereens and pick up the treasure from the debris. I..."

"A weak enemy blusters and threatens. We were taught that at the academy," Elk said and felt pain suffice through him again, heightened and extreme, erasing his perception and sensory input, causing his muscles to buckle and strain on their own. Had he still possessed his sense of hearing, he would have heard them straining. He fought desperately for control, but he felt his grasp on his mind slipping. He felt it slowly moving from his grasp and, with a loud scream, it all fell apart and his mind was laid out bare and open.

Ork saw, from the cameras they implanted to give him feedback directly from Andrew's eyes, the treasure as it sat in some kind of container, suspended from the bottom. It was a beautiful thing indeed. It was almost unbelievable how something so small, so seemingly common, could hold such unimaginable power.

Ork suspected that even Elk didn't know of the current location of the treasure. It was indeed in a secure place that would take some time breaking into. He was amused that the most powerful weapon in this war lay in the hands of the enemy, but they were losing because they didn't have the courage to use it.

Ork contacted his Captains mentally and sent a telepathic command to them. For this task, he chose the Wryu – lethal pilots and warriors from a subdued planet at the edge of the Andromeda galaxy. They were about the same height as a human child but extremely strong, aggressive, and accurate. They had also had their will taken from them by the fear of engineering he had created on their planet after their defeat, keeping them docile and subservient. They would bring back his treasure; he was sure.

***

Andrew watched as the light swirled before his eyes. He could have sworn that he hadn't seen anything quite as beautiful, or that exuded so much power. "You're saying that Olivia has used this before?" he asked.

Tekka kept the kind of silence that was affirmative in itself.

"I just can't believe that," Andrew said with something akin to wonder and fear.

"Believe it. She used it in a different timeline. She saved the world from Ork and created this timeline that is being threatened now."

"Wow. So… you're saying anyone can do that? That this thing can grant anyone the ability to change timelines?"

Tekka went silent as if he was contemplating the question, then spoke. "Well, changing timelines isn't the only thing that's possible with it, and of that I am certain. It was rumored that Vol changed appearances, saw multiple paths of the future, and was almost on the verge of destroying an entire galaxy before the treasure he was using rebelled. I think this one can grant something similar, but not just to anyone, it appears. It only reacts to Olivia's presence."

Andrew turned sharply to look at him. "What? You mean that only Olivia can use this thing?"

Tekka nodded slowly, still trying to get accustomed to that physical expression. "Yes. Only she can use this and, even then, it isn't a sure thing how it would react. After its last use, it needed time to recharge and, after it was fully charged, it became unstable. We're not sure the reason for this instability but… she could obliterate this galaxy or turn this whole planet inside out or maybe even create a black hole out of the sun or something. No one can be sure what is possible under these circumstances."

"If this gets into Ork's hands then…"

"Exactly," Tekka said.

Andrew shuddered a bit then turned away. "So what do we do? Just sit around and wait for it to gain stability? Doesn't seem like much of a plan. And, we don't know how much time it will take. Cosmic things take… cosmically large amounts of time. Time that we don't exactly have? Catch my drift?"

Tekka nodded slowly again. "I agree. We don't have much time. We were studying it and working on a way to induce stability, but we don't understand it. It confounds our scientists much the same way atomic theory would confound the ancient Egyptians of your kind. We don't have enough of the materials that are required to understand something such as this but we're doing our best. Another alternative is for Olivia's will to be proven strong. When she used it last time, according to Elk's analysis of her mental state, she just wanted everything to be better; for Ork to go away, for this nightmare to end, and the treasure found a way to make that happen. In its current instability, it might take… creative liberties with making her desires a reality, liberties that we cannot imagine. So, she must try to control it and something that's probably as old as time can't exactly be controlled by… a mere human."

"Olivia is far stronger than you know."

"Are you willing to risk the safety of this entire planet on that strength?" Tekka asked.

Andrew went silent and then said, "I, too, want this to end but, until we have an alternative, we must be very careful because we don't understand what it is that we're toying with. I don't think anyone does. It has tossed Vol to the edge of observable space, it wiped out the Virzutian civilization, and there have been rumors, stories, and talks about a civilization long before that was wiped from existence when they used a treasure. You must understand our hesitation."

Just as Andrew was about to nod, the ground shook. Tekka went very still, which meant that he was receiving some telepathic communication. Then, he turned to Andrew and said, "They have come."

"Here too? How do they keep finding us?" Tekka shrugged and gently picked him up, moving away quickly. "What about the treasure?" Andrew asked.

"It's safe here," Tekka replied as he ran quickly, but carefully, so as not to hurt Andrew too much. They ran into a hovercraft and when he set Andrew down, the man looked around in confusion.

"Aren't we evacuating the others? Where are the rest?"

Tekka shook his head slowly. "The others have long gone to safety. I'm sorry, Andrew," he said and knocked Andrew out with a slap to the head.

Tekka went to the pilot seat and flew the craft into the air just as Elk's soldiers were landing. He knew that they wouldn't chase after him because, from Andrew's eyes, they had seen the treasure still in the building. But, what seemed to be the treasure was a bomb that was fashioned to look just like the treasure. Tekka waited patiently. Then he felt a tremor and saw the bright flash of light that erupted upwards and outwards, obliterating all of Ork's ships in the area and his soldiers along with them.

Tekka felt pleasure from this victory. After their second discovery, his highly analytical mind realized that it was shortly after Andrew's arrival that they were discovered, and nothing else came in after him. Andrew would be the perfect place to plant a spying artifact and Tekka scanned him thoroughly to reveal the tiny chip embedded in his brain. Impulsively, he wanted to remove it but, when he thought it through, Tekka realized that he could exploit it to deal harm to Ork.

Ork watched with disbelief as his ships and soldiers were lost in the blast. He could feel their fear, surprise, and pain as they died and his rage soared. In a low, controlled voice, he spoke to the guard behind him. "How many of the Terrans do we currently have as captives?"

"Thirty-eight, Lord," the soldier replied.

Ork nodded, then gave his orders telepathically.

Elk felt brief relief, but refused to embrace it. He felt shame and pain. He had slipped for a short while and, though Vol hadn't seen enough to doom him, Vol had still seen too much and gathered ammunition for his next psychological torture.

Elk remained in his cocoon of endurance, fighting against his body's plea to find relief, because he knew that if he did he would have to build his endurance back up again. He wondered when it would end. Elk knew that his endurance would not, could not, last forever. He felt different types of shock and some pleasant sensations meant to draw him out of his cocoon, but he held on desperately. He held on with all he had.

Then, Elk perceived it. It was very faint and seemed to come from about a mile away, but he couldn't mistake it. He let his cocoon drop and let his defenses relax for a moment, then reached out tentatively with his already abused senses and smelled the fresh Terran essence; what the humans would call blood. He opened his eyes, hoping desperately that it wasn't what he suspected it was.

Before Elk was a flowing blue liquid. He traced it back up to a Terran body. It was coming from a tenderer, the softest, gentlest part of Terran society. Elk made a long sound of painful mourning as the life essence flowed down to where he was chained and pooled underneath him.

Elk felt its sticky thickness and could smell the blue blood. He looked up and Ork was standing beside Vol, both looking down on him. He looked at them and hated nothing more in the entire universe. He wanted desperately to murder them, to cause them infinite pain, and to torture them for several lifetimes. He felt his heart threaten to break and his mind slowly being swallowed up by the surge of emotions. He would lose his rationality soon if he kept up like this.

Elk fought for calm. He fought for the yellow sunlight of home and a leisurely walk through the gardens from his home atop the metal hills. He thought about his family, his parents, and siblings. He thought about peace and happiness, but it worsened his pain. What had been paradise was now reduced to all devasation and his people were being slaughtered before his eyes while he was left powerless to save them. The pain was raw and unending, It was not the physical pain, but pain that flowed in his very essence and cracked his soul.

"Look what you have caused, Elk. You have deliberately caused the death of one of your people. I offered you safety and peace, but you chose this," Ork said.

Elk kept silent because he knew that if he tried to speak, he would lose the delicate control he had. Causing him to thrash and curse, making his mind and resolve weaken.

"The offer still stands, Elk. Tell us where this girl and the treasure are and we will leave this planet like we were never here. And, if you want, I'll even give it to you to rule, to dominate, and to make a home out of. I respect you as a foe and as a soldier and we shared a planet before. This offer is a sincere one and this is the last time I'll make it."

Elk felt his body start to tremble involuntarily and he quickly pulled it back into control. Loss of control over his body made loss of control of the mind easier. "I deliver one of the most powerful objects in the universe to you and the key to it as well and you promise me safety for my people? Is that it?"

"That's it," Ork replied.

Elk became genuinely amused and made sounds of amusement, much to Ork's annoyance.

"What's funny?" Ork asked.

Elk shook his head and then said, "Only you would think that is a fair trade. Once you gain all that power, my people can never be safe. No one is safe. You could decide to go back on your word and no one would be able to do a thing about it. You could even change our realities in such a way that we forget this trade… so this deal never happened. You would call that fair?"

Ork hissed and stepped back. "It might not be fair, but it's the only deal you've got. Either that or I kill every last one of the thirty-seven remaining Terrans with me and still get the treasure in the end. The best part is that I would slit their throats right in front of you, so you get to watch them die, knowing that you've failed as a general, a leader, and a Terran. I can do that, don't you see? So you can take this trade or you can watch that happen."

Elk breathed, thinking of the past. He thought of his disappointment and pain when he failed his first academy test. He thought about the pride when he passed it the second time and the difficult work to become warriors in the academy. He thought about all the times he'd given everything he could in defense of his planet. He thought about all the pain since the destruction of his home and the trust that his people developed for him. They truly believed and said that he would never let them down. But, he had time and time again and he was doing it again now. He looked Ork square in the eye and shook his head. "My people are strong and they are loyal. They have made great sacrifices. We don't sacrifice each other for selfish reasons. And if those Terrans here will be sacrificed for the safety of the ones left, if they'll sacrifice themselves so that the treasure doesn't fall into your hands, they'll do it with eagerness and joy," he said.

Ork hissed long and loud, then gripped Elk's face, raising it and bending over so that they were a finger's width apart. "This is not some heroic deed that you have done. I will wipe out every last one of you. I will erase the very idea of your race from the minds of creatures everywhere. And, you will be gone for good. And, I will still get the treasure; making your sacrifice useless."

Elk withdrew into his cocoon, fortifying himself for more pain. Ork stormed out of the room, his temper had a presence of its own.

***

Andrew sat in the chamber that was made suitable for human beings, although he found breathing more of a task than he remembered it being before. It felt like he was being slightly squeezed; like the air in the room was giving him a hug that was a bit too tight. He watched as a soldier walked in, clearly impatient.

"What?" the alien soldier asked.

"There is a problem in my Commonwealth that hinders our common interests, a problem that would hinder me from aiding you to the fullest," Andrew said.

The soldier watched him with as much hostility as Andrew had ever seen. "What exactly do you expect me to do?" the soldier asked. He seemed to be a high-ranking soldier under Ork's service, so Andrew told him.

***

Olivia watched as the big man, whom she found out was named Henry, walked in and turned on the screen with a wave of his hand. He plopped down in front of it and sighed deeply like a man that had been waiting the entire day just for this moment. She turned her attention away from him, focusing instead on the book in her lap. She was there for what seemed like an eternity before she heard a long, loud string of curses from Henry, who was usually quiet.

"What is it?!" Olivia asked, startled.

The man increased the volume of the screen. "Earthlings, it has come to my attention that some of you have chosen the path of aggression. You have decided to fight me and disturb what I believed to be an understanding between us and, for that, I will remind you what happens when we do not have an understanding," Ork said.

The screen started displaying a city that seemed oblivious to what was happening. It showed streets and people just going about their daily lives. Some even watched the broadcast on roadside holographs and, then, all of a sudden, a blue light exploded from within the city and spread with great speed, vaporizing everything in its path. Buildings, people, and trees were pulled inwards and the entire city sunk into the ground, creating a vast pit where the city once stood.

Olivia's mouth dropped in horror as she watched what happened and she saw the rage and anger on Henry's face. His eyes were red and his muscles seemed to want to burst out of his skin. Some other members of the group had also arrived and were standing in shock. Ork's face appeared back on the screen.

"I'm currently in search of a person, a lady whose picture will be shown." As he spoke, Olivia's face appeared on the screen. She felt her heart fall into her belly and she began to tremble. "She is of great importance to me. And, for each day that she is not found, I will destroy one city. Bring her to me and your planet will be left safe and free from my wrath. I give my word."

His face flickered off the screen. Olivia sat in horror, then felt a delicate touch on her shoulder. She turned to see Akya standing there, staring at the screen. She looked down at Olivia and nodded a little. Olivia looked back at the group who turned to look at her.

"Well that's… something," Henry said, his voice still tight with anger.

A girl, whose name she learned was Eve, watched silently, seemingly looking deep into Olivia's soul. "Seems like a good bargain. We just give him one person and he lets the rest go? One life for billions," she said.

Henry looked at her. "Have you asked yourself why he wants her, Eve? Why he's willing to go through all of this? What if we would just be giving him a weapon?"

"We don't know that," Eve said.

One woman who was exceptionally thin, so much so that it seemed that her eyes had sunken into her skull, turned to Olivia and asked, "Do you have any idea why he wants you?"

Olivia started to open her mouth and Akya spoke over her. "She is the key to something that he desperately wants, something that would make him… well, a god. Something that would grant him limitless power."

Henry rubbed his face then shook his head.

"He said that he would leave the rest of us alone," Eve said.

"This is a creature that destroyed his own planet and most of his own people. This is a being that has destroyed planets just because he felt like it. Do you understand?" Akya said.

Eve frowned and rubbed her forehead.

"Well I guess that settles it then," Henry said. "Unless you would like to put it to a vote?"

Most of them shook their heads, agreeing with him. Eve shook her head and pointed at the screen that had now switched to something else entirely.

"Tens of thousands of people have died. They have died over this person. If we don't give her in tomorrow, then others will die. For every day that we don't, people will continue to die. Until we are doomed anyway, we should just give her to him. Because if we don't, it still makes no difference."

"You're wrong," Akya said. "It matters a lot. This galaxy, other galaxies, the universe, time, reality… everything that you can imagine would be under his control. Do you understand what that means?"

Eve went silent. Akya nodded, seeing that her point was made.

"We should take her out of here. She's not safe in this place," Henry said.

"Where else? She has to remain here while we wait for Tekka," Akya said.

Olivia sat stunned while they argued about her. She wanted to cry. She wanted to turn herself in. Thousands of people had died because of her. What was her life in comparison to the tens of thousands of people that died today and the people that would die tomorrow and after that? She wanted to scream, but she could only sit there stunned, scared, and confused.

Olivia sat in the compound that evening with Akya who was sipping something, but she didn't know what. She raised an eyebrow at Akya's cup. "Is that something I would be interested in drinking?" she asked.

Akya shook her head. "Not unless you want to maybe die."

Olivia smiled a little. "Maybe that would not be such a bad thing, you know?"

Akya spluttered over her drink and looked down at Olivia with anger and horror over her normally impassive face.

"Think about it. If I were to die, then Ork wouldn't have to kill so many people. There would be no need for all of that. He would relent and you would only have to focus on protecting the 'treasure'"

Akya nodded coolly and sipped from her drink. "That would work, you know? You could just die and the world would set itself right. You could just escape and be free. Ork would surely relent and wouldn't do the exact same thing for the treasure. He would still destroy cities until it is given to him," she said quietly.

Olivia suddenly felt horrible. She had been protected by Elk, Tekka, Akya, and the entirety of the Terran race and she wanted to fling it all away because she was feeling badly.

"I'm sorry," Olivia said quietly.

Akya nodded. "Don't ever say that to me again," she said. Olivia nodded.

There was a clearing of throat beside them and they turned to see Henry standing with his hand on his belt which held a laser gun, a rare piece of technology for someone of his status. "Tell me, exactly. In what manner did you come about being or possessing this key that that alien lunatic is so hot over? I was thinking over a drink and decided that was a story I would like to hear," he said.

Olivia sighed heavily. "It's a very long story, Henry."

The big man came to occupy the chair that was close to them.

"I don't seem to be doing much at the moment."

Akya sighed and began talking.

***

Andrew watched the explosion. It wasn't the explosion that the rest of the world was seeing. It was a smaller one, placed conveniently and strategically to wipe out every last member of the council. The only explanation that was given was that the militia was too much for their Commonwealth and the explosion was dealt as punishment. Andrew watched as their crafts left and he knew that it wouldn't require much for him to be seated as a replacement.

Andrew felt no happiness about this, but he knew that the current council was not equipped to do what had to be done in order to ensure the safety and security of the Commonwealth. He was ready to first order a manhunt, sending out soldiers and bounty hunters to find Olivia. A bounty worth a staggering amount of money had also been placed on her head.

Andrew hoped that he would be the first to find her, but he suspected that she was nowhere near his Commonwealth. Perhaps these militia men could be of use. They knew almost all there was to know about the underground areas and they would surely see the life of one woman as a small price to pay for peace and freedom. He adjusted his kaftan and walked out. He had an appointment that he must keep.

Andrew sat and watched the room. It was an immersive VR technology that made it seem like he was in a room with the other delegates while they were still in their respective Commonwealths.

"I say there is no choice here. We must find the girl. We must alert the military and turn the Earth inside out because, while we sit here discussing it, the countdown is on for another city which could be any of ours. With all the resources of the world pulled together, there's no crevice within which she can hide that we would be unable to find her. If we give her up to this… Ork, then he may leave us alone. He has said so himself," the man said.

Andrew nodded to himself. Finally they had some sense.

"But why, out of several billions of people on Earth, would he want one woman? So much so that he's willing to leave the planet unharmed if she's brought to him. She's obviously very important and we must ask ourselves if we aren't delivering a terrible weapon directly into his hands. Who knows what this woman possesses? She's an astrobiologist, so she may have some knowledge that would grant him some unfathomable power," another said and Andrew groaned inwardly.

"He has already given his word that he'll leave when he finds what he's seeking," Andrew said. "And, whatever she *has*, whatever advantage that will grant him, it would be turned away from us. Think about it; does he really need any extra advantage to ruin us? He has sent the Terrans into hiding. Tell me, do you think that he actually needs any more of an advantage over us? Whatever *this thing* he seeks is, it's not for us, so I see no reason why we should be arguing about this. We should send out every resource we have, devoted specifically to finding this woman," he added and there were some noises of agreement.

It was finally put to a vote which infuriated Andrew. He found it very annoying that every little thing was put to a vote. There was nothing done without a lot of talking that consumed time that they didn't even have. He stood and turned off his device then walked away. There were more important things right now than arguments that led nowhere.

***

Elk watched as the blood flowed towards him, pooling around his feet. He had deadened himself. He felt nothing, was nothing. The pain was him. It no longer hit him, it no longer pushed against him. It became him. He just watched as the eighth Terran bled out before him. This was a worthy sacrifice. It was the honorable thing to do. He knew that, but he was watching his race dwindle before his eyes. His heart had shattered and he was left feeling nothing. He just watched impassively as Vol slaughtered his people.

The Virzutian must have realized that the effects of his actions were lost because he stopped and came to stand over Elk. "My father was a laborer. He didn't have enough natural intelligence to work as anything else. And my mother was a mathematician. It was a high science, but she wasn't terribly gifted at it. She was just competent and, among the Virzutians, competence is… well, it doesn't mean much. We had very little and were at the very bottom of the ladder, but, as I grew, I became skilled in astro-engineering and manipulation. I was able to design engines faster than the speed of light when I was barely a middling. I mastered the art of designing space stations soon after, and I decided to devote my skills to the military."

"Why are you telling me this?" Elk asked quietly.

"Listen," Vol said. "I had some very… radical ideas and my thought patterns were quite different. On my planet, knowledge was literally power and, often, the superior leaders were four Virzutians who had achieved the peak of knowledge. I wanted that, though it seemed impossible despite my intelligence. I wanted to rule. I wanted to be the best and I was willing to do whatever it took; what the rest were not willing to do. When an underling planet challenged our might and killed some of our delegates, I designed a weapon that wiped the entire planet out in one sweep. I rose quickly and was known for my brutality. I became the youngest general in Virzutian history. I was loyal and I was fierce and I gave everything for my planet. But, when one of the superiors saw that I was well on my way to replacing him, he framed me for insubordination and disloyalty. I was forced to flee and my family suffered for crimes that I didn't commit. The planet and system that I had fought for conspired against me, and for what? I lost my life as a Virzutian. And when I came back and staged my coup, I knew that, one way or another, I would be the end of my own planet." He voice seemed weary, like it had taken a lot for him to tell his story.

"I'll ask again. Why are you telling me this?"

"You will die soon and this is something that I have always wanted to relate to another being. You won't be able to speak of it because you'll be dead very soon. I just wanted to tell it to someone," Vol said.

"You had no true loyalty to Virzutia. You never did," Elk said.

"And why would you think that?" Vol asked very slowly, like he was starting to get angry.

Elk didn't care. He couldn't care much about anything now. "You only served Virzutia because of the power and security it could offer you. Immediately, something went wrong and you decided to punish the entire planet because of that. You killed billions of people because you were betrayed. Innocent people. You were selfish from the beginning, and that's on you," he said.

Vol let some time pass before his gasses hissed and the air was saturated with a strong foulness that Elk had grown accustomed to. "I see. Thank you for that insight," he said and went silent for a while. Then he spoke in a very measured tone that was backed by the subtle buzzing of the Terran language. "I intend to restore my people with the power of the treasure. I intend to rebuild my empire."

Elk made sounds of amusement for a long time, during which Vol waited patiently. "Is that it then? You're lonely? Have you learned nothing? I thought that you Virzutians were supposed to be the smart ones. Look what the former treasure did to you and your people when you tried to use it on a large scale. Do you think it would be any different now?"

Vol shook his head. "I know more about the treasure than you could ever hope to. I've learned so much about it and my mistakes have been found out and eliminated. You'll see when I get the treasure. Now, I have had enough of discussing with you." Vol placed the chip on Elk's body again.

"I could make you an offer," Elk said and Vol stopped. "I could offer to reinstate your people in exchange for my release and your help in defeating Ork."

Vol made what must have been the Virzutian sound of amusement. "I didn't know you had it in you, Elk. But, that will not be enough, sadly. The treasure would still be in your possession. It would still be yours and it would do nothing for me. I have killed a number of your people, so I don't see you treating me with kindness if such a power is within your grasp. Surely you must understand."

Elk shook his head, feeling the strain in his muscles from such a long time of endurance. It seemed like it was several lifetimes ago that he was taken in for questioning. "I've never broken my word before, except the one I gave to keep my people safe. And, I just gave it to you now. The power of the treasure will not be used to harm you in any manner if you just do what I ask. The power wouldn't even be mine. It would be hers."

Vol made the sound again. "Do you take me for a fool, Elk? Surely, you mustn't. I've contributed to you breaking that one word that you did, so it wouldn't be a huge stain on the white robe of your honor if you broke your word to me. I cannot trust you."

"And you can trust him? You can trust Ork?" Elk asked.

Vol shook his head. "Sometimes I don't even trust myself, but at least I understand Ork. I can expect so much from him. We are equals at this time, but you… I know nothing of how your mind works. I can't expect anything from you and we're certainly not equals because, once I let you free, you go back to possessing one of the most powerful artifacts in the universe. See? Not a very attractive offer for me."

Elk shook his head. "What would Ork do if he were the one making you this offer and you accepted it?"

Vol seemed to think about it for a moment, tilted his head slowly to the side, made a sound of amusement, then spoke in his usual slow manner. "He would obliterate me the first chance he got."

Elk nodded. "He would do that, yes, but we're not the same. He is my opposite in every way and, with that, you can make a guess at what I would do. I could even bring back those of my people you…" He stopped, suddenly reminded of the hatred that surged within him, the hatred that he had tried to bury under the logic out of necessity but, he wasn't sure even as he said it, that he would be able to keep from asking Olivia to vaporize Vol as soon as the treasure was ready to use.

"It would be worth thinking about. But, for now, I'd like to test that endurance of yours and be sure that it will be easier to accept your deal. And, it's worth the fun that I have in testing your endurance," Vol said.

Elk pushed away his hatred and pulled back into his cocoon that was already badly battered. He only had to hold out one more time, or so he hoped. He wasn't sure that he could though. His mind and body were slowly failing. He knew that he would break soon and the pain grew inside him.

CHAPTER SEVENTEEN

"They know you're here," Akya said, wide-eyed.

Olivia's senses, still dulled by drowsiness, sprung into full wakefulness. "What?! How?"

"No time to explain. Get dressed quickly!" Akya ordered.

With all possible haste, Olivia pulled on a pair of jeans and a sweater. She wasn't even done when she began to hear gunfire. The door burst open and Akya almost jumped on the person that came through, but, to their great relief, it was Henry. He carried his laser gun in one hand and his face was beaded with sweat and radiating violent anger.

"Eve sold us out. We need to move now. Southern and northern exits are blocked, but we can still get out if we go south," he said.

"Thought you said the southern exit…"

"The other south!" Henry snapped.

Olivia understood that he meant underground. They moved swiftly with the noise of gunfire and grenades getting even closer.

"Idiot, stupid…. foolish," Henry muttered under his breath, moving so fast he matched Akya's speed almost effortlessly.

Olivia felt strange being carried on Akya's shoulder, but she didn't feel that complaining would be appropriate. They went down a flight of stairs and through mazes that were lit by single bulbs that Akya crushed once they passed each one in order to make the job of navigation much more difficult for whomever decided to follow.

They ascended another flight of stairs and opened the exit hatch. It was still early morning and everywhere was gray but, when they turned, they saw armored trucks coming straight for them.

"Go!" Henry shouted. "I'll keep them occupied."

He snarled at them, his strong face determined. Olivia wanted to protest, but she had no time to as Akya sped off with her. She only had time to see one blast from Henry's gun slice through a truck like a knife through bread. She wondered how many people had given and were going to give their lives for her. It wasn't worth it. It was definitely not worth it. She was tired of crying. She was tired of being protected like she was some egg. She wanted to fight back, and she knew the perfect way to do it. Down with what Elk and the rest of them thought.

***

Andrew walked over to where Tekka was, speaking in low tones over a holophone. Tekka listened for a while, then dropped it and turned to Andrew and said, "Akya and Olivia have been compromised. I have given instructions for them to be taken somewhere else." Andrew stood perfectly still, watching him. After a while, Tekka continued, "I don't have to read your mind to know what you're thinking, Andrew."

"You read minds too? I thought that was just Elk's thing."

Tekka shook his head slightly. "I'm far better at reading minds than he is. But, as a matter of principle, I do it far less frequently. I believe in privacy."

Andrew nodded. "You know that it's about time we used the treasure, yes?" he asked.

Tekka stood and walked off to the side a little, then faced the wall. "There is far too much risk."

"In about six hours another city will sink into the ground, obliterated. Are you sure that this isn't worth the risk?" Andrew asked.

Tekka was silent, staring at the wall. He was there for so long that Andrew was beginning to fear that he had perhaps entered hibernation before he finally turned around. "We have to get Olivia and bring her here. I'll have to talk with her to know how we'll proceed from here."

Andrew nodded, but he suddenly started feeling worried. What if Olivia wasn't able to handle the treasure and subdue it with her will? What if her thoughts were amiss? He maintained a calm face and nodded at Tekka.

***

Akya had been running almost for a full day, which both impressed and worried Olivia. She was bound to get tired soon, and what would happen then? Did she mean to run all the way to the next hid-

178

ing place? She thought back to the former place they were at and it seemed that they brought death everywhere they went, even to the entire planet. Olivia had heard that earlier, another city had been wiped out and, somehow, that had numbed her. She felt absolutely nothing, but she knew that it would soon hit her and it would be devastating when it did.

In the distance, she saw a truck coming at them and her eyes widened. It seemed that Akya saw it too because she tensed up and her speed increased. Running, her speed was the equivalent of a crotch rocket motorcycle and the scenery blurred past them as she ran.

Olivia watched as the truck seemed to set course for where they were and her heart began to hammer. She wondered if they had guns, if they would start shooting, if they would kill Akya or her in the process. So many thoughts flew through her mind which caused her to let out a slight yelp when she heard gunshots rattle out from the truck. So, they did indeed have guns. She had thought that Akya would increase her speed even more but, at that moment, she grinded into a halt and turned sharply to watch the truck with what seemed to be confusion. The gunshots sounded again and she seemed to relax.

"What are you doing, Akya? Akya run!" Olivia yelled.

But Akya remained standing where she was and Olivia began to fear that they had used some kind of hypnotic technology that only worked on aliens to freeze her to that spot. She tried to get down, but Akya held her still. "Wait, Olivia. These're not our enemies."

The truck grinded to a halt when it got to where they were. The door opened and Henry came out. Akya had never been happier to see a face as repelling as his before. "Get in," he said simply.

Akya nodded then carefully carried Olivia in. Then she proceeded to hop in the back because it was too small in the truck for her. Olivia saw that the other woman, the very thin one that looked like some sort of reptile, who spoke for her back at the hideout, was the second person in the truck. She sat with her back erect and her face emotionless. Henry also seemed weary and haggard. His hair was a mess and his eyes seemed to hold a storm of emotion. It must not have been easy getting away from the small army that had been chasing after her.

"Thank you," Olivia said.

Henry nodded before starting the engine and driving off. The sun was hot and, the way the scenery blurred past them, combined with the weariness in Olivia's bones, caused her to fall asleep. When she woke, night had fallen and they were still driving. She wondered where they were going but didn't bother to ask. It wasn't like she would know the place anyway.

They stopped at what looked like a garage. But, when they entered, it looked so much bigger than it did before with a fridge and a truck and a few cars inside. A few chairs and holophones were also there.

"Where do you guys find these places? I mean, who would leave a place like this for you to just… you know?" Olivia asked and heard Akya chuckle from behind her.

"Elk made a lot of preparations after the first war and he has places like this almost everywhere and knowledge of their locations is shared amongst militia men. But some are very secret like this one and given only to highly trusted members so that if there was any sabotage or other infiltration, there would still be someplace safe to go," Akya said.

Olivia stood stunned at the sheer amount of planning that must have gone into creating a system like this. "I don't know your name," she said to the thin woman.

Eyes that seemed so sunken into her face that they appeared to stare at her from afar looked at her, then a very predatory smile crossed the woman's face. "Scythe," she replied.

Olivia nodded, deciding that Scythe was not a woman she exactly wanted to remain in a conversation with.

"We've heard no word from Tekka," Henry said in reply to something that Akya must have asked.

She nodded and went to one of the holophones and began trying to make contact while Henry sat in one of the chairs. His eyes seemed hollow as well, like a man who had to endure so much in a very short period. Olivia was tempted to ask if he was okay, but she couldn't get the words past her throat. She went instead to sit on one of the chairs, realizing that she was desperately hungry.

"Hungry?" Scythe asked, and walked to the fridge and peered inside. She brought out a can of milk and something that was inside a plastic container. "I'll have to microwave this," she said and walked away.

Shortly after, she came back and placed the plate before Olivia along with the can of milk.

"Enjoy," she said and went back to her chair, carrying another plate and a can of milk as well.

She hadn't asked Henry if he wanted anything, and Henry didn't even say a word. It was as if he'd receded into his own world and didn't care about anything that was happening outside it.

"Thank you," Olivia said quietly.

Scythe raised an eyebrow as she pushed her food around her plate, almost as if she was toying with it more than eating it. Olivia suspected that was the secret behind her almost scary thinness. "For what?" she asked.

Olivia shrugged, swallowing the food that she had been chewing. "You know. You both risked your lives and lost a lot of your friends to save me."

Henry turned his eyes that seemed dead to her, then nodded a little in acknowledgement before turning back to face the wall.

"Tekka just made contact," Akya said. "I've given him our coordinates and a hovercraft will be here in a few hours."

"How will he keep from being spotted by radar and… whatever tech stuff that everyone in the world is probably using to search for us at this moment?" Scythe asked.

"Tekka has his ways," Akya said simply. Olivia couldn't help but envy her unshakeable faith and belief. Still, the system that Elk had created had kept her safe so far. She couldn't deny that he had proven himself trustworthy so far.

"Good. I say we get some sleep then?" Scythe said.

Olivia looked down at Scythe's plate. She saw nothing and the can of milk was empty as well. At first, she thought that Scythe must have thrown it away, but she realized that she had eaten it and she wondered where the food went. There was no way the woman ate that fast.

"Sleeping would be wise," Akya said, and came to where Olivia was sitting. "When you're done eating, there is somewhere down that small corridor where you can wash up and, if you push this button here…" indicating a small green button by the side of the chair. "It will straighten into a makeshift bed. Get some sleep. You need it," she said and walked to one of the biggest chairs there and straightened it, laid down, and faced the wall.

Henry still sat motionless, staring at the wall, his gun on his lap.

Scythe looked at him with something of concern, then she turned to Olivia. "He'll be alright. He gets into these moods whenever he finishes a fight. You should wash up and sleep. I stink too. Should go now." She packed up her plates then went down the corridor. It didn't take long before she could hear the running water and a sigh of relief from Scythe.

"You are an astrobiologist?" Henry asked.

Olivia wasn't sure that it was her that he was asking because his face was still trained on the wall, almost as if he was seeking to bore a hole through it with his eyes. "Yeah. At least I was. I'm not sure what I am now," she said.

Henry nodded and smiled a little, but it was a sad, flat smile. "I was an engineer in the army. Was pretty good at it, you know?" He laughed a little.

"How did you meet Elk?" she asked suddenly.

Henry turned to look at her and his eyes were less vacant this time as he remembered. "I was removed from the army because of a back injury that left me in a stretcher. Thought I'd be crippled for life. Well, Elk found me and patched me up real good and, apart from when the air gets too cold and I feel the whistling in my bones, I'm as fit as a teenage athlete. I wanted back in the army, but he gave me this proposal instead and the salary he offered was well... impressive, and I was literally doing next to nothing. Well, until now that is." He chuckled a little. It was dry, as if it came from the ribs.

"I am sorry. For everyone back at the hideout," she said.

Henry nodded. "They... they knew the risk. And it was for the good of the planet so... it was worth it," he said.

Olivia looked back at her almost empty plate, suddenly not sure if it was worth it at all. She heard something like a struggle; a sharp grunt, and the bang of a gun. She jumped up and out from her chair immediately to see Akya lying on the ground, bluish liquid flowing from her side, while Henry stood with his gun raised. It took more than a few seconds before her mind accepted and understood what was happening.

"Henry! What are you doing?" Olivia yelled.

Henry looked down at her, his eyes as hurt as she had ever seen anyone's. Beside him was Scythe, gun raised. "Stay down, Akya. I don't want to have to kill you," Henry said, but his eyes were on Olivia.

"What is this?" Olivia asked.

He nodded sharply to Scythe, who walked up to Olivia and bound her hands behind her back. She looked at Henry, wondering what had happened. They had spoken that night. She thought that they were on their way to becoming friends. She felt hurt, betrayed. She looked at

Akya, whose face showed only anger and she was making a sound that couldn't be compared to anything Olivia had ever heard. It sounded so mournful and hurt that Olivia knew that she felt betrayed as well.

The Terrans knew little of actual betrayal, and it made sense that it hurt them more than anything except the death of their kind. Olivia moved sharply and heard another gunshot. Akya crashed to the ground again with a freshly bleeding wound from her leg. She writhed a little in pain and Henry stepped back out of her reach as Scythe pulled Olivia up. She was way stronger than Olivia expected someone of her size to be. Scythe pushed her, carefully but firmly, towards the door and turned to look at Akya, wanting desperately to help her.

"They heal way faster than us," Scythe said, and pushed her into the truck, then pulled the door shut.

Olivia knew that there was no escaping both Henry and Scythe, but she began to feel rage welling up within her. She kicked against the door, fighting with all her strength until she burst into tears. The door opened and Henry entered the driver's seat, started the engine, and drove off.

After she had cried for a good amount of time, Olivia felt extremely tired and her throat was dry. She thought that she was numb, but every time she looked at the backs of Henry and Scythe, she wanted nothing more than to cause them great pain. She thought about Akya lying back there all alone. True, Tekka would come for her soon enough, but Akya was her friend and it hurt her more than she expected.

"You okay back there?" Scythe asked.

Olivia hissed in anger, surprised that she could even make such a sound. "You betrayed us," she said.

Scythe nodded as if Olivia had said the most profound thing ever. "We did." Scythe fell silent for a while. It was almost as if the conversation had ended before she spoke again. "Henry has a brother, and his brother has a family. He has a wife, two daughters, and all that. He lived in a nice clean house with a nice lawn and drove a black sedan and was your average square. He never got mixed up in anything shady and was a very soft-spoken man. Fun fact; he's dead." Henry winced a little as if the mere mention of it hurt him. "He lived in the same city that was destroyed yesterday. He and thousands of other families. They all died because of you, because we refused to offer up one girl to him. He has promised that he wouldn't do anything to us and we still keep you? Thousands lose their lives and Tekka, Elk, and the Terrans do next to nothing about it. He would take you and get the heck away from here. And, I don't think I would mind what he does to other planets as long as mine is safe. I don't see those other planets running to our aid right now. There's no need for us to sacrifice our lives and our home for them." The words coming from her in a rush.

Olivia shook her head. "I changed reality once." Scythe turned to look at her as Olivia continued, "You wouldn't know because you live in the new one, the one I created. This isn't the first alien invasion that we've had and it was even by the same enemy. If you give me to him, you would be handing him the key to do what I did at will and to do worse. He could erase it from your memories that he ever said something like leaving. But, he wouldn't even need to. He could manipulate your will. He could control this planet if he wanted to and you would hand me to him because he promised that he wouldn't do that? He doesn't have any moral obligation to us. He…" she stopped and shook her head in desperation. "You have not met him. You don't know him. I have seen him and I know that our lives mean less to him than you can possibly imagine. We have defeated him before. Do you think that he would just let that slide? That he would just let us go free after that?" Olivia finally asked.

Scythe turned to look at Olivia. "You've faced him before?" she asked and Olivia nodded.

"She's just spitting dust. I say we gag her," Henry said, but Scythe looked curious and her brows furrowed.

"What if she's telling the truth? We cannot be sure…"

"Scythe, my brother is dead. He's dead and he died because of that girl, because of something that he knew nothing about. And, if I give her to that psychopathic alien, it will keep that from happening to anyone else. And that is exactly what I'm going to do," he said, his anger showing from the vein on his forehead and the tension in his muscles.

"We have no way of knowing, Henry. We have no way of knowing if what he said is the truth, if he would truly leave us alone once he gets her. But, we do know that she is of importance to him or else he wouldn't be turning the planet inside out looking for her. And that validates what she's saying," Scythe said.

"Then tell me, Olivia, since you were able to send him off last time, since you are powerful enough to change reality, as ridiculous as that sounds, why have you not done it? Why wait for the world's population to die off?" he asked.

"There's something they refer to it as the 'treasure' and it's what enabled me to do what I did. It's said to possess unimaginable power, and there are four of them. This one is currently with the Terrans. I have to be near it in order to use it, but it has been unusable because it's currently unstable, and any attempt might lead to… undesirable outcomes," Olivia said.

The truck went quiet before Henry's voice came out low and tight. "You honestly expect me to believe that you didn't think that off the top of your head just now?"

Olivia groaned in exasperation. "Why do you think he wants me? Think about it."

Henry seemed to think it over for a while. He braked so sharply that they were all thrown forward, Olivia's shoulder slamming into the back of the front seats. "So you mean to tell me that the thing that could save us all has been in their possession since, and they have refused to use it? Do you know how many lives have been lost? Do you know how…"

"The risk is far too great. This thing makes a nuclear bomb look like a candle flame. The variety of outcomes that could come out of this might result in a change in the very fundamental laws of the universe. It could cancel reality as you know it. Then, lives that would be lost would be the least of our worries," Olivia said.

Henry turned to look at Scythe, whose face was both shocked and determined. "Is there a chance that everything would work smoothly and we would all be free from this disaster? That you could change reality into one in which my brother actually lives?" he asked.

"I was told of an alien that used it and wiped off his entire race by mistake. He himself was transported to the edge of the universe and his mental health took a severe blow. Yes, there is a chance, but the odds don't look good," Olivia said.

Scythe looked at Henry who bowed his head over the steering wheel, his breath coming in gulps as he seemed on the verge of doing something Olivia imagined she wouldn't enjoy. "Fine. I say we go and steal that treasure or we find a way to get her close, so she can use it," he said.

Scythe nodded almost immediately. Olivia's mouth fell wide open in shock. A part of her had wanted this but, now, confronted directly with it, she didn't think it was the wisest course of action. But what was the alternative? More people would die. And, by the end of it, the planet would be a mere husk. She thought about her brother and wondered if the city he was in would be the next to be obliterated.

"I will try," Olivia said quietly.

Henry nodded. Scythe turned to look at her and something similar to concern flashed across her face before she looked away. Henry started the car. Olivia worried about Akya. She knew that the Terrans would do something drastic to find her. And now, she was actually going back to them, to steal from them. She didn't know if they would be successful but, basically, all she needed was to get close enough to the treasure. And, it would be easier if Henry and Scythe just handed her over, but she knew that they wouldn't, as they didn't trust her to carry out the task, she didn't even trust herself to carry out the task. She closed her eyes, suddenly feeling desperately tired. Tired of everything.

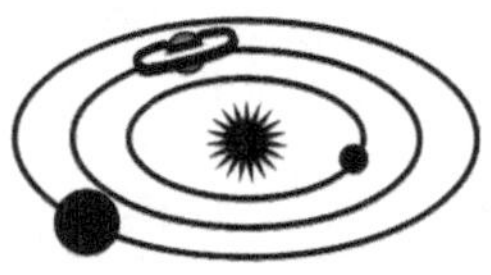

CHAPTER EIGHTEEN

"What do you mean she has been taken?" Andrew asked Akya, who seemed so beaten down and tired that it even seemed like torture for him to ask her questions.

Her wounds had healed up, but he could still see the blue stains around her and it made him soften his tone. Of course she would never have left Olivia to be taken if she could have done anything about it and, from the look of her, it seemed she had tried to do something about it.

"We were betrayed," she said slowly. Her tone in each word showed that she was hurt. Terrans didn't take betrayal or the idea of betrayal lightly. "Some members of the militia who were traveling with us suddenly had a change of heart and betrayed us. They took her and… we have to find her," she continued. Her breathing came in quick bursts because, although Terrans healed extremely fast, it took a lot of energy to do so and she seemed like she would pass out at any moment.

"I have people working on that at this very moment. She should be with us shortly," Tekka said.

"How can you be so sure?" Andrew asked, his anxiety peaking.

"They are two people traveling in a truck that will need to be recharged or refueled, depending on which kind it is. They'll need supplies, which means that they'll stop at one of the warehouses Elk created. And, once they do that…, we'll find them. I've also sent some very trusted militiamen within a one-hundred-mile radius of their last location in search of them. And, our own satellites are currently honing in on anyone resembling Olivia, Henry, or Scythe. It doesn't matter what it takes, we cannot let Olivia fall into Ork's hands," Tekka said.

Andrew felt a bit more comfortable, but then he thought how Olivia might feel when she returned. The trauma from knowing that hundreds of thousands have been killed because of you would be far too much for one person to bear. "Any progress with stabilizing the treasure?" he asked.

Tekka shook his head and said, "None. It seems that… we have to consider the more radical option, and find ways to make it even a little bit safer."

"What?" Akya asked from where she lay.

"We can't expect people to keep dying, Akya. The rebellion has even gotten into the militia and I can sense deep unrest among our own people. Soon it would be too much for them to bear."

She said nothing, but her displeasure was almost palpable. Andrew slowly walked away from their midst as they resumed their conversation in Terran.

He walked out into the new Terran home, which was cramped, but still ran efficiently, to Andrew's great admiration. Some of the Terrans buzzed in greeting and he waved at them. There was a sense of peace and comfort he felt among them that he felt nowhere else. It was because of the fact that he knew he could trust them. He walked slowly, his hands in his pockets, past the laboratories and workshops – as the Terrans never seemed to tire of research and innovation – past their storage facilities, and finally came to where he enjoyed being the most. It was the tendering facility.

When Terrans birthed their young, they groomed and took care of them in the beginning of their lives. It was the tenderers whose gender seemed to come with almost infinite patience and tolerance and a certain quietness that was almost hypnotic in its effect and it was just as well, because Terran infants were energetic, testy, and utterly destructive. Andrew sat among them and watched in the mandatory silence that was required of him. It was said that careless speech affected their minds at this stage, molding them in ways not suitable for some. Every sound was filtered and detailed in order to offer no effect on the newborns.

Andrew came here for the peace and the feeling of hope that he had when he saw that the Terrans had begun to reproduce. He hoped that they would get through this crisis and these little ones would grow along with others on the planet. Although the average Terran lifespan was four thousand years, they just stopped breeding when there was any threat of overpopulation.

Andrew thought about the kind of wonders that would come from the Terrans. The growth in culture and science and the mixture of ideas and behaviors to the point where it would be difficult to tell where the Terrans ended and the humans began. But, for that, a lot of sacrifices would have to be made and he wasn't sure that even that would be enough.

If Ork had his way, then the entire universe would be his empire and everything would descend into slavery with total loss of freewill. He felt both despair and hope at the same time. Andrew felt immense worry as he thought back to Olivia and his family. He wondered what he'd do if the next city that would be taken out would be the one his wife and daughter lived in.

He quickly shut the thought away from his mind, deciding that it wasn't what he wanted to think about in this peaceful place lit with soft yellow lights. He looked through the one-way glass wall that encircled the center where the Terran young were and let the peace wash over him.

***

Olivia felt Akya pull her into a hug. She had to remind herself of human attributes and also grit her teeth against the sheer force that Akya used to squeeze her. "I can't believe it. What happened? Who found you?" Akya asked. Olivia smiled wearily.

"Let the woman have a seat first," Tekka said.

He gently guided Olivia to a seat like she was of great status, or maybe just a toddler. Tekka handed her a glass of water and she took it in her hands, but did'ot drink. Her head couldn't think straight and her shoulders and back ached from being in an awkward position too long.

"You were lucky that our people found you first. What the heck were you doing hiking alone in the wastelands?" Akya asked.

Olivia gulped down her water and cracked her neck. "They let me go," she said quietly.

"What? They just let you go?" Akya asked.

Olivia nodded. "Yeah, they let me go. The only reason that they did it in the first place was because of Henry's mourning. The city that was taken yesterday was the one his brother lived in. He lost his brother and his entire family, so his grief drove him to do something crazy," she said.

Akya went very still for a long while and then said very softly, "I hope he's okay."

Olivia remembered that Akya's own family had been killed by Ork as well at some point. "I think I have to use the treasure now, Akya," Olivia said suddenly. Akya frowned down at her, then made a sound that Olivia had understood meant utter disapproval and displeasure. "People will die again in a few hours and the world will grow more frantic trying to catch me. Already, people have started torturing anyone that seemed to have any affiliation with me and, thankfully, that's a very few number of people. People are growing desperate, Akya. I'm growing desperate. And, I find it terribly exhausting and depressing to have to walk around with the deaths of so many on my shoulders. Please understand."

Akya frowned deeply. "It isn't me you have to convince," she said stiffly.

Olivia turned to Tekka, who had been standing perfectly still, listening unobtrusively. "Do you feel like you can do it? I warn you, the treasure will be very different from the first time you encountered it. It might be wilder, more furious. It will buckle against your will, but your will has to be stronger than it," he said. Olivia looked at his sculpture-like face and nodded slowly. "Come, then."

"I still think that this idea is foolish, reckless, and utterly irresponsible," Akya said in a very low voice just as Andrew was running in. He ran past her and pulled Olivia into a hug, wrapping his long arms around her. He pulled back then looked from Olivia's face to Tekka's, and to Akya's.

"Ah crap! You're doing it, aren't you?" Andrew asked. Olivia nodded. Andrew sighed deeply then nodded back. "I'm with you. Let's do this," he said and they walked away together.

Olivia felt her heart thump so hard, it almost seemed as if it was trying to break free of its imprisonment in her body. And, she suddenly wasn't so sure, but she gritted her teeth against the feeling and decided to move forward.

***

"Tell me something," Vol said to Elk, who had sagged against his restraints, his body utterly taxed from the ordeal and his mind finally reaching the limit of endurance. "Tell me how is it that you have the girl and the treasure, but you have refrained from using them. Why do you let yourselves continue to take so much punishment? I'm curious as to why you haven't used them?"

Elk shuddered and shivered; his mind seemingly incapable of any coherent thoughts as he fought desperately for a response. His mind and body had taken so much shock that he knew it would take a while before he responded, but he needed to respond, or else Vol would grow bored and go back to torturing him. And, he was certain that the next time would be the last.

"Let me guess. Could it be, perhaps, that the treasure is in a state of instability?" Vol asked.

Elk made himself look up at Vol who peered down at him from behind his black, flat mask. Elk wondered briefly how he knew, then remembered that he had been in possession of one before. "Yes," he finally managed to croak out.

Vol nodded and leaned back. "I supposed that was the case, and your caution is understandable. Use of it now by someone whose will isn't almost impervious would result in… less than desirable outcomes for all of us. And I feel that Ork's pressure will result in your girl using that treasure, and dooming this campaign anyway. I know how it can be made less dangerous, more stable," he said finally.

Elk's heart lit up with hope. He made himself look up at Vol who seemed to have briefly forgotten that Elk was in the room, seemingly deep in thought. After a while, he turned back and stared at Elk who said quietly, "She could use it in a specific way and reset all of this in a specific manner, and still have enough energy to help restore my people, though that would be the tricky part."

"Does this mean that my offer has been accepted?" Vol asked and walked past him once, and walked past him again, beginning to pace.

"There are too many variables. It's too great a risk for me, and for you," Elk said very slowly.

"But I have always enjoyed a good risk. I'll help you get rid of Ork, for whom I have no love. And, you'll restore my people, and… you'll discard the treasure. Send it away into deep space for all I care, such a power is an unfair advantage and must be gotten rid of," Vol said.

Elk thought about it and decided that once Ork was eliminated permanently, there would be no need for the treasure anymore. "I accept," he said slowly.

Vol nodded. "Now, I'm sure that you're a believer in the virtues of honor, but I have slain a number of your people in your presence and I have tortured you to extreme levels. If you double-cross me, make sure it's done in perfection. Otherwise, I will obliterate this planet, erasing it from the face of the universe forever."

Elk nodded his acceptance.

Vol patted him on the shoulder and continued, "By this time tomorrow, you should be with your people with instructions on how this shall be carried out if our reality is going to remain even vaguely similar to what we currently have."

Elk nodded again.

***

Tekka seemed, for the first time since Olivia had known him, agitated and afraid. He was on the verge of panic, and she could see that it was through supreme willpower that he kept himself in check. He was obviously sending a stream of commands to so many places at once she wondered how he kept his sanity. It must have been ridiculously difficult to be able to organize all these people in this moment of utter panic. The entire place shook again and loose sand rained down on them.

"We have to get to the treasure!" Andrew yelled over the noise. "Where is it?"

Tekka pointed distractedly in one direction. Olivia was mildly impressed that he even had the clarity of mind to point. The entire place shook again and it felt more like an earthquake as Olivia fell to the ground, but Andrew quickly helped her up.

They began to run in the direction that Tekka had pointed. As they ran, Andrew realized that he knew this place and there was nothing, no place of importance here except for the facilities for tenderers. They came to the wall that was the end of that section. Olivia felt a wave wash over her mind and, before she could put up her guard, it entered her very consciousness, which seemed to expand to accommodate and hurt her, but in a way nothing had ever hurt before. It could only be explained as a looseness of the mind, although it was obvious that wasn't the invader's intention. Whoever he was, was trying to be subtle and careful.

"Olivia, the young ones have been evacuated from the facility, go in." It was Tekka, but it wasn't merely his voice, it was an awareness of communication that had both emotion and personality. Like the

192

thought came from her own mind, but a part she had hitherto not been able to access.

She walked into the tenderer facility, followed by an obviously confused Andrew. She stood before the one-way glass wall and she heard the thought. 'Break it. Quickly now, there's no time.'

There was a tension, an urgency to the thought that frightened Olivia. There wouldn't be enough time for what she had to do. The inside of the wall was bigger than the outside and it was filled with things that were strange, but apparently were needed to raise well-adjusted Terrans.

'Go to the spot marked with a red dot at the center of the room.' Olivia heard the thought and, when she saw it, she was hit with a flurry of instructions and guides that meant nothing to her. It seemed the other consciousness was trying to pull away. She felt sharp pain and horror through the other consciousness, and the link was broken. Olivia was horrified.

"What had happened to Tekka?" she asked all of a sudden.

Andrew ran up to her and placed a hand on her shoulder. "Focus, Olivia, think," he said.

She stared at him wide-eyed, still feeling some of the pain from the other consciousness and some of the emptiness from the way it had been ripped apart from her. She knew that wherever Tekka was, he wasn't well. She fought with her mind, trying to order her thoughts, but she found them mostly useless because most of it was in the extremely complex Terran language. She needed a Terran to enter her mind and decipher it. She needed Akya.

The thought was still on her mind when she felt herself lifted up by powerful arms. "We have to get out… now!" she said, carrying Olivia on her shoulder.

"No! No! Read my mind, Akya. Please do it!" Olivia yelled and projected thoughts of what Tekka put into her consciousness. She felt another consciousness attach to hers, expanding her mind and she decided this wasn't something that she could get used to. Akya, however, didn't stop running. "What about Andrew? He's still in there! The treasure is still in there! Drop me this instant, Akya!" she yelled.

Akya stopped, then slowly dropped her and peered into her face with unreadable eyes. Then, she turned and ran back. Olivia's heart thundered in her chest and she felt her head get slightly dizzy, but she knew she couldn't remain here. She checked the thoughts that Tekka had left within her mind. Although most of it was in Terran, she picked up some bit of an awareness of how the tunnels were navigated. Most of it was in images and she decided to follow them. It was fairly difficult to navigate through, considering how complex Tekka's mind was and how their thoughts and even senses were heavily dependent on emotion and instinct.

Olivia ran through the tunnels and even when her breathing grew heavy, her throat burned, and her feet felt weighted with lead, she didn't stop. She finally came out of some place she didn't recognize and saw Akya's gigantic figure standing over someone smaller. She knew that it was Andrew, but something seemed wrong. She dashed towards them and saw that Andrew's head was bleeding. He seemed to have had a concussion.

"We have to help him. We have to take him somewhere and get medical help!" Olivia yelled again.

"No, we don't," Akya said quietly.

Olivia looked up with a tear-streaked face and she met an uncharacteristically cold face looking down at her. It seemed that with each misfortune her people suffered, Akya grew colder, angrier, more withdrawn, and now her face was indistinguishable from a sculpture. "We have to take you and get out of here," she said very slowly like she was talking to a child.

"Listen to me. He cannot die. Where is the treasure?" Olivia asked.

Akya tilted her head to the side, but not as a nod. She was angry and it was the kind of suppressed rage that seemed forced down on a string. If she were to let loose, Olivia knew that it wouldn't be a pleasant sight to see.

"Do you hear those explosions, Olivia? It won't take long before they find out you're not there and they come for us. Many of my people have been killed and they will be imprisoned, kept like animals, including the little ones. I want to save all of them, but I cannot. And that is a sacrifice that I have accepted, but you... you can't leave him? Do you know how much has been given to keep you safe? Do you think he'd want you kneeling there, wasting time? Wasting the sacrifices that my people have made for you? Do you understand that it isn't even the treasure that matters? What matters is you. You are the key to using it and your life is more important than you think, than you imagine. And you have to start acting that way!" she hissed.

Olivia froze. She'd never heard Akya speak with so much vehemence that it could be felt even through a relatively flat tone. "Where's the treasure?" Olivia asked slowly.

Akya stood perfectly still. Then, her shoulders began to shake and tremble. Olivia saw that it was with great willpower that she was able to force down what was undoubtedly a strong wave of emotion. "We can only hope they don't find it where it's hidden. I wasn't able to get it. And I don't think that I can now," she said.

Olivia thought about what she went through to convince Scythe and Henry that she would change things, that she would end this war. But the only thing that would enable that wasn't here. She sat there, suddenly feeling naked and tired, wanting nothing more than to sink into the sand and vanish, to become nothing.

Akya carried Andrew and moved a little distance, then hid him under the shade of a tree. She lifted Olivia very gently while she stared vacantly. She sped off. Olivia wondered where they were running to and what the point was. Would they run forever?

Ork had the resources to chase them to the ends of the universe, while they didn't even have the resources to get there. She buried her face in Akya's broad shoulders and began to weep and wail while the once Terran hideout was torn apart by the military, by the humans, by the very people they were protecting.

CHAPTER NINETEEN

Ork watched the softly shifting colors of the orb, which was basically blue, but it shifted in different shades. His eyes saw the colors and the underlying brilliance, the very complex swirls, and vortices of energy and he felt a bit of respect for whomever created this fake. He could see how it would fool the humans and some of his soldiers, but he could tell it was a fake. He took it and cast it to the ground, watching it explode in brilliant colors and waves of heat before dissipating into nothing.

"A fake," Andrew said quietly.

Ork could hear fear in the man's voice and, for a moment, he thought about taking his head clean off his shoulders, but a service had been given to him and it wouldn't be wise to reward it with punishment.

"An understandable error, my friend. It's something that your primitive eyes would be unable to capture," Ork said, and saw small relief in the man's eyes. For how fickle these people are, at least this one had acted with a bit more competence than the rest. "You have brought me all of the Terrans and I appreciate that. For seven days, no more cities will be destroyed but you'll have to find the girl before those seven days are up, or it will be two cities every day. Understood?" Ork asked. Andrew nodded repeatedly as Ork also asked, "Tell me, Andrew. What do you think about freewill?"

Ork saw Andrew open his mouth, then close his mouth and look at him. Andrew inhaled deeply then spoke with the measured slowness that showed that his mind was working overtime on what he was saying. "I think that freewill can sometimes be a burden."

Ork turned slowly to him, then nodded very subtly for him to continue. "When choices are many, we have difficulties picking. When there are many clothes in the wardrobe, one can spend hours deciding on what to wear. Whereas, a few clothes would make for an easier and faster decision. We have dilemmas over philosophical situations and, we wonder, after we have made the decision, if it was the right one. Then, very slowly, our minds and morals begin to waste away and we're unsure of anything. It would be freedom if our decisions were made for us and our consciousness and minds were shielded from decision making."

Ork watched him quietly and nodded again and said, "I'm in agreement. It's a burden and, many times, abused. It would be much better if it were merited and given only to the strong of heart and mind." Ork went silent for a while and waved at Andrew and said, "Leave me. Go find the girl and we'll discuss this matter further."

After Andrew left, Ork walked over to where Elk was held but, as the doors opened, he saw nothing. He stood perfectly still, looking at the manacles and chains that had bound Elk hovering in the air, inscribed in the lines and threads of Tuik writing.

'It seems that our partnership is at an end, Ork,' it said.

There was no explanation and he was surprised that a note was even left. Ork destroyed the message and rage bloomed within him again. 'Trust Elk to convert the most hardened criminal in the universe to his side.' He growled a little then stood up straight. With Vol loose and helping Elk, it would only be a matter of time before… he shook his head.

It didn't matter what Elk had on his side, Ork had the advantage. He had the population of this planet eating out of the palm of his hand, terrified to death of his whims. Ork inhaled deeply and gathered his thoughts, thinking what the Virzutian and Elk might do together.

***

Elk stood atop a small hill. His head ached and his body burned, but he remained perfectly silent. He heard some sound beside him and turned to see the Virzutian staring out as well to where the hideout had been.

"Everything… wasted," Elk said.

Vol bowed his head a little, although Elk was unsure if it was out of respect or remorse. "I understand how you feel," he said quietly.

Elk whipped around to face him and said, "You could never understand. You had no love for your own people. To you they were just a means to an end. There was no loyalty, no bond between you and them."

Vol shook his head in a very human way. "I spent a significant time of my life protecting them, serving them, and I employed all my faculties for the betterment of my people. True, there came a time when they revolted against me and I hated them, but nothing comes close to the feeling of seeing your own people destroyed. It's a common assumption that I went a little unhinged because of the treasure and… the curse. But, no, you see, I went unhinged because of that cold realization that it was the end. My kind would die out. There would be no face in this universe that's similar to mine. I was alone."

Elk peered at him, wishing he could see through the flat, smooth mask that was part of the armor he had chosen to hide himself in. "My people are still live. A good number of them still live. But, I must find the treasure first. Then, I must find Olivia and, with your expertise, we'ill see if we can't clean up this mess that we have made."

Vol hissed and his gasses fouled the air as he said, "I'm very interested in the manner with which you will infiltrate the area. It's crawling with Ork's ships, pods, machines, soldiers, and a few other things that would make our entrance infinitely difficult."

"I thought that you would be able to figure that out," Elk said.

Vol turned his mask to face him and asked, "Hmm?"

Elk shrugged. "You ruled the universe's mightiest empire and was named the destroyer of worlds. Surely getting into this place would be nothing more than killing a fly to you."

Vol made a sound of amusement. "The level of understatement in that entire speech shakes me. Elk, you will have that orb before they know they've lost it. But, I have a mind to give myself a bit of freedom. This life of rules and restraint is boring. Excuse me," he said and started walking down the hill.

Elk didn't follow. Not immediately, at least.

***

The clouds hung heavily outside. Olivia suspected that maybe the rainy season was about to start. She remembered sitting silently and listening to the rain beat on the roof when she was a little girl. She remembered the smell of sand and grass after the first rains, and she hoped that she would have the opportunity to experience those again.

It would be a comfort, a reminder that the world wasn't always on the verge of destruction and that hundreds of thousands of people didn't die every day at the hands of some alien, maniacal warlord.

Akya sat away from her, staring at nothing, looking like she was a piece of furniture rather than a living thing. Olivia wondered if maybe she should talk to her. Olivia wondered if she wanted to talk to her because she wanted to console her, or to console herself.

"You must be hungry," Olivia said flatly. Olivia wondered where the cheerful, enthusiastic Terran had gone but, then again, this war had changed all of them. She didn't even believe how she had changed from some obscure astrobiologist in once forgotten corner of the Earth to the most wanted human being on the planet.

"I'm not really hungry," Akya said, dust wafting slightly into her nose. It was already evening and they were sitting in what seemed to be an abandoned garage. Akya hadn't spoken until just that moment and she didn't look like she wanted to speak any further.

"You know that before you came, people used to think… some people, at least, used to think that aliens had come here before and had taught the human race, helped them build the pyramids, educated and ruled over them, and were worshiped as gods. That's what people thought about aliens," Olivia said and gave a hollow laugh that sounded so empty she winced a little.

"And what do you think?" Akya asked, turning to face her. Her eyes were still cold, but she seemed to be interested in what Olivia was saying.

"I mean," Olivia began, "the main reason why people didn't believe it before was that the very concept of alien life was one that was treated with skepticism and tentative thought. But now, knowing what I know, and seeing what I've seen, I think it's possible."

Akya nodded. "Consider the universe the entire human body and the Earth as one atom inside it. The edge of observability is maybe a cell or two wide, and they say that there is no alien life. Such small mindedness is almost amusing. The Krstychi were the ones that were in the habit of doing something similar to what you mentioned. Within them was a very strange and strong fondness for teaching and they were said to be the most enlightened race of their time. They traversed space in their machines that were faster than the speed of light and taught other life forms that were primitive, but possessed at least basic intelligence. They sowed the seeds of culture, science, and art even.

They stopped that when Virzutia attacked them. They held off as best they could, but they were more… scholars than warriors. And, they fell and were absorbed into the Virzutian empire. They're weakened now, but they continue to rebuild. Especially after the fall of Virzutia," she said.

Olivia was surprised that she said so much, and so fast, like she couldn't wait to let it out, like her words were a tool through which she let out her frustrations and pain without actually talking about them. "The Terrans will get their chance to rebuild as well," Olivia said softly.

Akya looked at her with something almost akin to loathing in her eyes. "We would have no home. I don't think that your people would want to harbor us after the trouble that alien life generally has given them. We would grow infinitely slowly and we'd have to rebuild the rudiments of our culture from scratch. All of our best engineers, doctors, scientists, even the makers of our art, and modifiers of our language are all gone."

Olivia pulled her legs into herself and tried to imagine how it would be if the human race had fallen to near extinction like the Terrans. All the books, learning, art, and culture would be lost. And, it seemed that was what Ork was on his way to do. "I could try and bring them all back," she said with uncertainty.

Akya watched her with wide eyes. Then, her eyes slowly lost their light again. Olivia began to fear that perhaps she had lost hope and will. The two people she had trusted completely were gone and she was cast adrift. Olivia couldn't imagine what she was feeling at that moment. "You can't do that. Bringing them all back, even with the treasure, is something that might be terribly tricky. Pulling time back in that way… would have consequences that we may not know of. It would be irresponsible and reckless. What if we affected something that would smash our reality into bits? Or, what if there was some modification or a slight mistake in your mind that would worsen matters? I find humans very fascinating and interesting and I see the great potential in them but, with something like this, I don't trust the willpower and strength that your kind has. They are quick to betray and harm. I would not trust them and, by them, I mean you, with something as important and delicate as this," she finished.

Olivia stared flatly for a while then nodded and looked away. There was nothing to argue. She knew how fickle humanity was. And, obviously, most other races evolved with better moral compasses than they did and with impressive mental strength. She had nothing to answer and, even if she did, it was an argument she had had many times within herself and had grown tired of.

"I'm sorry," Akya said and looked away.

Olivia nodded even though she still felt deeply insulted. She decided not to push it. She just went in search of something soft that she could sleep on.

***

"There's nothing here," Vol said to Elk as they stood at the spot that Tekka must have hidden the orb. Elk couldn't understand it. It should have been there. If it wasn't there, then did it mean that someone else got to it first? He knew that it wasn't Tekka. He had felt his death, and that was something he stashed away somewhere where he didn't have to deal with it. Then, Vol stated, "If someone else has taken the real thing then..."

"It must have been one of my people," Elk said. "There's no way that another person could have found out about where it hid. If Tekka shared the information with someone, then it would be one of my people."

"But they were all captured," Vol said with impatience and slight anger in his tone, but Elk ignored it. Elk knew his people, and he knew that some of them must have escaped. Olivia hadn't been caught, and at least one Terran must be with her.

"Akya," Elk said suddenly.

Vol nodded like he knew the name, then proved otherwise when he asked, "Who?"

"She must know where the treasure is. We must find her," Elk said, then stopped and looked around at the burning bodies and ships, the wrecked pods. He couldn't understand why Vol laid waste to the place and the ease with which he did it, using some kind of explosive that Elk couldn't even begin to understand as he had never seen anything like it.

"We have to find a ship with a good tracker. I can find her if…" Elk started to say. "That one," he said, pointing to a silvery-white ship in the distance.

Vol looked at him and he slowly nodded his mask. "I thought of the eventuality of us needing a pod, so I left one unspoiled. But if we leave, then we have to do it now, because it will not take long before we have Ork's soldiers crawling over every square inch of this place," he said evenly, then added, "They're very close."

Elk wondered how Vol could say it without any hints of concern. He strolled leisurely to the pod, broke into the access patterns somehow, and slipped in gracefully. Elk jogged after him, wondering just how vastly knowledgeable the Virzutians were.

***

Olivia was woken by a soft tap and, when she opened her eyes, she saw Akya staring down at her.

"Come with me," she said softly.

Olivia yawned, stretching herself. She had actually slept. There had been no nightmares and she hadn't even turned or tossed. Her breath would be horrible, judging from the taste in her mouth and her hair was a mess. Akya, however, looked perfect, everything in place as she walked slowly towards the entrance. Olivia climbed down, slipped her legs into her shoes and followed her, wondering where they were going and how extremely tired she was. Her head was throbbing and her feet could barely hold steady. She felt like she could fall asleep standing up, but she had to follow Akya now because she was the only one left who she still felt safe with.

The morning was soft and the gray hue that characterized it still covered everything. Along with it was the bone-chilling cold and breeze that made Olivia shudder. Waiting outside were people dressed like soldiers or something of that sort standing around. It seemed like Akya had managed to contact the militia and Olivia was silently thankful for how resourceful the Terran was.

There was utter silence inside the pod and even the noise of the engines didn't even get to them. It felt more like Elk's hovercraft, and she knew this to be a highly sophisticated pod. Sleep was around her eyes and her mouth opened in a very wide yawn. This pod was far too sophisticated to equip militia with and the weapons they carried were also very sophisticated. And, even though they carried no flags or emblems, she immediately realized that they were soldiers. She wondered if Elk had contacts that were willing to help them in the army and decided that he didn't, otherwise there would be no need to create the militia. Her eyes met Akya's and Akya looked away.

Olivia's kind didn't think it was possible because of the Terrans' orientation towards betrayal, and her mind still fought against the possibility, but as Akya avoided her gaze. Olivia realized, in that moment, that she had been betrayed.

"Why?" she asked Akya. She was, in truth, too weary to fight. And, it would have been futile anyway. There was nothing she could do. She couldn't jump from the air or fight at least eight fully-armed soldiers. She didn't even feel that much anger. She just felt a sense of resignation, utter weariness, and exhaustion. And, more than she could remember, she desperately wanted to sleep. "Why?" she asked again. Her curiosity had grown. There would have to be a powerful motivator to push Akya to go against the basic foundation of Terran society.

"You cannot use the treasure, Olivia. You don't have the will or strength to do so. I'm handing you over to someone who can, in exchange for the restoration of my people and, possibly, my family," Akya said.

Olivia nodded and leaned back with her head on the wall and closed her eyes, sighing heavily. "I'm sorry," she said. Akya turned away. "I'm sorry that I'm not strong enough and that my species are scum. I'm sorry that we evolved to be so thoroughly weak. And I'm sorry that I cannot help you save your superior species. I thank you for helping me all this while, for protecting and guarding me under Elk and Tekka's orders, both of whom you've now betrayed." She said this quietly and let sleep slowly take her. There was nothing else she could do at this point.

It was a while before Olivia woke up. She could see the silver ship and it was beautiful when the sun struck it. They must have been flying for hours because the sun was full and the ship was radiating brilliance. She could see some kind of massive structure going up. She could see pods and ships flying around in a manner that seemed disorganized, but was actually very organized and effective.

It was something beautiful, indeed, and it was such an irony to her that Earth's greatest crisis came from such a place. A few of the ships came close to them and surrounded them as they moved in to land. And, she saw that waiting for them were aliens who were undoubtedly from the same race as Ork.

For the first time, Olivia began to feel true fear. She remembered how his flat, lifeless eyes had stared at her, how her legs had burned under his grip. And the mindless creatures they had made out of people. She stepped out soon as they landed and, to her surprise, they didn't bind her hands or anything of the sort. They just came to stand beside her as they walked into the ship.

It didn't feel different as she walked in and she assumed that it had been adjusted to suit her. Akya walked beside her. When she looked at the Terran, she wasn't sure what to do. She wasn't even able to hate her. She just felt sorry for everything and wished she hadn't been caught up in this.

They continued walking for such a long time that she began to wonder how big this ship actually was. They came to a long corridor that led to a large door that had strange decorations similar to the carvings that she had seen in the Terran bunkers. But these were much more detailed, and made of a kind of substance that shifted and changed. She didn't merely see that it was beautiful with her eyes, she felt its beauty somewhere within her and she realized then what Akya had been saying about its emotional quality. The door opened as they approached and they walked in.

The room was bigger than anything Olivia had ever seen. So big that she couldn't even see where it ended. There was a slight curve as it tapered off, like the room was circular. Standing within the room was the inhumanly large, unsightly creature. His armor was adorned with normal carvings and some of the kind that she had seen on the door.

He turned to face her, his flat, black eyes seeming to reach deep into her soul. Suddenly, she felt his consciousness shove hers down and peer into every nook and cranny of it, searching for what she didn't know. It was painful, but in that strange, inexplicable way. But, it was worse because Ork was neither gentle nor subtle, it was as if he was trying to drive her insane with how he went through her mind, then quickly receded.

"You've had quite the journey," Ork said from deep within her consciousness. Olivia shuddered involuntarily. "But, like every other journey, it must come to an end. For a human, you have shown strength and determination, and I applaud you for that. But now, it's over and you will yield to me. And, after you have outlived your use… I'll decide on what to do at that time."

"Ork," Akya called out physically. Ork pulled away from Olivia's mind and turned to face the Terran.

"Ah, Akya. Just like your parents. It seems that the tendency for betrayal runs strongly within you."

Akya ignored the insult and took a few paces forward. "I brought her to you. Not the humans, not your own soldiers, but me. And, I'll be able to bring you the treasure if you agree to an offer that I will now make you."

Ork's soldiers started to move towards her, but stopped, like he had sent a telepathic order to them. Ork stepped down from where he stood and came to stand before Akya. He was a full foot taller than her, but it didn't seem capable of intimidating her.

"You're in no place to make demands, little one."

"From where I'm standing, it seems I am. Your soldiers are obviously unable to find the treasure. And, up until this moment, they couldn't find the girl. I found the girl and I'm telling you that I can get you the treasure that would otherwise prove an insurmountable challenge for you and your soldiers."

"I could take it from your mind. You're no warrior. It would be simple to take the location directly from your mind."

Akya stepped forward and looked up so their eyes met. Olivia had never seen her this way before and she couldn't help but feel slightly impressed even though she was the one being betrayed. She couldn't even care much about that anymore. It was a relief that at least people would stop dying on her behalf.

"You think I would be that foolish to leave the thoughts in my mind? To expose myself to its whereabouts so that you can take it from me? I'm not stupid. You will have to agree to what I propose if you want the treasure," she said.

Ork watched her silently for a while, then nodded slowly to himself. "What then is this offer you speak of?" he asked and stepped away from her, back to where he stood before.

"When you have figured out the way to use the orb, I need my people to be reinstated. I need them to have a home and a base. I need my family back as well," she replied.

Ork tightened his fist. "Your family? The rest is possible but that…"

"Anything is possible with the treasure. I have seen it work before. If time can be pushed back, that means my family can be revived," Akya said.

Ork watched her and she matched his gaze for such a long while that Olivia was beginning to think that they might challenge themselves to a duel. "A hard bargain, Akya, just like your father," he said slowly.

Akya's face didn't even shift. But weeks spent being close to Olivia had made her sensitive and she knew she was tense.

"Fine. I'll give you what you wish," he said.

"Do I have your word on it?" she asked.

He nodded slowly and said, "An oath as solemn as the one I gave your father."

Akya made a hissing and buzzing sound that was terribly loud. "Stop mentioning my father," she spat at Ork. He remained silent. She turned and began to leave. She turned and looked at Olivia, who was suddenly afraid, but decided to mask it under a blank exterior. "I am sorry," Akya said simply and left.

Her absence left Olivia naked. She was entirely in Ork's power again, like she was before. Olivia wanted to run after Akya, she wanted to plead not to be left behind. She wanted to do so many things, but she just stood there. She turned to face Ork, who had turned to look at her.

"I have a feeling we will come to know each other rather well, Olivia," he said, his voice low.

***

Elk's hands had begun to shake, his sight was beginning to go and his strength was failing him. He coughed up blue liquid and knew that Vol noticed but pretended he didn't. The Virzutian had gone strangely silent and it bothered Elk at how he could be there yet remain so still. It was almost as if he wasn't breathing.

"You might die soon. I know your kind heals well, but the damage done to you was more than physical," Vol said.

"I hate you," Elk said softly.

Vol nodded as if that was the most reasonable thing ever said. "As you should. But, I need you alive if our deal is going to happen. You don't seem to know the whereabouts of this girl and, I must say, that's not very reassuring."

The threat was veiled, but Elk could sense it nonetheless. "Are you going to return to Ork? He would never accept you. He would never work with you again," Elk said, feeling his mind and body growing increasingly weaker. He needed medical help, Terran medical help.

"That's where you are wrong, my Terran friend. It turns out that our friend, Ork, had no clue as to how the treasure works, which is why he enlisted my help in the first place. So you see, I'm indispensable to him. He might tinker with it, and try to figure it out, but let's be realistic here; who wants to take the risk of being erased from existence? He will accept me, albeit with more resignation. And, no one knows the machine better than he that attends to it. So, I will have my way no matter the situation. You, however, seem to be rapidly losing grip of the situation," Vol said amiably.

"When we find Akya, we'll find the treasure and Olivia. And you will have your deal," Elk said.

Vol fiddled with the controls and listened before he nodded and turned to stare at Elk through his flat mask. "You have lost all control of this situation," he said softly. Elk's eyes narrowed. He had learned to turn off his buzzing so it would be harder to interpret his emotions. "It would seem that your girl has been delivered to Ork's hands by a Terran. I thought that no Terrans were traitors. You must feel properly disappointed and betrayed now, yes?" Vol asked, and made a Virzutian sound of amusement that almost annoyed Elk.

But Elk just sat there, not knowing how to feel. He had taken many things into account, but he had always refused to distrust any one of his people. It must have been Akya. Her father had been a traitor; as was her entire family. He had trusted her, forgiven her, and helped her rebuild her reputation among the rest of the Terrans. But now, when it mattered most, she had utterly betrayed him. He closed his eyes and exhaled, clenching his fists.

"He doesn't have the treasure though, as it seems that Ork is not with it. It also seems that you don't have the resources to uphold your end of the bargain, Elk," Vol said quietly.

Elk knew that if Vol decided that he was useless, there was nothing that he could do. He couldn't fight. He couldn't do anything and he didn't even want to. He wondered what he was even fighting for and if it was even worth it. No one would know who he was anyway; no one would care. One of the very people he was fighting for had chosen to betray him. He found it all strangely amusing that he had taken such severe damage to his health all to keep the whereabouts of the treasure and Olivia away from Ork, only for them to be handed over to him by one of his own.

"It would seem so," Elk answered Vol after an extended period of time. He sank into his chair and exhaled heavily. He didn't care much what Vol did because everything he fought for had shattered. Tekka was dead and his people were disbanded captives. One of his own had betrayed him and it was only a matter of time before the treasure fell into enemy hands.

"We'll have to go fetch Olivia then," Vol said.

Elk opened his eyes to stare at him. "What do you mean?" he asked.

Vol looked back at him and Elk wished again that he could read his eyes, or attempt to read them at least. From what he heard, Virzutians weren't exactly pleasing to look upon.

"We have to take her from Ork. He had plans. Plans that are extreme, but it would seem that he actually took my betrayal into account, although I wouldn't call what I did betrayal. There was no deal in the first place. There were just lies. And with you, at least, there was a semblance of truth and trust, so I have decided that I will help you in getting this girl. And we shall find the treasure and end this," Vol said.

Elk watched him for a while, wondering why he remained. But then, he decided that he wouldn't make the Virzutian change his mind by asking too many questions. "Thank you," he said.

Vol made a sound that was clearly Virzutian from its ugliness and practicality. "The humans have tainted you so well. You've even adopted their cultures of gratitude," Vol said.

Elk shrugged, noting that the expression itself was human, and that, in a very little way, both comforted and amused him.

CHAPTER TWENTY

"Please. A glass of water will do," Andrew said as he sat in what appeared to be a family's garage, staring at a boy around twelve years old. His head felt like it was being pounded on by hammers on every side and his body kept on wanting to yield to the peaceful state of unconsciousness, but he knew that he couldn't afford that. He had done it once and Olivia was no longer with him.

He wondered where she and Akya went, but he also knew that someone must have carried him away from the madness that was happening. If so, then why did they leave him without any help, resources, or protection whatsoever? But, he understood the practicality of it. Olivia was more important and Akya's priority would be protecting her, and she herself didn't seem in top shape earlier. He groaned a little as the pain worsened and the lights before him seemed to swivel and dance, even the boy's shape had become distorted.

Andrew had woken up and walked a distance that he couldn't estimate and stopped at this open garage. His throat was parched and he wanted to rest. The pain in his body made groans and hisses occasionally slip out his mouth, substitutes for the screams his body so badly wanted to let out.

"Please. Just water," Andrew said to the boy, who had been staring at him suspiciously for the better part of a quarter hour.

The boy nodded and dashed out. Even speaking seemed to be taxing Andrew and he could only take deep breaths and fight against unconsciousness as he sat on the dirty floor. After a while, the boy walked back in with an elderly man with very blue eyes. He had a limp but looked strong enough to lift a man over his head. He gave Andrew a measured gaze as he gulped down the water that was given to him.

"You're in pretty bad shape. What happened to you?" the man asked.

Andrew's head was able to miraculously put together a passable story that involved him living close to where the aliens attacked and every other human either died or escaped; with him being one of the escaped ones. The man came closer to him and squatted before him, then reached out to inspect the wound on his forehead. After a while, he clicked his tongue and stood back up again.

"You'll need that stitched up good, and you'll have to sleep after. My wife's good with injuries. Can you walk? Come, I'll help you," he said.

Andrew nodded then proceeded to stand, but found that the headache grew more terrible. It was like his head was about to burst. He felt strong hands hold and slowly raise him up and he leaned on the man as he was slowly taken from the garage into the house. He would survive this. As long as he remained safe, then he would survive this.

***

Andrew stared at the instructions on the screen of his holophone and he felt a mixture of excitement and fear. This was the first direct order he was given by Ork. While it wouldn't be easy to do what had been asked, it was still an opportunity, and one he wasn't going to miss. The council had favored his opinions after he had bought them time without more deaths and they'd nearly turned the Earth inside out searching for Olivia. But now, Ork had told him that the girl had been found and he needed something else; the treasure. For one, he didn't even know where to begin looking and he thought that he might be able to interrogate some of the militia men that had been captured, but he suspected that they knew nothing either.

Andrew had riots and protests to handle, small wars were being held among people and almost all of the Commonwealths seemed to be on the verge of splitting apart again. He closed his eyes and forced some semblance of calm upon himself, but he knew that this was too much. The alien had spoken of no treasure before and it seemed like an excuse for him to go back on his word and stay, even though he swore that he would leave once the girl was given. A flicker of resentment started to grow in Andrew's chest, but there was nothing he could do about it. He sat in his office, his heart angry and his body tired, wondering where the end to this all was.

***

Elk stood before a group of roughly one hundred people. Each of them stared back at him with zealous eyes and he could almost feel their motivation from where he stood. He learned that some of the militia had betrayed him and, while that had hurt him, it had been overshadowed greatly by Akya's betrayal, so it wasn't more than he could cope with. These ones were some of the loyal ones remaining, made up of pilots, engineers, soldiers, and former criminals that he had helped personally and felt that they owed him a personal debt. And, they all had hatred for Ork.

Elk wanted to speak, but his head hurt so much from over-exertion that he wasn't sure whether words would form or if everything would just come out in a jumble of screams and groans and other sounds exclusive to his kind. He had arrived the day before and it only took a day for those one hundred to flock in. He hoped that the word of his arrival would bring more, but he wasn't entirely optimistic. Elk wondered why it took him such a long time to begin to take into account the fickle nature of creation everywhere. He thought about Akya again, but pushed that out of his mind for now; realizing that there was so much he was refusing to deal with and hoping that he still would have the ability to deal with them when the time came.

"Thank you all for coming," Elk said softly, mildly grateful that the words were able to come instead of groans of pain. "I know that you all have been wondering about my disappearance over the past weeks and I apologize for that, but I was taken by the enemy, captured, and tortured. Doesn't seem like he got much from it though. But, I realized something while I was there, something that I have failed to realize since I've been among humans. I'll be honest and say that, whenever I thought of humanity, it was with a little bit of condescension. I always thought that you weren't fast enough, not smart or willful enough to do what needed to be done. I felt that you would destroy yourselves even before any alien civilization came to destroy you,"

Elk noticed the shifting of feet and murmurs. He let that go on for a while as he gathered his strength and continued, "But, I've found that opinion to be terribly wrong. My eyes were opened to that after I was betrayed by my own. I saw that there was disloyalty in everyone, in every race, in every creature. But, there is also loyalty and fierce courage. Which you have shown when the militia stood and fought against the enemy and has given them enough pain that they now fear you. You have fought even when there was no hope of winning and, as a soldier myself, I know that the amount of courage it takes to do that is beyond anything else that requires courage." He then drew uncomfortable breaths that were quickly turning ragged.

Elk continued further, "And, I've come to realize how fearsome this species can be when united, how strong and loyal they can be. And, I've come to trust them with all my might. This fight that we fight… it isn't like any other that we have fought. It isn't to expand our territories, or because of differences amongst our own kind. It's a war of our survival against an enemy that would have us all removed from the face of the Earth. Our families and homes gone, obliterated with no one to remember or even whisper our names." He wiped the blood from his mouth with the back of his hand as he said this. He could feel the fire and energy from the people standing before him. Some were even cheering and pumping their fists in the air, while some showed anger and determination on their faces.

Elk added, "But this enemy doesn't know us. He doesn't know our capabilities and how strong we are; how strong you are. And, we're going to show it to him. We're going to show him that our homes won't be taken easily and this planet is ours. And, by the time that we're done with him, his men will get back into that silvery ship of theirs and fly back into whatever dark corner of space they came from with their tails between their legs while his head is mounted for all the world and beyond to see as a reminder that no one, no one can take our home from us."

The room burst into roars, cheers, and applause with men and women pumping their fists and guns in the air. Elk knew that, at this moment, they were in this together, and they would charge the entire enemy forces if needed. They were still cheering when he turned away and started to walk back, his head feeling so light he thought that he would fall down and die where he stood.

"Beautiful speech, General," Vol said and made that ugly sound of amusement that Elk was fond of. "And a very riling speech indeed. But, I wonder if this would be enough to even cause Ork a raise of one of his non-existent eyebrows. We need more men, firepower, planes, ships, and pods. We need everything we can get."

Elk nodded. The speech had been aired on militia networks and he was sure that they would get more manpower and resources, but even that wouldn't be enough. There was someone he needed to meet, but he wasn't entirely enthusiastic about how that meeting would go. He just wanted to rest and sleep. His body only had so much energy in it. As he was trying to heal himself, he was barely able to keep on his feet, and that was only because he was a warrior and was both genetically and physically modified for these things. But even he was reaching his limits.

"There's something else you should know, Elk," Vol said, his tone suddenly growing solemn.

"What is it?" Elk asked, knowing that, whatever it was, it wasn't something that would be to his advantage or that would give him any joy to hear.

"Ork started building something. He doesn't intend to leave this planet either way. He wants to turn it into some kind of military base that replicates the conditions that were on your former planet. He wants to rebuild Tuik here."

Elk had a brief moment of clarity as he turned sharply to look at Vol, who was staring off at the still-cheering soldiers. "What do you mean?" he asked.

Vol turned to face him and said quietly, "Exactly what you heard. No species enjoys solitude. I know that from experience. The entire reason that we formed as a species was because of coexistence. None of us were meant to be alone. And, Ork must see how rapidly he's approaching extinction because there isn't anyone among the Tuik left with him that can take female form. He hopes to use the 'treasure' to make some of them capable of that and turn this planet into some utopia. I'm telling you now that the humans don't seem to have much of a role to play in this world he hopes to create. So, if you want to do something, you must do it fast."

Elk turned his head forward very slowly and nodded, thinking what that meant. The part of his planet where Tuik lived was very similar to where the Terrans had resided. He thought that he'd like to see that again, but it was what Ork wanted, and Ork was a demon, a thing that shouldn't be allowed. He nodded to himself and wanted to move forward, but he wasn't sure if his legs would allow it.

"General?" Elk heard a voice call and he turned to see a lean woman that seemed like she had never eaten a good meal in her life. Her bones were painfully visible and her eyes were so deep inside her face that she looked like she was observing him from afar. But, there was something almost remorseful in her manner that made Elk listen, discarding his opinions on her appearance. "I knew Olivia personally and took part in her protection before, but… I also took her captive when I thought that this would never end. I understood that was a mistake and I returned her to the Terrans. But, I heard that the Terrans had been attacked and.... well, I just wanted to know if Olivia is still in Terran possession?"

Elk nodded and considered lying for a while, but he'd rather be honest with the people he led. "No. She has been taken by Ork and she is currently in the hands of the enemy. But, she and the treasure are needed to make whatever he wants to happen a reality and he doesn't have the treasure. Plans are underway to bring Olivia back. I could do nothing about what happened, and I apologize. But I'm back now, and we'll fight back."

She nodded, her face solemn. Then she looked at Elk again with narrowed eyes and commented, "I'm sorry sir, but you seem to be in bad shape. You need a doctor."

Elk nodded slowly, taking account of her perception. He might need it for later. He marveled at how he was able to think of tactics and individual strengths at a moment when he could feel his life draining from him.

"I trained as a doctor, sir. And, I took some courses on Terran biology by some lucky coincidence. I don't know much about your kind, but I can apply first-aid at least," she said.

Elk looked at her with fresh eyes and nodded gratefully. A man stepped up beside her and he looked powerfully built for a human. He silently walked up to Elk, who understood what he was offering. Elk remembered this one and he remembered recruiting him. He leaned on the man who bore his weight silently as they walked to a place where he would be attended to. He thought about the meeting he would soon have and Ork's plan, and what that meant for everyone.

***

Willows loved flowers, she always did. She thought that perhaps that was the only part of her that was sentimental in any form, but it wasn't. She liked to pretend that she cared little, or didn't care at all. But she did, more than most and, when she hurt, she hurt deeply. Seeing Elk abandon them in the midst of the battle had been unbelievable at first. Now, it was painful. It hurt her more than she could say. The one she trusted not to betray, that she trusted as an ally, left her in such a delicate position.

She hissed to herself and ran her fingers over the hibiscus flowers, which would soon die either way because she hadn't found herself willing to water them because she felt like everything was falling apart. The world was ending and its fate was almost sealed. It was either that humanity would be wiped out or live in perpetual servitude.

"A message for you," a voice called from the door.

Willows nodded. He walked up to her and handed her a note. She frowned at it and asked, "Who gave you this?"

"A boy, Madame. Said that it had information that you were after. I had it checked and it's perfectly safe," he said. She nodded and opened the note and, on it, in clean, precise handwriting were the words:

"The sands shift and the trees bend and the world is an ever-changing blossom of pain and beauty."

Willows narrowed her eyes at it for a while and almost decided that she didn't understand, and it didn't matter, wondering who would send her poetry, when it hit her. She nodded at the soldier who saluted sharply and left. She walked out and when her guards started to follow her, she waved them off. She walked past men working at the new ships that Andrew had issued them, given to him by Ork. Most of them saluted and she felt mild pain at their young, hopeful faces. Some of the older faces were weary and tired and seemed to understand the hopelessness of the situation. Thinking about it angered her more and her steps quickened. She swore to herself that when she saw Elk again, she would smash his face in.

Willows came to the tree that was almost dead. It was shriveled up and bent. It reminded her of an old lady, one who had seen all there is to see of the world and, now, sat viewing the landscape with weary eyes. She walked to it and looked around, seeing nothing. Then, she saw a figure in a black cloak hobbling to where she was. From its height, she knew that it was an alien, but of what race she couldn't tell. It was when he had gotten close enough that she realized that it was Elk, but he wasn't standing strong and proudly like he always did. He was bent and when he pulled off his hood, his eyes were as weary as she had ever seen them, with a pained expression on his face. It seemed that he had been through a lot, and thoughts of smashing his face in died in her mind.

"Marshal Willows. Pleasure meeting you again," Elk said. His voice had a different quality to it. Where it had been dry and detached before, it was soft and more emotive now, which lent it a different kind of strength and inspired a bit of trust.

"Elk," she said simply, anger clearly on her face.

He nodded at her and slowly lowered himself at the foot of the tree. "This world is beautiful," he said quietly.

Willows wanted to tell him to get to the point, but she found that she missed his lazy, poetic speeches. And, his condition inspired no anger from her. He seemed to be in so much pain already.

"It's almost as beautiful as my home planet. I had a house on a hill and I could see the entire town from there. The sun would shine directly into my room. I would watch the pods. Their buzz was like music to me, trying to tell which pilot was which from the string of their thought commands," Elk said.

There was such strong nostalgia in his voice that Willows' curiosity piqued. "You said before that you couldn't show emotions in the way that we do, but I hear how strongly you miss your home from your voice," she said.

Elk nodded. "That seems to be a habit I've picked up. And, I find myself picking up more and more of them. Your ways have mixed into mine and I find myself frowning at nonsense these days. Isn't that interesting?" He chuckled a little.

"You're a bad one, Elk," she said with sudden intensity.

He nodded slowly as if he had expected the outburst. Her anger increased even more at this reaction.

"You are a bad one and a coward," she said firmly.

He winced a little. She was glad that that had gotten to him. If there was one thing that she knew a soldier didn't like to be called, it was a coward.

"I understand why you would see me in such a light Marshal Willows and, I suppose I deserve it, after a fashion." he said slowly and began to draw patterns in the sand, lazy doodlings that were so geometrically precise.

"You left during a battle. You were the best pilot there and you just left, leaving all those men to their fate – leaving them to die. You don't care about our kind, about my kind. And, the only reason you fought for us is selfishness and self-preservation. And, soldiers, warriors, don't fight in that manner!" she shouted.

He took it all in silence although she could see that her words had an effect on him. It was a bit comforting to know that her words touched him and some of her anger went away.

Elk rubbed his face slowly, then shook his head like he was terribly weary. "I didn't leave the battle because I was scared or because I feared for my death, but because there were other fights that required my attention with far greater stakes than the one I was involved in at that time. Ork was, and is, looking for something that is beyond the subjugation of this planet. He wants Olivia because she can help him access a device that puts god-like abilities within the palm of the wielder's hands. With it, he would be able to manipulate all the physical laws of nature. Time, space, reality, you name it. Olivia has used it before to modify reality. In the other reality, you and I both died, but she brought us back. Do you understand?" he asked.

Willows frowned, wondering if there was truth in what he was saying and deciding that there must be some truth at least from the sincerity on his face. "Such a device really exists?"

Elk nodded, leaning on the tree with his eyes to the horizon. "There are four of them. And, many have searched for them, but imagine looking for four tiny things in the infinite universe. This one would grant Ork powers like no one has ever imagined and it has been in my possession for a long time. That's what he's looking for. And, it can't work without the girl. Apparently, it attaches to the person that used it first. That's why he wants her."

Willows' heart sank into her stomach. Ork already had the girl and she was now tasked with finding the treasure. She had known that the object would probably grant Ork some benefit, but she didn't know that it would be as much as this.

"My home was destroyed. I watched the lava eat up my house on the hill and I watched all the ships and pods crash to the ground. I watched my people burn and die, and watched from afar as my planet imploded; its beauty stripped and forgotten. One creature, one being, was responsible for this. He is the one you know as Ork. He took that away and he is currently building something to take yours away," Elk said.

Willow stood for a while, then sat down on the sand beside him. "So, this is how it feels?" she asked.

"How what feels?"

"I've devoted my life to defending first my Commonwealth, then defending this planet. Maintaining peace and standing between us and whatever would harm us. And now, I see that all I fought for will be lost…. All this beauty stripped away. And, I can only sit in the sand because I'm utterly powerless and can do nothing about it. It feels…."

"You can still do something about it," Elk said and a small smile spread across his face, but it was not from amusement. It was something else. Willows turned to peer at him as he continued, "I fought him down to the last available ship, down to the last drop of Terran blood. I fought against him for so long, and made his destruction of my home hell, even for him. You can do that here. And the thing is, you can even win."

"I'm listening," she said quietly.

Elk shrugged and rubbed his hand over his face again. "I've been gathering a private army since my arrival here, training and equipping them. You now know them as the militia. Well, most of them have suffered loss and oppression during this time, but they're still five thousand strong and they're flocking down to the base. There are pilots and engineers trained by my own people, and we have ships. But, it's not enough. We're not enough, Willows. We need the army, and you are the army. Their loyalty to you is far more than the loyalty they owe their respective Commonwealths. You have been in the flames with them and there is no greater loyalty than to one that has gone through suffering with you. Speak to them and they will follow you. They will fight with you." He sighed heavily, like his speech was taking from his strength.

"So you own the militia? I should have known, you rascal," she said.

Elk chuckled. "I don't own them. I employ them. They are loyal to me and to their planet. Who are you loyal to, Willows? Will you continue to let yourself be yanked around by the petty politics of men and women who enjoy nothing more than long, fruitless discussions? Or, would you act as a soldier should, and defend your home?" he asked. "This planet is truly beautiful and I'd hate to see it fall. I'd like to swim in the ocean and traverse the desert, climb Everest, and sail a ship across the Atlantic perhaps. I'd love to do all that someday. I wonder why I never did before," he added quietly.

Willows chuckled. "My father said that we don't appreciate life any more than we do at the time death knocks at the door," she said.

"A wise man indeed," Elk said.

Willows chuckled then nodded. "Yeah he was."

"Willows?" Elk said, his face turning solemn. She raised an eyebrow at him, and he matched her gaze. "I'm truly sorry for leaving," he said.

Willows shook her head and looked away. "Forgiven. You've made one heck of an explanation," she said and he nodded. She thought about her flowers and thought that maybe she would water them when she returned.

CHAPTER TWENTY-ONE

"Do you know what this is?" Ork asked, gesturing to what seemed to be a huge bed covered with some kind of glass with blue lights lining the sides and a low hum came from it. Olivia knew that, whatever it was, she wouldn't enjoy finding out. She just stood there and looked at it, perfectly silent.

"Take a guess," Ork said very softly.

In these moments, it was easy to think that he wasn't the villain. There were moments of tenderness that, although they were fake, were very convincing.

"Something sinister," Olivia said.

Ork looked at the machines again, like he was reevaluating them, then slowly nodded. "I suppose they would seem that way to you, wouldn't they? For someone so smart, you can be very obtuse," he said then stepped from her side to stand before the machines. He ran his finger across the substance that looked like glass. "I first saw these used in Asadam. Beautiful pieces of work and their genius caused me to marvel. I was truly impressed because there was a way for them to live for such long periods that they were considered immortal. They kept this technology hidden and had almost destroyed it before I came to them. I found only one piece of it, which I had my engineers work on. They replicated it and it was successful. I was keeping it for when this body aged. But now, it would seem that they were meant for a greater purpose."

Olivia's heart began to sink as she guessed what that might be.

Ork continued, "You see, the Asaal, natives of the Asadam planet had the technology to create the physical body, the flesh. It was mindless, of course, because creating something like consciousness requires a level of technology that no civilization I've heard of has acquired. But, they didn't need to create consciousness. They merely took the best minds of their race and installed them in the new bodies. That way, they were able to preserve the best of their mental resources. Their emperor was able to live countless lifetimes. I don't know what the 'treasure' has found in you, but when I take over your body, I'll use it regardless. There was a tweak as well, something you'd be impressed by, I'm sure. I took into consideration that your mind might play a part in the attraction, so I decided to occupy it, you see? There's no need to fear, as you'll be preserved, albeit muted. It's a good compromise, no?" Ork said this with such nonchalance, it seemed almost like he believed that he was doing her a favor.

"You are a hateful creature," Olivia said.

He looked down at her with black eyes that seemed to show no expression except condescension. "You think so? Why?"

Olivia hissed through her teeth. "You truly don't know, do you? You come into peoples' planets, ruin their way of life, enslave and kill them, steal from them, and use them to further your own agenda. Your soul is dark and empty," she said.

Ork nodded as if he agreed with everything she said and saw nothing wrong with it. "And what's wrong with the exploitation of others? It's hypocritical to hate me for that because it's a basic requirement of survival to exploit and use both nature and other creatures as tools to further our own aspiration. That's the truth of the universe, my girl. It's built in such a way that the strong rule. And, any system that's created in defiance of this truth is a system that will fail because it goes against a basic truth that is so deeply rooted. It's nearly a physical law itself. As you grow, you see that some people are made to be used. That's their sole purpose in the realm of things, and it would be arrogant to want to break out of that. You know this is true. The lion devours the antelope, the employer exploits the employee, and it's no different in any other place in the universe," Ork said slowly as if he were explaining to a child.

"You cause pain and destruction and then back it up with some weird, twisted ideal?" Olivia asked.

Ork shook his head, then said, "Nature itself is twisted and strange, and you know nothing of pain and destruction. I have known pain and I've known it so intimately that I've come to embrace it. I have endured torture in every form conceivable. I understand the meaning of pain. It's a reformer, it's a creator. The blade passes through the flame before it can be used. And, the soul of a creature must be cured through the fiercest of trials for him to be reborn. That is the nature of things. I create as I destroy. And, new things are formed from destruction; black holes, planets, the very universe itself. I'm merely a creator that seeks to spread the beauty of suffering and the reformation that it brings."

Olivia stared at him in wide-eyed shock. "You truly believe these things, don't you?" she asked.

He nodded solemnly. "I do."

Olivia looked at him again and realized that this creature had suffered. He had suffered in the worst of ways and it had twisted him. Instead of the fiery purification he claimed to have achieved, his soul had been blackened by pain and there was no hope of saving him.

She looked back at the machines and asked quietly, "What are they called?"

Ork looked down at her for a while, then looked back at the machines. He walked to them and ran a webbed hand over them very gently like they were more like pets than machines. "In your language they would mean mind-givers but, in mine, reduced to a basic form of speech, they would have the name Uikam. Neuro-transfer machines. Is that not beautiful?"

Olivia nodded. To some people it was.

***

Meanwhile, Andrew found it almost impossible to sleep. He was home and his wife was beside him, yet sleep eluded him at every turn. He wondered if it was the stress or if it was something else, an ailment, perhaps.

He looked over at his wife who lay carelessly in her usual manner, her hair spread over the pillows. Andrew smiled a little at how some things never changed and stepped out of the bedroom into the living room where he opened the big window to let in the night breeze from the desert. He sat down in a chair directly in front of it.

He had grown up here, in the desert. He had walked to school with shoes that were quickly overrun with dust and he covered his nose during the mild sandstorms, squinting over the horizon. He'd worked hard, gotten scholarships to schools his peers couldn't even dream of, and he had gotten here, to this place.

Andrew was a boy born in some unknown slum, a boy that had his lips severely broken by the harmattan every year. He had taken pride in those achievements, but not any longer. Not today. Today everything was futile and painful and he wondered what the point of anything was. What was the point of making art, music, of loving and caring and trying to leave an impact when something stronger could come and tear down everything that you have built in a single moment?

Andrew thought about how the Egyptians advanced in every field, but had all of it snatched from them by the Greeks. Or, how the Greeks built so much and the Romans just took it all. Nothing else had meaning if there was no strength to defend it, and humanity wasn't strong. They didn't have enough strength to fight this foe. They could only relinquish what was theirs and wait, hopeful that they might be allowed to keep some of what they worked for. He hated the thought deeply as the soft breeze caressed his skin. He had to find sleep, and find it soon.

"Andrew Jimoh," a voice said from behind him. He turned sharply to see a figure in what appeared to be a sleeker, modified version of a welder's suit. He faced the form, which was too tall and had a presence and an aura, an aura that marked him as an alien. Andrew went perfectly still, wondering what this one was doing in his home.

"I've started doing as he asked. His orders are being obeyed as we speak. We're currently searching for the object he showed us. And, I swear, that it will be made available as soon as possible," Andrew said, his voice shaking and causing him embarrassment.

His wife was inside and he feared for her, more than he feared for himself. He knew how casually these aliens, these demons, took lives.

"There is no need for all that. I believe that we've met before, Andrew," it said softly, and Andrew realized how true this was immediately.

The voice was even more otherworldly than the others and dripping with menace and madness. It was the one that had killed men like he was squishing an insect. This one that killed so casually, the one that Ork even seemed wary of. His heart pounded in his chest as he worried about his wife.

"There's no need to worry about your wife, Andrew. I have no intention to harm her," it said. Andrew felt slight relief, but then the words of these creatures could be trusted only as far as a man could spit. "I see that you don't trust what I say, but that is your burden to carry. I've told you the truth. I've also kept knowledge of your wife and daughter from Ork," it added.

Andrew's eyes widened with horror. He had carefully kept himself from thinking about his daughter who was in a far away corner of the Commonwealth, but this alien knew. Terror tore through Andrew's chest and he felt on the verge of tears.

"Why do you react in such a manner, Andrew? This is no veiled threat, and I truly have no desire to harm them. I've merely made an investment; one which I need your help securing. I've come to ask for your help, but you tempted me to get rash with your quivering and quaking. Control yourself," it said, then came to stand in front of him and continued flatly, "I want Ork dead. Defeated, forever."

Andrew's eyes widened.

"Yes. The investment I made requires Ork's death and I need you to help me achieve that," it said simply, like he was asking about the color of an orange or the weather.

Andrew's eyes widened even more in shock and he struggled to form his disarrayed thoughts into speech. "But... but you're allies. I mean..."

"And you have never heard of the act of betrayal? Which, I believe, is what you did to the members of the council of your Commonwealth. That was so cold-hearted that I almost admired it," Vol said. Andrew was stricken with shock. There was no way that the alien could have known except... well, they had their own methods of knowing everything.

"Please, please..."

"Why does your kind prefer to beg when there are dignified means of getting what you want? Nothing you have done is of interest to me at this point. I'm only interested in what you do from now on."

"Ork cannot be defeated. You know this. He has ships, he has soldiers and..." Andrew stopped when he noticed how quiet the alien had gone.

"My name is Vol, and I say that he can be defeated!" the alien said with such strength in his voice that Andrew knew that, whatever this one was, it was a leader. "You've been helping him blindly. Right now, he's planning to terraform your planet into a utopia for his people. Your kind will either be wiped out or be reduced to slaves, little more than livestock in the new system of things. Do you understand me? The only chance you have now is to help me and perhaps you will be able to win."

"But... but what if he finds out? He would have me...."

"Fighting him, you have a chance at survival. But serving him, your extinction and subjugation is certain, and do not think that he will pity you because you aided him in times past. I know I wouldn't," Vol said slowly.

"Why, why then are you telling me this? I'm the only one who gains anything from this," Andrew asked.

"Keep that tongue in your mouth before I yank it out. This is no deal. I make no deals with your kind. I make no bargains. My loyalty lies with another and you are merely a tool for its fulfillment. You will fight for your planet as you should and leave the talk of gains and benefits alone. Understood?" Vol hissed. Andrew cowered, knowing how close he presently was to death. "Do we have an understanding then?" Vol asked and a hiss happened then foul-smelling gasses filled the air, causing Andrew to momentarily gag.

"Yes. We have an understanding." Andrew could feel the threat and menace ease off of Vol like it was a cloth he merely discarded, but a heavy one nonetheless.

"Good. Now you will continue searching for the object, but when it's found, it will be given to me first. Also, you will fund the militia with money, weapons, parts, manpower, and anything else they require. Do you understand?"

"But, Ork…"

"Will be far too preoccupied to even notice," Vol said. Andrew nodded. "Andrew. This is for you, for your people, for humanity. I will assume that even you are not selfish enough to go against them, but if it turns out that my assumption is flawed, I'll take from you everything you hold dear and leave you to wander in the anguish that will be the reality of Ork's world."

Andrew nodded repeatedly and Vol nodded once and stated, "Good. The desert breeze is truly soothing. We never had anything of this sort back home. I wonder why we never thought of creating it. Take good care of your health."

Vol walked out through the front door. Andrew wiped his forehead, sweat flowing freely down his face. His room was so calm afterwards that he wondered if he had been dreaming, but this was no dream he knew.

Andrew breathed deeply and turned to face the window again. His thoughts were disturbed, but he began to see a ray of light within them. If he was able to do as this alien asked, then he would be seen as one of the people that protected humanity's freedom and victory over this outworldly foe. But, their victory seemed unlikely.

Andrew allowed himself to think of his daughter and he felt the pressure that he had endured bear on him. He had to fight for this last chance at least. If not for anything else, he would do it for her, because he was sure that whatever world that Ork was creating, it wouldn't be one that he would want his daughter in. The desert breeze blew on him and he achieved some calmness, but his heart was still in heavy turmoil.

CHAPTER TWENTY-TWO

Two weeks had passed and Andrew watched the cows with fascination. He'd never been on a farm before and it was exciting for him. He had first watched the goats, seen how they were fed, and how there was a semblance of a community among all the goats in the pens. He'd watched the chickens as well, although they didn't impress him much.

Now, he sat in front of the cows and enjoyed the relative silence broken only by the moo of cows and the bleating of goats. It was very easy to forget that a war was raging in the rest of the world. Not that it was much of a war. He said a silent prayer for his mother and sister and wondered whether he would see them again, whether he would see Olivia again. He knew that he couldn't stay here for much longer though. The treasure was now his responsibility and he had to protect it. He had to keep it until such a time came when more suitable, trusted hands took it from him.

There was laughter from somewhere to his side and he looked to see the boy whom he now knew was called Steve. He was laughing and bouncing around a tall, lean man with a strong face and long hair tied back with a single ribbon. The man's eyes met his, which caused Andrew to stare at them wide-eyed, standing up in preparation to run should the young man prove himself an enemy. The man raised a fist to him, then opened his palm and waved. Andrew still didn't trust him because it might be an act to get him to drop his guard and be captured.

"Ah, Josh is home!" The elderly man who had taken him from the garage said in a voice that was filled with pure happiness started walking very quickly towards the man who spread out his arms as they met in a long embrace. The young man walked with the older one to where Andrew stood.

"My brother says you're a refugee," Josh said.

His eyes were squinted and Andrew wondered if his job required him to either stare at the sun or look too long at small things.

"Yes. I am," Andrew said quietly.

The man nodded and brought out his hand. "My name is Josh. And I'm sorry for the losses you must have suffered," he said.

Andrew tentatively took his hand, half waiting for a gun to be pointed at his head, demanding the treasure. The gun never came. "My name is Andrew."

"Well, Andrew. You can smile a little easier now, because Elk has resurfaced and the militia has been revived," the man said and beamed proudly. He couldn't have been more than twenty-three years old but his eyes had a quality of someone that had seen far too much for their years.

"Elk's back?" Andrew asked, his heart beating a little faster, a tiny beam of hope streaking past him.

Josh nodded with pride. "Yes. I was there at his speech. It was powerful. He truly is back."

Andrew smiled a little, feeling a bit of happiness before he realized that he needed to take what he had to Elk, but he didn't want to take Josh from his family almost as soon as he arrived and he wasn't sure that he could trust him yet. He nodded and smiled and Josh smiled back.

There was a small feast and Josh's mother kept fussing over him in a manner that made Andrew slightly jealous and sad as he remembered his own mother. He wanted to see her, even if it was brief, but there was no chance of that. There were things to do.

Andrew tried to weasel out more information from Josh, but nothing came. The man was obviously trained to keep sensitive information silent. After dinner, Andrew walked out alone to watch the stars that Olivia was so fond of and had taught him about by association. He used to wonder why she chose to be an astrobiologist instead of an astronomer.

Olivia knew every constellation, cluster, and galaxy there was to be known, and she certainly had the will and brains for such a thing. He felt a powerful wave of sadness when he thought about her. In their time working together, he had come to see her as a sibling. And now, he didn't know where she was or what had become of her.

"What did it feel like to work with Elk?"

Andrew heard a voice ask from behind him. Even though he was startled, he didn't turn back. "How did you know that I worked with him?"

"Because of this question you asked," Josh said, coming with a foldable chair to sit beside him.

"I guess that was stupid of me, huh?" Andrew asked.

Josh man smiled a little. "You also asked questions that were oddly familiar to…"

"Ah. Stupid indeed," Andrew said.

Josh laughed then brought out a cigarette pack from his pocket and gestured at Andrew. "Mind if I smoke?" he asked. Andrew shrugged.

Josh went about the business of popping one stick into his mouth, lighting it, and drawing long and deep. He puffed smoke through his nostrils and looked up.

"You know, we always guessed it. We always guessed that there were other things out there and loads of movies were made about it, scientists argued their heads off, and it turns out that we're not alone. And not only that, there are maniacs that make Hitler look like a child with a toy gun."

Andrew laughed a little and shook his head.

"Is that picture funny to you?" Josh asked.

Andrew shook his head, then said, "Not really. You just talk like someone I know."

Josh smiled a little then turned back up, drawing smoke and blowing it out slowly.

"I really need to get to Elk," Andrew said.

The man looked at him with discerning brown eyes, then nodded. "I should have stayed at least a week but you seem to be in a hurry?" he asked.

Andrew nodded.

"I hate to take you away from your family, but it is of cosmic importance… literally," Andrew said.

Josh narrowed his eyes and furrowed his brows, then nodded. "I see," he said softly. "We move very early in the morning. You should get some sleep."

Andrew exhaled slowly in relief.

"Do you know what's happening? What's really going on?" Josh asked.

Andrew raised an eyebrow at him. "I do," he said simply in a manner that suggested that he wouldn't divulge what it was that he knew. But then again, he felt that Josh had to know something. "What I have to show Elk is very important and might determine if we win or lose," Andrew added and that seemed to satisfy Josh because he nodded.

"I actually think we can win. I mean, I didn't believe it before. It all looked hopeless. But morale is high and the camps are flooding with soldiers and we're getting equipment and resources. Even though no one knows how Elk and his new friend managed it. But, whatever they're doing, it's working. I feel like we actually have a chance this time."

"His new friend?" Andrew asked.

Josh shrugged. "Some alien called, Vol," he said.

Andrew's eyes widened. What was Elk doing with Vol? He really needed to know what was happening, but he suspected that Josh wasn't the right person to ask. Instead, he nodded and leaned back in his chair. He looked back up again. "It is beautiful," he said.

Josh smiled, eyes to the sky and said, "It really is… and scary."

Andrew smiled and said nothing.

***

"We still don't know where the treasure is, Elk. Ork doesn't have it, but I'm uncomfortable with it being adrift for such an extended period of time. Those things possess their own consciousness," Vol said.

Elk nodded, watching the pods being fixed and checked by the engineers. They were part of a new batch that Andrew and some of his close Commonwealth friends had donated to the cause.

"We have people looking for it. Even Jimoh's efforts have been given to us. How you managed to convince him is a tactic I think I can guess at, but wouldn't enjoy employing. I'm, nonetheless, impressed," Elk said.

"It was a little thing involving threats and promises, but I suspect those are foreign concepts to you."

"You'd be surprised," Elk said flatly.

The thin woman whom Elk had now made his assistant walked in and nodded at Elk. She had something against saluting, but Elk wasn't sure what it was and didn't mind. Soldiers didn't salute on his home planet either.

"There's a man requesting to see you. Says his name is, Andrew, and that you know him," she said.

Elk nodded quickly. "Yes, I know him. Please, bring him in."

"Who's Andrew?" Vol asked.

"A friend," Elk said. Elk was surprised when he saw Andrew. The smooth faced, almost attractive young man that he had known had morphed into a weary-eyed, strong-faced man with short hair and a very thin build. He was no longer handsome, just merely tired looking, but his eyes lit up when he saw Elk. It almost seemed as if he would run and hug him, but he walked slowly to him and took his hand in a handshake. Elk pulled him into an embrace.

"It has been a long time, my friend. I feared that you went down with the bunker," Elk said.

Andrew shook his head. "I'm sorry about... even Tekka..."

"It's okay, Andrew," Elk said, his emotions threatening to rise again. "I'm glad you're okay."

Andrew cast his eyes on Vol and seemed to almost shrink away from him, but more out of revulsion than fear. He turned back to look at Elk. "May we speak privately?" he asked.

Elk nodded, signaling for Vol to follow, but Andrew remained rooted to the ground. He looked at Vol and dipped his head.

The alien turned to Andrew. "I can't believe it!" Vol exclaimed. Elk turned to look at Andrew, narrowing his eyes in puzzlement. "This man has the treasure!" Vol said.

Elk's eyes widened in surprise. Andrew seemed annoyed and surprised that Vol found it out, but Elk came to place a hand on his shoulder. "It's okay, Andrew. He's an ally now. And what was our agreement about reading minds, Vol?" he asked.

Vol was so subtle with his mind reading that the victim almost didn't realize until after it had happened.

"You have the treasure?" Elk asked softly when Vol had made it obvious that he wouldn't reply. Andrew nodded and Elk nodded in return. "Follow me," Elk said and walked off.

The excitement in his chest knew no bounds as he walked. It had worried him greatly as there was still a wildcard factor in his preparations; an undesirable variable that would be difficult to plan for. But now, he had it and a sound of happiness escaped him.

"What do we do now?" Vol asked. "I say we strike now."

Elk shook his head. "I don't think so. We have to wait until the right moment. If we attack now, then we pour the element of surprise down the drain. We have to wait a little longer."

Vol shrugged to himself and remained silent, but finally said simply, "You're the General."

Elk nodded in agreement. "Yes. Yes, I am the General."

CHAPTER TWENTY-THREE

Akya knelt before the mirror, her body trembling from exertion. She had barely rested since she left Ork's presence. She no longer had anybody. She knew Elk was alive and free but she couldn't go back to him.

There was only one place for Akya to go and she saw the path open up before her just like it had for her parents. She looked down at the note in front of her and ripped it into shreds. It wouldn't be easy to go against everything she'd ever believed in and to pledge her loyalty to the creature that had caused her so much pain and loss, but it was her last option. It was either that or live as a fugitive, hated by humanity and hunted by everyone else.

Akya took the little hovercraft she had stolen from one of the houses of some wealthy idiot that still chased after luxury on the edge of an apocalypse and rode it towards the silver ship. Her entire being was fighting against her, her heart breaking, but her logic powering through.

"Ah, I see the traitor returns, fruitless," Ork said.

Akya forced herself to remain calm as she met his gaze. Her entire body wanted to burst out of anger but she knew that he would merely belittle her and all she did would just appear to be nothing more than the tantrums of a child.

"I am no traitor. What I do, I do for the benefit of my people," Akya said.

Ork nodded, then spoke with a measured, heavy tone that made her see the invisible threats that lay within, "But you have done relatively nothing. So there is no benefit for your people."

"I have brought you the girl. That must count for something," she said.

He leaned forward, his flat, black eyes locked on her. "What do you want? I do this in remembrance of your father and his services to me during the war. Not because of anything that you think you did."

Akya bristled at his tone, but reigned it in. There was no point now. She had lost anyway. The only chance she had was to mold her loss in such a manner that it bore what little fruit that it could. "I would like for the remainder of my people to be safe and treated with dignity, absorbed into whatever areas of service that they might deem suitable. And, if their sense of loyalty proves too rigid to make them able to serve, then they are treated respectfully nonetheless, until a time when they have become more receptive to the idea of servitude."

Ork made a sound of amusement then leaned back. "I suppose that would cost me nothing. But, bringing the girl is not enough in exchange for all of that. You must give more," he said.

Akya gritted her teeth in hatred, then narrowed her eyes, straining for control. She had never been so at odds with the very essence of herself before. "I would also pledge myself to your service in whatever capacity you deem fit."

Ork went silent for a moment and Akya saw that she had surprised him. After a while, he nodded and said, "I accept. I will accept you into my service as my mouthpiece to these races and people that have been conquered by me, starting with the humans. I don't much enjoy having to sully myself with their inferiority." Ork was taking charge of the situation and she responded like he expected her to answer.

It made perfect sense to Akya that he would take her in as what was essentially his public relations officer. It was a high enough position that made her useful, yet be easily monitored, as she would be given assistants who were no doubt fiercely loyal to Ork or had their will manipulated by him.

Ork got up from his chair and walked down the steps to where she stood. He observed her quietly for a moment before walking past her so that his back was turned to her. "You are so much like your father. But, you look like your mother. She fought his decision to ally himself with me for a long time, but gave in in the end. I see both sides at war inside you. And, I advise you to think about your people whenever that internal battle starts. Think about what would happen to them if I so much as get a whiff of disloyalty and insubordination from you. You will prove useful in the days to come."

The door opened and he walked out of the room. One of the creatures in the purest tones of the cleanest white came to where Akya was and communicated telepathically that she was to be shown to her quarters. These creatures seemed timid and reserved and unnaturally docile; a marker of lost will and it was upon closer inspection that Akya realized that she was in the presence of an Asaal, native of Asadam and one of the first to fall under Ork's control.

They walked through crisscrossing corridors and winding stairs when they eventually came to a row of doors that seemed to be cut from some foreign metal, left unadorned – which was in fashion – an adornment.

The door opened and she was led into a room that reminded her painfully of her home. The light was soft and yellow and the bed was made from a soft, but firm, material that was used for both beds and cushions on her home planet. And, there were soft emotional sounds in the background with compilations of threads on classics that were famous back home.

It had been built for a Terran and it evoked such a strong feeling of nostalgia that a sound of mourning escaped her. The guide communicated that she should contact them if she needed anything and promptly left, the tentacles from its head writhing in different directions.

The door was about to close when a small figure stepped through and Akya looked and saw Olivia. Guilt and shame washed over her, but she masked it with a straight face and stood looking at Olivia like she'd never seen her before.

"Must be comfortable," Olivia said softly, running her hand over the cushion. She wore a kind of suit that was both comfortable, fashionable, and efficient; Ork's engineers were impressive.

"What are you doing here?" Akya asked in the most hostile voice she could summon. It didn't even seem to faze Olivia.

"Is it comfortable?" Olivia asked and looked at Akya.

There were so many emotions in her eyes that Akya looked away, focusing her attention on the wall that was decorated with some drawings and paintings that seemed to shift on their own and soothed the mind just by looking at them. Akya guessed that it was an Asaal creation as they were obsessed with the mind.

"I suppose it is. I just got here," Akya said.

"It is interesting what you did to get it," Olivia said.

Akya whipped her head around sharply and advanced two steps towards Olivia, who stood with so much nonchalance it worried Akya a little. She wondered what had happened, but her anger made her put the thoughts aside. "You know nothing…"

"Actually, I've heard so much it's beginning to sound like it's all on replay. I know you sold me out. You betrayed Elk and you betrayed Tekka. I trusted you. I thought that you were my friend. Elk and Tekka thought the same as well. But, what do you do? You take all that trust and flush it down the toilet because you think that my inferior will and inferior mind is good for nothing. You say that you trust and believe in Elk so much, but you ignore the fact that he trusted me with whatever powers that 'treasure' possessed in the beginning, powers he didn't even understand. Your superior mind wasn't able to handle it, but mine did. You don't care because you're a prejudiced, traitorous piece of filth," Olivia said, the words coming out in a rush. She was breathing hard now, her fists clenched, and her eyes dripping tears of malice.

Akya stepped back and towards the bed then sat on it, her eyes focused on the soft rug. "I… my people were dying. This was the only way for me to save them. Elk is… gone. Tekka is dead. And, there's nothing I can do but this. I'm helping my people the best way I know," she said softly.

Olivia stood there, looking at her with eyes that were both unforgiving and hurt. Akya inhaled then slowly let it out.

It was strange how the very atmosphere and mixture of gasses Akya was used to now felt foreign to her. It calmed her, but that calm made her weaker, made her softer, made her want to cry, be vulnerable, and speak of things she had never spoke of before. "My father bought into Ork's vision. I don't know why but he did, he and my brother. My mother tried to talk them out of it for a while. And sure, she could have gone to the authorities, but she lived with my father far too long for that and joined them in their betrayal, becoming the first set of Terrans to break faith in over a millennia. I didn't know anything about it. It was only after the war, after Elk rescued me, and we were drifting aimlessly in space that the truth came out and everyone hated me. They hissed at me and made sounds of disgust when I walked by. Only Elk and Tekka cared for me and looked at me like I was a person, without the stain of my parents' betrayal. The others kept saying that I should be thrown into deep space because they felt that the tendency of betrayal lay strongly in my blood. I tried so hard to prove them wrong…. but it turned out they were right after all. I have broken faith. I am a traitor."

As soon as the words left her mouth, sounds of sorrow and pain welled up from her and Akya shuddered as they came in waves. When her grief had passed and she sat in a room that felt more like a prison than anything, she realized that the strangeness was because it didn't feel like home anymore.

The harsh sun, the harsher air, and the roughness of foam underneath her mattress felt like home. Sitting with militia warriors and Olivia and arguing, with an occasional laugh or shout dropping into the conversation, that was what felt like home. When she looked up, Olivia was sitting with her on the bed.

"He plans to take my body, to force his consciousness into mine, so the treasure can respond to his commands. He would suppress my mind with the force of his own and then… I would be a prisoner in my own body, a passenger of sorts. Isn't that funny?" Olivia said and laughed a little.

There was resignation in her eyes. Olivia was in a battle of wills against Ork, a creature that had been tested and strengthened by the worst of trials, and this wasn't one that she could have any hope of winning.

"I wish I could see Eric again and, at the same time, I'm glad that he won't see me… like this. If Ork had his way, then Eric…" she stopped as her voice broke and she leaned back until she fell on the bed and blew out through puffed cheeks. "I'm tired, Akya."

Akya reached out to hold her hand which felt so small and delicate. She wondered if she could help Olivia, if she could help Eric, if she could somehow make this any better, but she knew that she couldn't. She tightened her grip a little, still staring at the rug, but seeing nothing. "I'm tired as well, Olivia. I'm very tired."

Akya laid on her back beside Olivia, looking up at the ceiling that was made in the resemblance of the Terran sky.

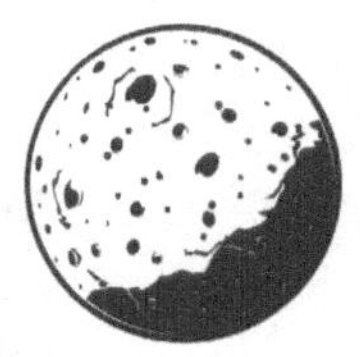

CHAPTER TWENTY-FOUR

Elk watched the array of pods, planes, and hovercrafts before him like insects. He could barely see the men that were checking and preparing them. There was no joy or pride in his chest, but there was something else; a weight of purpose and determination. A sense that this would be his last battle with Ork.

Whatever the outcome, he would make sure that there was only one of them left alive. And, it was that weight that he held on to. It seemed to cross him, permeating the very air around him because people unconsciously stepped out of his way and avoided his gaze as he walked and he was mostly left alone when he stood to view the final preparations. He wondered where Vol was off to and decided that he didn't really want to know. There was a battle to be fought and the rest of this war would be decided by how well this first battle went. He inhaled.

"Nervous?" Scythe asked.

Elk was impressed by the woman's stealth. He didn't even know when she came to stand beside him. "I have fought a thousand battles, Scythe, and every time there has been so much on the line. But, never as much as this. So yes, I'm nervous."

Scythe chuckled a bit and said, "Didn't think that you would admit that."

Elk nodded and then remarked, "My father once said, when I asked him why he never seemed fazed before a battle, 'You are bound to feel some measure of fear and nervousness of that which has the potential to erase your existence, but it is how well you master that fear that makes the difference between courage and cowardice.'"

Scythe nodded then grinned and replied, "Wow. I feel like I should write that down."

Elk laughed a little. "Perhaps you should. I wrote it down and had it memorized." They both laughed. He knew that she had deliberately drawn him out and he was thankful for that. "Is my armor ready?" Elk asked. He had given the engineers designs of armor that would resist firearms or at least dull their effect and he had asked for one specifically suited to his needs and proportions.

Scythe nodded. "Want to see?" she asked.

Elk followed her. In the adjoining room was an armor of beauty and simplicity. It was efficient, yet adorned in the manner that his own personal armor that had been ruined before was. In his head, Elk blessed the engineer that wrought this.

"Will it do?" Scythe asked beside him.

"Very nicely," Elk replied.

***

They crouched in the dust. The dust had risen to epic proportions as they watched the shield mechanism Ork had around the silver ship that served as his base. Elk had elected not to join the pilots and flyers, at least not for now. He was the only one fast enough to lead the charges and the time wasn't right yet.

The man beside him was stone-faced and had tattoos on his face. Elk knew such men and endeavored to keep them near himself in battle. He waited patiently; his eyes barely seeing through the dust that was raised by a mechanism devised specifically for this purpose. Masked to be impervious even by the best of radar technology, they were hidden perfectly.

The main shields started to go up as they always had during this time of day and Elk calmed himself, inhaling once then pushing off his right foot with all his might. He propelled himself into the air farther than any man could leap. He made several such leaps, bringing himself to a point where he could fire the ribbon of light at the shields.

Elk started to run back, but an explosion of light crashed behind him that was so bright his eyes had to close for protection. A sound like a long, loud whistle emanated from around the shield structure and the light went out. Ork's shield had fallen. Immediately, the men behind Elk pushed down their trigger locks and beams of energy shot from their weapons to shatter the structure that had served as a base for the shield.

At that moment, hundreds of battle pods oozed out from behind Ork's fallen structure and headed directly for the soldiers in the sands.

This was the signal for the militia pods to advance. They had hidden behind the mountains, but Elk had anticipated that and had required that their range and speed be prioritized over every other feature. Even from a distance they engaged Ork's pod.

Elk watched as the first wave of Ork's aircrafts fell like stones from the sky. He placed his palm on the ground, feeling the movement of underground trains that carried the foot soldiers and he nodded to himself. The battle had begun.

***

Ork hurt the soldier that had reported that the shield had fallen. He wondered how they had missed them, how they got enough technology and manpower to stage such a thing. It must have been the combined efforts of Vol and Elk.

Vol was a genius engineer, a master weapon maker, and a Virzutian nonetheless; a race known for their thirst for knowledge. He hissed to himself as the soldier's body lay before him, motionless. He had to accelerate his plans.

Ork watched as the battle raged outside. Elk's pilots seemed to have a madness about them. That, combined with the maneuverability and speed of their ships made them lethal and dangerous. The militia didn't seem to care for their own lives as they took down wave after wave of Ork's pods.

Ork nodded to himself. That was what happened when a species was driven to desperation. The fiercest fights came from cornered animals. He tried to initiate his bombers, sending telepathic orders to his soldiers but there was no feedback. Their minds registered that they were no longer alive. There was nothing where they were supposed to be.

Ork felt a small sliver of worry creep up his spine and he moved quickly away from the center. His generals could control the details of the battle but, for him, there were other details to attend to. He mentally checked where Akya was and found that she was still in her room. It was good that she remained there for now and he mentally ordered an Asaam to lock her in.

Ork had sent orders to the lab and, when he came, he saw, to his great relief that his mind-givers were still intact.

"Where's the girl?" Ork asked. He mentally searched for Olivia and found her seated in her room, facing the wall, resigned. It gave him great pleasure to know that she'd chosen to give up because it would make the work of devouring her mind that much easier. But for now at least, he had a meeting to attend.

"Load them up on the ship," Ork instructed the technician who nodded in response.

Ork walked slowly to the room where Olivia was and, while he did, he thought about Elk. He thought about Vol. And, he thought about all that had happened. He knew that he should never have let Elk live. Elk was always a danger to him, an unpleasant variable that managed to soil his plans, but this would be the end. In his world there would be no will, no variables, and certainly no Elk.

Ork opened the door to Olivia's room and stepped in. She looked only slightly larger than a child and was wearing a white T-shirt that seemed too big with baggy pants. "It's time," he said.

She nodded then stood to face him. Her eyes held something in them that he hadn't seen before. There was a certain defiance, a simmering hatred, and resentment, but in her mind was resignation. He wondered exactly how that was possible, but he didn't have the time to linger on it. She walked with him as they proceeded to his ship. He had loaded the mind-givers there so that the transfer would take place when they had arrived at their destination. A ship was no suitable place to transfer consciousness.

***

The battle raged all around Elk, who had a clear space around him formed out of the fear of the enemy soldiers when they saw how effortlessly Elk overpowered their comrades. It was a small challenge for Elk to both fight and give orders at the same time; telepathic orders that were sent directly to machines that the pilots and commanders wore around their heads that converted his commands to languages that could be understood by them.

Elk spread his awareness, his consciousness, all over the battlefield, observing it like an organism that changed, moved, and breathed. It was because of that awareness that he perceived Ork walking into a ship with Olivia.

Elk couldn't get to them on time, not on foot. He couldn't let Ork take Olivia away. She was far too important. The fate of the entire universe rested on that astrobiologist and Ork had her.

Elk gave a mental command for a pilot to come down to where he was and, in a few breaths, a light high-speed pod dropped low enough so that, when he leaped, he was able to reach it and climb into its already open doors.

***

Andrew sat in his room and stared into the middle of nothing, his eyes focused on the space between his feet and the wall, yet he saw nothing. His entire body was wracked by nervousness and he wondered if he made the right decision to listen to Elk and stay. But, it wasn't his decision anyway, not really. He wasn't a warrior and he would be more of a liability on the field than an asset.

Andrew rubbed his head and stood, then sat back down, his body seemingly unable to remain still for any stretch of time. He hadn't prayed in a long time and it stemmed from the fact that the older he grew, the less religious he became, but he knew that he had to pray now. He had to pray to something, to someone. He didn't care if anyone was listening.

When he muttered the words, he felt a little weight lift off his shoulders. He walked out of the room into the long corridor that was part of a network of corridors that ran along the entire base of operations of the militia. He frowned as his mind picked up on something. His instincts told him that something was wrong and he immediately became wary. He had been on the run and in hiding long enough to know that his instincts were seldom wrong.

The entire place was too quiet. There was no sound of machinery or chatter. True, Elk had moved most of them out for the safety of the treasure, but a few remained and there should've been some noise at least. He stepped on something that hurt his bare foot and he looked down at something that resembled pieces of coal. He looked around to see that they were all around him, clustered around tables and pieces of equipment, and it hit him. Andrew had seen those pieces of charcoal before when Ork first arrived and they weren't pieces of coal, they were charred human flesh. The engineers that remained were all dead.

Fear wrapped its arms around him and he almost froze, but the knowledge that the treasure might be in danger spurred him into motion and he ran for where it was. To his even greater horror, the door was open and it seemed that it was opened by force. They had obviously been betrayed and Andrew didn't have to think long to realize who it was, the one person that had nothing to lose from betraying them.

"Nice seeing you here, Andrew." He heard the voice say from behind him. Andrew turned to see Vol standing right behind him. His hands folded behind his back, his posture entirely relaxed.

"You," Andrew said, anger rising in his chest and sending a bitter taste into his mouth.

"Yes, me. I realize that," Vol said mildly.

"I knew that we never should have trusted you."

"Your words are far too predictable, my friend. Of course, you knew and our friend Elk knew as well; at least in the beginning. But, considering the way I devoted myself to the creation of all those fancy technologies that allowed him to be able to stand a chance against Ork and how my interests seemed to align with his, he forgot at some point and trusted me. I earned his trust and I have now used it for what I want. Don't bother making a dash for the treasure. It's in my possession already," Vol said very calmly, clearly enjoying himself.

Andrew suddenly felt tired. The treasure wasn't supposed to be in Vol's hands. It was wrong. It was so wrong, but there was nothing he could do about it. He couldn't fight him. He was even lucky to still be drawing breath at this point. A fact that made him suddenly curious.

"Why not just kill me then?" Andrew asked. His heart thundered in his chest. He knew that it would be an easy thing for his flesh to be turned into coal and Vol would feel no remorse doing it. He thought that being close to dying on different occasions would make him less afraid of death but he was wrong. He was still utterly terrified by the possibility that he might die.

"Because, I have read your mind," Vol replied. Andrew looked at him, puzzled. "You seem to have a connection to Olivia. You are one of the only people that is currently available to me that has that connection to her. In fact, there's a variable that I hope to solve with your presence. See? I have seen what you humans can be capable of when… properly motivated and I intend to give Olivia such motivation."

Andrew was now confused and more than worried. '*What would be done to him? What would be done with Olivia?*' He was still thinking when he saw a body lying at the far corner of the room. He looked from it to Vol, who followed his gaze back to the body.

"Ah yes. That is the second motivation. You can see if you want."

Andrew's heart caught in his throat and he began to run for the figure, hoping desperately that it wasn't who he thought it was. He turned the body over and saw that it was a handsome young man with raven-black hair. It was Eric.

***

Akya looked at the door, which was locked to bar her in and she looked at the Asaam that now lay unconscious on the floor. She had waited for an alarm or soldiers or something, but she'd seen nothing. She had begun transforming her figure into that of a male because it was much more durable and stronger than her female form and she would need that strength.

Akya mentally searched for Olivia but didn't find her, which meant that they had left the ship. She wondered why Ork would leave his ship as she jogged out.

There were no soldiers in sight and she knew that the battle had begun. Elk had attacked. She felt a mixture of fear and exhilaration, but didn't react as she ran for the holding cells at the lower levels of the ship.

Akya rounded a corner and came face to face with a Tuik soldier who seemed in a hurry. She didn't hesitate. She didn't have the time. Her reflexes took over and she rammed into him with her elbow, feeling her strength rising already as she took the gun from him and fired it.

When he dropped, Akya felt a sudden fear and hesitation as she had never killed before, but she shoved it down. She had to get to the dungeons.

Akya got to the door that led to the lower levels where she encountered another Tuik soldier. He stared at her and she projected her position as Ork's relations manager; asking for him to open the pod.

There was a moment of hesitation and Akya reminded him that there was a battle happening outside, so there was no time for a delay. He had opened the doors when, due to something that she couldn't see, he turned quickly and, without thinking, she fired first and a few more times to make sure that he was no longer alive.

Akya jogged in and had seen the holding cells when her weapon was slapped from her hands by a force so great it almost snapped her wrists. She felt a force connect with her jaw. Her feet left the ground and she smashed into a wall.

Akya punched wildly, reflexively, and hit something and heard a hiss of pain. She struggled to her feet and felt a hand grip her leg and pull her back. She kicked blindly in its direction, feeling her legs connect with something solid. She heard what sounded like a snarl and she threw herself away from the sound, her eyes finding enough clarity so she could see her surroundings and, almost immediately, as her eyes opened, her side took a hit so painful, she felt the air leave her body.

Akya felt a weight press on her and she looked up to see that it was a Tuik soldier, even bigger than Ork. His big, webbed hand circled her throat while the other pressed down on her buzzer. She shrieked in pain while her buzzer was almost crushed.

Akya gathered all her strength and raised her leg, catching him on the side with her knee then piercing his eyes with two fingers. She scrambled away from him, gasping and spluttering, whimpering from the pain of her buzzer.

Akya shoved into his mind and winced from the pain and madness there before she dug deeper to find the lock patterns for the cells that held the Terrans. She picked up the gun from the ground and shot him. She knew that she was beginning to turn masculine. Her form had almost completely changed. Her strength was yet to peak but it was coming along well.

Akya unlocked the hatches that held the Terrans and the sight of them almost made her release sounds of mourning even though she doubted that she could. She needed treatment for her buzzer.

The Terrans were huddled in corners and some of them were walking around, giving comfort to others. When they saw their cells open, they stared at her in shock. Then, she sent a wave of their freedom into their minds and asked for help from some of their males who could have the strength to help the others out to find pods. She was sure that as soon as Elk became aware of their presence, they would be safe. She, however, needed to find Ork and Olivia.

***

Ork stepped through the gigantic door. His eyes looked around and his senses heightened for any sign of a trap, but didn't find any. He slowly approached Vol, who stood with his back to him.

"Vol," Ork said.

Vol turned as if he just became aware of Ork's presence. "Ah, Ork. Right on time."

"Do you have it?" Ork asked.

Vol went silent for a while and Ork feared that he didn't have it when he slowly nodded. "Yes, I do have it. My plan worked," he said.

Ork scoffed. "A bit too well on Elk's side. He possesses such weapons that I've never encountered," he said with some anger slipping into his tone.

"And all that won't matter when you have the treasure and the ability to wield it. Speaking of which, is the girl here?" Vol asked.

Ork nodded as well. Then, the mind-givers were brought in on machines that levitated them a little then placed them at the center of the room.

Ork's scientists went to work. Standing with them were a few soldiers that were brought along for the sole purpose of keeping Ork safe while he was in the machine. Ork knew that Vol knew this, but the Virzutian showed no reaction, which worried Ork slightly. He knew that Vol might easily dispose of them, but he hoped that his logic would overpower his greed.

"They're ready, Lord," one of the Asaam scientists said.

Ork nodded, mentally ordering Olivia into the room. She walked in slowly, her suit taken off and her body covered with a simple brown robe. She walked to the machine and climbed in quietly, then laid down and shut her eyes. Vol showed nothing. He didn't even look at her for longer than a second.

Ork walked slowly to his side of the machine, took off his armor, and was about to climb in when his reflexes took over and he ducked just before a beam of light passed where he was. He looked around and his eyes fell on Vol. He wondered what ambush the Virzutian had planned. The soldiers that he brought to protect him fell after a brief exchange of fire and Ork's eyes rested upon the source of the disturbance.

Elk stood at the entrance, flanked by a spider-like woman and a man that was much more huge than the average human.

Ork barely had time to register Elk's presence before the Terran was upon him, firing at such close range that Ork kept retreating. Elk threw out his guns and brought out a laser knife instead.

Ork pulled out his own laser blade that was attached to the belt. They crossed blows with such speed that their arms and feet almost became a blur and Ork felt himself begin to tire from the sheer strength and stamina that Elk displayed.

It soon became clear who was the superior fighter and Ork began to feel fear creep into his chest. '*Would he die this way? Would his goals fade into nothing?*'

He made a slash at Elk but the Terran dropped down, stabbing towards his bare chest. He reversed his blade to block it when Elk threw the blade to his left hand at the last moment and stabbed it onto Ork's side.

Ork felt the pain course through him as he began to bleed. Elk held his hand that had swung outwards and pulled his blade out, raising it to stab at him again when he suddenly froze, gasped, and fell to the ground, blue blood coming from his back. Vol stood behind him, obviously strained. Around him lay the bodies of the spidery woman and the muscular man.

"Get into the machine, Ork. We have little time. It's already been initiated," Vol said.

Ork pushed past the pain and climbed into the machine. The machine locked around him and, immediately, he felt it.

It was like he was being ripped apart, but not his body. It was his mind that was being torn to shreds and recoupled together. Ork was being shrunken, expanded, squeezed, and the pain was more than any he had ever experienced. He tried to scream but it was like he was left incapable, utterly powerless and he slipped into the darkness and pain.

Vol stood over Elk, who now bled from his lower back. But, he was already healing, Vol knew. Out of all the species he had ever encountered, he had never seen any with the ability to heal as fast as Terran warriors.

Vol raised his blade, aiming for the heart when he felt a bullet hit him from the back. It couldn't pierce his armor, but it was enough to throw him against a wall. He stood almost immediately and caught another bullet and another. They kept raining on him, threatening to pierce his armor until he released his suit, releasing it outwards, and a part of it hit the assailant.

The harsh atmosphere tore at his skin, but years of genetic modification made the Virzutian virtually indestructible. The sensor tentacles attached to his back were let loose and he was almost blinded by the unfiltered light that hit his four eyes. He was running short of breath, but he could last without his own mixture of gasses for three Earth hours.

The pressure made him feel much heavier, but he was still fast enough to launch an attack on the Terran that was now struggling up from where he had fallen.

Vol rammed his shoulder into the Terran who gripped his side as both of them smashed against the ground. He felt the pain of blows as Elk hit his sides in a frenzy and he gripped one of Vol's arms, pulled it away and broke it. There was no sound of pain, but Vol received a kick that sent him sliding across the floor.

Elk scrambled to stand, but Vol was much faster and stood first, dashing for the Terran who threw himself directly to the ground and brought Vol down with his sheer weight.

Vol locked onto him with both legs and used his sensor tentacles against him, an act that made the Terran make a loud, angry sound. He looked and saw that the buzzer was wounded and he bit into it, making the Terran squirm from the terrible pain.

Elk placed his feet firmly on the ground and lifted Vol's entire body up and slammed against the ground, breaking one of Vol's legs.

***

Olivia could feel the invasion. She could feel the suppression. She could feel herself pushed into a corner of her own mind, her consciousness reduced to nothing and thrown aside.

But, there was something weak about the invader, something wounded; as if he too had suffered losses from the transfer. Her eyes opened. She didn't want to stand, but she stood and tried to push against this new force that overwhelmed her. It was like trying to move a brick wall.

The machine opened and Olivia slipped out. She saw Elk's form bleeding on the ground and she wanted to help him, but the force held her back, filled with hatred and anger. To her right, two beings were struggling in a desperate fight. She knew one of them. It was Akya but she wasn't concerned.

Olivia found that she could reach or rather, that he, could reach into their minds. Olivia heard him call out to the hideous one, the one she knew to be Vol and ask him where the treasure was, but Vol ignored him and spoke to Olivia instead, putting thoughts of her brother and of Andrew into her mind. Her eyes widened. Eric would die, Andrew would die.

Olivia began to scramble against the wall, desperately pushing against it, but it beat her back and back again. This was a will forged in fire. She had no strength compared to it.

Olivia thought about Andrew. She thought about his smile and how he took care of her in her moments of instability. They were her family, her brothers, and she would never see them again. The thought wasn't one that she could beat. She pushed against this will, this consciousness that sought to smother her. She strained against it although she felt her mind crack in the process.

Olivia strained in pain and misery and she began to see that even though it was strong, it was brittle. It was weary from the transition and it was beginning to buckle and budge. She pushed and kept pushing. She pushed farther and farther until she felt it start to give way.

Olivia sensed Vol's disbelief, sensed him fighting her and she sensed his weakness growing until he started to falter. With one last push, she shoved him down, tore him to pieces, and shoved him out to the corners of her mind.

Olivia was broken. She was weary. She couldn't think. She turned to the two struggling and saw that Akya lay dead and those four eyes from the darkest corners of the universe were staring at her. Then she felt it. The force came over her mind and encircled it, controlling and manipulating her already weak mind. She tried to fight, but she was much too weak from her previous mental exertion.

Vol guided her to the treasure and it leaped to life immediately as she came close, glowing even brighter. He made her move to it, made her reach out for it and suddenly he was gone. She weakly turned to see him lying on the floor, oozing steam and foul smelling gasses while Elk managed to bring himself to stand.

She turned to the treasure. '*Why was it called that? Why did they call it that when it had caused so much hatred and death and loss?*' She had changed reality before. She had removed these happenings from the mind of the world. She had made them forget, but she wouldn't do so now.

The world needed to remember their place, to remember what had and was happening. They needed to know that their wars and bickering were nothing within the infinite universe. And so, she reached out. Her mind was clear and she placed her hand on the orb.

***

Elk sat, watching the water flow and he breathed and accepted the unfiltered air of nature, letting himself rest. Olivia sat beside him. Her head was resting against a pillow on the grass but she wasn't sleeping. Her eyes were open, lost, and seemingly distant.

It had been three months since she obliterated Ork's armies and helped restore some semblance of sanity to the world, but she had taken nothing away. The world was damaged, the world was hurt, but they were wiser.

They were rebuilding as Elk's own people were rebuilding, but the use of the unstable treasure, combined with her own battles had taken its toll on Olivia's mind. She spoke less, preferring to withdraw into silence for extended periods. She was weary.

Elk thought about Tekka and Akya, who had redeemed herself in both his sight and the sight of the other Terrans. He felt their loss every day and he suspected he would for as long as he lived. He reached out to hold Olivia's hand. She'd sent the treasure off to where no one knew where it was and he found himself unable to penetrate her mind any longer.

Ork was gone, removed by Olivia and the treasure. But, Elk felt hollowed out, empty and tired. He looked back at Olivia. Perhaps he would go mountain climbing with her or they would traverse the desert or sail across the ocean. They would bring Andrew and Eric and perhaps she might smile again. He looked up at the sky. At least for now, the Earth was safe.

Naif Makmi is a bestselling author known for his novels in fantasy, sci-fi, crime, and romance with an ever-growing readership. He began writing in his teen years and published his first full-length novel at the age of 34. It started as a hobby that evolved into a passion, a career, and wild success that he now shares freely with all who are interested through his books.

Naif lives in Saudi Arabia and his hobbies include writing books, traveling, and watching movies. His friends and family know him for his extremely imaginative short stories and novels. He is always eager to share his ideas and thoughts with like-minded individuals.

Writing for Naif is more than simply a job; it's his life, soul, passion, hobby, favorite pastime…it's what he would do even if he were not paid for it. He wouldn't be the same person without writing. Writing has been a part of his life for as long as he can remember. At times, he has used writing as a way to cope with difficult situations and stress. He wants everyone interested to be able to benefit from the magic of writing as well.

TW: @NaifAlruwaili2

Coming soon by Naif Makmi

Chronicles Of Anne

Historical Ghost Mystery/Fantasy

Thirteen years after the cruel death of her parents that were killed for breaking the rules for falling in love, Anne is born and grows up in an orphanage home without a trace of who she really is.

Living in a world full of sorcery, Anne has a passion to become a witch. She gets the opportunity to become one, but strange things begin to happen when she realizes that she has a destiny to fulfill - liberating a nation in another dimension from the hands of their enemies in another dimension.

When Anne realizes what her identity is, she is left with accepting her fate or running away from a bloody war that has come to take the lives of those who live amongst her.

How far can she go as a girl with no idea of the powers she has, to win the war and how many sacrifices will she face to become the chosen one?

Coming soon by Naif Makmi

The Irone Games Series: Dark Age

Futuristic Robot Thriller: Sci-Fi

Science has a new definition as Dylan tries to replace humans with robots, drones, and cyborgs. Every day, humans are taken from their homes and taken to his facility where they were turned into cyborgs and slaves. They were made to perform hard jobs meant for machines.

Dylan's actions were cut short when he fell in love with one of the slaves, Vivien. Her compassionate nature drew him in and made him see humans as humans rather than slaves and machines.

They set out to start a new life together, but this new life is destroyed after Dylan found out his brother, Phineas was coming for him. A tussle for power ensures as Phineas tries to thwart Dylan's efforts of being a better person. Will Dylan fall for Phineas' games, or will he triumph?

Also available by Naif Makmi

Hurdles

Two Hours Mystery Crime Thriller

Marco was betrayed by his brother due to the accidental death of their mother which lands him in jail for the next decade. His anger festered into hatred during those hard years and he swore to take revenge when he got out but due to circumstances outside his control, he had to delay his vengeance. It was only time before he would collect his pound of flesh.

Marcus is then caught in the unforgiving grasp of the underworld by his estranged uncle, forcing him to learn the ways of the street. Eventually, his father's past catches up to the family as everything they know and love quickly begins to unravel. In his search for the truth, secrets will be revealed, lines will be crossed, and old wounds will be reopened. Is history doomed to repeat itself?

AUTHOR'S NOTE

Congratulations you just finished the book. Since readers usually rely on reviews, so, if you kindly can give feedback to this book on Goodreads or Amazon, it will be a great help.

Reviews

https://www.naifbooks.com/the-books/

If you would like to contact the author, feel free to email to Naif@naifbooks.com